Two Sides of a Coin

An Egyptian Story

Um Daoud

Two Sides of a Coin
by Um Daoud

Printed in the United States of America

ISBN 9781615796175

www.xulonpress.com

This book is dedicated to all those striving
to live for Jesus in Egypt
and to those who minister among them.

I will put in the desert the cedar and the acacia, the myrtle and the olive. I will set pines in the wasteland, the fir and the cypress together, so that people may see and know, may consider and understand, that the hand of the Lord has done this, that the Holy One of Israel has created it.
(Isaiah 41:19-20)

Chapter One

A women's beauty salon is an ordinary enough place. It should be safe to say that in most places in the world, they are filled with women hoping to leave better looking than they arrived, enjoying a moment of self-endearment and an opportunity to talk or gossip with members of the same sex. It is the one place where a woman can be vulnerable and not ashamed of who she is.

In Egypt, however, even the beauty parlor can be a place of division in this country of two distinct people groups—Christian and Muslim. How can this be? Women are all the same when they are washing their hair and having manicures. While the open-minded person may think so, the reality in this society is much different.

Phardos, on her weekly visit, enters the Chez Louis salon and greets the employees by name:

"Bonjour, Carmon, how are you?" she rings out in her melodious Egyptian Arabic, mixed with just enough French to reveal her past education.

"Bonjour, Madame Phardos," replies Carmon. "It is good to see you. How are you today?"

"I'm fine. Good morning, Alex. Good morning, Simone. How are you?"

"Good morning, Madame Phardos. We're fine."

"Would you like your usual, today?" asks Carmon.

"Yes, but I need a little more highlighting in the front. I'm noticing some grey coming in."

"That's easy to take care of," replies Carmon. "Simone will get you started with the wash."

Thus begins the ritual for Madame Phardos, a veteran patron of Chez Louis, and a well-known member of the local Coptic Orthodox community. She easily allows each member of the beauty salon staff to work on her in various ways. Simone washes her hair; Alex gives her a trim and does the highlights, and then the younger Gigi works later on her nails. They each know her well and appreciate her good tips.

While Madame Phardos and other customers sit in the open area of the salon, where there is a small waiting area and four chairs in front of mirrors, Chez Louis also contains an extra area for coiffures behind a partitioned wall. It is to this private room that Carmon calls Madame Fatma, another regular patron, but of Muslim persuasion. Unlike Madame Phardos, Madame Fatma would never allow the general public view her with her hair uncovered nor would she even think of having Alex cut and style her hair. It is forbidden for a good Muslim woman to show her hair to a man not in her immediate family. Therefore, when she enters the salon, with her hair veiled, she waits patiently in the waiting area until the private area is cleared and she can be seen to by one of the female employees.

As she earlier entered the salon, her greetings also differed from those of Madame Phardos:

"Peace be upon you," she said upon stepping over the threshold, not directed at anyone in particular, but to the inhabitants of the shop.

"Unto you be peace," replies Carmon, knowing Madame Fatma well. Though a Christian Egyptian, Carmon does not find it difficult to adjust her greetings to meet the needs of her customers. "I hope you are doing well today, Madame Fatma."

"Praise be to God," comes the reply.

"What can we do for you today?" Carmon asks.

"I just need a wash and trim."

"Please wait, and Simone will be with you shortly."

This is the routine at Chez Louis and in most beauty salons in Egypt—same service, given two different ways.

A land of history, a land of contrasts, Egypt has been home of two unique groups of people for over 1300 years. During the decline of the Pharoanic Empire, with the arrival of the Apostle Mark, Egyptians began to turn to Christianity, and it is this group of people, primarily as seen in the Coptic Church, that has maintained a presence in the country for nearly two millennium. Following the Prophet Muhammad's death, Arabs from Saudi Arabia swept through Egypt, spreading Islam in the late 700s. As Muslims came in, Christians, not willing to change their religion or pay the *jizya* (ransom), fled to the southern part of the country and stayed free from Islam's grasp.

Thus Egypt became home to two peoples defined both by race and religion. The relationship has varied over the centuries in their ability to live with one another, and yet, whether they agree or not, they have each affected the other. Why else would a Christian beauty salon owner have a partitioned area for Muslim customers?

This book, however, is not a history lesson, but a story, a story of the lives of the members of two families, that of Madame Phardos and of Madame Fatma. They are different and yet similar, sharing the same struggles and joys, the same history and future, the same city and country. One could say they represent two sides of the same coin.

Chapter Two

Phardos is an old Orthodox name, meaning Paradise, and when any Egyptian hears such a name for a woman, he knows immediately that she is from that particular background. Phardos knows this and is proud of it. She likes to be distinguished as a Christian, and is not ashamed to wear her large gold Coptic cross around her neck or hang a wooden one on her rearview mirror in her car. Identity is everything to her. She has fought for it from her early childhood in the upper Egyptian town of Minya. Though traditionally a Christian area, Minya eventually became subject to the migration of the growing numbers of Muslims from the north of the country over the centuries. As the Muslim population increased, Christians began to feel the pressure on their work as farmers. Hostilities flare from time to time, leading even to deaths among members of both communities. When Phardos was only a young girl, she saw her father killed by a group of Muslim men as a result of an argument over a piece of land. When the police did nothing to bring the perpetrators to justice, Phardos' mother took her and her five siblings and fled to Cairo, fearful that they would come to take their home as well. In the eyes of Phardos, her father died a martyr for his faith. The least she can do is to wear her cross proudly to proclaim her heritage to all around, even though they may curse her for it.

While life was not easy in the big city for her widowed mother, aunts and uncles rallied around to help provide Phardos, her two brothers and three sisters with an education that allowed them to rise in the academic and economic circles of the day. Phardos even went so far as to obtain her Masters in Education from Cairo University, and was preparing for doctorate studies when she met and married Girgis Philemon Wahba Marcos, an engineer and the owner of a prominent jewelry store and an outstanding member of the Orthodox church in Heliopolis, a suburb of Cairo. It was the perfect match for such an ambitious woman, and while she did not continue her education, Phardos did begin teaching and rose to become the director of a local French-language Christian school.

Only two children were born to Phardos and Girgis, as work and their social life led them to refrain from having as many as were normal in past generations among Christians. Their oldest was a son, Philippe. They named their daughter Marianne. They live in a modest three-bedroom apartment on the fifth floor of a building built around 1950. The brother of Girgis, lives on the floor above them, while his mother lives on the floor just below. As the eldest son, Girgis has gone to great pains to make sure that his mother's needs are met as well as those of his younger siblings. Now, however, that each one is married and well-established in life, his responsibilities lie only with his mother and his own wife and children—making life much easier as the years pass by.

Upon her return from the beauty salon, Phardos begins preparations for dinner for her family. Though she has Samia to help with housework, Phardos still prefers to cook the main meal of the day, as she has always loved to be in the kitchen. Her upbringing in Upper Egypt would have never allowed her to "put on airs" and give in to the luxury of having a cook as well as a housekeeper. Besides, her children and husband are always abundant in their praise of her meals, which encourages her to keep up the practice despite her busy work schedule.

It was in the kitchen that Marianne found her mother that warm spring afternoon when she returned from school and greeted her with a kiss:

"Hi, Mom, how are you? How can you stand this heat?"

"Hello, my dear, I'm fine," replied Phardos. "You know I can handle the heat of the kitchen when I know I'm able to provide a wonderful dinner for my family."

"That's so sweet, Mother. You really do spoil us. What are you cooking, anyway?" asked Marianne, as she opened the lid of a pot to peek in.

"Your father's favorite—*moloukhiya* with chicken and rice."

"Smells wonderful!" replied Marianne. "Do I have time to take a nap before we eat? I'm so tired from school."

"Yes, you can rest about an hour. Don't forget you have a lesson tonight with Dr. Marcos," Phardos reminded her daughter.

"Why do I have to have lessons? I hate them! Is everything in life about school and studies? When will this ever end?" Marianne ranted.

"I know you don't like them, dear, but that is the way it has to be. You know you can never pass your baccalaureate without extra studies," Phardos said consolingly. "There is too much competition and simply too many students to just try to get along in school. You have to be better than the best. You have a great chance to get into the American University of Cairo, Marianne, just keep up the good work and persevere."

Marianne threw up her hands in disgust and said, "Who cares about AUC, Mother? I will go anywhere just to get a degree. It really doesn't matter in this country anyway."

"You know that's not true, Marianne," Phardos replied almost in shock. "Your degree is everything. Employers are looking only for the top notch in their businesses; otherwise, you are out on the street, though of course, your father and I would never let you end up there."

"I know you wouldn't, Mother," Marianne said, as she again kissed her mother's cheek. "I'm too tired to have this conversation anyway. I'm going to take a nap."

As she watched her daughter leave the kitchen, Phardos was overcome with a feeling of depression and remorse. She thought to herself: How will Marianne ever survive if she is not motivated? Why is life such a struggle? She reflected over her own life and remembered the difficulties she faced since her childhood. If she had not been highly motivated, life would have overwhelmed her completely.

Though among the top in the intellectual and business community, Christians have always had to work extra hard to maintain their position in Egyptian society. If they did not make the highest marks, the millions of Muslims who studied beside them would easily monopolize all sectors of employment and society. Therefore, the Christian community put all their hope and energy into earning the best education in the country. This did not come without a price, but few are the families who are not willing to give all to enable their children to not only study at the best schools, but have private lessons as well.

While deep in these thoughts, Girgis had entered the house and quietly come up behind his wife in the kitchen. "This is where I want my wife to be!" he exclaimed as he grabbed Phardos around the waist.

"Oh, Girgis, you scared me to death!" shouted Phardos, while dropping the spoon she was using to stir the food. "Why did you sneak up on me? Shame on you!"

"Just having a little fun," replied her husband sheepishly. "You must have been somewhere far away not to have heard me come in."

"Yes, I was. I just had a small argument with Marianne about her lessons, and was thinking to myself how really hard it must be for her. However, we have no choice but to push her. I just hope we don't push her over the edge."

"She's a good girl, *Habibti*, don't worry. She'll do what is required of her, as we all have."

"Yes, I suppose we're not asking more of her than our parents did of us, and yet, somehow it seems so much more difficult these days. There are just too many students, not enough schools, and definitely not enough jobs for them all," Phardos said in exasperation. "I just wish we could make it easier for her. It's such a load on her, and not a small one on us—financially, that is."

"I know. We're paying almost as much for the private lessons as we are for the tuition for her school now," agreed Girgis, "especially now that she's taking physics. That professor is charging outrageous prices for his lessons!"

"Well, at least Philippe is almost through college," encouraged Phardos, "another two years and it will be only Marianne's expenses."

"Yes, but then come the marriages!" added Girgis.

"Oh, let's change the subject," urged Phardos, "I can't take any more of this depressing conversation. How was your day?"

"Fine. We had some good business mid-day. I'm hoping the evening will be good as well. With Mother's Day coming up, that should encourage sales, even though business has been down overall."

"Will it last long?" asked Phardos, though she didn't usually ask much about the business.

"I don't want to talk about it now," replied Girgis, "I'm ready for lunch and a nap."

"It will be another 30 minutes. Can you wait?"

"I'll take a shower to cool off while you finish."

"Thanks," replied Phardos, "I'll have everything ready soon."

As he went into the bedroom to change and then head to the shower, Girgis reflected on the question asked by his wife. Business was down. In fact, it had been down for over a year. How long would it last? Forever, it seemed. So much had changed in the jewelry business since the days of his father in the 40s and 50s. In those days, the Christians had a monopoly on the market. All of the jewelry stores in the Salah al-Deen area of Heliopolis were run by Christians. They were the ones even the Muslims came to for business, knowing them to be trustworthy and honest in business dealings. The value of the pound was strong in those days, and gold had strength. His father earned a good living for his family of six and allowed each of his children to be educated in the best schools.

Now things were different. Though President Mubarak had brought political stability to the country, the economic problems long under the surface were rising and ready to lead to a mass explosion in all areas of life for Egyptians. The pound had been steadily losing value, making it more difficult to purchase the gold at decent prices. The higher prices were keeping customers away. Even though gold was still viewed as a source of investment and a safe way to keep one's money, there were simply fewer Egyptians who had enough income to put anything aside, especially in gold. Gone were the days when a woman would buy gold bracelets, enabling her to wear her savings, and thus keep it safe until the time was needed for quick cash.

Not only was the country's economy rapidly going down, but Girgis could not ignore the fact that the growing number of Muslims entering the jewelry business was also hurting his own. In the past it was rare to find a Muslim-run business in the Christian dominated area of Salah al-Deen and Midan al-Gamaa, but now the area had become known as the

"Islamic Island" of Heliopolis, and Muslims were rapidly becoming the dominant owners of local businesses, including the jewelry stores. Though many still trusted the Christians more in the area of gold and silver, Muslim loyalty drew many customers to like-minded store owners. Where would this lead for his own struggling business? Girgis did not want to think about it now. He tried to wash out these depressing thoughts with a cool shower.

Chapter Three

Madame Fatma, or Um Muhammad, as her friends knew her, also had a story. She originally came from the Delta region of Egypt, where the Nile branches out like a fan, enriching great sections of farmland, making it rich for crops of all kinds, but especially well-known for figs. Her father, a hired laborer for a large landowner, was famous for his abilities in tending fruit trees. Though poor and without anything to their name, Fatma's parents were hard-working and provided for the needs of their nine children, of which Fatma was the third oldest. Not having means to send them anywhere else, she and her brothers and sisters were all educated at the local public school. Fatma proved quite intelligent, and at the urging of her uncle, was sent to a technical school where she learned secretarial skills and typing. When two of her brothers left the Delta to find work in Cairo, their mother sent Fatma with them to take care of their flat and cook for them. This was not enough for Fatma, however, and she began looking for a job of her own. She was hired to become the receptionist and secretary at a doctor's office, where she worked until her marriage.

Being from a strict Sunni family, her brothers maintained a close eye on their sister, as they were expected to protect her honor. For her part, Fatma was expected to veil and keep herself sufficiently covered, in order to avoid the unwanted attention of strangers in Cairo. While her brothers did the best they could, they understandably became occupied in their own lives and work and could not always be aware of their sister's actions. After living in Cairo for a couple of years, Fatma realized that one of the patients who came occasionally to the doctor's office now began to come more frequently, and not always for an obvious ailment. His name was Ahmed Muhammad Rachid Abdullah, and he was the son of a prominent professor at Al-Azhar University.

Though his father would have disapproved of his methods, Ahmed had become enthralled with Fatma. Though she was covered, her face still showed, revealing beautifully round brown eyes, an angular nose, and plump lips that led him to fanaticize about the possibility of kissing them. Fatma was unaware of Ahmed's rising emotions, until the day that Dr. Ibrahim called her into his office.

"Fatma, will you please sit down," began the doctor. "I would like to know if your parents will be coming to Cairo in the near future."

Not sure of what he was wanting, Fatma replied: "I don't know of any plans for them to come soon. I hope to see them during the *aied*"

"No, I was hoping they could make a trip to the city."

"If it is something urgent, I can send them a message to come," answered Fatma, now afraid she was in trouble.

Seeing her nervousness, the doctor rose to assure her by saying: "Fatma, please don't worry. It is a good thing. There is a young man interested in marrying you."

"Marry, me? Doctor, I have no idea who you are talking about. I have done nothing wrong. Please don't blame me."

"Calm down, Fatma, you've done nothing wrong. I just wanted to see if I can help in arranging a meeting, as I know the young man. If your parents are not able to come, then I am sure he can make arrangements to travel to them. I just thought it would be better if I am present, to reassure them that there has been no foul-play."

"Oh, I see," replied Fatma, only slightly reassured. "I will send a message to see if they can come. I do think it would be better if they hear it from you."

"Thank you, Fatma. Let me know what you find out."

"Yes, Doctor."

Fatma left his office and returned to her desk knowing that a man wanted to marry her, but not knowing his name or anything about him. She would be left to wonder for another month as it took that long for her parents to be contacted and make arrangements to come to Cairo for the appointment. Though she had done nothing to instigate this, Fatma feared her father's reaction to the proposal from a total stranger. She decided not to tell them what the doctor wanted, but simply told them that he wanted them to come for a visit to meet them.

Upon hearing the proposal via Dr. Ibrahim, after over an hour of greetings, introductions and small talk were complete, Fatma's father did indeed explode.

"How dare you bring me down here to hear such an indecent proposal!" I realize now that my daughter has been exposed to all kinds of immoral humans in this office. I knew I should never have agreed to let her work! I will hear no more of this!" He stood to leave.

Dr. Ibrahim rose to calm the old man. "Please, please, sir, you have misinterpreted the situation. I can assure you that your daughter has been nothing but an upright and moral girl while working in my office and moreover that no one has ever made an indecent proposal to her or spoken to her in a way which is not of the highest moral standards. I would never have allowed it. I know all my patients personally, and can stand up for their character. Please, please sit down and allow me to share with you more about the young man. I believe you will find him of fine quality and very suitable for your daughter."

Having convinced her father of the character of the intended groom, Dr. Ibrahim made arrangements for the family to meet him the following evening. Though he had still not given his consent, Fatma's father did seem more willing to consider the proposal, especially after learning of Ahmed's family background and his father's position at Al-Azhar. For the daughter of a poor farmer to marry an educated man's son was indeed an honor not to be passed up.

All of this was done while Fatma remained in the apartment she shared with her brothers. It was not until three days later that she was given any information about the man, who was now her intended husband. Though he sounded like a good match, what did she really know about him? And what did he look like? She racked her brain trying to recall the faces of each of Dr. Ibrahim's patients, but could not place the young Ahmed. It was not until she went to work following her parents' departure that she actually saw him as he came for an appointment. When he entered and gave her his name, he smiled shyly and greeted her by name. Fatma blushed, realizing that this was the man to whom she was now promised in marriage. She lowered her gaze and asked him to wait in a nearby chair.

This is how the life of the now Madame Fatma had suddenly changed—from that of a Delta farmer's daughter to the wife of an educated man. Though he could have progressed to the upper levels of the Al-Azhar institution like his father, Ahmed shunned the notion of teaching and all the politics entailed in being a part of the most famous Islamic university in the world and chose instead to do what he enjoyed—work with electronics. Not only smart intellectually, he was also extremely handy and enjoyed taking things apart and designing new things from an early age. This led him to open an electronics store in the growing, middle-class area of Heliopolis. Ahmed was already 30 when he became interested in Fatma, and was thus well-established in his business, enabling her to quit work and concentrate on establishing a home. The children were fast in coming. They had five in quick succession: Muhammad, Rachid, Abdel-Karem, Nawal and Eptisam.

It was Muhammad who bore the duty of carrying on his father's business. Though his interests lay elsewhere and he studied accordingly, earning a degree in law, the pressure was too heavy from his father for him to do anything but begin working alongside him at the store. His father could never understand that Muhammad would do anything but take over the business, and when his son tried to express a desire to practice law, Ahmed burst out in anger, telling him that he had no gratitude for all his father had done for him or was giving him. Why should he want to practice law when the store could provide him a great future? Though he submitted to his father's will, Muhammad's resentment continued to rise and their relationship sour.

Rachid did not know this pressure, nor did he have any desire to help out with the business, though he could have been useful. As the second son, he was free to pursue his own interest as long as it remained within the framework of an acceptable occupation according to his father. In most Egyptian homes, that meant engineering or medicine.

Since medicine was out of the question, because of his distaste for dealing with anyone ill, Rachid chose engineering and worked hard to earn a degree as a civil engineer from Ain Shams University. Upon graduation, his older brother begged him to take the family business, but Rachid selfishly refused.

"Why should I work for father?" He asked in response to Muhammad's request. "He's got you. I can go and work for a firm. Why should I kill myself with your schedule?"

"You think of no one but yourself, brother," spouted Muhammad. "At least you're good at electronics. I hate it. I'm dying in that store all day long, every day."

"Well, maybe you can get Abdel-Karem to take it."

"Yeah, and wait at least another 4 years before he graduates from college!"

"Maybe you'll like the work by then," joked Rachid.

"You're useless," Muhammad said with a sigh. "Go on and enjoy life. I'll do my duty."

"You're a good man, brother," replied Rachid, patting Muhammad on the back. "God will reward you."

"God," snorted Muhammad, "where is he? If he cared anything about me, he'd get me out of this."

"Don't blaspheme God like that, Muhammad," warned Rachid. "This is obviously the way he wills it."

"Will. I'm so sick of his will."

Rachid was really taken aback by his brother's words. "Muhammad, be careful. You do not want to bring his wrath. Maybe you need to go to the mosque more. Have you been praying lately?"

Muhammad, though named after the prophet of Islam, had never been a devout Muslim. Though his father kept the regular practice of prayer, especially on Fridays, he did not pressure his children to attend mosque. Muhammad had long grown disillusioned by the Faith and cared more for his studies and music than he did for religious duties. Rachid, on the other hand, had come to know a group of religious boys in high school and became increasingly devout throughout college, never missing a prayer time. He was far from being called radical, but on the edge of making a decision about important matters in relation to the practice of his religion.

Muhammad tried to brush off his brother's worries, but kept them in mind as he left him and went out to be with friends. He was so discouraged by the direction his life was going and felt hopeless with the future. Perhaps religion was what would give him hope. He would think about it later.

Um Muhammad was not unaware of these tensions in her home. While pleased that her two oldest sons had earned college degrees, she knew that Muhammad was not happy in working at the store, and she was increasingly concerned that Rachid seemed to be hanging out with an extreme group of friends. The fact that he was talking about growing a beard was a tell-tell sign that he was becoming more fundamental in the practice of his faith.

She was a good Muslim, in her own eyes, though she had not always been found to pray the five daily prayers. Her devotion usually surged during Ramadan, which was the most important time for Muslims to exhibit their faith anyway. She prided herself of the fact that she would read the entire Qur'an during the month of fasting and practiced the fast itself to the letter. While many Muslims over ate during the breakfast times, Um Muhammad always made it a point to serve her family a light soup and not an overly heavy meal in the evening. Though she cooked a lot, she felt that she was better than others by not being extravagant in the foods she served.

Yet when it came to the idea of being fanatical about the faith, Um Muhammad became worried. Her fear was not so much of being a better Muslim but of what the government might do to Rachid if they found him to be too radical. Though Muslims were the majority in the country and the president a Muslim, there were pressures from all sides to maintain moderation in relation to religion. Anyone found to express too much of a radical ideology usually was quick to begin to speak against the government, so such persons were known to be watched and many times taken into custody.

While preparing the evening meal, Um Muhammad heard her two oldest sons arguing again, and she worried that Ahmed would come home to find his house in an uproar.

She quickly turned the fire down on the stove and went out into the salon to reprimand her children:

"Boys, boys," she screamed, trying to get above their own voices, "please stop arguing. If your father comes home and finds you like this, we will all feel the consequences."

"I don't care, Mother," declared Muhammad, "Rachid insists on pushing his religious beliefs down my throat, and I'm sick of it."

"Mother, forgive us for fighting," Rachid tried in a calmer voice, "but Muhammad is blaspheming the Prophet, peace be upon him, and our faith. He must be brought to reason, or God will bring his wrath on this family."

"The only wrath that will come is my fist into your face," shouted Muhammad to his brother.

Um Muhammad was appalled at such threats between her sons. "How can you say such things, either of you? Rachid, you know your brother is a good Muslim. He may have different ideas from you, but he is not bad. And Muhammad, Rachid is your brother; blood ties are stronger than any other. You need each other." She came between them and put her hand on each of their shoulders.

Muhammad pushed her away. "Blood may be a strong tie, Mother, but Rachid holds his friends closer than his brother, and they are polluting his mind."

"That is not true!" replied Rachid, his voice now rising. "I am warning you because you are my brother. I would not want you to bring disgrace on this family."

"Disgrace, what disgrace?" shouted Muhammad in return. "I'm the one who's actually doing what Father wants. I'm upholding his honor."

"It's not Father's honor that is the problem, but God's," retorted Rachid. "You are in great danger because you are not being faithful to the tenets of Islam."

"I'll give you tenets!" and Muhammad moved again toward his brother.

Um Muhammad came between them again, but did not stop Muhammad throwing a punch toward his brother. When she tried to remain between them, Muhammad pushed her out of the way and shouted: "Get out of the way, woman! This is not your fight!"

Falling to the floor, Um Muhammad began to cry as her sons struggled together. A scream had just begun to come out of her mouth when the door open and her husband came in. Having heard the voices from outside the flat and now seeing his sons engaged in battle, he threw himself between them in a rage:

"What is this? Have you gone mad? Get off each other!" and he pushed each son in the opposite direction of the other. He then realized his wife was on the floor and looked in her direction with contempt.

"God forgive them, Abu Muhammad," came a small voice from his wife. "They are young and cannot yet control their emotions."

"Nothing forgives such behavior in my house!" He yelled, then looking at his sons, without helping his wife up, he continued: "Do you want to bring disgrace on our family by having the entire neighborhood hear such outbursts? Well, what do you have to say for yourself?"

"Father, forgive me for allowing Muhammad to push me to such behavior," began Rachid in an overly meek voice. "He, however, was provoking me by blaspheming the Prophet and our religion."

"Provoking him?" rebuffed Muhammad, pulling himself up tall. "He is the one who was accusing me of shaming you. Have I ever shamed you, Father?"

"I'm ashamed of both of you right now," replied Ahmed. "I'm tired and want to eat and take a nap. I'll let this go for now, but if I find you at it again, there will be consequences." He turned and walked out of the room.

Um Muhammad, all this time, was still on the floor, both in fear of drawing undue attention to herself and acquiring the wrath of her husband and also out of simple disbelief that he would not even be concerned about what her sons had done to their mother. As her husband left to his bedroom, and her boys now stared at each other in loathing, she slowly rose, and without a word to either of them, returned to the kitchen. She was both humiliated and angry that her home had become a battleground. What had she done to let this happen?

Chapter Four

The evening was a time of respite for Phardos. Girgis, though a good man and kind father, was disengaged from the family. Though he came home for the afternoon meal and a nap, he always returned within a few hours to his shop, where he continued to work late into the night. Cairo never sleeps, so they say, and the jewelry business is only one of many of the industries that remains open until midnight or even later in the summer months. Even if he closes relatively early, Girgis spends his extra hours with longtime friends, having a cup of coffee or playing backgammon at the neighborhood coffee shop. Friday was the only day that Girgis really committed to his family, and Phardos worked hard to keep that completely free for him and the children. After sleeping late, they would take either a nice brunch or wait until later and take a lunch out at a local restaurant, then relax together for the rest of the afternoon.

Now that the children were older, Girgis did not feel as compelled to remain with them all evening and again found ways to become occupied with friends instead of family. This made for a lonely life as a wife, but Phardos resolved herself to this fate. She was certainly not alone among Egyptian wives whose husbands were basically absent from the home. At least her husband did not work in the Gulf, leaving her and the children for months or years at a time, as many men did their families. She had a friend whose husband worked in Dubai. She saw him only for a few months each summer, and she was the one who went to visit; he never came to Egypt to see his family. What a life that must be. Yes, Phardos felt she had much to thank God for. Her husband was good, not home much, but good, so she could not complain. He never hit her and only rarely raised his voice. And of course, he went to mass with her and the children every Sunday morning. As a good Orthodox, Girgis would never have allowed himself to stray from the Church. Phardos would not call him devout, but he did go to church. He made sure he took communion at least once if not twice a week. If he went on other days without her, he always brought home some of the *corban* that she would be able to partake of the Body of Christ and receive a blessing.

Though she wanted to be more active in church activities, her work at the school did not allow her the time to become any more involved than an occasional activity. She did, however, make sure her children attended Sunday School every Friday when they were young and went on all the church retreats and events. It was only within the community that they would find real acceptance and eventually mates, and she did everything within in her power to ensure they were seen as active Copts. Having the priest's stamp of approval was important for those looking for potential marriage partners. Knowing her children were well-liked by the priest helped when good candidates for marriage came around.

The church was not just a place to go for mass, but was also the source of most Copts' social world as well. Along with Sunday School for children, most Coptic churches had their own basketball and soccer courts, where young people could play sports and hold large social gatherings. It was basically a club, a Christian club, but a club, and the center of the majority of activities for growing Orthodox children and youth. Parents knew their children were safe if they remained within the confines of the church property. While the growth of malls and more "secular" distractions had begun to lure Christian youth away from the traditional church ground, for concerned parents, like Phardos, the church was still the only place she allowed her impressionable children to go without her accompaniment. While Philippe could manage on his own, she would never allow Marianne to just "go out" with friends to any location outside of the church.

Life in Egypt was not easy for Christian girls who tended to dress in a much less restricted way than their Muslim counterparts. Harassment from Muslim boys was commonplace, and required most girls to travel in pacts to avoid attacks. Though Marianne sometimes baulked at her mother's protectionism, Phardos held her ground and refused to let her daughter risk abuse from the majority, though she realized, as Marianne approached college, she would have to let her have more freedom.

The other option besides social activities at the church for her children was simply to have their friends come to their home. As Philippe entered high school and then Marianne, it became a commonplace occurrence to invite friends to the house. They might begin under the pretense of studies, but it usually turned into a time of watching TV or listening to music. Though Phardos had her fill of children from the school, she willingly accepted this duty as a mother in order to maintain a close watch upon the friends of her own.

So it was to be the same this evening. Girgis was already out of the house, having finished dinner, napped, and taken a quick coffee with his wife before telling her goodbye to leave again for the shop. Since it was Thursday, Marianne and Philippe would be going to the regular youth meeting at church, so Phardos was completely alone. She decided to turn on the television. She enjoyed watching the Christian satellite stations because they many times had programs about raising children. She did not look at these as a mother, but as an educator, and was able to glean many helpful hints to use as she worked with the teachers under her supervision. Though her school was a good learning institution in general, not all the teachers had a good understanding of how to deal with children in the classroom. They knew their subjects, but did not know how to handle the children in a way that would enhance their learning and not stifle it.

Tonight, however, as she flipped through the various stations, she came across a program by an Orthodox priest, Zakaria. She had heard a lot about him, but had never seen his show. He was, as many described him, a kind-looking man, wearing his long, black robe and round head covering, as per his station in the church. The most noticeable part of his attire, however, was the large cross hanging from a chain around his neck. At first view, a typical Coptic priest, and yet the words she heard come from his mouth were anything but typical Orthodox.

"Tonight, my dear Muslim friends, I want you to open your minds. I want you to think for yourself," he was saying. "Look at the books I have read from tonight; they are your books, written by known Muslim scholars. Read them and know that what I am speaking to you is the truth. Then I want you to think about this subject and realize for yourself that what you have always been taught is not right. Now, Brother Ahmed, does that answer the question?"

Across from the priest sat a man in a suit who responded: "Yes, thank you so much for explaining that to our listeners. It is good to see the entire picture in relation to this issue, and we know that many who are watching tonight will be changed by what they have learned." He turned toward the camera and said: "Thank you for being with us tonight, and we ask in the Name of the Lord Jesus Christ that you may come to see the Truth and accept it. Good Bye."

As the screen began to show the credits, Phardos, sat in wonder. She only caught the very end of this program, but it made an impact on her. What was an Orthodox priest doing talking about Islam? Why was he talking to a man named Ahmed, who obviously was a Christian? Can a Muslim be a Christian? No, she shook her head. She had never heard of such a thing. Besides, all Muslims, in her mind where destined to Hell, and that is where they belonged as far as she was concerned. She made a mental note to find out more about this priest. He could really cause a lot of troubles for the Church, talking with a Muslim and criticizing Islam. What is he thinking?

These questions troubled her deeply. Who could possibly answer them? The first person who came to her mind was Father Andraous. Surely he knew about this man. Though she knew she should not bother her local priest, she felt this was urgent. She picked up the phone and called his cell phone number. He had given it to her anyway and told her to call him anytime. Well, this was an emergency. He must help her understand. After the phone rang twice, she heard his voice on the other end:

"Hallo," came the clear, firm voice of the priest.

"Hallo, Good Evening, Father Andraous, this is Madame Phardos, do you remember me?" She asked hesitantly.

"Can you remind me please?" requested the priest.

"Yes, I am the director of St. Anne's, my husband is Girgis Philemon."

"Oh, yes, forgive me, Madame Phardos. How are you?"

"Thanks to God, fine, Father."

"And your husband?"

"He is well too, Thanks to God," she replied again and continued on quickly, "I hope I am not disturbing you."

"No, no, my child, not at all. How can I help you?"

"Father, I was watching a program on the television and it disturbed me greatly. I felt that perhaps you could help me to understand more about it."

"I will do my best."

"Have you heard about Father Zakaria?"

Suddenly, a great change came over the voice of Father Andraous, so much so, that when he spoke, Phardos almost dropped the phone.

"Blasphemer!" he yelled into the phone. "This man is a fraud and up to no good. The Church disclaims him totally, and you are in danger of your salvation if you watch him." When Phardos did not instantly reply, he continued in an agitated voice: "Did you hear me Madame Phardos?"

"Yes, yes, Father, I'm sorry," she tried. "I only saw him this once, please do not think that I have been watching him every day. I was only confused about what he was saying and then talking with that man, Ahmed, who seemed to be acting like a Christian." Before the priest could respond, she added quickly, "Can a Muslim become a Christian, Father?"

"I want you to never watch that program again," the priest replied. "Do you hear me?"

"Yes, yes, Father."

"It can bring you nothing but trouble and jeopardize your salvation and relationship with the Church. Good-bye, Madame." The phone clicked before she could finish: "Good-bye, Father."

As she closed the phone, Phardos leaned back in her chair, her hands actually shaking. What in the world? She thought. Never had she heard the priest raise his voice like that. It terrified her. Was this Zakaria so horrible? As she thought more, she realized—he did not answer her question. Can a Muslim become a Christian? Why didn't he answer? She closed her eyes and tried to make sense of what had just taken place, but the more she thought, the more she became troubled and confused. Perhaps it was better to just push it all out of her mind and forget it. One thing was for sure...she would never watch that show again!

Chapter Five

The afternoon meal was eaten in silence at the home of Um Muhammad that day. Following Ahmed's rampage against his sons, no one dared open their mouth at the table. Even when Abdel-Karem, Nawal and Eptisam came home from school, they realized something was wrong, but not daring to ask, also kept quiet during the meal. It was not until she was helping her mother clear the table that Nawal approached her about the situation.

"Mama, what happened? Is there a problem? Baba looked so mad at the table."

"It is none of your concern, my dear," replied Um Muhamamd, "your brothers were fighting and your father came in on them. It's all over now."

Nawal put down the dish towel she was preparing to use to wipe off the table and put her hands on her hips. "Don't they know better than to make Father angry? When will they ever stop fighting?"

"I don't know, Nawal, I don't know," exclaimed her mother in exasperation. "Nothing I do helps. They are just so different, and nothing one does pleases the other. I am ready to wash my hands of them both."

"They are still your sons, Mama, you can't do that."

"Yes, they are my sons, but they are adults now and need to learn to live in this world in peace. If they were good Muslims, they would be able to do it."

"But Rachid is a very good Muslim, Mama," replied Nawal. "I've seen him praying. He is so faithful. And he reads his Qur'an all the time."

"Well, maybe there is more to being a good Muslim than just praying and reading the Qur'an," exclaimed her mother with a sigh of frustration in her voice.

"I am sure that Rachid is following the teachings of the Prophet, peace be upon him, very closely," replied Nawal. "Maybe it is Muhammad who is provoking the situation."

"No, I cannot believe that," Um Muhammad retorted quickly. "He is my eldest, and I know him best. He has a good heart. Even though he may not be as devoted as Rachid seems to be, I know his heart is pure. I can never doubt him."

"You know best, Mama," Nawal said with some doubt in her voice.

"Yes, and now I know that the best thing is for you to forget all this and go work on your homework."

"Yes, Mama." Nawal rolled her eyes and left the kitchen.

Though her husband did not discuss the issue further that night, Um Muhammad could not get it out of her mind, and as she cleaned her house the next morning, she kept replaying the horrible scene in her mind. Two questions bothered her the most: Why do her boys not love each other? And why did they and their father treat her with such contempt?

Did not Ahmed marry her out of love? After all, he was the one who saw her in the doctor's office and asked for her hand. There was no prearrangement made between families. He saw her, he liked her, and he married her. They had a long life together. They had five children. Could there really not be love in his heart for his wife? She had to know the answer.

But did she dare ask him directly? What if he said no? Would that change anything?

No, she knew she would never leave him, nor could she. Muslim women just do not leave their husbands, even if they are cruel, because a Muslim woman knows she will never get the custody of her children. Yes, there are laws, but the reality is not the same. No, for the sake of the children, she was needed in the home, whether they realized it or not. She would put the need for love behind her, move on and not look back. It was always for the woman to sacrifice. She must accept this fact.

While Um Muhammad was cleaning her house and contemplating the issues that faced her, Ahmed was sitting in a coffee shop, having his morning cup of tea with the *Al-Ahram* newspaper. Never did a day pass that he missed this ritual of life. A businessman was required to know what was happening in the country, and the greatest source for this was Egypt's oldest and most well-known newspaper. While many other newspapers were also on the market, *Al-Ahram* was the most respected and widely-read. Others had a tendency to promote religious or political views to the extreme, but Ahmed wanted nothing to do with extremism. That was the main reason he did not want to follow in his father's footsteps at Al-Azhar.

It was in the routine of his life that he found pleasure. He knew every man who entered the coffee shop that morning. For a man to be recognized by his peers brings great satisfaction, and even these daily greetings from men so familiar to him lifted his spirits. Yet, as he read the paper, a headline caught his eye and brought him distress. A Muslim man had brought a case against the government suing for the right to change his identity card from Muslim to Christian. Ahmed almost spilt his tea as he brought the paper closer to his eyes in order to focus better on the smaller print.

Could he be understanding the report correctly? A Muslim claimed to have converted to Christianity many years ago. He married a woman who also claimed to have been a Muslim convert to the religion. They, in turn, now had children. Because they were supposedly Christians they did not want their children to have Islam as their religion on their identity papers, but wanted them changed. What blasphemy! Ahmed could not believe any part of this article could be true. A Muslim convert to Christianity? Never. It was deserving of death. And, if it was true that he had actually been a Christian for several years, why was he not already dead? How could his family or friends have allowed such heresy to take place and not fulfill the requirements for the crime?

And how dare such a person even think he could come before the mighty Egyptian government and raise a case. Does he not realize that the government is based on the Sharia, the law of Islam? What impertinence, what a disgrace to the good name of this country. Someone must have put him up to it. Ahmed thought of possible scenarios: Perhaps the Christian church is paying him to raise such a case to push the government. Maybe he is just looking for a way to immigrate to America or Canada, by bringing on himself an impossible situation. Or, maybe Israel is using him to destabilize the country by creating chaos in the system.

Ahmed wished he had his father to discuss this with, but he had been dead now for three years. Though they were never really close, Ahmed respected his father for his knowledge of the Faith and ability to teach it to others. Since his father was not a possibility, he would have to settle for his friend, Mahmoud, and decided to call him once he opened his shop. This was indeed an important piece of news, and Ahmed knew it was one that could cause great problems for the country, his country, which did not need any extra problems right now. He tucked the paper under his arm, paid his bill and headed for the shop.

Chapter Six

Although Phardos had tried to put all she had just experienced out of her mind, she was unable to do so. Perhaps the words of the priest were true and she was in jeopardy of losing her salvation. She had to act. Since everyone was out of the house, she decided to walk to church and light a candle and pray, trusting that God would accept her repentance, forgive her and give her comfort.

The walk from the house to church was not a long one, though it could be tricky. Sidewalks were not conducive to pedestrian traffic as in most countries of the world, between the trees planted in them and cars parked on them; few permitted a person to walk the length of even the block. Therefore, most walks were delegated to the street itself, which brought its own set of trials. The growing population of Cairo and lack of sanitary services left the streets to become recipients of huge amounts of trash. Avoiding this was a challenge in itself, not to mention the cars which passed continuously down these once-wide, but now crowded roads, forcing pedestrians to be aware at all moments for fear of serious injury. Therefore, as Phardos walked to the church, she was not able to spend time reflecting on her own thoughts, but instead focus on each step she took and all that was in her path.

She arrived safely at the church fifteen minutes later, but with sand in her shoes, which made her uncomfortable.

Before entering the church, she slipped to the restroom on the side of the building to take off her shoes, shake out the dust and wash her hands. Because it was Thursday, the church yard was packed with young people, but since their meetings were in the building with classrooms, the main church sanctuary only revealed a handful of parishioners.

Phardos pulled a scarf from her purse and put it on her head. As she entered the church, she moved her hands in the sign of the cross, the symbol of her faith and the cause of so much strife between the two major religious groups in Egypt. She then moved toward a group of candles found at the back of the church.

"Dear Lord," she prayed, "may the scent of this beeswax be a sweet fragrance to you. Forgive me, Lord, if I have done wrong. Hear my prayer."

After placing her lit candle in the holder, she moved toward a bench to continue her petition:

"God, you are my light and my comfort. When answers do not come, I turn to you. Lord, help me to understand why listening to that priest is wrong. Help me to know why that Muslim man was talking like a Christian. Is it possible, Lord?"

She shifted in her seat and looked up to the front of the church to see the face of the Lord Jesus staring down at her from one of the prominent icons. His face seemed harsh, and she was taken aback. "Lord, am I wrong to ask you such things? Am I wrong to bring such selfish requests to you?"

Phardos sought out the icon of the Virgin Mary with baby Jesus in her arms. "You, Mary, Mother of God, be merciful to me, that I may hear his voice and know his will."

Tears began to flow from her eyes. She could not help it. Never had she felt so rejected by a priest and confused about her faith. She searched in her purse for a tissue, but realized she had neglected to put any in. Suddenly a hand touched her shoulder and a tissue was offered. Phardos looked up to see the kind face of an elderly woman smiling down at her. She accepted the tissue and wiped her tears.

"Thank you," she said softly.

"You are very welcome, my dear," came the reply. "Are you all right?"

"I think so," Phardos began but found herself adding, "No, not really."

"Why don't you come outside and have a cup of tea with me?" the lady offered.

Though she wanted to refuse, Phardos felt drawn to this woman. "Thank you," was the only thing she could say, and they rose to leave the sanctuary.

Because it was a social center, the church naturally had its coffee shop, complete with several tables, where members could have a snack and drink as they waited on children or were between meetings. As she guided Phardos to a table, the woman went to the counter to order the tea. Lost in her thoughts, Phardos did not even attempt to argue over paying for the drinks. As the lady returned and sat beside her, Phardos began:

"Thank you so much. I really should have served you."

"Do not worry about it, my dear;" replied the older woman, "you will have time in your life to do a kindness to many, I am sure."

"I hope so," said Phardos weakly, though she knew that her busy life kept her from having time to meet the needs of others. "What is your name?" She asked, hoping not to dwell on her on frailties long.

"My name is Naema," replied the woman.

"What a beautiful name," said Phardos, "and you obviously live by it, as you showed me much grace today."

"Because the Lord has shown me so much grace, I cannot help but show it to others. But, what is your name?"

"My name is Phardos."

"Well, you see," said the woman, "we both have meaningful names. What could be better than a constant reminder of our eternal hope through Jesus."

"Yes, I suppose," replied Phardos weakly. "Actually, I've never thought of it like that. To be honest, I've never really liked my name at all!"

"Oh, it is a beautiful name, and you should carry it with pride," offered Naema.

"At least now, perhaps I'll think about it differently," Phardos said with all honesty.

"I'm sure you will," agreed Naema, but then asked, "Now what is it that has you so upset? I trust it is not a family problem. Please do not think me nosey. I just want to encourage you if possible."

"You already have, thank you so much. I don't know why I was crying. It seems so trivial. I really shouldn't have."

"Nothing is too trivial for the Lord, my dear," replied Naema with a pat on Phardos' hand. "We can bring anything to him. Tell me what's troubling you, perhaps together we can find his guidance."

With that, Phardos began telling Naema about all she had heard on the television program and then the response of the priest to her questions. Naema did not interrupt, but let her share everything that was on her heart. When she finished, Naema said: "Phardos, let's pray and ask for God's wisdom." And without waiting for a reply, right there in the coffee shop, Naema bowed her head and raised this prayer to God:

"Our dear Heavenly Father, you are so rich in mercy and love to give all your children desire. I pray to you now on behalf of my sister Phardos. Her heart is heavy with questions and confusion. Ease her mind, give us your answers, that we may know your truth in all these matters and be drawn closer to you. In the precious Name of Jesus our Lord, I pray. Amen."

It was a short prayer, and definitely more personal than Phardos had ever heard voiced, but it touched her heart. There was something different about his woman. She just did not know what. She lifted her head as Naema said *amen* and listened with expectation at what the woman would say next.

"Do you know where I like to go for answers to life's questions, Phardos?" began Naema.

"No, where do you find them?" Phardos asked with sincerity.

"If God wants to speak to me, then I believe the first place to go is his Word, the Bible."

"Oh, yes, of course," replied Phardos, but then found herself asking: "Does his Word talk about things like this?"

"Let's see," said Naema, and she took a small black book from her handbag. It was a well-worn leather-bound Bible, quickly revealing to Phardos that it had been read over and over again through many years. As Phardos watched, Naema flipped through the obviously familiar pages to find exactly what she was looking for. She smiled as she looked up at her new friend and began to speak.

"I like the words of Peter, when he became the first to proclaim the Risen Lord and the Good News of the Gospel to the Jews on Pentecost. Listen to this, Phardos:

> *Repent and be baptized, every one of you, in the name of Jesus Christ for the forgiveness of your sins. And you will receive the gift of the Holy Spirit. The promise is for you and your children and for all who are far off—for all whom the Lord our God will call.*

That is how a person becomes a Christian, by repenting and then being baptized in the name of Jesus Christ. When we confess our sins and surrender our lives to Christ, we are saved. It is a simple message and yet the most powerful one.

But look at this: Peter said this is the promise for you and your children. Who is he talking to?"

"The Jews," replied Phardos, "Isn't that correct?"

"Yes, Phardos, that's right," responded Naema, "but then look at what he says. This same promise is not only for the Jews and their children, but for 'all who are far off'. Who would he be referring to there, do you think?"

Phardos knew she would quickly show her ignorance at Bible knowledge. She had never taken the time to seriously study the Bible, but relied heavily on whatever the priests said about it. She had to admit her fault: "I don't know, Naema, tell me."

"Peter is referring to the Gentiles, my dear, anyone who is not a Jew. Now, look, he will say almost the same thing with another group of Jews in the next chapter." She turned a page in her Bible and read again:

> *Repent, then, and turn to God, that your sins may be wiped out, that times of refreshing may come from the Lord...Indeed, all the prophets from Samuel on, as many as have spoken have foretold these days. And you are heirs of the prophets and of the covenant God made with your fathers. He said to Abraham, "Through your offspring all peoples on earth will be blessed." When God raised up his servant, he sent him first to you to bless you by turning each of you from your wicked ways.*

Naema then looked up from her reading and asked: "Are we Jews, Phardos?"

Somewhat taken aback by the question, Phardos replied: "No, of course not."

"Then that means we are Gentiles."

"Yes, I suppose it does."

"So you see, Christ revealed himself among the Jews first, but his ultimate purpose was to be made known to all peoples of the world, including us. Do you find it hard to believe that an Egyptian can hear this Good News and accept it?"

"No, if so, we would not have the Church."

"That's right," replied Naema smiling. "So if it is not hard for you as an Egyptian to accept this news, then why should it be hard for an Egyptian Muslim to accept it?"

This simple truth and logic hit Phardos hard, causing her to simply stare at Naema with her mouth open. Naema laughed and continued: "It's all right, my dear, many times the simple truth is the hardest for us to accept."

Now Phardos was angry at herself for not seeing this earlier. "But if that is true, then why would the priest become so upset with me?"

"Now that may take a longer visit," replied Naema. "I would not presume to understand the priest's feelings, but I have some possible ideas why he reacted that way. However, maybe this is not the best setting to express them." As she spoke, she looked around to the surrounding tables, making obvious to Phardos the presence of several priests and monks in the area.

"Yes, I understand," Phardos acknowledged. "I would love to have you in my home."

"That would be lovely," smiled Naema. "I must leave you now, however. My grandson will be coming out of his meeting just about now, and I need to return him to his mother."

"Can I please have your telephone number, then?" asked Phardos. "I will call you to arrange a time. I work during the week, so it will most likely have to be on Friday or Saturday, once I see my family's schedule."

"Yes, you have many responsibilities. Here is my number," and she handed her a small piece of paper. "Call me anytime. It has been such a pleasure to meet you, and I trust you will return home in a better state than you came."

Phardos could not help herself, but moved toward the older woman and warmly kissed her on both cheeks. "I will never forget this time," she said. "Thank you for what you have done."

"I have done nothing, Naema replied humbly. "God has simply revealed the truth through his Word."

"Yes, but he has used you," added Phardos.

"Then I am blessed because of it," said Naema. "Good-bye, my dear."

"Good-bye, Naema." Phardos watched her walk away. She stood in the same spot for a few moments, just watching the old woman and then realized others were watching her. Catching herself, she quickly picked up her purse and moved toward the gate.

She had not gone far when she heard a familiar voice call: "Mother, Mother, is that you?"

Phardos turned to see her son and daughter coming toward her.

She smiled when she saw them. "Hello dears, how were your meetings?"

Philippe responded first: "They were fine, Mother, but what are you doing here? Is everything all right?"

"Oh, yes, of course, darling," she replied while kissing him on the cheeks. "I was just out for a walk and decided to come by to pray. Everything is fine now. Are you ready to come home?"

"Yes, Mother," said Marianne as she too kissed her mother, "we were just heading out."

"Will you let your mother walk with you, then?"

"Of course, we would not have it any other way!" replied Philippe warmly, and he took her by the hand.

Chapter Seven

The thoughts of enjoying his familiar routine were now completely out of Ahmed's mind as he arrived at his shop. Though he still had to unlock the metal grill, lift the heavy barrier, and then unlock and enter the shop itself, he was not focused on what he was doing, but on what he had read. He still went through the motions, giving the floor a quick sweep and straightening the things from the night before he had not yet finished repairing, but decided he would let everything else wait until he was able to contact Mahmoud. Was it too early? Maybe, but it was important. He dialed Mahmoud's cell number and waited:

"Hallo," came a voice still fresh with sleep.

"Mahmoud, peace be upon you, this is Ahmed."

"And to you be peace. How are you? Is everything all right?"

"Yes, yes, everything is fine. I'm sorry for the early hour of the call," Ahmed apologized.

"No, I should have been up long ago, but we had a wedding last night. Please tell me what is it?"

"Read the morning paper and then come by the shop when you have a chance. I want to discuss something with you."

"I think I already know what has caught your attention." Mahmoud replied. "Everyone is talking about it, but you are right. Let's talk about it face-to-face and not over the phone. I will try to come by soon, Lord's willing."

"Thank you, Mahmoud. You are a true friend. I am sorry for the disturbance."

"No disturbance at all, my friend. I will see you soon."

As he said goodbye and closed the phone, Ahmed felt better just knowing that Mahmoud already knew about the situation and was willing to talk. Now he could at least face the work of the day knowing that help was on the way.

As with many businesses in the country, Ahmed's was suffering. He was no longer the only electronic store in the area, but now just one of hundreds that had moved into Heliopolis over the past 20 years. Business now became all about reputation and loyalty from clients. If he sold or repaired a piece of equipment for not only a good price but at the best quality, clients tended to remember him and shared his name with friends. He also learned that he had to know the needs of the people. In the old days, he could carry anything and it would eventually sell, because goods were limited and demand high. Demand was still high, but the amount of goods on the market was vast and the quality even more so. Many businessmen settled for selling the cheap Chinese imports, with full knowledge that they would break within a short amount of time. They did this, knowing that most people would just go and buy another, because of the low price.

Ahmed learned that the customers who mattered were those who were willing to pay a little more for better quality equipment. When and if that equipment did break, they then would bring it to him to repair, because they were not willing just to throw it away and buy another one. So, he benefited in two ways from this—he gained more from selling higher-priced goods, and he earned money from repairs on them as well. Equipment in Egypt was notorious for breaking. The idea of taking care of an appliance was unknown, and with the harsh heat and dirty, sandy air quality, lifespan on equipment was drastically shortened. This, however, made a repairman happy, and Ahmed enjoyed repairing equipment much more than merely selling it, for it gave him a chance to work with his hands and explore the inner workings of each machine.

Today, he was working to finish repairs to a cd player that *Hajj* Ibrahim had brought in last week. It was a simple job, but he had allowed other work to come before and thus he was now behind on his delivery to the client. If he wanted returning customers, he had learned the hard way to have work finished on time. While he worked he reflected on this concept. It drove him crazy to hear other friends in business tell clients that they would finish a task by such and such a day and then add that all important *in sha Allah* to the end of their statement. This is where he and his father had differed in applying religion to life. While it was true that the Qur'an was clear in teaching Muslims to say *in sha Allah* when making a statement to show that everything is under his ultimate control, everyone knew that most Muslims said this to simply take the responsibility off of themselves for ever completing anything on time!

It was after he had been in business about five years that Ahmed, having been screamed at by a customer for being late with work, swore to himself that he would never say *in sha Allah* when telling them when he would finish the job. Actually, it was not only the screaming customer which made him take this decision but a television program he had seen on one of the Christian stations. He was not one for watching Christian programs, but was repairing an air conditioner at the home of an evangelical family when he heard a pastor say on the television: "God's Word says, Let your 'Yes' be 'Yes,' and your 'No,' 'No.'" He then went on to say that believers in Christ should be people of their word. A person does not have to swear to prove that he will keep it, but should show by his actions that he is worthy of people's trust. This gives glory to God.

These simple words made a profound change in the way Ahmed dealt with people, and even though he never told others that it was because of Jesus' words that he changed his way of doing business, he did change nevertheless. Even as he recalled this in his mind, he awoke to the realization that even he had been affected by Christian teaching...just like that man in the paper. This troubled him, but he did not know how to deal with the thoughts. Perhaps when Mahmoud came, he rationalized, he would help me him understand why all this is happening.

The morning dragged by as he waited for Mahmoud. The newspaper story was not the only thing that bothered Ahmed this day. He could not help thinking about what had happened the night before with his two sons. Disappointment and disgust where the only words he could think of when remembering how he could hear their voices from the stairwell, long before he arrived to the door. Then, upon entering his own home and finding them at each other's throats and his wife on the floor, he could not help but shake his head at the deplorable state of his household. What could possibly have provoked his sons to act like that? And to treat their mother in such a disrespectful manner?

He caught himself as soon as the thought came to his mind: I actually have no idea what they were fighting about. I never asked. Fatma, what must she think of me? I did not even see if she was all right. She must hate me. What have I become? What are my children becoming? I need to be more committed to the Faith. God must be judging me for my lack of obedience; otherwise, this would not be happening.

Ahmed determined in his mind as his hands continued working that he would make every effort to attend prayers more regularly and to follow the tenets of the Faith with more diligence. A good Muslim would not have such problems in his home. He made a note in his mind to take a break for prayers that very day. Sometimes he let work get in the way of the call to prayer, and he was now resolute to do better.

However, shortly before the mid-day call to prayer, Mahmoud arrived at the shop.

"Peace be upon you," he said as he entered smiling.

"And to you be peace, and the mercy of God and his blessings," replied Ahmed, as he moved toward his friend to greet him with a kiss on the cheek.

Returning the kiss, Mahmoud continued: "How are you, my friend?"

"Thanks be to God, I am fine, Mahmoud. How are you?"

"Thanks be to God, all is well," came the reply.

"Please sit down," said Ahmed, pulling up a chair for his friend. "What can I get you to drink? Some tea?"

"Yes, tea would be great."

Ahmed called out into the street:

"Ya Hamdy, Hamdy, come."

A small boy came running into the shop. He could not have been over 10 years old. He wore worn slippers and was poorly dressed. Hamdy was the errand boy for the street.

"Hamdy, go get two teas from Abu Ibrahim."

"Yes, sir," came the soft reply, and he was off.

Turning back to his friend, Ahmed sat down in a chair and began:

"Mahmoud, I'm so glad you came. So many things are disturbing me today."

"May the Lord protect you, Ahmed. I trust that it is no more disturbing than this simple newspaper article."

"Yes, that bothers me, but I also have worries at home," replied Ahmed. "I am sure God is judging me because I have not been a good enough Muslim."

"How can you say that, Ahmed?" Mahmoud replied, putting his hand on the shoulder of his friend, "You are a model for many. I am sure that problems at your home are no fault of your own."

The call to prayer rang out over the neighborhood through the loud speakers of the nearby mosque:

"God is the Greatest," began the muezzin with a strong voice. "God is the Greatest. The witness is that God is One. The witness is that God is One and Muhammad is the Prophet of God. Come now to pray. Come now to pray." The voice was musical, yet firm. Ahmed began to notice men moving past his door heading toward the mosque.

Though he had just made his resolution to be better in his prayers, he could not be inhospitable to his friend. He decided that if Mahmoud moved or made the suggestion to go to pray, he would. Otherwise, he would try to make this prayer up later. He returned his focus on his friend who did not seem to catch the irony of what he had just said and the call to prayer that was just heard. That was the problem of something happening five times a day, every day of one's life. It became so routine, that it was no longer noticed.

"It's my boys," Ahmed began as he took up the dialogue again, ignoring his thoughts about prayer time. "They are at each other's throats all the time. I fear they may disgrace the family."

"Oh, I would not worry about them," Mahmoud said soothingly. "Don't you realize they are becoming men, Ahmed? They just need to get married, that's all. Their hormones are too active. They need to find release for that energy."

"Do you think it is as simple as that?" asked Ahmed with a queried look on his brow.

"I'm sure that's it," replied Mahmoud. "How old is Muhammad now?"

"He's twenty-five now."

"Don't you see, my friend?" Mahmoud asked with a smile. "He's ripe for marriage."

"No, I think it's too early. Besides, weddings cost money. I'm not ready for that."

"Well, you had better begin to put something away," Mahmoud replied seriously, "you have several in line, and they will not wait on your finances when they want to marry."

Hamdy arrived with the tea cups on a silver platter, and placed it on a small table between the two men. Ahmed paid him for the tea and added a little for a tip for the boy and sent him away. His head was spinning at the thought of any of his children marrying, much less all of them, but he realized that Mahmoud was right. He needed to be ready. He was not. This almost made him sick at his stomach. God seemed to want to torment him today. He should have gone to prayers.

"Can we change the subject, Mahmoud. I do not want to think about the children any more today."

"I'm sorry if I disturbed you, my friend," Mahmoud replied as he patted Ahmed gently on the knee. "The Lord will provide everything in the right time. Do not worry yourself."

Mahmoud sat up straight and quickly made the change in conversation. "Besides, I believe you called me about something you read in the paper. Am I not right?"

"Yes, yes," Ahmed replied, as he took up his tea glass and took a small sip. "Look, here is the article. What do you make of it?"

Mahmoud only had to look at the headline, since he had already read the paper that morning. "Yes, I knew that was what you were referring to. Everyone is talking about it."

"Well, what does it mean?" asked Ahmed, urging his friend to tell him more. "Do you think it's true?"

"Yes, it is true," replied Mahmoud. "I have a friend who works in Security, and he assures me that the story is accurate."

"But how can a Muslim raise such a case?"

"Well, there are a lot of pressures on the government these days from the West and from organizations that promote human rights. They are what have allowed people to think they can do things which are so obviously against Islam and our laws."

"But will the government allow the case to be tried? And what about Security, can they not arrest him and put him in jail?"

"I am sure the government will try to postpone the case as much as possible in an attempt to try to appease the outside forces and yet not allow a verdict to be made, hoping that something will happen to the family in the meantime or that people will get tired and forget about it. As for Security, they cannot find the man. He has gone into hiding. Some say he's fled the country, others say he's moving around from place to place, being supported by the Christians. In either case, they can't locate him."

"What a mess!" exclaimed Ahmed. "Don't they know that if one person does such a thing, others may get the same idea?"

"Of course they do," replied Mahmoud. "That's why they are trying to either find and kill him or keep the case out of court."

"What is the world coming to?"

"I don't know," Mahmoud said, shaking his head. "I still can't figure out why a person would even think of leaving Islam in the first place and to follow that blasphemous Christian religion. He must have been paid off for converting."

"Yes, I'm sure. Christians always seem to have more money than Muslims anyway. If they can't grow their numbers by births, then they must be trying to buy the increase."

"Babies would be easier!" Mahmoud said with a laugh. He then took on a serious look and said: "However, I cannot help but think that days of great change are coming in our country. I don't know if they will be for good or bad, but I feel as if they are coming."

"I miss the old days," replied Ahmed. "Why can't they just go back to the way it was when we were young?"

"Because it is not God's will."

"God's will...is that what this is?"

Chapter Eight

The days since her encounter with Naema had passed all too quickly. Phardos wanted so much to have called her new friend right way, longing to hear more from this woman of wisdom. Unfortunately, her duties as school director occupied many hours of each day, and the evenings were devoted to the family. The words of Scripture Naema had read began to fade in her mind, and Phardos wanted to find them again, but could not remember from which book she had read. She increasingly became discouraged and began to put the entire episode out of her mind.

She did not even think to discuss the incident with Girgis. He seemed overly preoccupied with the business these days, though he never shared his worries with his wife. They each earned a living, but spoke little about how much was coming in or going out. Phardos put her paycheck into their bank account each month and Girgis always made sure she had plenty to take care of the needs of the family. Otherwise, she had no idea how much was in their account. Girgis knew she would be shocked to know that there were some months when she earned more than he did. Such knowledge would only hinder their marriage and make her think less of him. It was better left alone.

It was not only the business that worried her husband during these days. The papers were full of articles on the conversion and court case of this Muslim-background family. Girgis read not only *Al-Ahram*, but several other local papers as well, including the fundamentalist Islamic papers. He felt it was important as a Christian to be aware of what they were saying about the minority, as it affected everything in the country, especially the economy and business relationships. If negative reports were published about Christians, then business always dropped at the store. Sometimes, when there was fighting between Muslims and Christians in Upper Egypt, problems would pop up in Cairo as well as a reaction to one side or the other.

Already rumors were rampant in Midan Al-Gamma about this case. For the most part, Christian businessmen were trying to keep a low profile and not talk openly about it. Several Coptic priests had published statements disclaiming any knowledge of this family and attacking them for their brazen disrespect for the law. Girgis knew this was propaganda and just an attempt to keep the Church from being caught in the backlash of the case. Everyone in the Church knew that Muslims were coming more and more to Christianity, though the Church made a great effort to hide them in various ways and even get them out of the country.

Though admittedly not an active member of the Church, Girgis could not help feeling that something was wrong in the way the priests were responding to this issue. Though he had never personally met a Muslim convert to Christianity, he had a friend who knew some. He also had talked at length with another jeweler in the area who read widely and attended an Evangelical church. Joseph told him that Muslims all around the Middle East and North Africa were converting to Christianity, or being *born again*, as he put it, and that they were even starting churches made up completely of believers from Muslim backgrounds.

Girgis pondered over all this as he put the papers away and began drinking his tea. A young man, Marcos, was cleaning the jewelry cases in preparation for the shop to open. Once he had finished his work, Girgis would be forced to put these thoughts behind him and focus on getting out the jewelry and putting it in the window and cases. Watching Marcos at work, Girgis secretly wished to himself that he could be as carefree as the young man and content with his simple labors.

The business that morning was slow. Only a handful of customers came in, several of them being people who wanted to sell their own gold jewelry. This was a common practice in the Middle East, as gold was always considered an investment and not a luxury item intended for keeping forever. One young woman entered around noon. She was fully veiled in the black abaya and niqab. Girgis always hated dealing with these women, because you could never see their eyes to see if they were telling the truth, nor could you hear them well behind the veil. However, he did his best not to appear too rude.

"Peace be upon you," she said softly as she entered the shop.

"And peace to you." Girgis replied evenly. "Can I help you?"

"Yes, I want to sell some jewelry." She pulled out a small cloth bag from her black purse and opened it up on the counter.

Girgis was shocked when he saw the contents—a beautifully cut one-carat diamond wedding ring and an engraved gold band to match. It also contained a bracelet of high quality diamonds and a necklace with a single solitaire of its own.

"These are yours?" he asked, trying to determine the age of the young woman, though it was hard through the veil.

"Yes, they were," she replied and continued with bitterness in her voice, "but I no longer need them."

Girgis was never one to give counsel to women, and especially to a completely veiled Muslim one. It could bring great wrath from family members, especially of the male persuasion. However, he could not help himself, as he felt this particular woman was obviously in a bad situation.

"Are you sure you want to sell them?" he began. "I mean, please, do not take this in the wrong way; they are beautiful. Do you really want to part with them?"

Even through the veil, she looked straight at him, allowing her eyes to be revealed through the thick cloth. "What are jewels if there is no love?"

"I am very sorry," tried Girgis. "Please forgive me for prying. I will be glad to accommodate you any way I can."

"Thank you. You are kind," she replied, and took a tissue from her purse. She took it and lifted her veil slightly to obviously wipe the eyes beneath.

"Please, sit down," offered Girgis. "Let me get you some tea. It will take me a few minutes to inspect these and give you an appraisal. Please," he said again, pointing to the chair, "sit down."

The woman sat down in the chair, returning the tissue to her purse. Girgis hurried Marcos out to get the tea and then took the jewels to his desk to inspect them through his eye piece. Propriety would not allow him to approach her again about the reason she was selling the jewels, but he could not help but wonder about her situation. He made an effort to focus on the jewelry and not their owner and began taking notes as to the approximate price he would be willing to offer for each piece. Marcos returned with the tea and offered it to the woman, who sat quietly and refrained from looking in Girgis' direction as he worked.

Eventually, Girgis finished his calculations and shared with the woman his conclusion.

"That is a very good offer," she said as he handed her the piece of paper.

"I try to be honest and straightforward in my dealings," he replied.

"Yes, that is why I came to you."

"Have we met before?" Girgis asked.

"I have come in here several times with my mother, Um Fethi."

"Oh, yes, I know Um Fethi, but..." then Girgis caught himself, as he realized the only daughter he ever saw with Um Fethi was not covered at all.

"Don't worry. I know what you are thinking. No, I was not covered before marriage. This was an expectation of my husband. However, I will no longer need to worry about that. It was not to be. I only wore the veil today, so that no one would recognize me as I came in your shop."

Girgis could not help himself now that he realized who the woman was: "Why don't you hold on to the jewelry. Surely, you do not need to sell it all at once."

"If I am to start a new life, I will, I'm afraid," she replied. "Mr. Girgis, I know that I can trust you. You are a Christian man. Please do not let my family know that I was here."

"No, no," he stuttered in reply, "you have my confidence. Is there anything else I can do to help?"

"No, you have done more than enough in giving me an honorable price for the gold."

"Well, they are beautiful pieces, and will be easy for me to resell, to be honest," he said, looking at her and smiling. "Can you come back tomorrow? I will have the money ready for you. It is a large sum, so I will need to go to the bank. Keep the jewelry with you, but I will have the money for you tomorrow."

"No, I trust you, Mr. Girgis. You keep the jewelry. I have no need for it now," she said in a sorrowful tone. "I will be back tomorrow about the same time, is that OK?"

"Yes, I will have everything ready for you."

"Thank you for your time and for the tea. Good-Bye."

"Good-bye, Madame."

Girgis watched the black creature flow out through the door, and as it shut behind her, a heaviness weighed him down so that he felt forced down into his chair. How many times had he seen those black abayas flowing through the streets of Cairo, and never had he thought of the person beneath them... never. Now here was a woman with feelings, emotions, needs, and yet hiding them all under that same cloth. It made him realize that things were not always so black and white as they seemed. He felt intensely for the needs of this woman, and yet, he should have no reason to be involved in her personal life. It was an odd, surreal experience.

He tried to push aside the emotions and made a note to go to the bank first thing in the morning. He then picked up the jewelry, held each piece in his hand. What a beautiful wedding band. She must have married a man of great wealth, he thought. However, as she so quickly found out, great wealth without great love is nothing. This notion made his mind flow to his own wife and marriage. God had been very good to him indeed by granting him Phardos. She was an intelligent, hard-working woman and a good mother to their children. She also made sure they went to church. Yes, God was good. He must remember to do something special for her. After all, Mother's Day was coming up. Hopefully, he would be able to sell one of these pieces quickly and make a good profit to buy her something special.

Chapter Nine

Um Muhammad never did talk with her husband about what happened that night with the boys. Since he did not mention it either, she decided it had made no impression on him and was not worth it. It had been several days since, and life was back to normal. She did note a slight change in Ahmed's behavior toward her, however. He seemed to be making an obvious effort to show his appreciation for her work around the house. A few days before Mother's Day, he surprised her with his comments.

"Fatma, you are a good mother."

She was so taken aback by the simple statement that she could not speak, so he tried again.

"Did you hear me, wife? I said you are a good mother. I just wanted you to know that I think that."

"Thank you, Ahmed," Um Muhammad replied with hesitancy.

"I will be out the rest of the day."

"All right, husband. Go in peace."

"Peace to you," he said, and he was out the door.

Um Muhammad stood in the same spot for several seconds, simply staring at the door from which her husband had departed. What was that about? She wondered. Maybe his conscience was bothering him about the other day. She shrugged her shoulders and returned to her housework.

Rachid had been in the kitchen eating his breakfast. He came out into the living room where he mother was standing.

"Mother, was that Father leaving just now? I heard the door."

"Yes, my son, he was just leaving for work."

"Too bad," he said, "I was hoping to get some money from him."

"Are you going to be doing some more interviews today, my son?" she asked. "I can give you some pocket money if you need it."

"No, I was needing something more, Mother, but that's all right," he continued, "the Lord will provide."

"Where will you interview today?"

"No interviews," he replied quickly, "I am meeting some friends at the mosque."

"Rachid, my son," Um Muhammad tried.

"Mother, do not start with me. I am sure through my connections at the mosque a good job will come."

"Rachid," she pressed, "you have been out of college some time now. It is time you found a job. You are spending too much time with friends. Please look harder. Your father will not be pleased if you do not find something soon; even if it is not engineering."

"Well, if you must know," he said to her condescendingly, "I am not looking into the area of engineering anyway. I am leaning toward other areas. There are many opportunities out there for good Muslim men."

"My son, I prefer that you discuss this with your father."

"Father does not understand my desires. All he is interested in is making money. There is more to life than material gain. God's way is the straight path."

"I fear you are walking in dangerous waters, my son," said Um Muhammad, and she moved toward Rachid to take him by the arms.

He moved away from her suddenly and said: "You do not know what you are talking about, woman. God's way is always the right way. I will do what he requires, not you or Father." Rachid pushed past her and went down the hall to his room, slamming the door behind him.

His mother sat on the couch and put her head in her hands and cried in a loud voice, "Oh Lord, oh Lord, how can you let this happen? Stop him, Lord, stop him from this path of evil in the name of religion."

No sooner had the words come out her mouth than Rachid came back out of his room, but this time with a back-pack in his hand. He threw it over his shoulder and said, as he moved toward the door: "I may be gone for a few days. Do not worry about me."

Um Muhammad rushed toward him and caught him by the arm: "No, Rachid, don't do this. It will only lead to trouble."

"Leave me alone, Woman. I'm a man now, not a child. I can make my own decisions. Besides, everything I do now, I do for the good of Islam. It is my destiny, and you would do well to follow the same path. Now, let me go."

"No, Rachid, no my son, please!" begged Um Muhammad, but he was too strong for her and pulled himself from her grip and ran out the door. As it slammed shut, she fell to the floor and cried.

Muhammad had been in his room, but heard the commotion between his mother and brother, and came into the foyer just before Rachid left. "Good riddance," he exclaimed with a loud voice, when the younger brother left. His mother heard his voice and looked up through her tears.

"Muhammad, how can you say that about your own brother?"

"Mother, don't you see that he has chosen the path of the Brotherhood? Can you not see it? He's been changing for some time now. It was obvious that he would leave us eventually; and it is better for him to be away from us if he is going to follow them. Otherwise, we will have all their troubles on us as well."

"I don't know, I don't know," cried Um Muhammad. She then sat up on her knees and looked at her son directly. "Muhammad, you must tell your father. He will want to know."

"No, Mother," replied Muhammad, "that is something I will not do. If you want him to know, you must tell him. He will only think that I am saying that because of our fight the other night."

Um Muhammad picked herself up off the floor and moved to the living room. Her son followed her and watched her as she sat down on the couch.

"Yes, yes," she said after a few silent moments. "You are right. It will have to be me. I will go down to the store right now. It cannot wait. I would not want him to hear it from someone else, whatever the consequences may be for me."

"I can walk down with you," Muhammad offered. "I have to go to work anyway. Just give me a few minutes to get ready."

"Thank you, my son. I need to get myself together as well." And she went into her room to find her veil and a more appropriate dress.

They walked down from their apartment and into the street. The family did not own a car, as public transportation was a common way of life for the majority of Egyptians. Cars were a luxury, though the number of them in the city made it appear that every citizen owned one. However, with a population of over 20 million, even a minority of car owners made the streets congested beyond belief.

Um Muhammad and her firstborn son walked briskly down the street until they reached the metro line. This tram system, which wove its way through the suburbs of the city, connecting neighborhoods with one another and ultimately downtown, was a product of the 1940s. Though expanded with the growth of the city, maintenance was only enough to keep it running. The cars themselves appeared never to have been refurbished or painted since the day they were installed. Millions rode the cars (inside and out) day after day, paying their few cents to travel the system. Though there were taxis and buses of various sorts, the metro was the easiest for Muhammad and his father to use to get to work from their home. Heliopolis was not large, and they could travel the few stations with relative ease, though not much speed, as long as they did not catch it at rush hour.

As it was later in the morning now, the cars were not too full, and Muhammad was able to find his mother a seat. They sat together in silence, watching passengers get on and off at each stop, until they reached Salah El-Deen station. Muhammad rose and helped his mother get safely off the tram. Crossing the road from the metro to the next sidewalk was always a challenge, but Muhammad put his hand up to keep approaching vehicles from running them over as they quickly maneuvered across. They walked along for a few more blocks and then turned into the main thoroughfare of the area. Another short turn and they were in front of her husband's electronic store. Before they entered, she could see Abu Muhammad sitting at his table, working on a small television. He looked so content, she actually regretted that she had come, but she knew she must, and as Muhammad opened the door, her husband looked up in surprise.

"What are you doing here?" he asked, empty of the kind tone shared earlier in the day.

"I have something important to share with you, Abu Muhammad," she replied. A Muslim wife never referred to her husband by his familiar name in public, and some would never do so in private either.

Before he could reply, Muhammad spoke up: "Father, I am going to go to pick up those transformers we needed.

I will be back later." He was out the door before his father could object or comment.

Um Muhammad looked back from where her son had stood, and took a deep breath. She knew he would leave her to do this alone. She must be brave.

"Abu Muhammad, something has happened, and you must be informed."

"What is it, woman?" he replied sharply; then caught himself. "Here sit," as he pointed to a chair, "tell me what has happened."

"It is about Rachid," she started.

"What about Rachid?" he asked with a worried look on his face.

"He told me this morning that he was going to the mosque, and that the people there would find him a job. Oh, Ahmed," she exclaimed without realizing her mistake, "he has taken a bag with him and has left. He said he would be gone for a few days. He said he was following the straight path."

"Careful, woman, how you speak to me," began Ahmed, "Remember your place."

"Yes, forgive me, Abu Muhammad," she cried; "I am just so upset."

"This is not the place to air our problems."

"No, no, I know that," she replied, trying to dry her tears, "I just did not want you to hear it from anyone else. I did not know what to do."

"Yes, yes, you did fine. Just go home now. There is nothing more to be done."

"Nothing more to be done!" Um Muhammad exclaimed. "How can you say that? You must do something. We cannot let him go with such a group!"

"Control yourself, Woman! I do not need more problems from this neighborhood as well. Dry your tears and go home. You have done all you can. I will take care of our son. Do not concern yourself. You have other children to think of." He rose and took her by the arm, walking her toward the door. "Now, go home. Put yourself together. All will be well."

Um Muhammad knew it was useless to say anything further. She quickly wiped her tears and straightened her veil to make sure she did not look out of order. She offered a soft, "Good-bye, my husband," and walked out the door and into the light of the mid-day sun.

Chapter Ten

When Girgis got home that evening, the thoughts of the veiled woman were still in his mind, but were quickly pushed aside as he faced the frantic activity that greeted him.

"What is happening in this house?" he exclaimed as Marianne flew past him, running down the hall.

His wife was coming out of the bathroom, wrapped in her terry cloth robe. "Good evening, Girgis, welcome home. I completely forgot that we had a wedding this evening at church."

"What wedding?" he asked.

"The daughter of Marianne's youth group leader, Nadia Philemon."

"Who is she marrying?" Girgis asked.

"The groom is from Alexandria. I don't know him."

"What time is the wedding?"

"In an hour."

"You won't be ready," he said with a smirk on his face.

"I will, but I will have to fix my hair myself. There is no time to go to the salon now. I have your suit out and ready."

"No, I'm not going," he said with determination in his voice.

"Girgis, you must. It is Marianne's teacher. People will be expecting you."

"You know how much I hate weddings, Phardos."

"I know, dear, but it is an obligation we must face. Please, for me?"

As her parents made this last exchange of conversation, Marianne was bursting out of her room and headed toward the kitchen with a scarf she wanted to iron. She hurried past them but then yelled back over her shoulder: "Yes, Papa, for me too, please!"

Girgis could never say no to Marianne. She was his special girl, and he knew, though he hated to admit it, that she had him wrapped around her finger. He shrugged his shoulders at them both and headed for the shower. A wedding! How boring. He would have to console himself that at least he could see some friends and catch up on the news of the community.

Though it took some effort, they made it out of the house within the next hour. They knew that it was not necessary to be at the church at the time written on the invitation...brides were never on time. As they walked to the church, they laughed together about the bride who was a whole two hours late. Problems at the coiffeur was the excuse given, but it did not make the guests any happier, who were eager to leave the church and get to the reception. They all prayed it would not be the case tonight. Neither Girgis nor Phardos wanted to stay up later than necessary. Both were tired from a long day at work. Though they were all invited to the reception at the Sheraton, Philippe and Marianne were the only ones going. Receptions were loud and long, and the older they got, the less the parents enjoyed such events. It was enough to attend the wedding.

As they neared the church, they could see that a large crowd was attending the wedding due to the double and triple-parked cars in the street. Thankfully, they had arrived before the bride, and they greeted several friends and family members as they entered the building. The church was crowded, but they managed to find a pew that held the four of them and took their seats.

Marriage is one of the sacraments of the Orthodox Church and thus taken very seriously. Yet, Phardos could not help but think, as she looked around at the beautiful flowers and decorations, that all too many marriages these days were falling apart. She could not understand what was happening to this new generation. Actually she did realize that fewer young people were dedicated to the church as they had been in her youth. Though they married in the Church, they were not really a "part" of it. Maybe that was the problem. She hoped this young couple's marriage would be a lasting one.

A noise came from outside—the sound of the *zuggarit,* as the bride's arrival was being announced by village women. It never seemed to matter the class or religion of the bride, there had to be this high shrill sound made by moving the tongue back and forth in rapid succession. It could not be a proper celebration without it. So many things crossed cultural and religious boundaries in Egypt, and this was obviously one of them. Everyone in the church turned in anticipation and then began to stand as the procession began.

The first thing Girgis noticed about the bride was her dress, which was much too revealing for his taste, though she had a body to be proud of. He looked at her in shock and then realized as he stood and took in the rest of the congregation that the majority of the women were also dressed in tight and revealing soiree attire. He now worried about Marianne going to the reception. He would remember to speak to Phardos about it once this ceremony was over. He did not like the look of the crowd, though he knew many of the older adults present. It was the young ones who concerned him.

There were no less than four priests officiating the marriage ceremony, which meant that the father of the bride obviously had a good income. Everyone knew that it was money that drew the priests to the weddings. Girgis remembered the good old days when priests were honest and really served the people; now it was all about money. He noticed a rather overweight priest who had obviously come from the groom's church in Alexandria, since he did not know his name. He chuckled to himself as he recalled the joke about the Orthodox priest who entered the priesthood skinny, but came out of it fat. Oh, the temptations they faced as they accepted this position of responsibility. He was grieved that so many used it to gain power and money. The poor can hardly find a priest to perform their ceremonies and funerals. What a shame to have four!

All these thoughts were going through the mind of Girgis as the ceremony got underway, requiring the congregation to stand or sit at appointed times, whether for prayer or the reading of Scripture. Girgis prided himself on knowing a fair amount of the ancient Coptic or Hieroglyphic language, so at least he could follow the liturgy as it flowed between the largely unknown tongue and the more modern and understood Arabic. However, this was a well-rehearsed routine to all Orthodox Christians, and whether they understood the language or not, they knew exactly how to respond and what to do.

It was as he stood for about the third time that Girgis caught a glimpse of several Muslims in attendance. Remembering his encounter earlier in the day, he looked at them intently to see how they were reacting to the service. Some were not bothering to stand, but remained seated throughout the service, smiling politely but obviously at a loss as to what was really happening. Others were making serious efforts to follow the crowd, but had looks of confusion each time the language switched from Arabic into Coptic. Girgis realized that truly we must look like a strange people with odd customs to Muslims, and he thought to himself how little we really understand each other.

As the time for the rings to be exchanged approached, Phardos could not help but remember her own wedding. Did this young girl know her groom as little as she knew Girgis when they married? She has no idea what she's doing. Phardos didn't. Yet, somehow God brought good out of it and she could not really complain about her husband. He was by her side, wasn't he? She looked around her and took notice of all the women who were obviously without their husbands tonight. She looked at Girgis and smiled. He smiled back to her. Where were his thoughts? Was he thinking of her?

Neither would know what the other was thinking that night, for they would never talk about it. Long past were the days when they confided deeply in each other. Girgis never wanted Phardos to worry unnecessarily, so he chose not to share his troubles with her. Phardos wanted to show Girgis that she was a strong woman and could handle any crisis that came her way and not fall apart. Slowly, but steadily, the communication stopped. They lived two separate lives under one roof.

The ceremony lasted a full hour, as each priest took part in the liturgy and made remarks about marriage. Finally, however, the couple was able to sign the book which officially joined them as husband and wife, and upon finishing their vows, where released to the world as a married couple. The shrills began once again, as the procession left the church, and smiles filled the crowd. Girgis took his wife by the hand and leaned over to speak to her:

"I am not sure about letting the kids go to this reception."

Phardos looked at her husband in surprise and asked, "Why not, Girgis, is something wrong?"

"I just think the crowd is too wild for Marianne."

"I am sure that her teacher would never let things go too far. We cannot keep her from going, *Habibi*. All her friends will be there."

"Well, then I want to make sure Philippe watches out for her," Girgis replied with a serious look on his face. "Where is he?"

"They went out the door as soon as the service finished."

"Well, let's find them before they leave."

"Yes, husband," replied Phardos with submission.

After congratulating the bride and groom and their families, the couple found their children and warned them of the temptations that would face them at the reception. Both were indignant at the worries of their parents.

"Oh, Papa, I know there will be drinking, but you know I would not do that," exclaimed Marianne.

"Well, just the same, you need to be careful when there are men around who have had too much to drink," warned her father.

"Papa, I will stay close to my friends," replied Marianne, "plus Philippe will be there. He will not let anyone bother me. Please don't worry."

"Yes, Papa, you know that I will watch out for my sister," assured Philippe.

"You behave yourself too," said his mother as she gave him a kiss, "and watch out for fast women."

"Oh, Mama, please!" Philippe replied as he rolled his eyes.

"Call me before you start home," Phardos added.

"You'll be asleep, Mother," Marianne offered.

"Wake me up! I don't care. Just call."

"Yes, Mama," both children echoed obediently.

"Make me proud," added their father. "Don't give in to shameful behavior."

"Yes, Papa," came the required response.

They kissed their children again and left them at the church with the crowd. As they began to go out the gate, Girgis saw several of his friends and stopped to talk. Phardos looked around for her own friends and spotted several, whom she also greeted. It was another half an hour before they began the walk home. Girgis held his wife's hand as they walked home in silence.

Chapter Eleven

It was several days before news would come of Rachid's whereabouts. Though his brother knew he went to mosque regularly, he was not sure which one. Ahmed sent his oldest son all around the area to inquire about Rachid. Finding information was difficult, as imams were cautious about letting strangers know about their more radical activities. In the end, it was his friend, Mahmoud, who was able to locate the young man. He was more highly connected in the religious community and was able to make more effective inquiries into the matter.

Now that he knew where Rachid was, Ahmed was not sure what to do. If he went in and simply claimed his son and dragged him off, he knew that Rachid would hate him forever and possibly just run away for good. However, if he let him be, he feared the worse and had concern about the repercussions on the rest of the family. He decided in the end, after counseling with Mahmoud, that he would send Rachid a letter to let him know that the family knew of his location, were concerned about his health, and preferred that he come home. If he wanted to pursue this path in life, his father requested that he come home so they could at least talk about it openly.

Though he did not want to do it, Muhammad was chosen by his father for the task of delivering the letter. The mosque was in a different area of town, so he had to take a minibus and the underground to get there, but after an hour of travel, he finally found it. Taking a deep breath, he walked through the large main doors. To his amazement, there was Rachid sitting with his legs crossed in a circle with several other young men all listening to a bearded imam, who appeared to be giving them a lesson. Muhammad did not know what to do and simply stood there and stared at the group for a few moments. One of the young men, however, noticed him and rose to greet him.

"Peace be upon you," he said as he neared Muhammad.

"And upon you be peace," came the reply.

"Have you come to pray?" the man asked.

"No, to see my brother," Muhammad answered with more confidence than he actually felt.

"And who would your brother be?"

"Rachid," and Muhammad nodded toward the group.

"One moment please," said the young man. He returned to the group and whispered something in the ear of the imam.

Now the entire group was looking in Muhammad's direction. Rachid, who had not previously noticed his brother, now realized who he was. He made an effort to rise, but the imam put out his hand to stop him. It was the imam who then rose and came over the Muhammad.

"Peace be upon you," he said.

"And upon you be peace," Muhammad said again, but continued quickly. "I would like to see my brother, Rachid."

"Yes, I am sure you would," replied the imam. "However, Rachid is in the midst of intense studies and cannot be disturbed. I will be glad to take him a message."

"You will not let me see my own brother?" Muhammad's voice began to rise.

"You will see him soon enough, *in sha Allah*," replied the imam. "Right now, however, he will not be able to talk with you."

"I have a letter for him from his father," insisted Muhammad. "It is very urgent."

"I will be happy to give it to him."

"He will be expecting a reply," Muhammad said with persistence. He noticed in the corner of his eye that the group was rising. They all, including Rachid, wore the same uniform—a light *galabiya* and the shorten pants of the Sunni. Each had his head covered with a small white skull cap. Each was sporting a short beard. It was obvious the direction his brother was headed.

"He will receive one, rest assured," said the imam. "Now, if you will excuse me, I must return to my students."

Muhammad handed the letter hesitantly to the imam and turned to leave. Before he went out the door, he turned around to look again at his brother. He noticed the imam had walked back to the group, but instead of giving Rachid the letter, was putting it into the pocket of his robe. Rachid was not looking in his direction, but had his gaze fixed directly on the leader. He was obviously under his spell.

Muhammad turned and went quickly down the steps of the mosque, furious that Rachid was allowing himself to be drawn in by such a group and mad at himself for being so easy on the imam. However, he knew that if he had gotten angry, the men in the group would quickly come to the imam's defense and possibly rough him up. Rachid was not worth that, so he had controlled himself. What his father would say, he did not know. What was sure was that his younger brother was bringing a great deal of trouble on the family. What a mess!

He knew his father would be waiting to hear the news, so he quickly found a minibus to take him to the underground station. It was not too crowded, and he sat next to a well-kept man about the same age as himself. He was obviously a Christian, as he noticed his distinct features and the small cross tattooed on the inside of his wrist. The man greeted him as he sat down,

"Good morning."

"Good morning," replied Muhammad without a smile.

"My name is Fouad."

Muhammad realized that he was not going to be able to ride the bus in peace, so replied obligingly: "My name is Muhammad."

"It's nice to meet you, Muhammad," continued Fouad, "how are you today?"

Under normal circumstances, Muhammad would not have given the man the time of day, but he was full of emotions and was glad to get some of them off his chest.

"Do you really want to know, Fouad?" he asked, looking at him directly in the eyes.

"Yes, I would not have asked if not."

"I am terrible," admitted Muhammad quickly. "I hate my life, my work, and now my brother is bringing trouble on our family and I had to find him."

"It seems the Lord has put us together today, my brother," said Fouad surprisingly. "Did you know that God does not want you to have such a miserable life?"

"I don't think God cares about my life at all," replied Muhammad. "If he did, I would not be going through all this."

"I am afraid you are wrong in that assumption, my friend," said Fouad, "God is very interested in your life and even wants you to live it more abundantly. He said himself in the *Injil*: 'I have come that they may have life, and have it more abundantly.'"

"An abundant life, I don't believe it."

"Well it is true. Our Lord, *'Isa* the Christ said it himself."

"I don't remember anything like that in the Holy Qur'an," replied Muhammad, though he did not want to admit that he had not really read the entire Qur'an, but he was sure that if something so great was in there, he would have at least heard about it.

"Our Lord *'Isa* has many words in the Qur'an, but many more are recorded in the Holy *Injil*," said Fouad. "Have you read it?"

"No, never," said Muhammad.

"Would you like to?" Fouad asked with some hesitancy and with a lower voice so the other passengers could not hear.

Muhammad did not know how to respond to the question. He knew the *Injil* was the book of the Christians, and from what he had been taught, was corrupt. However, he was intrigued at reading something that might make his life better. He thought to himself: What would it hurt to just read it? He responded openly, "Yes, I would. Where can I get one?"

A smile came across Fouad's face. "You can take mine." He pulled a small green book from his shirt pocket and handed it to Muhammad.

Muhammad looked at the book and then up at Fouad. "Thank you, but are you sure you want to give me your copy?"

"Oh, I have another at home, don't worry," said Fouad reassuringly. "Muhammad," he continued, "I have to get off at the next stop, please take my number and if you have any questions about what you read, feel free to call me." He handed him a small piece of paper.

Muhammad took the paper and again said thank you. Fouad told the driver to stop at a nearby corner. As he prepared to get out of the van, he turned to Muhammad and said again: "I know the Lord has put us together today, Muhammad, and I know he will speak to you through his Word. Good-bye."

"Good-bye," was all Muhammad could say as he watched the man get out of the van.

Another man got in as Fouad left and took the seat next to Muhammad. Realizing that he was still holding the *Injil*, Muhammad quickly slipped it into his shirt pocket. His own stop was shortly thereafter, and he descended the van onto a crowded street in front of the metro station. As the metro was crowded with afternoon riders, Muhammad did not have time to look at the book again before arriving at home, but his mind kept going over the words he had heard from the stranger: *I have come that they may have life and have it more abundantly.* Abundant life, what an absurd notion! There would be no abundant life with the troubles that were about to rain down on his house. He thought with dread about what he would have to tell his father.

Chapter Twelve

The wedding ceremony was merely something everyone endured in the Orthodox Church in order to get to the reception. Of course, no respectable friend would show up at the reception if they had not first been to the church, but it was not easy for the many young, basically heathenistic guests to sit through the entire mass. Most had no clue what was happening, and many were quietly texting their friends on their cell phones as the couple took their vows. Though Philippe and Marianne had grown up in the church and were therefore deemed religious, they too were impatient to get to the hotel for the party. Philippe had been to weddings before without his parents, but this was a first for Marianne. She could not wait to see what would happen.

Philippe had money from his father to take a taxi to the hotel, but he knew if others joined them, they could share the cost. He found two of his friends who were going and asked them to ride with him and his sister. After they hailed a taxi, Marianne got in first and went to the far side of the back seat, Philippe sat next to her and then one of his friends, making the back seat full. The other friend sat in front next to the driver. Marianne was worried her dress would get dirty in the taxi, as they were never clean. She leaned over to her brother and said:

"Philippe, I want to go to the bathroom as soon as we get into the hotel. I am sure my dress will be ruined!"

"Oh, you'll be all right, Marianne, don't worry," responded her brother with some exasperation, "but you can go to the bathroom anytime you want."

"I know I can," she whispered back loudly in his ear, "but I don't want you to run off and leave me before we even get into the reception hall."

"I won't, I won't." Philippe was already regretting having his little sister along. It was obvious she was going to cramp his style. Oh well, he resigned himself to her presence and assured himself as well that once she got with her friends, he wouldn't have to be so watchful of her.

Upon arriving at the hotel, passing by the bathroom, and then showing their invitations at the reception hall, they each took in a big breath as they saw what lay before them. The room was full of round tables, set up for dinner, and each with a large crystal centerpiece full of flowers. There was a wooden parquet dance floor in the center of the room and a stage behind it with a band just setting up. To the side they spotted four young women dressed in matching skimpy outfits who were obviously going to be part of the show on stage. More flower arrangements were set around the room, and at one end was an area of couches and small coffee tables. A bar was also set up near this area, and boxes of drinks of all kinds were set against the wall behind it. A lot of money had obviously been spent.

It took another hour before most of the people actually had arrived. They began sitting in groups at the tables. Waiters started taking drink orders. Philippe, Marianne and their friends took a table near the couches. Finally, a friend of Marianne's showed up, and Philippe was happy when she left him to join her at her family's table. What Philippe did not notice was that his sister looked very beautiful that night, and as she left the table, his friends frowned at her departure. Brothers seldom see their sisters in any light but that of sister, and it was so with Philippe. He should have noticed, however, because Marianne was already gaining the attention of many that night. Perhaps it was her long hair that she pulled up into a loose bun, allowing her slender neck to be revealed in all its splendor. Or, it may have been the black dress she wore that fit tightly to her body and hung low in the front. She did have a good figure, after all, and the high heeled shoes that she wore gave her an appearance of maturity that may not have been there in years.

However, it was not just Philippe who was oblivious to this, but Marianne herself. She had always been a strong, self-confident young girl, but was only just beginning to learn about what it was to become a woman and was still naïve when it came to the intentions of the opposite sex. Since she did not dress like this every day, she had never really experienced the attentions she was already receiving.

All this was forgotten as the bride and groom made their entrance, and what an entrance it was! The band was playing, smoke started rising and then a sudden burst of sparklers heralded the couple's entrance. The Master of Ceremonies made the grand announcement and everyone clapped and cheered. The couple went immediately to the dance floor and began the first dance to the applause of all in attendance. People began to leave their tables and surround the dance floor to watch the couple. Philippe and Marianne and their friends joined the crowd, pushing to the front to get a good view. Once the first dance was finished, others moved to the floor to begin the next song. Though Philippe stayed off the floor with his friends, Marianne moved with her girlfriend onto the floor to dance. In such a segregated society, even among Christians, it was not unusual for a group of girls to dance together or boys for that matter. So Marianne was perfectly content to let herself go with the music in front of her girlfriends. What she did not realize, however, was that many eyes were on her as she did so.

After watching several dances, Philippe moved back toward his table with his friends, since he was hungry and hoped the dinner would be served before midnight. Marianne kept on dancing, but eventually returned as well to eat at her friend, Gigi's table. When the waiters finally brought out the food, Gigi leaned over to Marianne and said quietly:

"Did you see those guys watching us?"

"What guys?" asked Marianne.

"Oh, come on Marianne, you can't be serious." Gigi said louder. "There was a whole group of them watching us on the dance floor."

"Really? I never noticed," responded Marianne in all honesty.

"You are so clueless, sometimes, Marianne," Gigi said, shaking her head. "After dinner, let's go back to the floor and see if they follow us again."

"Sounds like you are looking for trouble, Gigi, and your parents are right here," Marianne said, now lowering her own voice.

"My parents don't really care what I do," Gigi replied with a little sadness in her voice. "Besides, we're among Christians, so they figure that if someone takes an interest in me, at least he'll be from the church. That is all that matters to them."

Marianne shrugged her shoulders at her friend and tried to concentrate on the food now on her plate. However, new thoughts and even emotions were rising inside her that she had not experienced before. Some even frightened her. Until now, she had not bothered with thinking about boys. School was an all-consuming occupation for most Egyptian young people, and since she was not yet in college, marriage was not important to dwell on. She suddenly realized, however, that she was close to graduation, which meant that marriage talk would begin soon among the women in her family. Even among Christian girls, marriage was the goal of life. But could it be true that guys were interested in her? She knew she was decent-looking, but surely there were other girls here tonight who were much more mature and attractive.

Though she did not drink, she did take some of the wine that was poured into her glass during dinner. Everyone drank, and her parents were not so strict that they would deny her a little wine. She did not anticipate the effect, however, and as she and Gigi finished their meal, they both became more relaxed and even giggly. As the music continued to blare, Gigi gave Marianne a nod and they excused themselves from the table and headed to the dance floor.

The music varied between western popular music and well-known Arabic selections. The girls on the stage had a routine for each kind and provided a good diversion for many of the older men present, who remained at the tables with their wives. When yet another Arabic song began, Gigi and Marianne began the familiar and natural movement of their hips and hands and were caught up completely in the music. The floor was crowded, as people danced together in groups or as couples. It was not unusual then that a young man ended up close to Marianne as she danced. What was unusual was the way he was obviously engrossed with her presence. He could not take his eyes off of her as she moved seductively to the music. Marianne was not even aware of his presence until she turned a circle and looked up to find him dancing to the music with the same movements of his body. She caught herself, but he quickly leaned in and spoke in her ear so he could be heard over the music:

"Don't stop, you are beautiful. Dance with me."

Marianne was too shocked to know what to say, but as she looked into his eyes, she found herself continuing the dance and allowing him to remain close to her body. He smiled and they remained in motion, but without touching until the song came to an end. As soon as the music slowed, she came out of her revelry and looked around for Gigi. Unfortunately, her friend had already taken the hand of another young man and was being led off the floor toward the couches. Marianne had no intention of that happening, and as the music quickly began again, she returned her eyes to the man before her.

"My name is Marianne," she said quickly before the music got too loud.

"My name is Emad," he responded with a smile on his face.

"Nice to meet you."

"You too," he said. "Shall we dance another?"

"I'm game if you are," she said as if she was so self-confident.

The song was a western pop song, fast and loud, requiring those dancing to adjust their movements accordingly. Emad kept his eyes fixed on Marianne as she did her best to dance to the music. She was not used to wearing high heels, and struggled to keep her feet moving without falling on her face. The floor was so crowded, mostly with young people that she was well hidden from any adults who might know her, and her brother was still with his friends close to the bar. She and Emad were both relieved when the music changed to a slower beat. Though Marianne had considered excusing herself, Emad moved in quickly as the beat changed, putting one hand around her waist and holding her right hand in his left. This move startled Marianne, but as she looked into his eyes, she found herself relaxing in his arms as their legs moved simultaneously to the music. It was the first time she had ever actually touched a man before and it sent a new sensation through her body. As they danced, Emad smiled and whispered in her ear:

"You are the most beautiful woman here tonight, Marianne."

Marianne could not think of anything to say in reply, but simply allowed him to squeeze her tightly to his body. She was lost in a new feeling and enjoyed it. The music changed yet again, and they hesitantly separated from one another.

"Would you like something to drink?" Emad asked, leaning in closely in order to be heard over the noise.

"Yes, thank you," Marianne replied, grateful to be able to take a break.

Emad took her by the hand and led her off the floor. When they reached the area where the tables began, however, she pulled hers from his and simply walked behind him toward the bar, afraid that someone might see them. As they neared the bar, she spotted Philippe. He had not seen her coming, so she quickly maneuvered through a table, separating herself completely from Emad and walked over to her brother.

"Hi, Philippe," she said as casually as possible. "Are you having a good time?"

"Hey sis," he replied, startled by her sudden presence, "are you? I haven't seen you in a while."

"Oh, I've been dancing," she smiled. "The music is so great."

"Yeah, it really is tonight. What a band! Do you need anything?"

"No, no," came the innocent reply, "I have a bunch of friends here. I just wanted to say hi."

"Thanks. Have fun."

"You too," and she turned to walk in the direction of the bar. As she moved away from her brother, she could see Emad standing at the bar watching her. He smiled as she came up.

"Someone you know?" he asked. "I thought I'd lost you."

"That is my brother," she replied as she took a drink from his hand. "It is better that he not see us together."

"I understand," he replied, looking over her shoulder to make sure her brother was not looking. "Would you like to go out into the hall for a while. It is so stuffy in here."

"That sounds good. I need to use the ladies room anyway."

"You go ahead then, and I will meet you out there in a minute. We would not want to look so obvious, now, would we?"

"Good idea," Marianne smiled. "See you soon."

Emad watched as she turned and wove her way through the dinner tables to reach the main door. Her tight dress allowed him to enjoy every move. He finished his drink, took a deep breath and followed the same path.

They were not the only guests enjoying the quieter and more airy halls of the hotel. When Marianne came out of the bathroom, she found Emad leaning against a large marble column obviously deep in thought. He motioned to her to follow him, without speaking. He walked through the large hall and then went into a smaller hallway, further away from the wedding party. He spotted a door and opened it, Marianne following without question. She did not read the "house-keeping" sign on the door before he closed it behind her.

Emad pulled her quickly to himself as soon as she entered.

"Marianne, please, let me kiss you," he said with such a deep pleading in his voice.

"Emad, you shouldn't," came the protest, but a weak one.

He moved his head toward her and began caressing her neck with kisses. He could feel her wilt in his grasp. His lips moved toward her mouth. She did not resist. The kisses continued as did the caressing, but this time with his hands. He wanted to feel every part of her body.

Voices were heard coming from the hallway. Marianne suddenly came to her senses.

"Emad, stop. We mustn't." She pushed him away. "I don't even know you!"

"I want you to know me, Marianne," he replied, trying to keep her in his grip, "to know me in every way."

"No, Emad," she said, becoming rigid, "This is not right. Not like this. Besides, I could get into big trouble."

"No one can see you. Please let me kiss you one more time. We'll go back, I promise." The voices had faded outside the door. Marianne was trying to straighten her dress, but when he asked for the kiss, she looked up and was immediately taken with the pitiful look in his eyes. She smiled. After all, his eyes were so handsome and kind-looking. How could she deny them? Emad drew closer to her once again, but in a gentler way this time. He put his arms around her back and moved her toward him. Their lips joined for a long and passionate kiss, something that Marianne only thought happened in the movies. She was lost in love.

They came out of the closet several minutes later. Emad put his head out first to see if anyone was around. When he found it to be clear, he drew Marianne out and they returned to the main hall. She again excused herself to the bathroom, and he said he would find her inside. She entered the women's room and closed the door to a stall to try to straighten her dress and get herself composed. She then went to the sink and almost gasped as she saw her makeup. Thankfully she had put some things in her purse, so she began to repair the damage when she heard a voice:

"There you are! I've been looking everywhere for you."

Marianne turned to see Gigi coming toward her. "You scared me to death, Gigi!"

"Well, you scared me. I couldn't find you anywhere."

Trying to act nonchalantly about the whole thing, she replied: "Well, it's easy to get lost in that crowd, and besides," she continued as she lowered her voice, "you seemed to be very occupied with a certain boy, if I'm not mistaken."

"Oh, that was Michael. He's a friend of my cousin. I've known him forever, but tonight, he really showed some interest. I don't know if he's serious. He's a real playboy."

"You, with a playboy, Gigi?" Marianne replied slyly. "I never thought you the type."

"Now, listen, stop picking on me." Gigi countered with agitation. "What happened with you? I saw that guy come up to you. Did you keep dancing with him? He was so cute."

"Oh, I danced a couple of songs with him."

"That's it? No, I can tell you are not telling me something. What happened, Marianne? What's his name?"

"His name is Emad," came the reply without further details.

"Emad? I don't know any Emad here."

"Do you have to know every Emad here?"

"Well, most of the guys are from the church. A few came from Alexandria, but not many. The only Emad I know is a Muslim guy who came with Reda."

"Muslim?"

Chapter Thirteen

Muhammad did not want to go directly to his father but avoided the urge to stop by a coffee house for a drink and snack. He knew he would never hear the end of it if he did not see his father first; thankfully, he found him alone in the shop.

"Peace be unto you," Muhammad said upon entering the store.

His father replied without looking up, "And unto you be peace." Realizing it was the voice of his eldest, Ahmed looked up and changed his tone: "Well, what news do you bring me?"

"I found Rachid, Father," Muhammad replied without emotion.

"And?"

"And he sits at the feet of a radical imam, completely under his spell."

"Tell me everything," his father said dispassionately, "and don't leave out a detail."

Muhammad took his time and explained to his father everything that occurred in the mosque. As he finished, his father put his hands on top of his head and closed his eyes. Muhammad did not dare speak or move. After a long silence, Ahmed raised his head and looked at Muhammad:

"It seems the Lord has chosen to deprive me of my second son," he said with resoluteness in his voice. "I fear that if we do not consider him dead to us, he will come back to haunt us as a family and bring us much shame. Muhammad, speak of this to no one until I have had time to make my final decision."

"Yes, Father," Muhammad replied with sadness in his voice.

"Muhammad, I know you are tired. Go get something to eat and bring me a coffee when you finish. We have a lot of work to do."

Muhammad turned and left his father without saying another word. He knew it was useless to really try to discuss the issue with him. His father would never consider his opinion to be important. Children were always to yield to their elders, even as adults. As he walked, he thought to himself that maybe Rachid had chosen the better way. Just escape to something so radical that your family would have to disown you! Oh, how he wished he could escape. He held his thoughts in check long enough to order two sandwiches from a small shop. Fried eggplant had always been his favorite, but he added a fava bean sandwich and some French fries as well. He was really hungry after all that traveling. He took the small plastic bag that contained his lunch and headed for the nearby coffee shop. He sat inside, so he could have some peace from the noise out on the streets, and ordered a bottled drink. Once served, he opened the food bag and began to eat, allowing his mind to turn again to Rachid and his escape.

It was then that he remembered the *Injil* in his pocket. He looked around the shop and saw that he was only one of a few customers, and they were at tables farther away. He pulled the small book from his pocket and opened it to the first page. It began with the words: "The Gospel according to Matthew." Muhammad began reading and found that it contained a list of the ancestors of Jesus Christ. He recognized many of the names, since they were also listed in the Holy Qur'an. He never realized that the Bible and Qur'an had things in common. As he read on, he found the book giving a history of the birth of Christ. The Qur'an talked about this as well, though not in such detail.

As he read on, he realized that this book of Matthew was a history of Jesus' life, though more than just a history. It read like a story and was easy to understand. It flowed from one event to the next with continuity. Every time he had tried to read or especially memorize the Qur'an, he struggled to comprehend what it meant. Of course the local sheik at their mosque had interpretations of what each sura was to mean, but if he visited another mosque, he would find that the next sheik had a completely different interpretation. Now he read a book for himself that made sense—and he was not even a Christian!

Muhammad lost track of the time, and it was not until several cars erupted in loud honks due to a traffic jam, that he looked up from the book. Startled, he quickly put the book back in his pocket, ordered a coffee for his father as he paid his bill and then tried to run back to the shop without spilling the drink. He knew as soon as he entered that his father was not pleased.

"Must I have two sons that disappoint me today?" he said as Muhammad, obviously out of breath from the run, handed him the coffee.

"I'm so sorry, Father," he apologized. "I lost track of the time."

"I don't want to hear any more," Ahmed replied shortly, "just take this cd player and check out the motor."

"Yes, Father."

The rest of the afternoon was spent between the inner workings of electronic machinery and the occasional customer. Muhammad handled most of the customers, as his father really preferred to deal only with the non-human element of their work. Perhaps it was this part of his personality which led him to study law. Muhammad was a natural with people, and could sell almost any piece of equipment to anyone who entered. Because his father never showed appreciation for his gift, Muhammad himself did not readily recognize it in himself. Yet it was his enjoyment of talking with people that kept him from going insane in his father's shop.

The busyness of the work kept him from thinking longer about what he had read in the coffee shop or of Rachid. It was only when he and his father went home late in the evening that the events of the early morning came back to either of their minds.

Um Muhammad had not slept a wink since the day Rachid left the house. Though his subject was not discussed further between her and her husband, she knew that Ahmed was trying to find him. As soon as she saw him and Muhammad enter the house that night, she sensed something had happened in relation to her second son.

"Peace be unto you," came a tired greeting from Ahmed.

"And unto you be peace," she replied, but then continued, "Are you well, my husband?"

"I am tired. It has been a long day."

"Yes, I was worried about you when neither of you came home for lunch. I am sure you need something to eat now." She cast a look at Muhammad.

"I just want a cup of tea, Mother," he said in response.

"I want nothing," Ahmed said curtly, and began walking toward the bedroom.

"Abu Muhammad, are you not well?" She called to him with concern in her voice.

He turned quickly to her and cast an agitated look. "I am well, woman, it is your second son who has made me lose my appetite today." With that, he walked into his room and closed the door.

Um Muhammad turned quickly to her son for answers: "What happened, Muhammad? You must tell me!" She moved closer to him and put a hand on his arm.

"What is there to tell, Mother?" Muhammad replied. "Rachid will bring shame on us all for following a radical sheik. You should have seen him today, Mother. He already wears the short pants of the Sunni and is developing a good beard. We have lost him, Mother, lost him."

"No, no!" she screamed, "it is not possible! You must get him back, Muhammad. You cannot let him be lead astray by those criminals! What will this mean for us?"

Upon hearing her scream, Ahmed rushed from the bedroom now wrapped in a robe as he was preparing to take a shower. Even Abdel-Karem, Nawal and Eptisam came into the hallway from their bedrooms, where they had been studying, but hesitated to move closer since their father stood between them and their mother. They remained well behind him as he lashed out at her.

"Control yourself, Woman!" he yelled. "Do we need the whole neighborhood to hear our problems? We do not need to discuss Rachid in this house again. I will deal with this issue, but you are to remain silent. I will not have such outbursts again. Do you understand me?"

Um Muhammad had backed herself into a corner during her husband's tirade and was visibly shaken by his reaction. She could say nothing in response to his question, but merely nodded her head. As soon as he saw her response, he turned and headed to the bathroom. Muhammad, who was standing by his mother throughout the scene, felt a sudden compassion for his mother as the anger for his father rose. He took her by the arm and led her into the kitchen. He put her next to a chair by a small table, and she obediently sank into it. Completely out of character for her oldest son, he began filling the tea pot with hot water and sat it on the stove to heat. He took two cups out of the cabinet and placed a tea bag in each along with a spoonful of sugar. He then sat down at the table and looked his mother in the eyes.

"Don't mind him, Mother," he cannot help himself. "This thing with Rachid is driving him crazy. Just put it out of your mind."

"How can I put it out of my mind, son?" she replied, tears beginning to well up in her eyes. "He is my son, your brother. He is one of us."

"The direction he is choosing tells us that he does not want to be one of us, Mother. You may have to let him go."

"I cannot do that, Muhammad. It would be like giving you up, or your brother or sisters."

"I know, Mother, I know. Just try to leave it to Father. He will do what's right, I'm sure."

"Maybe this is God's will," she said wiping her tears with a tissue.

"I find that hard to believe, Mother, but who knows? God seems to be coming up a lot lately. I just don't think God wants us to follow him like Rachid is doing." He rose to take the water from the stove and poured it into the cups. As he handed his mother her tea, she took him by the hand.

"My son, I don't know what God wills either, but I do want to thank you for giving me comfort tonight. I have always known you had a good heart."

"There has to be more to life than yelling and strife, Mother. I just want to get past all this junk and have a decent life." He sat down again and took his tea cup into his hands, just looking down into the steaming drink.

"That is my wish for you as well, Muhammad. May the Lord grant you all your desires."

They sat in quiet, drinking their tea and contemplating the life laid before them. Muhammad's mind wondered back to the book that still lay in his pocket and again remembered

Fouad's words: abundant life. He stared at his beaten-down mother and doubted that either she or he would ever know what that would be like.

Chapter Fourteen

Marianne was at a loss for words as she felt the weight of this news crash down on her. Here, her first experience with a boy had already become a disaster. What would her mother do? What would Philippe say? She had to get out of this place.

"I want to go home, Gigi," Marianne said in a soft voice.

"Are you all right?" Gigi looked at her with concern.

"I'm fine. I just want to go home. I've had enough."

"Let me help you find Philippe." Gigi took her by the hand and led her back to the reception hall. The music was still blaring and the dance floor full. Marianne kept her head down, trying not to look to see if Emad was watching for her. Eventually, Gigi worked their way through the tables to the back area near the bar where she found Philippe sitting on a couch with his friends. As they approached, he stood up and came toward Marianne.

"What's the matter?" he yelled, trying to get above the noise.

Gigi answered for her friend: "She is not feeling well. I think you need to take her home."

"Are you all right?" he asked his sister.

"I just want to go home. Please take me home, Philippe," Marianne said with pleading eyes.

"All right. It's getting late anyway. Just let me say good bye to my friends."

"I'll wait."

Philippe moved away from her and Gigi gave her a kiss good bye and said she would call her later. As she was left alone, she moved toward a wall for support while she waited for her brother to return. A hand touched her arm. Marianne jumped at the contact.

"Are you all right?" It was Emad.

"I'm going home," she said coldly.

"You can't leave now."

"You are a Muslim." It came out of her mouth as a mere statement of fact. She wasn't asking.

"So, what if I am? What does that matter?"

"My brother is coming. You need to leave."

"I don't want to leave you Marianne, and I won't let you go."

"You will, because I don't want to have anything to do with you."

"I know that's not true." He forced her to turn her head and look him in the eyes.

She looked at him, but only with a cold stare. "Please leave now."

"I will leave, but this is not the end, Marianne. I will see you again."

He walked away. She did not know if he left because of her harshness with him or because Philippe was actually coming toward her. He came up to his sister and took her by the arm, leading her out the main door of the hall. As soon as they were in a quieter corridor and heading toward the elevator, he looked at her and asked:

"Are you all right? You look pale."

"I'm fine. It's just so noisy in there and the smoke was heavy. Maybe all that with what I ate has made me not feel too well. I'm sorry to make you leave."

"No, it was getting late anyway. It's better to be home at a decent hour, since this is your first time out with your brother."

Marianne was relieved that she did not have to explain anything from the events of the evening to Philippe. It was better just to go home and forget all about it. There was no reason she would have to see Emad again anyway. She was sure they moved in completely different circles. However, she did have to admit that he had given her feelings that she had never experienced before. The way he kissed her, touched her. "But why, O Lord," she thought to herself as they road back home in a taxi, "did he have to be a Muslim?" Then a new thought came into her mind. "Did I sin for kissing a Muslim?" She said a quick prayer asking God to forgive her and promised him she would do a service for him at the church this next week in order to cover for the unintentional sin.

Emad, left behind by Marianne at the reception, had watched as she left with her brother. Though he should have been completely turned off by her insulting attitude, he found himself totally mesmerized by her beauty and sweet lips. Once she was gone, he searched for his friend, Reda, who had come with him to the wedding. They were both friends of the brother of the bride, having gone through high school and now college together. He found him standing by the door of the hall, trying to get some fresh air but not wanting to leave the music behind.

"Hey," began Emad, as he walked up to his friend, "what are you doing?"

"Just trying to breathe," replied Reda. "The smoke is getting thicker by the minute. It's bothering my asthma."

"Do we need to go?" asked Emad with concern.

"Maybe we should, but I don't want you to leave if you're having a good time."

"No, it's OK, my good time just left."

"Oh, who was that?"

"Did you not see that girl that just left with her brother?" Emad asked.

"Do you mean Philippe's sister?"

"Well, I don't know her brother's name, but I know her's."

"What is it then, man?"

"Marianne," came the name with a touch of music off his lips.

"Yeah, that's her," replied Reda smiling. "She's really grown up. I've never seen her looking so good."

"So, you know her?"

"Well, not personally. I know her brother. He's a year ahead of us in college. We're in the same meeting at church of college students. Come on," Reda said, taking Emad by the arm, "let's go."

They headed toward the elevator and continued out of the hotel and into the night air.

"We can take the same taxi and I will get out at Triumph and you go on to your house, OK?" Reda suggested.

"Sure that's fine," Emad replied. As Reda put his hand out to hail a cab, Emad continued with his questioning concerning Marianne. "So, do you think you can help me see her again, Reda?"

"Are you crazy, Emad? You know she's Christian! Wait," and he put his hand down and looked at his friend, "does she know you're Muslim?"

"She does now," Emad said sadly.

"And..?"

"She dumped me." He put his head down.

"See, it's impossible. There is no way she would see you again. Forget her, friend. That's just the way things are. You would never let me date your sister."

"Well, now that is where you're wrong, Reda. I'd let you date my sister, but you would just have to convert first!"

"Are you ready to convert for Marianne, Emad?"

"I thought she might convert for me," he replied seriously. "I'd make it worth her while."

"Yeah, I'm sure you would," laughed Reda.

They stepped into a taxi that had pulled up. Emad got up front with the driver and Reda in the back. They told him the directions and began their ride home. As they wove in and out of traffic on the crowded streets, Emad turned around in his seat and again addressed his friend: "I have to see her again, Reda." He was serious this time.

"Well, I cannot help you there, my friend," came the reply. "You are treading on dangerous waters and I want no part of it. As a matter of fact, I will do all I can to prevent you from seeing her. We're friends, and you know that, but when it comes to our women, the friendship stops. I know you understand, Emad, so please don't push it."

Emad did not respond right away but turned back in his seat and considered what he was hearing from Reda. He knew the driver, who was Muslim, would have an opinion on the matter, but did not want him to add to the problem. Without turning around, he simply said: "I understand, Reda. I understand."

Neither spoke the remainder of the way to where Reda got out; both were lost in conflicting thoughts about this common predicament. While Christians and Muslims can be friends as long as they are of the same gender, there is an understood line against Christian girls being allowed to become friendly with Muslim boys or Muslim girls with Christian boys. The problem is, as Reda knew, that legally, a Muslim man can marry a Christian girl, because by doing so he is helping Islam; whereas, it is illegal for a Muslim girl to marry a Christian man. He knew, if Emad were encouraged to pursue Marianne, he could easily win her over and convince her to marry him. Why, some Muslims went as far as to kidnap Christian girls in order to marry them and increase the Muslim population!

Emad, for his part, was frustrated with his friend because he would not help him, allowing centuries of Muslim-Christian hatred to surface in his own, previously carefree relationship with Reda. This was so typical of Christians, he thought. They keep to their own and think themselves so pure—the true Egyptian race and descendants of pharaohs. Muslims were only invaders, outsiders. He would show his friend! If he wanted Marianne, he would stop at nothing to get her. And if she ended up not pleasing him, he could always throw her back to her Christian family.

He watched his friend get out of the taxi.

"Bye," Reda said, as he leaned toward the window once he had closed his door.

"Good-bye," offered Emad.

There was no, "See you later" or "I'll call." It was as if a wall had risen between them, and neither could pull it down.

Chapter Fifteen

It was Mother's Day. Um Muhammad sat at her kitchen table, having risen early to fix lunches for Nawal and Eptisam. Maybe her girls would remember their mother on this day, though she had no assurance that any of her children would care to honor her. She had already lost one son. Was she destined to lose them all? Why? She had done nothing but serve her children, hand and foot from the moment of their births. They were all she lived for, but what did she get for it? Sons who argued and fought, and now one who was willing to bring disgrace and shame on his family. Though the three younger ones still submitted to her influence, she was nothing but fearful that they too would soon leave her. Muhammad, her oldest—what had changed in him? If all she had for Mother's Day was a son caring enough to serve her a cup of tea and bring her comfort, she would be content.

Nawal was the first to enter the kitchen. She was rubbing her eyes and wrapped in her bathrobe, her hair a mess. "Good morning, Mama," she said sleepily.

"Good morning, my dear," smiled Um Muhammad. "Did you sleep well?"

"Just not long enough," Nawal replied with a yawn.

"You are studying far too late in the night, my daughter," began her mother. "You know I want you to do well on your exams, but not at the expense of your health."

"Well, classes will be over soon enough, and then I can study without having to worry about going to school. That will be a relief."

"The water is hot on the stove, my dear. Can I fix you a cup of tea?"

"I can do it, Mama," replied Nawal. "Oh, by the way," she added, "Happy Mother's Day." She bent down and kissed her mother on the cheeks.

"Thank you, my daughter. It is kind of you to remember."

"How can we forget our mothers?"

"I'm sure many people do, my dear," Um Muhammad said with a touch of sadness in her voice.

"Well, I could never forget you." Nawal put her arms around her mother's shoulders. "You are the greatest mother in the world!"

"Now those are big words, Nawal. I'm a very poor mother at best."

Nawal let go of her embrace and returned to the stove where she began fixing her tea.

"That's not true, Mama," she said. "You are so good to all of us and put up with so much from the boys, especially."

"The life of a mother is not always full of joy."

"By the way, Mama," Nawal began, bringing her tea and sitting at the table with her, "what is happening with Rachid? Abdel-Karem told me he has run off to join a fanatic group."

"We are not to talk about him, my daughter," Um Muhammad said, with a blank stare on her face.

Nawal leaned toward her mother at the table and touched her hand, "Mama, you cannot just not talk about him. Anyway, the rest of us need to know what happened, in case it affects us later on."

"I'm sure it will affect us all eventually, I'm afraid, Nawal," her mother replied, coming out of her stare and looking back at her daughter. "If he attracts the attention of the authorities, it will put stress on us as well. I'm also fearful he might try to pressure us into conforming to his new way of thinking. If that happens, he would never approve of us allowing you to attend that Christian school."

Nawal's eyes grew wide: "Surely he would not go that far? Father would never let him."

"My dear daughter, you have to understand, when young men become part of such groups, they are like a mob or gang. Rachid would no longer face his family alone, but surrounded and supported by a large group of young, angry men. It is that kind of pressure I'm talking about."

"The Lord protect us," Nawal responded, considering the scenario.

"Yes, it will have to be the Lord," agreed her mother.

They sat in silence for a few moments, each considering this weighty subject. Eventually Nawal looked up at her mother and said: "I'm sorry, Mama, if I ruined your Mother's Day by bringing it up. Cheer up. You still have two great daughters!"

"And two other sons," replied her mother with a forced smile on her face. "I'll be fine, you have not ruined my holiday at all, so don't worry."

"I need to go and dress for school," said Nawal, rising.

"You go on, my dear, and please wake your sister as you do."

"Yes, Mama."

The remainder of her children rose, dressed, ate breakfast and left the house over the course of the next two hours. Eptisam was up and out with Nawal, as they attended the same girls school together. Because her sister had reminded her, Eptisam gave her mother a sweet kiss and hug with her Mother's Day wish. As they walked out, they talked together about getting her some flowers on the way home from school that afternoon.

The boys, however, lived up to their mother's expectations and completely forgot the holiday. Abdel-Karem was up before Muhammad as he had a nine o'clock class. He had not allowed himself much time, so he rushed into the kitchen still buttoning his shirt.

"Good morning, Mama," he said breathlessly, "Do you have something I can take with me to eat?"

"Morning of flowers, my son," she said, rising at his entrance, "Here is a cheese sandwich you can take." She handed him a large pita bread, rolled with cheese in the middle. "I made it for Muhammad, but I have time to fix him more. Will one be enough for you?"

"That's more than enough," he replied. "I am going to be so late! Bye." He was out the door.

So much for a Mother's Day wish from Abdel-Karem, she thought, as she began to make another sandwich for Muhammad. She straightened up the kitchen and began moving to the living room to dust, when her husband came out of his room.

"Who is that slamming the front door so early in the morning?" he asked with a grumble.

"Abdel-Karem was running late, so he went out too quickly and forgot to be quieter. I'm sorry, my husband. Can I get you some coffee? Your paper is there on the coffee table."

"Yes, coffee, please," he responded as he sat down on the sofa and picked up the paper.

Ahmed skimmed over the headlines, but would not read it in detail until he was at the coffee shop. This was just a preliminary perusal. He really was not awake enough to read, anyway, as he had not slept well last night. The worries over Rachid were weighing heavy on his mind.

His wife brought his coffee but knew better than to attempt conversation with her husband in the morning. He was not a morning person and thus not ready for deep conversation until he had his coffee and was dressed. Since he was now in the living room, she moved toward their bedroom to straighten the bed and arrange his clothes for the day. She left him deep in thought. He too had forgotten what day it was. The day was still young, though; maybe he would remember to bring her something special later. Once he finished his coffee, showered and dressed, Ahmed left the house. He was never one to eat breakfast, so his wife had no more contact with him prior to his departure.

Though Muhammad worked with his father, he did not have to leave as early, as he knew his father spent at least an hour in the coffee shop before work. This allowed him to rise, breakfast and dress at a leisurely pace, not bothered by the other members of the family. He spoke to his mother as he came out of his room:

"Good morning, my Mother."

"Morning of jasmine, Muhammad," she replied. "Did you sleep well?"

"Yes, I actually did."

"I have some eggs and pastrami I can fix for you this morning, my son. Would you like that?"

"That sounds wonderful! I'm starving, since I didn't eat last night."

"That's right," she said and added, "so I'll add some extra to fill you up. Just come in once you've had your shower, and it will be ready."

"Thank you, Mother," he replied, heading toward the designated room.

Um Muhammad found it easy to cook for a grateful child, and as she stood over the stove, she smiled thinking of her sweet moment with Muhammad the night before. Maybe his good demeanor would remain now that Rachid was out of the house. Perhaps it was his brother that was the cause of his struggles, though she knew that he was also not happy with having to work for his father. How she wished she could help change that, but unless Abdel-Karem became an electrician following college, she doubted that her husband would ever release Muhammad from the family business. If only there was something she could do to help him. Maybe he just needed a wife. If he lived out on his own, had a wife and began having children, he would not feel so down about being under his father all the time.

As she spooned the cooked eggs and pastrami onto his plate and added two pieces of warm bread, she determined in her mind to begin to look for a wife for Muhammad. How she would go about this, she did not know, but God would provide. Her son walked into the room shortly thereafter and sat down at the table in front of his meal. Um Muhammad was washing the skillet in the sink.

"This looks great," he said. "Thank you, Mama."

"To your health," my son," she replied, smiling over her dishwater. She decided to take a chance and see how her son felt about marriage in general. She began with a casual tone: "May the Lord give you a wife who can provide for you."

"Wife?" questioned Muhammad, his eyebrows raised. "Now where did that come from?"

"Oh, I was just thinking that it is about time for you to be thinking of marrying, Muhammad."

"You were? Are you ready to get rid of me?"

"No, no," she responded, wiping her hands on a dishcloth, "I just realized that you are getting to the age where you can think about it. Do you not want to marry?" She sat down across from him at the table.

"I suppose I do," he responded, "but I don't know how I'll find a wife. Do you have anyone in mind, Mama?" A smile came on his face.

She knew he was playing with her, but decided if she kept it light at least he was willing to talk. "No, I don't have anyone in mind, my son, but I'm sure God will show us the right girl for you."

"Well, you'd better start looking for her," he responded, the smile still there, "because I can tell you there are not many who come into the shop in Midan Al-Gamaa!"

"Oh, Muhammad, you're teasing me!" and she laughed. It felt good to laugh, she thought.

"Yes, I am, but I promise to open my eyes if you will," he said.

"Oh, I will start to look, my son, don't you worry," replied his mother.

"I wouldn't think of it, Mama. I know you'll have it all under control."

He finished his breakfast and began to leave the house for work. Um Muhammad was again trying to dust in the living room as he passed her on his way out. The door opened and her son turned toward her suddenly: "Oh, by the way, Happy Mother's Day!" He closed the door before she could respond, so she just stood there with her mouth open. "Will wonders never cease?" she said out loud to an empty house.

Chapter Sixteen

Though it was a normal school day for both Philippe and Marianne, their mother knew that neither of them would be motivated to get up and go to school. Maybe it was good for them to sleep. They both study so hard; they needed a break. She would never understand why weddings were in the middle of the week in Egypt. She remembered hearing her friend, Fadia, tell her about a cousin in America who went to a wedding there and gave her a report. She said they were almost always on the weekend, so people would be off from work. They also only had one pastor do the ceremony! That was amazing in itself, as good Copts with any amount of money usually had several priests. She also said that this particular wedding had a small reception at the church itself, and they served only punch, cake and nuts! Unbelievable.

Phardos knew that the reception for last night's affair had to have been spectacular. She could not wait until the kids woke up and told her all about it. Though they made it home before two o'clock last night, she was already in bed. Girgis had stayed awake, watching television until they came in. She was simply relieved they made it safely and on time. She had been a little nervous about allowing Marianne to go without her, but had to trust Philippe to be a responsible brother.

Even Girgis slept later than usual this day, so Phardos had a nice quiet morning and decided to take her tea on the balcony. It was still cool for March, though the days were warming up. She wore a warm, flannel pajama set and wrapped her terry cloth robe over the top. The sun was bright, and she thought she had never seen a clearer day in Cairo. It seemed the days were becoming rarer to actually see the sky or spot a cloud. Pollution had settled in the city and it seemed no effort was being made by the government or industries to make it better. This was having a horrible effect on the people, and even Philippe had developed some mild asthma as a result. Therefore, she considered a clear sky a gift from God and determined to enjoy it as much as possible.

Her mind began to wander back to the woman, Naema, she had met so many days before at the church. It seemed she was so much at ease with the Bible, and found the passages she wanted so quickly. I really should read my Bible more, thought Phardos. She realized this was as good a time as any, and she went quickly into the living room to retrieve a Bible. Where should she start? She did not know her Bible well. Though she was weekly in the church, she realized that Copts were not really encouraged by the priests to read their own personal Bibles, and they therefore relied heavily on the teaching that came from their leaders. She did not know if this was good or bad, but knew that it would not hurt or anger the Lord to read his Word more on her own.

She knew that the New Testament was toward the back of the book, and since it was about the life of Jesus and the church, she thought it would be easier for her to handle. She hoped to be able to find the same verses that Naema had read, but realizing the chances were slim, she just began to flip through the pages. Her eyes landed on some verses in the book of the apostle Matthew:

You are the salt of the earth. But if the salt loses its saltiness, how can it be made salty again? It is no longer good for anything, except to be thrown out and trampled by men. You are the light of the world. A city on a hill cannot be hidden. Neither do people light a lamp and put it under a bowl. Instead they put it on its stand, and it gives light to everyone in the house. In the same way, let your light shine before men, that they may see your good deeds and praise your Father in heaven.

Phardos looked up from the reading and squinted as the sun hit her face. She closed her eyes and thought about these verses. Obviously these were the words of our Lord Jesus, she realized, but to whom was he speaking? Was she meant to be salt and light to the world? She did not feel that she was much of a light to anyone. What did she have to give? It was clear from the verses that the good deeds of the followers of Jesus were to lead others to praise God, the Father. She did not recall anyone ever praising God because of something good she had done. What was wrong with her life? She could not help but feel that God was not pleased with her. She tried to drink her tea and think about what she had to do.

Girgis came out to the balcony with a coffee cup in his hand.

"You seem deep in thought this morning, my dear."

"Oh, good morning, Girgis," she said, trying to cover her concerned look, "I didn't hear you come up."

"Can I join you?" he asked hesitantly, noticing the Bible on her lap.

"Oh, of course, come, sit down." She pointed to a chair next to hers.

"Happy Mother's Day, Phardos." Girgis leaned over and kissed her as he sat down.

"Oh, thank you, *hayati*, I completely forgot about Mother's Day."

"We cannot forget our mothers," he said smiling.

"That is very sweet, Girgis."

"Well, I hope you will think this is even sweeter, and he pulled out a small box from the pocket of his robe."

"What is this?", as she took the gift with her hands.

"Just a little something to show you how much I appreciate the mother of my children."

She opened the box to find a pair of diamond earrings. "Girgis, this is too much," she said, tears coming to her eyes. "I know we cannot afford this."

"You just leave it to me to know what we can afford. Besides, remember I'm the jeweler!"

Phardos leaned over and kissed her husband. "They are beautiful, Girgis. I love them."

"I should have given them to you yesterday, so you could wear them to the wedding."

"No, no," she replied, shaking her head, "it means much more to have received them on Mother's Day and on this balcony. Isn't it a gorgeous day?"

Girgis looked out at the sky and breathed deeply. "You're right. It is a lovely day, but you are even lovelier." He looked at her with an expression she had not seen since their early years together.

"I know you're teasing me, but I appreciate the compliment all the same."

"I am talking seriously, Phardos. You have not changed one bit since the day we married. I don't think I've ever told you how much I appreciate the way you look after yourself."

"There is a lot more for me to look after these days, but I do try."

They sat for a few minutes without talking and then Girgis changed the subject completely. “You would never believe what happened the other day.”

“What’s that?” asked Phardos, curious that he would want to tell her anything that happened during his days at work.

“A woman in full *niqab* came into the store.”

“Oh, really, what did she want?” Phardos was really interested now.

Girgis proceeded to tell her about the entire incident with the Muslim woman. He had never intended to share this episode with his wife, but he could not get her out of his mind, and especially since he was giving his wife a gift as a result of the money he made off the sale of her jewelry. Phardos sat in silent awe as he retold the story, complete with his feelings on the matter. As he finished, he asked her: “Isn’t that amazing?”

“It really is,” she replied, “and so sad too.”

“Yes,” he answered with a faraway sound in his voice.

“Girgis,” Phardos began.

“Yes?”

“Do you think a Muslim can become a Christian?” The question came out of her mouth before she realized it. She almost wanted to take it back as soon as she heard it come out.

“What?” he asked, not sure of what he had just heard.

“Do you think a Muslim can convert to Christianity?” The fact that he had not reacted with harshness encouraged Phardos to ask the question again.

Girgis looked away from his wife and out into the scene around them. They were surrounded by buildings full of Muslims. Though they lived in what was once a Christian neighborhood, they were forced to admit that it was no longer the case. Muslims had moved in by the thousands over the years. They were here to stay. It was hard for him to think of those same Muslims as being Christian like him. After all, Christianity was part of their identity. He turned back to his wife.

"I really don't know Phardos. I find it hard to accept. Maybe you should ask the priest."

"I tried that already," she replied sheepishly.

"Well, what did he say?" Girgis asked with curiosity.

"He refused to answer the question and hung up on me."

"You asked him over the phone?"

"Yes, why?" She looked at her husband with a furrowed brow.

"Of course, he would not want to answer such a politically sensitive question over the phone. I don't blame him, really."

"I never thought about that," she said. "Do you think I should ask him again?"

"Maybe not the same priest," he replied smiling.

The couple had to go to work, so they parted and headed their separate ways shortly thereafter. Phardos was walking on air as the joy from her morning on the balcony lingered with her for several hours. She received many well wishes for a happy Mother's Day from colleagues and children at the school, which kept her mood lifted, but it was the beautiful bouquet of flowers and prepared meal that met her at home, which really brought the day to a perfect ending. Since they did not go to school that day, Marianne and Philippe decided to surprise their mother with a special treat for Mother's Day. Marianne was not a great cook, but she knew how to make a salad while Philippe ordered a couple of chickens and other side dishes from a local restaurant. They had a great time going together to pick out the flowers.

"Happy Mother's Day!" came the shout as Phardos entered the house that afternoon.

"I am blessed!" she said, as they hugged her and showered her with kisses.

Chapter Seventeen

The thought of marriage was not only on Muhammad's mind these warm spring days, but on that of his sister as well. Nawal was a maturing eighteen-year-old and finishing her last year in high school. She had the self-sufficiency of her mother and level-headedness of her father. It made her unusually ahead of most girls her age, who only thought of superficial pleasures. Though marriage was in their minds as well, it would not be for the same reason as it was in the mind of Nawal. Perhaps the school she attended all these years also had an effect on her. Schools led by nuns were known for their high academics and strict discipline, but what some parents were not aware of was that the nuns could not help but influence their daughters on a spiritual level as well.

While they did not teach Christianity to their Muslim pupils, the students did learn about the basic principles of the faith and most would leave their primary schools with a more accepting attitude toward Jesus and the Christian religion in general. Attendance at Christian schools especially led for more mixing between Muslim and Christian students, and Nawal had several classmates with whom she was particularly close. It was not uncommon for her friend, Nancy, for instance, to invite Nawal to her house to study. Um Muhammad at first was hesitant to allow her daughter to go to the home of a Christian, but after Nancy visited her one afternoon, she became convinced that Nawal would be in good hands. Besides, they lived in the same neighborhood. What could happen?

What happened was that Nancy had a brother, Emir, who was in college. It was not an instant attraction between him and Nawal, especially since on his part, he was put off by the fact that Nawal was a Muslim and covered her head. Yet, as the years passed and she became more comfortable in Nancy's home, Emir found himself hanging around more during his sister's study group time. Since it was a group of about six girls on average, no one seemed suspicious of Emir as he came in and out of their room as they worked together. Even Nawal was not fully aware of his intentions until one afternoon in early April. She was in the kitchen, helping Nancy prepare drinks. Nancy left to carry a tray of snacks to the other girls. Emir walked in and greeted Nawal.

"Hi, Nawal," he began casually, "how are you today?"

"I'm fine, thanks."

"What are you all studying?"

"We're trying to prepare for a physics exam. It's so hard."

"I'd be glad to help you. I'm very good at science."

"Oh, thanks," she replied with hesitation, "I'm sure we'll figure it all out."

"Well, you know if you don't, you can call me anytime. I'd be glad to work through it with you."

Nawal felt nervous at what she was hearing. "I'm sure the other girls would appreciate that."

"I'm not talking about the other girls." Emir moved closer to her as she stood against the counter. "I'm talking about you."

"I don't think this is wise, Emir." Nawal tried to move away.

"We have to take risks in life, Nawal."

"Some risks are too hard to take."

"I'm willing if you are," he said, taking her hand.

"The risk is much greater for me, Emir, you know that." Nawal pulled her hand away. "You can't ask that of me."

"If it's meant to be, God will show us a way. At least tell me you will think about it."

"I cannot promise you that." She picked up the tray of drinks and left the kitchen, thankful for a reason to flee.

Now as she thought back on this incident, Nawal realized her resistance had been in vain. She had done nothing but think about Emir over the past two weeks since the encounter. Everything about it told her to put him out of her mind. While she could avoid going to Nancy's house, she could not avoid thoughts of Emir. It was true that she had grown comfortable with Nancy's family over the years of their friendship. Seeing a Christian family up close did wonders for tearing down the stereotypes that most Muslims had created in their minds against Copts. She found Nancy's parents very accepting and easy to be around, and they did not judge her or the other Muslim classmates who joined Nancy for studies. While they did have several icons up in their home, she did not find any of their ways as a family to be scary or abnormal. The best thing she liked about them was their willingness to let Nancy, Emir and their other siblings make their own choices—from what clothes to wear to their careers. She would never know this in her own home. Not even Muhammad could choose his own line of work!

Yet there was no denying the impossibility of the situation. She was Muslim, he was Christian. No country in the entire Middle East would marry them, if he was even thinking that far. She really should just forget the entire thing, but could she ever go back to Nancy's again? She would miss those special times. Nawal found herself realizing she would also miss Emir.

Nawal was walking to the metro with all this in her mind, when she suddenly heard her name called out. Turning, she saw Nancy and two of her friends running toward her.

"I'm so glad I caught you, Nawal," said Nancy, out of breath from the fast pace.

"Hi, girls," replied Nawal, "I'm sorry I didn't see you."

"That's OK; I just wanted to make sure you could come over tonight. We are going to try to review the history notes at my place and have some pizza. Please tell me you can come."

"I can't promise. I'll have to ask my mother. I'll call you."

"You have to come," ordered Nancy. "I haven't seen you in ages."

"It hasn't been ages, Nancy, just a couple of weeks. I'll try really." She kissed all the girls on the cheeks. "Bye, now. I have to run."

"Bye!" they called in reply.

Nawal waited for the metro still deep in thought. Would she really be able to not go? No, she knew that Nancy would call her until she relented. Nawal determined in her mind to go and be indifferent to Emir. Anyway, she did not have any feelings toward him, and why should she? They had never been alone more than two minutes in the kitchen that one time. Why was she working herself up so? He was just a guy, nothing to worry about.

Um Muhammad willingly gave Nawal her permission to study at Nancy's. Her daughter had proved herself a good student, and perhaps it was these study sessions that helped her the most. At any rate, it was saving them from having to pay for a tutor for private lessons. Nawal kissed her mother good-bye that evening to face her fears at Nancy's.

The group of five girls studied diligently for almost two hours. There was so much information to get into their brains before the final exams. History was not an easy subject for Nawal—too many dates. She wondered as they analyzed yet another Muslim war, what her Christian friends thought of studying so much Islamic history. Frustrated by the overlapping dates, Nawal told her friends:

"I just don't think I can remember another date tonight. I can't believe how many wars there were."

"Yes, this is too much information for my brain too," agreed Mary. "Plus, why do we need to remember all these wars anyway?"

"I don't know," replied Nawal. "Do Christians have this many wars in their history?"

Nancy looked at the other girls for a minute before answering. "We wouldn't know. We never study Christian history."

"You don't? Why not?"

"Because we only study the Egyptian curriculum. It doesn't include the Christian era."

"You know, that's right," replied Nawal. "I don't remember learning anything about Christianity in Egypt."

"We probably shouldn't discuss this issue," said Fatma. "Let's just stick to what we know we have to learn."

"Why shouldn't we talk about it, Fatma?" asked Nawal. "Just because we're Muslims and they are Christians, doesn't mean we can't have a civil conversation about religion."

"No, but once we do start talking about religion, something will happen and we won't remain good friends. I've seen it happen before."

"I can't believe that's true," Nawal responded. "Besides, I've never seen anything but understanding from the Christians I've known, like Nancy and her family."

"Thanks, Nawal," Nancy said, smiling, and then changed the subject. "Why don't we see if that pizza has come?"

The conversation ended there. Everyone knew that Nancy was keeping the peace and were glad for it. Nawal however, had become uneasy with her Muslim friend's attitude and began to feel resentment for it. As she went into the kitchen with Nancy, she asked her:

"Nancy, why do Muslims have to be so hard to get along with?"

"You are asking me, Nawal?" replied Nancy with a surprise look on her face. "I think you will have to find someone else to ask that question to."

"No, really," insisted Nawal, "you, Mary, and Yvonne never get nervous about religious questions. I just think Christians are so different from us—much more accepting of differences. You know, sometimes I wish I could be a Christian."

"Nawal, watch out what you are saying," Nancy whispered. "What if Fatma heard you?"

"She would probably go and tell her imam, and I'd be in big trouble!" She smiled.

"So, we don't want that," replied Nancy with assertion. "Here, help me cut this pizza."

Nawal took a knife and started working on the pizzas. The other girls began coming in and out of the kitchen to carry plates and drinks to the table. As the last item was carried out and Nawal and Nancy walked toward the dining room Nawal looked at Nancy.

"I meant what I said."

Nancy did not reply but just looked at her friend with her mouth opened. As they neared the other girls, she was brought back to reality by their voices. They ate their pizza, talked and laughed like nothing had happened, but both Nancy and Nawal knew things had changed. A line was being crossed, and it scared them both. As if it was not enough for this emotional charge to be going through the air, another soon entered the room—Emir.

"Hello, ladies," he said as he came in the front door and saw them at the table.

"Hi, Emir," called Nancy. "Want some pizza?"

"Don't mind if I do," he replied. "I'm starved."

"I'll get you a plate from the kitchen," his sister offered and left her spot next to Nawal.

Emir quickly put his backpack by the couch and claimed his sister's chair. Nawal felt the hair tingle on her neck as he pulled up beside her. "How is the studying going?" He asked the girls, avoiding addressing anyone in particular.

The girls offered their opinions on the subject, and then he turned to Nawal: "Is it as hard as the physics exam?"

"No, much easier," she replied calmly.

"I thought you said you could never remember all the dates?" Mary interjected.

"Well, yes, that's true, but it is still not as hard as physics," Nawal replied, irritated.

"Well, I'm no good at history either," admitted Emir, smiling. "Good luck."

Nancy had returned with her brother's plate. "Hey, you took my chair."

"Sorry," he said, standing. "Thanks for the plate." He put a couple of pieces of pizza on the plate. "I will leave you ladies to your party."

"Bye, Emir!" They called in unison. Nawal sighed in relief.

Chapter Eighteen

The days went by and Phardos completely forgot to ask her children about the wedding reception. Neither Philippe nor Marianne desired to open the subject with their mother, knowing that what she did not know would not hurt her. While Philippe could easily forget the now foggy events of that evening, Marianne had a harder time pushing the experience out of her mind. Several times she found herself dreaming of Emad and the taste of his kisses and then awakening at odd hours of the night unable to return to sleep. Her mother noticed the darkening circles under her eyes but attributed them to long hours of study. Marianne did nothing to dispute this impression.

In an attempt to push Emad out of her mind, she sank deeper into her notes for the upcoming exams. She had to maintain focus in order to pass, because more than anything she did not want to have to repeat a course. Her private lessons increased as the last days of school drew nearer. She had no desire to be distracted by a Muslim boy of all things! How could she have let that happen? She felt unclean and corrupted by it all.

As for Emad, he was now a man with a mission. It was not clear in his mind if it was because he really did like Marianne or his irritating conversation with Reda that night in the taxi. Reda had been so incredulent of the idea of a Muslim being with a Christian girl. It had really soured their friendship. Who did he think he was, taking such a stand? She should be honored to marry him. Why was it that Christians always thought of themselves as better than Muslims? He would show Reda—he would make Marianne fall for him!

It had taken a while, but he found out from some other friends that had been at the wedding where Marianne went to school. He spent a week just watching the gate, to see if he could spot her leaving in the afternoon. Several times she came out with other girls, but he realized that on Tuesdays and Thursdays, she came out later and alone. He would make an attempt the following week to talk to her.

Marianne was completely unaware of Emad's presence around the school. When she began her walk home on Tuesday, her surprise was immediate upon the sound of his voice.

"Hi, Marianne," he called out, as she passed a corner.

She jumped and then looked down the street to see Emad walking quickly toward her. She wanted to run, but could not get her feet to move.

"What a surprise," he said as he drew closer.

"Emad," she stuttered, "What are you doing here?"

"I was going to meet a friend in the area. What are you doing here?"

"This is my school."

"It is?" he replied innocently. "Are you going home now?"

"Yes." She started walking again.

Emad kept in step with her.

"Emad," she stopped and looked at him. "I thought you were going to meet someone."

"He can wait."

"You cannot walk with me." She started moving again. Emad did as well.

"I really enjoyed that night we had together."

"Well, you need to forget it."

"How can I? It was magical."

"You are playing with me."

"I'm being honest."

"You were not honest with me about who you were."

"You never asked, and it didn't seem to matter."

"Well it does matter. It matters a lot."

"How can you say that?"

"I can say that because being with you would be a disgrace for my family." She stopped once again. "Please, Emad. Just leave me alone."

"What if I said I would convert for you?"

She looked at him in disbelief. "What did you say?"

"I'm willing to change my religion...for you."

"Emad, do you know what you are saying?"

"I know exactly what I'm saying and I know the cost. You are worth it, Marianne. From the moment I laid eyes on you that night, I have not been able to get you out of my mind. Please think about it and give me a chance. We can just spend some time together, if you are not comfortable with more. Then if you are still not in love with me, I will leave you alone forever." He paused to let it sink in. "Please, just think about it?"

Marianne was shocked. She did not know if he was telling her the truth or not. His face seemed sincere, but how could she be sure? It was such a risk. But in reality she too had not been able to forget that night. What would it hurt to agree to consider the issue?

"I am not making any promises."

"I'm not asking for any. Just some hope."

Before she could reply, he changed his tone completely.

"Oh, there's my friend," he said, motioning at a man walking on the opposite side of the street. "I have to go. I'll find you again. Don't worry. Just think about what I said. Bye."

She stood alone on the sidewalk just watching him cross the street. Before he reached the man he had indicated, she came to herself and hurriedly entered a small side street to make her way home. Completely lost in her thoughts she did not bother to look back or notice that Emad continued past the man who was to have been his friend.

Emad smiled to himself as he made his way and circled back to watch her walk home. He was able to follow her the entire way, noting the building into which she entered. He felt confident he had succeeded at the first stage of his plan—to get her to believe that he loved her and was willing to do anything to be with her. As she disappeared from his sight, he began humming to himself, perfectly content with his success.

Phardos was not long behind her daughter in arriving home that afternoon. While she saw Emad across the street from their building, she only noted that he was a handsome young man, but otherwise a stranger. She went up to their flat and found Marianne lying on the couch.

"What's the matter, Marianne?" she asked concerned by the distress exhibited on her daughter's face.

"Nothing, Mother," Marianne replied, startled by her mother's sudden entrance. "I'm just tired. It was a long day."

"Yes, it was for me as well. Why don't you take a shower and rest for a while? Your tutor is not coming until seven tonight."

"Oh, I can't even think about studying now! I'm so tired." She made an effort to get up from the couch, leaving her books strewn on the floor as she walked toward her bedroom. Her mother stood with her hands on her hips, dismayed to see the lax attitude of her daughter.

As she removed her clothes and put on her bathrobe, Marianne let her mind return to Emad. She tried, but was not able to come to a rational conclusion as to his sincerity or whether she should continue to see him. Everything in her heart and mind said no, but a small part of her kept the memory of those moments alone with him at the wedding. It was neither intellectual nor emotional but hormonal. While he had not touched her during this latest encounter, every part of her body tingled with the attraction that had been between them. Though her mind could not understand this feeling, it was clear that the sexual element of their relationship was the major force in leading her to continue to contemplate his request.

She moved from her room to the bathroom. Removing her clothes and getting under the hot water, she recalled the sensation of his touches from that night. She was feeling something completely overwhelming and she did not want to stop it.

"I have to see him again," she said aloud, as she soaped up her body.

Chapter Nineteen

Mothers hear stories, but it is amazing how difficult it is to apply such tales to one's own situation. As Um Muhammad, sat with her sisters, who had come to visit, she found their words hard to believe.

"You cannot tell me that a girl would fake her own death!" she exclaimed to Amal, the closest of her siblings.

"I am telling you the truth. I know the girl's cousin, and she told me that in order to keep her family from being disgraced by the fact that she was in love with a Christian, she would simply die to them."

"How did the cousin know?" Myriam, Um Muhammad's oldest sister asked.

"Well, now, listen and don't be shocked."

"What?" her sisters asked together, their curiosity peaked by this secrecy.

"Her cousin is a convert to Christianity."

"You have got to be kidding!" exclaimed Um Muhammad. "How do you know that?"

"Well, she told me, Fatma," Amal replied sheepishly. "I've known her for 20 years at least. We worked in the factory together. I knew something had changed in her life about seven years ago. It took her a long time to confide in me, but she knew I would never tell anyone, so finally she shared with me the reason for the change. She follows the teachings of *'Isa* the Christ."

"Now, Amal," said Myriam. "Why would you even continue to keep company with her then? Certainly I would not believe what she tells me. Maybe she's trying to convert you!"

"Do you know what's strange, sister?" Amal looked at her elder sister straight in the eyes. "She has never tried to push her beliefs on me, and I respect her for that. I must tell you, she is a really different person. She never takes advantage of a situation, like some of the other girls used to. She's honest and hard working. More than any of the rest of us ever were. In reality, I admire her. She took a big risk to change. I don't think I could ever be that brave."

"Let's go back to the original story," offered Um Muhammad, trying to change the subject from this one that made them all feel uncomfortable. "I still don't understand how she actually got away with faking her death."

"You see, the guys were ready in the water to pretend they saw her drown. When she was far enough away from her family, she swam under the water, and as she kept going and eventually came up behind a rock to get away with her boyfriend, the guys in the water started screaming that they saw her drown. Since the family didn't see anything, they had to believe she was lost at sea. Very clever really."

"It may be clever," agreed Myriam, "but I don't see how she got away with marrying the boy. She's Muslim, he's Christian."

"Even I know the answer to that," replied Um Muhammad before her sister could answer. "Everybody knows that the Church gives fake identity cards to Muslims who turn to Christianity."

"They do?" Her sister seemed shocked.

"Myriam, I'm surprised you didn't know that," said Amal. "Some say that the Church has a big business of selling identity cards for Muslims. Not even Christianity comes free. I've heard that they can go for even up to 30,000 pounds."

Even Um Muhammad was shocked at this news. "Really? That is disgraceful."

The three sisters sat quietly for a moment. There was much information to take in, and it affected each one in a different way. Amal, however, having been exposed to a Muslim convert friend for several years had obviously thought many of these issues through previously. It came out in her next statement:

"You know, in reality, it doesn't surprise me that the Church charges for making those identity cards."

"How can you say that?" asked Um Muhammad.

"Think about it. It is illegal for a Muslim to change his faith and to change his identity card to become Christian. However, it's perfectly legal for a Christian to change his to become a Muslim. The Church is taking a big risk for people they don't even know. Maybe by charging them, they can know if the person is really sincere about becoming a Christian."

"I've never heard anything so ridiculous in my life!" exclaimed Myriam. "How can you side with the Church and even with the people who want to leave Islam. Do you realize what you are saying? They are blasphemers, Amal! Blasphemers! And I want you to stop seeing that woman. I can tell she's had a bad influence on you! If I had known this earlier, I would never have allowed it to continue."

"Calm down, my sister," tried Um Muhammad. "I'm sure that Amal is no longer in relationship with the woman. She hasn't worked at that factory in a couple of years. Am I not right, Amal?"

"Yes, I do not see her all the time, Myriam. I just said I've known her for a long time, that's all. I'm sorry if I upset you. I've just been trying to see the situation from another viewpoint. Don't worry; she's not going to convert me."

"Well, you just better be careful," warned Myriam, slightly mollified.

The sisters changed the subject and remained together for a few more hours, enjoying the opportunity to visit and catch up on each other's news. Myriam, however, left by early afternoon to pay a visit to her mother-in-law, who lived in Cairo. Amal would stay with Fatma until Myriam was ready to return to their town in the Delta on the late bus.

With Myriam gone, Amal and Fatma were working together in the kitchen, preparing lunch for the family who would arrive home in a few hours. Amal was the first to return to the subject of earlier that day:

"Fatma, I'm sorry if I said things I shouldn't have with you and Myriam."

"No, no, don't worry," replied her sister, patting her hand. "Myriam is just being overprotective. Don't mind her. Anyway," she continued, taking a carrot to peal, "it was a very interesting story and gave me a lot to think about."

"Really?" asked Amal, "I'm glad to hear you say that. I think about it a lot too. What a risk that girl took."

"Yes, it's amazing what lengths people will go to for love."

"What bothers me is that the girl had to go to such a risk at all." Amal pushed a bunch of cut tomatoes into a large pot with a knife. "Why should it be illegal for certain people to marry each other?"

"Amal, you're asking dangerous questions."

"I know, I know. Things will never change in this country. I just felt sorry for the girl."

"That's the choice she made for wanting to leave Islam and marry a Christian."

"Yeah, but I've never heard of a Christian having to do such a thing or be disowned by his family for wanting to change his religion."

"Our religion is different, Amal, you know that."

"It seems to me that if Islam and Christianity are from the same roots, then they should look at things the same, but obviously they don't. What does that say to you, Fatma?"

Suddenly uncomfortable with the direction of the conversation, Um Muhammad turned toward the stove to stir the okra that was simmering. It smelled wonderful, and she would have preferred to simply talk about recipes with her sister. Why talk about religion? She was not a Muslim scholar, nor did she care to really go into the depths of her religion. She did what she had to to be considered a good Muslim, and that was enough. She turned around to her sister.

"It doesn't say anything to me, Amal. I really don't think much about religion. I don't have time. Can't we change the subject?"

"We can, but I think you'll have to think about it one day, Fatma. Things are changing in this country, and we can't help but be better informed about the world and her religions, especially our own."

"I suppose you're right." She thought about Rachid and his drift toward fundamentalism. "Maybe I should do some real study about Islam. I hear they have classes for women at the Islamic center."

"Yes, they do have classes for women in most areas," replied Amal, "but just be careful with what you hear. Not all of it is true."

"What? The teacher would tell you things that are lies."

"Well, let's just say he may look at it from a certain perspective. Also, don't forget to study Christianity as well."

"Now where would I do that?"

"My best suggestion is to read their Bible. It has all the teachings of Jesus in it."

"Where would I get one, if I wanted to do this?"

"Find a Christian bookstore. You're in Heliopolis; there have to be some here."

"I suppose so; I've never noticed. Have you ever studied the Bible?"

"Well, only part of it. My friend gave it to me. It's very interesting."

"You had better not let Myriam know."

"No, I won't." Amal smiled at her sister. "I love cooking with you!"

"Me too." Um Muhammad gave her sister a hug. "Oh, look the rice is done."

Chapter Twenty

Being the director of a school was not a job for the faint-hearted. If there was not one problem there was another. On good days, Phardos was able to face them with confidence and determination. On bad days, however...

It was getting close to exam time, which meant that teachers were stressed, pupils were stressed and even parents were stressed. Phardos expected parents to come to her once exams were over, many pleading with her to see a grade raised or a teacher disciplined. What she did not expect was the irate father who stormed into her office that morning, before she had even had a chance to drink her tea.

"Madame Director," he began with a shout, "you must do something about this!"

Phardos tried to keep her cool and lower her visitor's temperature as well. "Please sit down, Mr.?" She pointed to a chair.

"I will not sit down until I know what you are going to do!" He stood defiantly in front of her desk.

"I will be happy to attempt to respond to your request, but I really must insist you take a seat and again, please tell me your name."

"I am Engineer Ahmed Abdullah, the father of Eptisam Ahmed."

"Can you please remind me what class Eptisam is in?"

"Aren't you the director? You should know that!"

"I direct a school of over 900 students, Engineer Ahmed," she responded, trying to keep her voice even, but feeling it crack. "It is impossible for me to memorize the names and classes of every child, try as I do."

"She's in KGII," he responded briskly.

"Thank you." Not feeling comfortable with the man continuing to stand, Phardos rose and moved to the corner of her desk. "Now, what is the problem, sir?"

"Her teacher has given her hardly any work to prepare for exams."

Phardos tried to keep herself from bursting out laughing. Oh, what stupid parents we have, she thought. The poor child is only in kindergarten, and he wants her to be studying as a college student. She took a deep breath.

"Engineer Ahmed," she began, "While I understand and appreciate your concern for your daughter's education, I encourage you to realize that she is only in KGII, which in reality is a class designed to prepare children for school. Therefore, the material covered is not nearly as detailed or time consuming as in other grades. I have complete confidence in our kindergarten teachers that they are giving Eptisam and the other students plenty of preparation time in class and that the children will all do well on their exam, which is not difficult at all. Eptisam will have plenty of years ahead of her for studies. Allow her to enjoy these early years."

"Are you telling me what to do?" His voice rose and was carried out the room through the windows.

"Did you hear what I just shared with you, Engineer Ahmed?"

"I heard you all right," he retorted. "If this school is going to play around with my child, maybe I had better take her somewhere else where she will get a proper education!"

"That is your decision, sir, but we will miss Eptisam and would be sorry to see her leave."

"You did not even know her two minutes ago!" He exclaimed. "What does it matter to you? You just want the money we pay. You Christians, you always have such expensive schools. It's killing me and I don't see that she's even learning anything." He stomped toward the door. "I may make a complaint to the Ministry of Education for this!" He walked out the door.

Though she should have run after him, Phardos could not make herself do so. She knew that if he came true on his threat and complained to the Ministry, she might have troubles. All she could do, however, is collapse into her chair and put her head down on her desk.

Her assistant, Magdy, ran into her office. "Are you all right, Madame?" he exclaimed, giving her a start. "Did he hurt you?"

"No, no, Magdy, but maybe you could run out there and catch him and try to smooth things over. He threatened to go to the Ministry."

"Yes, I'll go right away," and he was out the door.

It bothered her that she would resort to sending Magdy after the irrational father, but sometimes she had to admit that men listened better when another man spoke to them. She had no problem being the director, where the mothers were concerned. They could talk to her and she to them without misunderstandings, but fathers were another matter, especially the Muslim ones. "Wouldn't it be nice if all the children were from Christian families?" she thought to herself. She hated having to deal with the Muslim ones. They made so many demands of her and the teachers, as if they were doing her a favor by putting their children in a Christian school. She felt it was the other way around just accepting them. In the end, however, she knew that the reality was that she would take anyone who paid. Schools only survived when there were students. While she had a good 40 percent Christian students, she was watching that percentage go down each year as Christians were willing to pay higher prices to get their children in better schools.

Magdy tapped on her door this time before entering.

"I think he'll be all right," he said as he sat down in front of her desk.

"Thank you, Magdy. He was really looking for trouble."

"Just because he works for a foreign company, he thinks he can push people around."

"Yes, he pushed hard, but I kept my cool and thought the matter was closed, but he obviously wasn't listening to reason and the comment about the Ministry scared me."

"Isn't his daughter only in KGII?"

"Yes, can you believe it? Making a fuss for a kindergartener! What is he going to do when she faces her high school exams?" They laughed together and it felt good to release the pressure.

Phardos decided to take some time from her schedule that day and check on her students and teachers. While Magdy and her other assistant did this regularly, she felt it was important for the teachers to know that the director was also checking up on them from time to time. She began in the KG area, coming into each open door and greeting the class. The school was a large square of rooms, three stories high, with a large open place in the center for physical education and assemblies.

All was going well, and she smiled to herself as she reflected on how well-behaved the students were and the quality of her teachers. Finding good, qualified teachers was a challenge that never lessened with the passing years. She had a good core of veteran Christian teachers, for which she thanked God every day. They kept the standard for all the newer ones. She even had a handful of Muslim teachers who were liberal in their thinking and had been able to adapt to her leadership and teaching directives. It was some of the newer teachers who were proving to be a challenge in training and guiding.

As she rounded a corner on the second floor she heard a sound she never wanted to hear from her classrooms.

"You stupid pigs! You are unteachable! I cannot believe you do not understand this! You will all fail the exams for sure!"

Phardos quickly walked toward the door of the classroom and stood in the open doorway. The screaming stopped immediately as the teacher stared at his boss in shock.

"Mr. Saeed, may I have a word with you, please?" Her voice was firm, but calm. She heard snickers from the back of the class. "Children, you will take your notebooks and write the following line: 'I will not laugh at my teacher.' Fill one full page please. No talking."

She walked with the teacher into the hallway, trying to position herself in an area where children would not hear the conversation.

"Mr. Saeed, I will not tolerate such outbursts in my school. What do you have to say for yourself?"

"The children were being extremely unruly, Madame Director. They are not studying and I saw that the only way to get them to do so was to humble them."

"Did you not attend our teacher training courses prior to your employment, Mr. Saeed?"

"Yes, I did."

"Was it ever suggested that yelling and abusive language was an acceptable method of teaching?"

"No, but."

"Yes or no, Mr. Saeed."

"No."

"That will do. You are suspended for one week without pay, effective today. I will see to your class. I want you to review your notes from the training time and return next week ready to teach in a more effective manner."

"But, Madame, you can't."

"Is there anything not understood, Mr. Saeed?"

"No, Madame."

"Thank you. Please go in your class and remove your briefcase and personal items. I will see you next week."

When it rains it pours, she thought as she followed him into the classroom.

Chapter Twenty-One

Muhammad had a moment alone at the shop. His father had gone to pick up some replacement parts in another area of town. Since he was caught up on his work, he took the opportunity to pull the *Injil* out from his pocket, where he kept it since the day Fouad gave it to him. Because he shared a room with his brothers, he never had the privacy to allow him to read. The shop was also a risk, but Muhammad felt the pages would burn a hole in his jacket, if he did not read what they contained. Though his parents believed his problems would be solved with the acquisition of a wife, he knew that was not the answer, as good as it may sound.

Oblivious to the noise of the neighborhood — the honks of cars going up and down the street, venders calling out about their wares, and pedestrian traffic in front of the store, Muhammad moved behind the back counter, sat down and held the small *Injil* where it could not be seen from anyone who might enter. He returned to the pages of the book he was reading when he left off last, Matthew.

Time after time, Jesus seemed to reach out and touch people, no matter their status in life. He healed the sick and performed many miracles. It was clear to Muhammad that the religious leaders were not happy with Jesus and accused him of blasphemy. He liked the way Jesus stood up to them and never let them trap him. As he neared the end of the book, however, things started to change. Jesus, himself, told his followers he was going to die. Muhammad could not figure out how he knew this or why he would have to die. It did not make sense. Then he came to a verse which read:

> *Whoever wants to become great among you must be your servant, and whoever wants to be first must be your slave—Just as the Son of Man did not come to be served, but to serve, and to give his life as a ransom for many.*

"Ransom", thought Muhammad, "ransom from what?" Muhammad wanted to understand what Jesus was talking about, but it was hard. He read on, but the next few chapters were parables that Jesus told about the kingdom of heaven. They did not seem to answer his question about the ransom, or why Jesus had to give his life. Though he did not find that answer, he did find another passage that really surprised him. When Jesus was asked what the greatest commandment was, he replied:

> *Love the Lord your God with all your heart and with all your soul and with all your mind. This is the first and greatest commandment. And the second is like it: Love your neighbor as yourself. All the Law and the Prophets hang on these two commandments.*

He tried to compare these words with what he knew of the Prophet Muhammad. While Muslims are to submit to God, the idea of loving him was not stressed as far as Muhammad remembered. Though we are to do good to our neighbor, the concept of loving one's neighbor as you loved yourself—well, that just would not work! That would be too radical!

Muhammad looked up from his reading to allow his mind to take in these thoughts, as he did, he saw his father standing before him, having just walked into the shop. He quickly put the *Injil* into his pocket.

"Praise the Lord for your safe return, Father," he said haltingly.

"And peace be upon you," replied Ahmed, not noticing his son's actions. "I picked up this radio from Engineer Medhat as I was coming. He wants it by tomorrow."

"Yes, Father."

"Did you take Madame Suzanne her mixer?"

"No, I'll take it now since you are back."

"Oh, yes, well, that's fine. Go ahead and do that. The bill is stapled to the bag."

"Yes, Father." Muhammad stood up to locate the mixer and leave.

Ahmed settled behind his worktable to examine the radio. Muhammad took the repaired item and headed for the door. A thought, however, came to his mind, and he turned again to his father.

"Father."

"Yes, son?"

"Would it be all right if I left early today? I have something I would like to do."

"Well, since it is already almost seven, I think it's all right for today. Just don't make it a habit."

"No, Father. Thank you. I'll just deliver this and then go on."

"Fine."

"Good-bye."

"Good-bye."

It did not take long for Muhammad to make the delivery and collect the money for the job. He put the cash in his wallet and headed to the metro stop. What he wanted to do he did not want to do so close to home. Once on the tram, he put his hand in his pocket, feeling the book that was capturing all his thoughts. After passing three stops, he exited the tram and started looking around the area to which he had arrived. He walked up and down a couple of streets before he found what he was looking for—an internet café.

When he was in college, he heard his friends talking about chat rooms on the internet. Of course, many of them had to do with ways to meet girls. Oh, the stories he had heard! However, it was not those kinds of chat rooms he was interested in tonight. The one he wanted to try was on PalTalk. A friend had told him once of how he had found an answer to a question he had about Christians through that site. Apparently there were Christians who would talk to you in their chat rooms about religious subjects. Muhammad thought that maybe he could find a Christian who could help him understand what he was reading in the *Injil*. By doing it on the computer, he could be totally anonymous and not get into any trouble. No one knew him at this internet café, and he would only use it the one time.

Internet cafés were everywhere in Cairo and through them young people were accessing a world of knowledge and information, both good and bad. Of course, the government did as much as they could to block sites which were not deemed politically acceptable, but there was really too much out there to stop access to everything. As he entered this particular café, Muhammad was happy to see that it was crowded, with only a few computers available. He checked at the main desk to register his time and then took a seat behind a terminal.

All he knew to look for was the PalTalk site. He did a Google search and found it easily. He looked under religion and spirituality and found a site for Christianity. Knowing that he would need it in Arabic, he found there were chat rooms for Arabic groups. The biggest one was for Father Zachariah. He knew all about that from the television, but he did not want to be seen getting on that group. He instead chose a smaller group that looked willing to answer questions. He clicked on the group, took a deep breath and began typing.

Deciding to start simple, he merely told his cyber pal that he was reading in Matthew and wanted to understand what it meant when Jesus said he was a ransom for many. As soon as he entered his question, he began to look around to make sure no one else could see what he was doing. Everyone seemed very occupied with their screens, so he relaxed somewhat. He was startled to see that a comment had already come up on his computer.

"Hi, I'm Thawrat," it read.

"Hello. My name is Muhammad." Muhammad decided there were enough people with his name that it did not matter telling the truth.

"You have asked a really good question."

"Thanks," typed Muhammad, "Can you answer it?"

"Yes," came the reply.

Muhammad did not type again but just waited. In a few moments some words appeared.

"Jesus had to come as a ransom for man, because of sin. Since the fall of Adam in the garden, men have been born to this earth with a sinful nature. No matter how hard we try, we cannot do good. Mistakes always happen, sin is always committed. Because of this sin, we cannot have fellowship with God."

Muhammad read these words, but then typed a question:

"Fellowship with God? What is that?"

The answer came:

"When God created Adam and Eve, they were perfect. The Bible tells us that God would talk with them in the Garden of Eden. They had a close relationship. However, when they ate of the tree and sinned, God could no longer come to them."

"Why," asked Muhammad.

"Because God is holy. Sin cannot be in the presence of a Holy God. Now that man was full of sin, he had to be separated from God. That is why God put them out of the garden, and that is why we cannot go to Heaven to be with God when we die."

"But can't man get to heaven by good works? That is what the Holy Qur'an says."

"Yes it does, and I respect that, but I must disagree with that based on what the Holy Bible tells us. Sin is not a material or physical act, but a spiritual one. We cannot cleanse ourselves from this spiritual act with a physical one. We had to have something higher to cleanse us of our sins—a blood sacrifice that would be acceptable to God. It had to be something perfect, and the only perfect thing is Jesus, because he came from God himself. That is why Jesus said he came as a ransom—he was the sacrifice for our sins. He paid the price on the cross; gave his life for ours. We were the ones who deserved to die, not him, but he accepted that task because he knew that was the only way God would ever allow man to come back into his presence."

Click. Muhammad turned off the PalTalk page and abruptly left the computer, paid his bill and then left the shop. It was too much for him to think about. He was grateful for the easiness of turning off the internet, not realizing that there was a live person on the other end, who, though shocked by the quick exit of his new friend, was now down on his knees in prayer for the Lord to work on his heart.

Chapter Twenty-Two

It was a warm day, and it was obvious that summer was coming early. Marianne stood on her balcony in her bathrobe trying to decide how hot it would actually be by midday. The weather could be so unpredictable until it finally decided to get hot and stay hot. She decided to wear a short-sleeved blouse with her school skirt, and though she still put on her sweater, she knew it would not be long before she was wearing it around her waist. She hated wearing a uniform; she felt she had definitely outgrown this aspect of school. After all, she was graduating and would soon be going to college. College! What a horrible thought. Why did life have to be so hard? She turned back into her room with a sigh, wishing she could just escape it all.

There was an avenue of escape being offered to her—Emad. If she married him, she would not have to go to college and could just enjoy being someone's wife. She had no idea what that entailed, but anything seemed better than more studies at this point in her life. If she could just get through this last week of classes, maybe she would survive and not have to worry about the future.

After dressing, Marianne went to the kitchen, where she found her mother drinking coffee and eating a croissant.

"Good morning, Mother," she said, kissing her lightly on the cheek.

"Morning of jasmine, my dear," replied her mother. "The water is hot and there are some fresh croissants on the counter. Do you need me to help you?"

"No, Mother, I can take care of it. Enjoy your breakfast."

"I will, thank you, but then I need to get myself to school."

"Yes, your work is never done."

"I could not agree with you more, my darling."

The day was normal enough. Marianne met up with her friends at school and they suffered through what was thankfully their last Monday of their high school experience. The teachers seemed to work extra hard at piling new information into their brains that would be covered on the exams. By the end of the day, with her head aching, Marianne began her walk home. The weather had warmed up, and she was now wearing, as predicted, her sweater around her waist. She was joined on the walk by her friend, Lola. They complained to each other of the trials of school until arriving at a small kiosk, where Marianne offered to buy Lola a Coke.

"No, thanks, Marianne," she replied to the offer. "I need to get home. Mom was sick this morning when I left, and she will want help with my baby brother."

"All right," Marianne sighed. "I'll just have one without you. I hope you find your mother feeling better when you get home."

"Thanks. I'll see you tomorrow."

"OK. Bye."

Marianne watched Lola walk away and then went around to the side of the kiosk to pick out a drink from the cooler. She jumped when a hand stuck a Coke out to her.

"Let me buy you a drink."

"Emad!"

"Hi, Marianne," he said smoothly. "How are you?"

"What are you doing here?" She looked around to see if there was anyone she knew watching.

"I was just hoping to catch you on your way home." He left her side to go to the front of the stand to pay for the drinks, and then came back to her. "Let's walk a while."

"Emad, I really shouldn't."

"Oh, don't be so afraid, Marianne. It is broad daylight, and we're just walking and talking." He started moving away from the kiosk. She followed him hesitantly.

"My house is that way." She pointed in the other direction.

"That is why we're going this way. It will give us more time."

They walked for about a block in silence. Marianne tried to appear preoccupied with her drink, almost choking as she accidentally took a big gulp. Emad laughed to himself, but appeared to ignore it. They passed by the big Orthodox church.

"That was a beautiful wedding," he said off-handed, remembering the reason for their meeting.

"Yes, it was very nice," replied Marianne.

"You would make a beautiful bride."

"That's the farthest thing from my mind right now," she said, trying to repress the feelings she remembered from the early morning.

"Is it?"

"Emad," she said with irritation in her voice, "I am about to take my bac exams. I cannot be thinking about marriage!"

"Yes, I'm sure you're right. You do need to study."

"Yes I do."

"Don't you get tired of it though?"

"Of course I do, but I cannot let myself get distracted right now. I have to pass those exams."

"Why?"

"Why?" The answer seemed obvious to her. "Because I hate school, but I have to get through this or I'll never get out."

"So, you're not thinking about college?"

"I don't want to, but my parents for sure will."

He could sense the hopelessness in her voice and that was what he wanted. Emad knew this was the chance he was looking for. They came to a corner, and he turned to have them walk up a narrower and quieter street. He threw his Coke can into a rubbish bin.

"If you married me, you would not have to go to college." He took her hand in his.

"Emad, you know I cannot marry you. Please don't start." She did not release his hand.

Though he kept walking, he spoke with the same intensity that she heard in that small closet at the hotel. "Marianne, you know I'm crazy about you. I cannot let you go."

"It's impossible, Emad, really."

"No, I don't believe that," he replied. "We can marry, and I told you what I was willing to do, if necessary, to have you. Either way, we can have a wonderful life together."

"Wonderful life?" She replied, with a mock laugh. "I'm a Christian, you're a Muslim. Neither of us have a job. One of us would have to change our religion. Our families would both kill us. What do you see wonderful in that?"

"You."

It is amazing how logic can disappear upon a word. Emad knew he had her by the silence that followed. He longed to kiss her to seal the effect but could not find a private place anywhere. Cairo was not made for lovers! He settled for squeezing her hand.

"Marianne, if I did not think I would get you in trouble, I would take you in my arms and kiss you right here in front of everyone. You will have to just take me at my word that I want to. I know you may think that by marrying me we would have a miserable life, but I refuse to believe it's true, and to prove it, I am going to find a job, and not just any job, but a job that will provide for you in the way you deserve to live. You go home and study for your exams. Do your best. Pass them. When you have your results, call me, and I will tell you what the next step is. What do you think?"

"I don't guess I can argue with that."

"Good. Take my number and put it in your phone." He raised his cell phone up so she could read his number and enter it into hers. "I won't bother you from now on. I want you to put your mind on your exams. I will be putting my mind on finding a job. Then, we'll be able to put our minds together for the future."

They walked along until they came back to a main street which led to her home. Emad stopped at the corner and let go of her hand.

"I love you, Marianne," he said, looking into her eyes.

"I love you, Emad."

He smiled, and she began walking down the street to her house, oblivious that she had just been caught in the biggest web she would ever experience.

Chapter Twenty-Three

While a mother's work is never done, it is really on the father that the burden lies for the welfare of the family, and Abu Muhammad was feeling this burden more than ever. As he had his morning coffee and read the paper at the coffee shop, he could not focus on the article before him, even though it should have grabbed all his attention. Egyptians had lived off of government subsidies for decades, but now the Ministry of Social Solidarity was considering either revoking some of the subsidies or revising the way they are handled. Rumors were already rampant as to the impact of this on the common man, and with the ever-increasing cost of living, the effect could be devastating.

Ahmed had more immediate issues on his mind, and he sighed as he put the paper down and picked up his coffee cup. He had heard nothing of Rachid in the weeks since he had left home. Mahmoud promised to keep his ears open and inform his friend as soon as he heard anything. Ahmed was growing impatient. He felt it imperative to keep some kind of tab on Rachid, in order to prevent his actions from damaging or shaming the family.

He also was concerned for Muhammad. Though he was a good boy in general and worked hard for him at the store, he knew that in reality he was no longer a boy and needed a wife. The question was how to find one? He thought of his sister, Yasmine. She was very social and knew a lot of people. Perhaps there was even someone in the family that would be good for Muhammad. Yasmine was much more connected with the family in the village, than he was; maybe one of their cousins had a daughter. A girl from the village would not have big expectations either. "Yes," he said aloud to himself, "I'll call Yasmine."

Finishing his coffee, Ahmed left the shop, leaving his paper for the first time in his life. His mind was set on the task before him and the cares of the country were the least of his worries. He crossed the street, weaving in and out of cars, arriving to the other sidewalk only to avoid the traditional greetings to his colleagues and friends in the various shops along the way. He came to his shop; quickly unlocked the grill, pushed it up, unlocked the door itself, and entered the small space. Turning on the light, he moved immediately behind his desk and picked up the phone.

"Hallo," came a sleepy voice on the other end.

"Peace be upon you. Yasmine?"

"And to you be peace. Yes?"

"Yasmine, this is Ahmed.

"Ahmed! What's wrong?"

"Nothing, nothing," he said quickly. "I'm sorry to call so early. I thought you would be up with the children."

"Ahmed, my children are grown! I don't have to wake up with them any more. It has been a long time since we've visited."

"It's my fault. I wasn't thinking. Maybe this isn't a good time."

"No, no. It's fine. I'm glad to hear your voice."

"Yes, it's good to hear yours too. My sister, I need a service from you."

"Anything, Brother."

"Do you have anyone who might be appropriate as a bride for my Muhammad?"

"Muhammad? Is he old enough for marriage already?"

"They grow up fast. Yes, he's already 25."

"Amazing. The years go by so quickly. I still can't believe I'm a grandmother."

There was a pause. Abu Muhammad could not take the silence.

"Yasmine, Are you there?"

"Yes, yes, I'm here. I was just thinking."

"Well?"

"Have you ever met your cousin Hekmet's daughter, Noura?"

"I didn't even know he had a daughter.

"Yes, she's about 18 now, but very pretty and bright. Or, there is also Nevine, Iman's daughter."

"Which Iman?"

"Iman, your Aunt Fatma's daughter."

"Oh, yes," he replied. "I do recall her."

"My sister, I would be obliged if you would check into these girls and let me know who might be the better one. Then we can visit and make a decision. Would you mind doing this service?"

"Of course not, Ahmed, I would be glad to," came the kind response. "As a matter of fact, Karim is driving me to the village next week. I can visit Iman, then I'll see Hekmet on Tuesday. If you want to come with me, you can check them out yourself."

"Let me think about it. I will let you know."

"That's fine."

"Thank you, Yasmine. I hope everyone is well in your family and your health is good."

"Yes, we are all fine, Praise the Lord."

"I will call you in a few days."

"I will await your call."

"Good bye."

"Good bye."

Ahmed hung up the phone, very pleased with the outcome of this first attempt. Maybe the Lord would smile on them and provide a good wife for Muhammad without too much trouble. Before he could make his second phone call, his eldest son entered the shop.

"Peace be upon you," Muhammad said as he entered.

"And upon you be peace and the mercy and blessings of God," Ahmed said smiling.

"Your health is well, Father?"

"Praise God, my health is very good."

As Muhammad prepared to begin the day's work, his father decided he needed some privacy in order to make the second call.

"Son."

"Yes, Father?"

"Will you go to the bank for me?"

"If you need me to."

"Yes, I want some more change. Take these and get me smaller bills to make change for customers?" He handed his son several large bills.

Ahmed quickly picked up the phone as soon as his son left the shop, fearful that he would be interrupted before he finished his second important task of the day. He dialed Mahmoud's number.

"Hallo."

"Peace be upon you."

"And upon you be peace," came a strong reply. "How are you my friend?"

"You recognize my voice easily. I'm fine, praise God."

"Do you think I don't know your voice after so many years?"

"No, I suppose your right," replied Ahmed. "How are you?"

"I'm very well, praise God."

"And the family?"

"Everyone is fine. And yours?"

"We are fine, praise God." Ahmed paused, thinking how to ask this sensitive question. "I'm sorry to bother you early in the day, but I wanted to catch you before you left the house for work."

"You can call me anytime, my friend."

"I know. Do you have any news, Mahmoud, any news at all? I'm desperate to hear something."

"Will you be in the shop this afternoon?" Mahmoud asked.

"Yes."

"I will come to see you."

"I will look forward to that. Thank you, Mahmoud."

"I have done nothing. Good bye, Ahmed."

"Good bye."

The day went by quickly. Even before Muhammad returned from the bank, his father had to wait on two customers, which was unusual for the early morning. One bought a CD player while the other left the same item to be repaired. This made the fifth CD player Ahmed would be working on that day. They were notorious for breaking and required constant maintenance. Muhammad came and joined his father in reparations, but was interrupted several times by customers. Overall, it was a good day. Several sales were made and requests for repairs made. At the sight of his friend's entrance about four o'clock that afternoon, Ahmed made a surprising gesture to his son.

"Muhammad, why don't you take the rest of the afternoon off? I can handle things until we open again later."

Muhammad looked at his father, but before he could reply, Mahmoud spoke up.

"Ahmed, I think it is better that both of you hear this, especially since Muhammad knows about the situation."

Shocked at what this meant, Ahmed replied with hesitation: "Well, if you think that's best, my friend." He then turned to his son. "Sit down Muhammad. Mahmoud has something to tell us both."

As Muhammad sat down behind the table, his father offered a chair to Mahmoud and then he went to the door and closed it. This would eliminate eavesdroppers and anyone entering without being noticed. Sitting on a stool beside his friend, he indicated for him to begin.

"I have hesitated coming to you, I'm afraid," began Mahmoud. "I wish it were that the news I had is better."

Ahmed shifted uneasily on the stool and Muhammad looked at his father with a worried face. Mahmoud continued:

"The group that you saw at the mosque, Muhammad, has disappeared."

"What do you mean disappeared?" asked Ahmed with fear in his eyes.

"They are no longer meeting in that mosque. The question is whether or not they have been taken by police or simply have moved their location. My sources are telling me that the authorities have not yet intercepted them, so it must be that they have changed locations. The odd thing is that even the imam is gone. He called in sick one day and they haven't seen anything of him since. Of course, this is the story we are getting from those working in the mosque. They may be covering up for him too, who knows. The point is there is no information coming from the people there."

"What do we do? Do you think we'll find them?" Ahmed was clearly distraught at this news.

"It is difficult to get more information without alerting the police that something is amiss," replied Mahmoud.

"Wouldn't the police already know that this imam is missing as is the group of men?" asked Muhammad.

"Yes, that makes sense," added his father.

"I think you're right, but the police are acting like there is no problem yet. This could mean they are playing dumb so people will eventually talk or they already have someone on the inside who knows exactly where they are."

"Where do you think they may be?" Muhammad asked again.

"They have to be somewhere besides a mosque. They've obviously gone underground with their teaching and training. Finding them will not be easy, I'm afraid. We'll just have to wait until they take an action."

"An action?" Ahmed's eyes were wide with fear. "What kind of action?"

"We'll know when they do it."

"Is there no way we can protect our family from what Rachid is doing?" Muhammad was again asking the right questions.

"The only possible way you can do that is to submit a report on him to the police. This would at least show the authorities you have no relationship with him and count him as disappeared or dead."

"Dead?" asked Ahmed. "Do we have to go that far?"

"You need to consider the rest of your family, Ahmed," replied Mahmoud. "That may be the only option you have."

"And to think," Ahmed said, "this had started as such a good day."

Chapter Twenty-Four

Though he should have been studying for exams, Philippe could not stand being locked in his room for more than a few hours at a time. The weather was great for an afternoon game of basketball, and when Sherif sent a SMS on his cell phone to see if he wanted to play, he did not have to think twice in responding in the affirmative. He passed his mother in the salon, where she lay with her feet up on the couch, and told her he was taking a short break.

"Don't make it too long, Philippe," she warned. "You need to apply yourself now before the time runs out."

"I will, Mama, I promise," he shouted, as he ran out the door.

As he walked the few blocks to the church where they would play, he met up with Stephen, another friend from the university.

"Hi, Philippe," Stephen called as he fell in step with his friend.

"Hey man, how are you?" Philippe asked, patting Stephen on the back.

"I'm fine. It's been a long time since I've seen you. Are you studying for exams?"

"Yeah, even though I don't want to."

"I know what you mean. Sherif just called to see if I wanted to shoot some hoops. I was ready for the break."

"He called me too," said Philippe. "Great. It will be fun to relax together."

"Yeah, it's been a while since I've played basketball. I'm glad for the chance."

They walked into the gate of the church basketball court. Sherif had not arrived yet, so they started stretching to warm up while they waited.

"I don't see you here on Thursdays?"

"I don't go to this church," replied Stephen. "I go to the Evangelical church just down the street."

"Oh, I didn't realize you weren't Orthodox."

"Well, I was at one time, but now I'm not."

"What? Your family is Orthodox?"

"Yeah, but I left the Church."

"Why?" Philippe asked in all sincerity and curiosity.

Stephen began looking around them as if to see if there was anyone listening. There were lots of boys on the court, but everyone was engrossed in his own game and friends. There should be nothing to hinder him talking.

"I left the Church because I made a decision to have a personal relationship with Christ."

"A personal relationship? What does that mean? We all believe in Jesus."

"I would really like to explain it to you, but this doesn't seem to be the right place."

"Hey you guys!" A shout came from over by the gate.

Philippe turned to see Sherif and some other boys coming toward them.

"Hey, Sherif!" he called.

The conversation between Stephen and Philippe was interrupted by the arrival of their friends. After they greeted one another, Sherif produced a basketball and they began to play. The activity was fierce and fun, as each young man was ready to release all the pent-up energy stored while studying. A good 45 minutes went by before they stopped for a break.

Walking to the kiosk across the street, the guys compared notes on the exams coming up and their varying degrees of difficulty. Each bought a bottle of water and began the return trip across the street to the court. Philippe pulled Stephen back from the crowd.

"Can I go with you sometime to your church?" he asked in a low voice.

"Sure," Stephen replied with hesitancy, "but are you sure your family would approve?"

"What they don't know won't hurt them. I just want to see what the difference is anyway. I'm so sick of the masses here, and I heard you Evangelicals have great music."

"Well, that's true, but music isn't the reason I changed churches."

"Yeah, I know," replied Philippe. "but it's a reason to check it out at least."

"Sure, you're welcome to do that. Our service is at 7:30 on Sunday night," said Stephen. "Do you want to meet me here at the kiosk?"

"No, this is too close to this church," Philippe whispered. "I'll just meet you in front of yours."

"OK, I'll be waiting."

"Sounds good," replied Philippe, raising his voice. "Now, let's play some more ball." They hurried through the gate to catch up with the others.

Later, as he sat at the desk in his room, Philippe put his head down on his books and thought about what had happened that afternoon. He did not know what possessed him to invite himself to go to church with Stephen. It was true that he had long been dissatisfied with the Orthodox Church. It was not simply the fact that much of the mass was in a foreign language, but that even when he attended Sunday School and the youth meetings, he felt like the teaching was reaching his head but not his heart. And it was in his heart that he felt a huge void.

When Sunday night came, Philippe tried to look inconspicuous standing in front of the Evangelical church on Cleopatra Street. Since his main concern was someone from his own church seeing him, he stood somewhat to the side of the front gate, trying to look like he was just waiting for a friend or ride. He was grateful it was not long before he spotted Stephen. They greeted each other and Philippe followed his friend inside the newly renovated building. Instead of a somber, iconic clad room, he was faced at once with the brightness of the church, illuminated by a single large chandelier and a yellow stained-glass cross positioned behind the pulpit. There was no holy of holies in this place, no separation between the priest and people.

The service had already begun as Stephen led him up to the balcony, where he could get a better view of the people and building. Lively music was coming from the front stage, where young people of his age were playing instruments and singing.

Lord, the light of your life is shining; in the midst of the darkness shining.
Jesus, Light of the world, shine upon us; set us free by the truth you now bring us.
Shine on me, Shine on me.
Shine, Jesus, Shine. Fill this land with the Father's glory.
Blaze, Spirit, blaze, set our hearts on fire.
Flow, Spirit, flow, flood the nations with grace and mercy.
Send forth your Word, Lord, and let there be light.

Between the light of the auditorium and the theme of the song, Philippe was overwhelmed with the light that seemed to flood the place and people. They sang with feeling and movement, and he could see many closing their eyes as they allowed the music to flow through them. It was a touching first experience. The song service continued, interspersed with prayers and words of encouragement from the Bible. It all seemed so personal to Philippe, who never felt truly part of the mass before.

When the last song was completed, one of the ministers rose to introduce the speaker for the evening. He was not their regular pastor but a guest speaker. He was Egyptian but had immigrated to America over 25 years previously. Even so, the last 15 years had been spent in the Middle East where the Lord had called him to return as a missionary. Philippe wondered what this man would have to say.

The speaker began by sharing his testimony, telling the congregation that he came from this very church and was raised to be a good church goer. He did go to church and even at one time considered becoming a priest, but he did not have a personal relationship with Christ. It was not until he had immigrated and lived the American dream that the emptiness in his heart became impossible to ignore.

"I fell on my knees in my home. I had been drinking, but my mind was clear. I told the Lord that I wanted to give my life completely to him and asked Jesus to become Lord of my life. As I lifted my head from my prayer, I knew that I would not drink again. I would never smoke another cigarette. There would be no more girlfriends. It was as if I saw my life before me, and God told me that I would stand before churches in the Middle East and proclaim Christ. I was never the same."

He went on to share how the Lord called him to serve among the majority population in the Middle East and North Africa, and how the Lord had allowed him to see many come to know Christ as Savior.

"Now as I am growing older and near retirement," he continued, "the Lord is asking me to share with boldness this message to the Church in Egypt. *From everyone who has been given much, much will be demanded; and from the one who has been entrusted with much, much more will be asked*. Will the Lord come back to find those of us who have been blessed to be raised in Christian homes and within the loving arms of the Church remiss in having shared the Good News of Jesus Christ with the millions around us who do not know him as Savior? Or will he come back and say to you: *Well done, good and faithful servant*?

I want the Lord to find me ready and able to give an account to him with confidence of what I did as I waited his return. Will you be a proud servant or one that hangs his head in sorrow?

You may say: I have time to do all that. I warn you my friend, do not grow complacent in obeying the Great Commission. Who can quote me the Great Commission?"

Philippe was shocked when the congregation said in virtually one voice:

> *Go and make disciples of all nations, baptizing them in the name of the Father and of the Son and of the Holy Spirit, and teaching them to obey everything I have commanded you. And surely I am with you always, to the very end of the age.*

"So you do know it!" shouted the speaker. "That is commendable. Now," and he lowered his voice, "how many of you do it?!"

There was silence. No one moved. Philippe was afraid to breathe. The speaker did not continue but allowed the silence to hang, making sure the congregation felt the impact of the moment.

His voice rose again with a suddenness that made people move in their seats: "Do you not fear the wrath of God?!" he yelled. "God has entrusted us with the Good News! We have the cure for the cancer of the human soul! Are we sharing it with those around us?! You have been entrusted much—Much will be required!"

Again the preacher allowed his words to sink in. Philippe could see heads bowing throughout the auditorium. As he continued, his voice was this time soothing and consoling.

"'But preacher', you may be saying, 'I don't have what you have. I have nothing to give. I am just a pew warmer like you were.' Well, I understand that and believe there are quite a few out there tonight. But do you know what?" and again he lowered his voice and stared deeply out into the audience, then rang out in a strong, clear tone, "You are not off the hook!

Yes, here you are, forced to go to church since you were a child, though never having made a personal commitment to Christ. Well, I'm sorry to tell you, but you are in a worse case than the millions around you. At least they have an excuse! What do you have? You have the Truth!! You've heard it every week for all of your life, though you may have done your best to avoid living by it. Oh, how God will judge you!

I challenge you now to give, no surrender your life completely to the Lordship of Jesus Christ. Yes, you need him to be the Lord of your life. Give up control yourself, so he can take control completely. Otherwise, my friend, you will wind up in the same place that you accuse those around you of going. Your church going won't save you, your parents' faith won't save you, your grandmother's prayers won't save you. Only Jesus will save you! But you have to ask him. I'm going to tell you how, and this is the greatest thing about the Good News—it's easy, it's free, it's a gift.

If you have never given your life to Jesus Christ, close your eyes right now and pray this prayer. Remember, we don't know when he will return. I don't want you to get caught in church but lost on the day he comes back. I not only want to see you saved, but busy for the Lord too! Wouldn't that be even better to know that when Jesus returns, he'll find you reaching others for him? If that's what you want tonight, pray this prayer with me:" Philippe saw everyone bow their heads and close their eyes as the preacher prayed:

"Heavenly Father, I'm a sinner. I admit that I can do nothing on my own. I confess tonight that I believe that Jesus is the Son of God, who came to earth to die for me, and by believing in him I can have eternal life with you in Heaven. Forgive me of my sins, dear Lord, and fill me with your Holy Spirit. I ask Jesus to come into my life and be my Lord and Savior. Thank you, Lord. In Jesus' name I pray, Amen."

The preacher raised his head and said: "Now, this sermon is not over, there is still more." He smiled. "If you prayed that prayer with me, I want you to make sure before you sleep tonight that you tell someone about it. Find a friend or family member that you trust and share with him or her what you did. Then I want you to start reading your Bible every day, for now you will see it in a different light."

He took a deep breath. Philippe did not know what would come next out of this very unusual man. After taking a drink of water, the message continued: "Now I trust that the number of believers in Jesus Christ has increased here tonight." *Amens* rang out from among the congregation. "If our numbers have increased then I believe our ability to reach this city and country for Jesus has also increased. Amen?" he asked, looking for another response. "Amen," came the answer. "Now, the real question is..." and he paused for effect. "Are we going to be found worthy of our Father's praise by becoming true ambassadors for Christ? Are we going to get busy doing the work he entrusted to us from the beginning? I'm not talking about committee meetings, choir practice, teaching children in Sunday School. Yes, we can do these, as they do help to build the church from within, but if we do not get outside our walls and reach out to those who are destined to hell without us, I am afraid the Lord will come and rebuke the Egyptian Church for the sin of apathy. For this reason I am asking you tonight to make a personal commitment to the Lord for what your part will be in reaching the lost for Christ. If you do this and the Lord brings fruit, then perhaps the person next to you will be encouraged and begin sharing as well. This is how it will multiply, and how not only Egypt but the Arab World and beyond will be changed forever. Pray with me."

As the sermon ended and the congregation bowed in prayer, Philippe felt like his insides would burst. He felt sweat on his hands, as he stood up and grasped the pew in front of him. Not knowing what was happening, he slipped out of the pew and hurried quietly down the stairs and out of the building before Stephen could follow.

Chapter Twenty-Five

"Fatma," the voice called out as the door slammed, "where are you woman?"

"I'm here Abu Muhammad." His wife appeared from behind the kitchen door. "Praise God for your safe return."

Her husband returned the obligatory greeting and then sat in a nearby chair, took a Kleenex from the table and began wiping his forehead.

"Sit down, Fatma," he said, pointing to the couch, "I want to tell you something. Are the children around?"

"They are in their rooms," she replied, wondering what this was about.

"Fatma, Yasmine may have a girl for our Muhammad."

"Really? That's wonderful, Ahmed."

"She wants us to go with her to visit the family."

"When?"

"Tonight."

"Tonight?" replied, Um Muhammad, in shock. "Who are they, my husband?"

"The first one is my cousin Hekmet's daughter, Noura."

"The first one? Are there more than one?"

"Yes, she has two possibilities, but we'll start with this one."

"Do you really think Muhammad is ready for this?"

"When is a man every really ready?" asked her husband in reply. "The important issue is that he needs to be married. It's time."

"It will cost a lot of money, Ahmed."

"We will face that challenge when it comes. God will help us."

This first visit was preliminary to see if the parents liked the girl. There was no thought in telling Muhammad about their plans. Why get his hopes up before they actually met the girl? Of course, as they saw their parents preparing to leave together later that night, there were questions.

"Where are you going, Mama?" asked Nawal, who was watching TV in the salon.

"Your father and I have a visit to make?" came the flat reply.

"Will you be gone long?" Eptisam chimed in.

"We could be a few hours, Lord's willing."

"Go in peace," the girls said in unison.

"Go in peace," replied their mother.

The girls looked at each other on the couch. Abdel-Karem was sitting there as well, but had not entered into the conversation previously.

"Where do you think they are going?" he now asked his sisters.

"I don't know," replied Nawal. "They never go anywhere together. Maybe there's been a death."

"No, if it was a death, they would have told us," her brother asserted.

"Maybe it's a wedding," tried Eptisam.

"No, if it were a wedding, Mother would have worn a different galabiya," said Nawal.

As their children pondered the purpose of their parents' outing, Abu and Um Muhammad made their way far across town to the area of Giza in order to meet Ahmed's cousin and her daughter. It was a tiring trip, requiring transfers from minibuses to the underground and then a short taxi ride through winding streets until they arrived almost two hours later to their destination. Ahmed reminded his wife as they walked up the stairs to reach his cousin's apartment:

"Remember I will do the talking." He knocked at the door and stood back.

The door was opened by a man of some height, dressed in a manner which immediately revealed his social class. He wore neatly ironed trousers with a white shirt and tie. Though it was still warm, he showed no sign of the heat.

"Peace be unto you," offered Ahmed, upon seeing his cousin's husband, Abdullah.

"And upon you be peace," replied the host. "Welcome, welcome. Come in." He moved back to allow the guests to enter, and then bent over to greet Ahmed with a kiss on both cheeks.

This was the first time for Ahmed to actually be in his cousin's home, as they most often saw each other at his grandparent's home in the village. When Hekmet came out of the kitchen, she rushed with enthusiasm to greet her cousin and his wife. Unlike Um Muhammad, her head was not covered, since she had grown up with Ahmed and they knew each other well. This also revealed to Um Muhammad that this was not a strict Muslim home, which encouraged her. She feared for her son to marry into a fundamentalist family, as this would limit the freedom he would have in directing his wife and own home.

As she sat on the couch next to her husband, she tried to observe the house without looking conspicuous. It was evident, from even this quick perusal, that this was a family with more money than her own. Neither she nor her husband could remember what Abdullah did for a living, but it was obviously a substantial position. Would this hinder them being willing to marry their daughter to her Muhammad? Maybe he would not be good enough for them. She tried not to look worried as her husband carried on his conversation with their hosts.

Of course, no mention was made of the purpose of the visit for some time. Otherwise, it would seem very rude. They therefore talked about the weather, traffic, work and the family in general for over an hour. During this time, Hekmet went to the kitchen and came out with a beautiful platter of cakes and cookies and soft drinks. She had also taken the flowers they brought and put them in a vase, sitting them on a side table for all to admire. As the refreshments were finished, Ahmed straightened up and cleared his throat to speak.

"Abdullah," he began with confidence, "you know that our eldest son, Muhammad, is now 25 years of age. He has a degree in Law, but works with me in my shop, where he is very effective and useful. I rely on him heavily and see a great future for him in the business. Perhaps my sister, Yasmine, has already spoken to you about our desire to see him married?"

Hekmet nodded her head, while her husband remained still and without emotion. Ahmed stirred uneasily in his seat and continued:

"It is the belief of my sister that your Noura would be a good match for our son. What do you think?"

Hekmet looked at her husband, knowing that she was not allowed to give an opinion on such an important matter. This was an issue left between husbands.

"I do not know your Muhammad," began Abdullah, "but I do know you and your family. Though I am sure that Noura could marry higher up, I prefer for her to be within the family rather than married to a rich man. However, before I could give my consent, I would want to meet your son. It is no reflection on you, Ahmed, but you must understand my caution where it comes to my daughter's welfare."

"Yes, of course," nodded Ahmed, relieved that at least the preliminary idea had been accepted. "I would expect nothing less of a man who loves his children."

"Thank you," replied Abdullah.

"May I ask of you to meet your daughter?" Ahmed asked with a crack in his voice. "I too want to know that Muhammad would be pleased with his new bride."

"Hekmet, go get the girl," Abdullah ordered his wife, but then added, "but have her cover."

"Yes, my husband," Hekmet replied. She stood and left the room, returning a short while later with a petite and demure young girl, who did not look up to the eighteen years Ahmed's sister had given her. She kept her eyes down as her mother brought her in, but looked up after being nudged by Hekmet to greet the guests.

"Peace be upon you," she said in a soft voice.

"And upon you be peace," replied Abu and Um Muhammad at once.

"Come, sit with us," said her father.

As the girl sat in a chair near her mother, Um Muhammad could not but help notice how pretty her face was. She thought to herself how pleased Muhammad would be with such a sweet girl. Though she hoped to hear the girl express herself, she was to be disappointed as the men continued their conversation without acknowledging there were any other people present. In a normal family setting, Um Muhammad would have offered to help Hekmet in the kitchen or they would have moved to another room, but since this was an official visit, she did not want to do anything to displease her husband. She therefore sat quietly on the couch, listening to the men talk, while trying to watch the girl's facial expressions and take note of her physical appearance.

After being served coffee and visiting for another half an hour, Ahmed rose to take their leave. He and Abdullah had made arrangements for Abdullah to meet Muhammad in a downtown coffee shop later that week.

"You did what?!" exclaimed Muhammad to his father, as he sat facing his parents in their living room several days later. "How could you? Without even asking me?"

"You are an ungrateful son!" came the rebuke from Ahmed. "How dare you yell at me!"

"Muhammad, try to calm yourself and listen to your father," tried Um Muhammad with a soothing voice.

"Mother, how can I calm myself? You are changing my life without even taking my opinion. What if I don't want to get married?"

"What?" both parents exclaimed.

"Or, what if I prefer to choose my bride?"

"Calm down, son," replied his father with a slightly different tone. "Of course, we will let you choose. We are just trying to help you get started. You have so little opportunity to meet girls, and what is better than to have one from a family we know?"

"This is so archaic," Muhammad said with a huge sigh.

"It has been done this way for centuries," tried his mother.

"And look at what has happened as a result," replied Muhammad, opening his hand toward his parents; "marriages not based on love or mutual respect but on convenience and ultimately misery."

Ahmed rose from his seat, "How dare you make such a statement to your parents!"

Muhammad looked at his mother and asked, "but is it not true?"

His mother replied with a smile on her face, "My son, you must know that your father chose me because he loved me." She looked up at her husband, "Isn't that right, Abu Muhammad?"

Her husband sat down and looked his son in the eyes as he replied, "Yes, I married her not out of convenience or family ties, but out of love."

"Would you not want the same for me, then, Father?" came the pleading question of his son.

"Of course I would, my son. Please do not misunderstand our intentions here, but you rarely go to the doctor," he turned to his wife and actually winked, then continued smiling, "we are just trying to give you some options. Besides," he said, leaning closer to his son, "she is a very pretty girl."

As the tension in the room settled down, Muhammad finally agreed with his parents to at least meet the girl's father first, but he insisted that he be allowed to see the girl herself and make up his own mind about whether to entertain the idea of marriage.

While Muhammad and his parents had come to an agreement, convincing Noura's father of this idea was another matter. It took several cups of coffee and heavy negotiations on the part of Ahmed before his cousin's husband would agree to the proposal. It was finally decided that Ahmed would host a family dinner, allowing Muhammad an opportunity to see Noura and make up his mind. A date was set for later in the week. Now the pressure was upon Um Muhammad to come up with a wonderful meal.

After cooking all day, the kitchen was full of platters of food. Nawal and Eptisam had helped their mother prepare many well-known Egyptian dishes such as stuffed grape leaves, squash and peppers; moulokhia, a leafy, green soup; macaroni with béchamel sauce; kebab and kofta; a big green salad and rice. It was not only a feast but took a big part of Ahmed's monthly income to prepare, as the price of meat had risen sharply in the previous months.

Muhammad had arrived home from work early that day to take a shower and prepare himself both physically and mentally for this event. He was very anxious about the possibility of meeting his future wife, and did not know how to settle his nerves before her arrival. His eyes moved to the drawer which held the *Injil* he had received on the minibus. Could it offer him comfort? A word of hope? He quickly moved across his room and removed the book from the bureau and sat on his bed to read.

He had been secretly reading from the book at every possible moment and thus remembered a passage that mentioned something about prayer. He flipped through the pages until he found what he wanted in the Gospel according to Luke.

> *One day Jesus was praying in a certain place. When he finished, one of his disciples said to him, "Lord, teach us to pray, just as John taught his disciples."He said to them, "When you pray, say: 'Father, hallowed be your name, your kingdom come. Give us each day our daily bread. Forgive us our sins, for we also forgive everyone who sins against us. And lead us not into temptation.'"*
>
> *Then he said to them, "Suppose one of you has a friend, and he goes to him at midnight and says, 'Friend, lend me three loaves of bread, because a friend of mine on a journey has come to me, and I have nothing to set before him.' Then the one inside answers, 'Don't bother me. The door is already locked, and my children are with me in bed. I can't get up and give you anything.' I tell you, though he will not get up and give him the bread because he is his friend, yet because of the man's boldness he will get up and give him as much as he needs.*
>
> *So I say to you: Ask and it will be given to you; seek and you will find; knock and the door will be opened to you. For everyone who asks receives; he who seeks finds; and to him who knocks, the door*

> *will be opened. "Which of you fathers, if your son asks for a fish, will give him a snake instead? Or if he asks for an egg, will give him a scorpion? If you then, though you are evil, know how to give good gifts to your children, how much more will your Father in heaven give the Holy Spirit to those who ask him!"*

He moved to the floor and touched his head to the ground.

"God," he said in a soft but audible voice, "if you really are my Father as this book says, show me whether this girl is to be my wife. I'm asking; I'm knocking. If Jesus' words are true, make it clear to me."

The doorbell rang. Muhammad quickly rose from his position and finished dressing. He looked at his face in the mirror as he brushed through his thick hair. A peace had come over him. He did not know exactly why, but felt it had something to do with the words of Jesus and the prayer. "All would soon be revealed," he said to himself as he walked toward the door.

Chapter Twenty-Six

It was a warm Sunday morning when Phardos began walking to church to attend mass. Philippe had agreed to go with her, though he was not particularly inclined to do so after his experience at the Evangelical church. That, however, was not something he wanted to share with her, and though it had troubled him for several days afterward, he worked hard to suppress his feelings and return to normal life. They walked in silence for several minutes, before his mother started to speak:

"Philippe," she began, looking at him with concern, "are you feeling all right?"

"Yes, Mother, I'm fine."

"You've been awfully quiet the last several days, and I've hardly seen you. Is there something bothering you?"

"Nothing, Mother, I'm fine," he said again.

"Well, I'm glad you are going with me to mass this morning. It should help in any case."

"Yes, Mother."

The church was not very full when they entered and separated for Philippe to sit on the side with the men and his mother with the women. Phardos found a friend to join. Philippe, however, stood in front of a pew a good distance away from the only other person on the bench, who was a very old man in a galabiya. The liturgy was already underway, and the priest was reading from the Gospel in Arabic. This was the one portion of the service Philippe actually liked and understood. Today, the priest was reading from the Gospel of John, which held, as he briefly explained, Jesus' final prayer before his crucifixion.

> *After Jesus said this, he looked toward heaven and prayed: "Father, the time has come. Glorify your Son, that your Son may glorify you. For you granted him authority over all people that he might give eternal life to all those you have given him. Now this is eternal life: that they may know you, the only true God, and Jesus Christ, whom you have sent. I have brought you glory on earth by completing the work you gave me to do. And now, Father, glorify me in your presence with the glory I had with you before the world began.*

As the priest finished, Philippe repeated with the congregation: "Glory be to God forever." The congregation sat down as the priest began his sermon. Unlike the words he heard at the Evangelical church, the priest was not able to catch Philippe's attention as he spoke without excitement about the passage of the day. Hard as he tried, Philippe was not able to concentrate and found his eyes wondering to the church building in which he sat. Though it was a big auditorium, there were no bright colors here, even with the sun shining through the windows. He focused on the icons which represented stories of the Christian faith. In spotting the icon of the Christ, Philippe was struck by the sadness in his eyes. He realized that he had always been rather afraid of Jesus because of the way he was illustrated in Coptic artwork. Though the Christ child seemed welcoming, the adult Christ did not. He remembered another icon he had seen of the Christ, which a priest had told him showed the justice and mercy of the Lord. Half of the face was dark and angry, and in his left hand he carried the book of the Law. The other half of the face was lighter and more sympathetic, and the hand of the right was raised in blessing. No, Jesus was not someone in whom he felt he could ever confide. The Virgin Mary, on the other hand, was always painted as soft and kind. It was to her that most Copts raised their prayers for intercession. She was the mediator who could reach Jesus with their concerns.

Philippe continued to work through these thoughts as the service progressed and the congregation rose and sat as designated, the scent of incense increasing with each ritual and reading. It was now time for the holy communion, and the priest began the process of blessing the bread and wine, called the Lamb, in reference to the sacrifice of Christ on the cross. The priest made the sign of the cross over the bread three times, each time saying a different phrase and the congregation saying "amen". Holding up the bread, the priest proclaimed:

> *He broke it and gave it to His own holy disciples and saintly apostles saying: Take, eat of it, all of you. For this is my Body, Which is broken for you and for many, to be given for the remission of sins. Do this in remembrance of Me.*

He continued with the cup of wine, with the congregation responding as required. The priest then moved into a ritual in which Philippe understood that the bread and wine are changed into the actual body and blood of Christ. Though he accepted this act by faith, he never fully understood how or why this took place. However, a good Orthodox Christian never questions the liturgy or priests, yet for Philippe, he felt the nagging uncertainty of many things within the traditions of the church.

Before the congregation could partake of the communion, many more prayers were offered, covering everyone from the Pope Shenouda to the actual church building, to the saints of old and even the dearly departed of the church family. The liturgy continued with the recitation of the Lord's Prayer by the people and then the priest prayed for the absolution of the sins of those present, that they would not bring a curse upon themselves in taking the Holy Communion in a sinful state. Finally, the deacons were served the Holy Communion and then the congregation was allowed to participate. Philippe went forward to receive the bread and wine. As the priest gave him the bread, he said:

"The Body of Emmanuel our God. This is true. Amen"

Philippe responded, "Amen".

The priest then gave him the wine to drink, saying, "The Blood of Emmanuel our God. This is true. Amen."

Again, Philippe responded, "Amen".

Returning to his seat, Philippe savored the taste of the wine and again tried to figure out how it could really be Christ's blood. He knew that he would never be able to ask the priest about it, but wondered anyway. Watching his mother take communion, Philippe was now ready to leave the church but had to wait until a few more prayers were offered. As they bowed their heads, the priest lifted this prayer:

> *Your servants, O Lord, who are serving You, entreating Your holy name, and bowing down their heads to You, dwell in them, O Lord; walk among them; aid them in every good deed; wake their heart from every vile earthly thought; grant them to live and think of what is pertaining to the living, and understand the things that are Yours; through Your Only Begotten Son, our Lord, God and Savior, Jesus Christ, unto Whom we, and all Your people, cry out saying, "Have mercy upon us, O God, our Savior."*

Philippe liked this prayer, and as the priest continued with the final blessing, he lifted his own prayer to the Lord:

> *Heavenly Father, I do ask that you help me to understand the things that are yours. It is so hard to know what is from you and what is not. Show me, Lord, that I may walk in your way. Amen.*

The congregation began leaving the church following the priests through the open doorway. Philippe quickly did his duty in greeting the priests and then stood a distance away to wait for his mother. She joined him carrying a loaf of the sanctified bread in order to share it with her husband and daughter and anyone else who came her way that had not had the opportunity to take communion.

"It was a nice mass, wasn't it?" she asked her son as they began the walk home.

"I suppose so."

"What, you did not like the sermon?"

"Mother, how can you like such a sermon?" responded Philippe with agitation. "You could tell he was just going through the motions."

"No, my son, you cannot criticize the priest."

"Why not? Do we have to just accept everything they do and tell us?"

"They are the spokesmen of God, my son."

"Then we are never to question? Have you never questioned something a priest did, Mother?"

Phardos felt a struggle inside her, but knew she had to tell her son the truth. "Well, I have tried not to."

"So you have questioned them?" Philippe looked his mother in the eyes.

"Yes, my son, I have," she admitted.

"Good," he replied, "because today I felt myself questioning so much of what was happening; not only the sermon, but other things as well."

"Like what?"

"Like, how the bread and wine actually turn into the body and blood of Christ," he said. "Don't you find that hard to believe? I mean it tastes the same, how can it be his actual blood?"

"These are things we accept by faith," his mother responded.

"But why do we have to?" Philippe asked again, raising his voice. "Is there anything in the Bible about these issues?"

"We have the traditions of the Church as well to follow, Philippe. You know that."

"Well, I worry about accepting anything except what is specifically in the Bible."

"Maybe you should talk to the priest about your questions."

"Maybe I will."

They completed their walk in silence, each lost in thought about the discussion. While Phardos could easily dismiss such questions because of her lifetime of training to do so, Philippe could not. He was of the new generation that was learning to question everything, from education and government to church and religion. It was a worrisome sign to his mother, who feared her son would be disciplined by the Church for doubting things of faith. Maybe it was time to get her husband involved in the matter.

Chapter Twenty-Seven

The house was full of noise as Muhammad found family members busily greeting one another in the foyer.

"You bring light to our home!" rang out Ahmed as he kissed first Abdullah and then his cousin, Hekmet, on the cheeks. "Please come, come, our home is yours." He led them into the living room.

Muhammad watched from the hallway as the parents, then Noura and her three siblings followed his father into the other room. Though his parents were not yet aware of his presence, Noura turned and looked at him as she passed by. Here warm, brown eyes were striking as her face was enveloped in an auburn veil. She smiled in his direction but then quickly dropped her eyes and turned toward the direction she was headed. Her sisters giggled behind her, knowing what was happening. Muhammad quickly broke from his trance and moved toward the children who were yet within his reach.

"Welcome to our home," he said. "My name is Muhammad."

"Welcome to you," came the reply. "I'm Nisrine, and this is my sister Selwa and brother, Sayed."

"It has been a long time since I've seen you all," said Muhammad. "You have really grown."

"I'm six now," came a proud little voice from Sayed.

"Wow, six! You're a big man!" laughed Muhammad.

A voice came from the salon, "And this is our son, Muhammad," he heard his father proclaim. Muhammad looked up from Sayed to see everyone in the room looking at him. He came into the living room and went first to greet Abdullah and then his wife, to whom he refrained from touching but nodded politely.

"It seems you have already met our younger children," Abdullah proclaimed and then added, "And this is our oldest daughter, Noura."

As he was once again confronted with the penetrating eyes of his relative, Muhammad had to force himself to act normal and nod appropriately without giving to all in the room the impression that he was already smitten.

"Welcome to our home, Noura," he said.

"Welcome to you," came the soft reply.

Muhammad went to sit with his father and their male guest as the women began talking on the other side of the room. Though the older men were able to proceed as if no one else was in the room, Muhammad could not help but try to snatch glimpses of Noura in conversation with his mother. However, the interruption of Abdel-Karem into the circle of men forced him to keep his attentions elsewhere as the men began discussing various subjects of business and politics. When he again tried to look her way, he realized the women had actually gone into the kitchen.

Having maintained conversation for over half an hour, Muhammad was now ready to move on to the meal so he could have more opportunities to observe the lovely Noura. How was it, he wondered to himself, that in such a short moment he was already intrigued by this creature? Was this God answering his prayer or just his hormones being overactive? Finally, the meal was on the table and everyone was called to eat.

Abdullah raved over the expansive feast set before them, which gave Um Muhammad hope that things would go well for her son and his future bride. As plates were filled and guests began eating, she watched for signs of interaction between Muhammad and Noura. She was not disappointed.

If Muhammad had hoped to hear Noura carry on a long conversation, this however, turned out to be the wrong occasion. It was to be the adults who dominated that area. Yet there were moments when he caught glimpses of her personality as her younger sisters and brother requested her help to cut a piece of meat or serve them some food from the table. Noura smiled as she met their needs and talked to them briefly. He detected a tenderness in her that attracted him immensely, for if there was anything in a wife that he desired, it was a kind and tender heart.

Following the meal, as the men adjourned to the living room for tea, Muhammad excused himself to the restroom. Noura was helping the women clear the table. Muhammad retreated to his room, desperately trying to figure out a way to have at least one minute's conversation with this girl. What he did not know as he deliberated was that Noura had finished helping her mother and asked to go to the restroom. She was just coming out as Muhammad opened his bedroom door to return to the living room.

"Oh, excuse me," she said, as she almost bumped into him.

"No, no," he stuttered back, "I'm sorry. After you." He quickly added as she turned toward the living room: "I hope you have enjoyed yourself here tonight."

"Yes, very much," and she stopped to look at him in the face, "your mother is a very good cook."

"Yes, she is," Muhammad agreed. "Noura," he said quickly as he took a deep breath, "will you please forgive me for being so bold, but I know you know why your family is here tonight. I see no reason to go on with this if you are not interested in me. I will be honest with you that I find you a beautiful and kind person, but perhaps you do not have the same impression about me."

Muhammad knew as soon as the words came out of his mouth that he was doing something risky. Would she be shocked and repulsed by his advances? Maybe she did not even like him in the first place. He could not tell by the way she handled herself at the dinner table. Now, here she was, in the small hallway, so near to him that he was tempted to reach out and even kiss her. She was silent for a few moments, yet never deviated her gaze from his. Slowly she lowered her head, took a deep breath, and then again looked him in the face to speak.

"I have always asked the Lord to provide me with a kind husband," she said. "I have few expectations about looks, job, and money, but I do have many about how he is to treat me, and that is with respect. My mother tells me that your father is a good man, but that does not mean that his son will be. I know nothing about you, Muhammad, but if you prove to me that you are kind, then I have no other objection."

Voices rose from the living room, as the women had returned to join their husbands. Both Muhammad and Noura realized that they might be found in a compromised position if the adults realized where they were.

"Thank you, Noura," Muhammad said quickly, "I will do my best to prove myself worthy of your desires. Now, you go into the room alone. I will return to my bedroom and come out shortly. I do not want them to suspect anything wrong."

She turned without speaking further and went into the other room. Muhammad watched her go and then turned and entered his bedroom again, closing the door without making a sound. As soon as he was in the privacy of his own room, he collapsed on the bed, looking up at the ceiling. "Thank you, Lord," he sighed out loud. He remained in his room for another 15 minutes before getting up and returning to the others.

"Where were you son?" his mother asked, as he came in.

"I took a short rest. I just could not keep my eyes open," he replied. "Mother, is the water still hot in the kitchen? I would like a cup of tea."

"Of course, son," she replied as she rose to her feet, "I'll get it for you."

"I can do it, please stay."

"Come, we can do it together." And they walked to the kitchen, leaving the others to enjoy the fruit she had set on the table earlier.

As soon as they got into the kitchen, Um Muhammad turned to her son.

"What do you think, my son?" she asked, taking him by the arm.

"I cannot believe I'm saying this," he replied, "but I believe that God is smiling on me today."

She kissed her son on both cheeks and then went to the stove to check the kettle. Finding it hot, she began to pour him a cup of tea. "Praise be to God," she said.

"What do you think of her, Mother?"

"I like her, Muhammad. She seems very decent and mature for her age."

"I think you are right, Mother. Now what do we do?" He took the teacup from her hand, blew across the top, and took a sip.

"We will leave that to your father," she replied. "Come, we mustn't keep them wondering what we are doing. Bring your tea, and let's join them."

The evening continued with lively conversation between the men, but with growing input from the women as well. Abdullah turned out to be a great teller of jokes, and even had Noura smiling and laughing before he finished the second of many that night. Things turned more serious as Abdullah began asking Muhammad some direct questions about his studies and plans for the future. Though he had done some of this during his earlier private visit, he was aiming now to have the women hear from the young man and to gain further insight into his character.

Muhammad must have pleased the man with his responses, for after an hour of directing questions, Abdullah finally said:

"You have done well by your son, Ahmed."

"Praise be to God," Ahmed replied. The father then looked at his son and asked in front of everyone: "My son, do we continue?"

Shocked, though happy to have been asked, Muhammad replied, "Yes, Father."

Ahmed turned to his cousin's husband: "Now, cousin, what do you think of our proposal?"

"I am in agreement," replied Abdullah, matter-of-factly.

"Praise be to God," Ahmed exclaimed.

A loud shrilling sound rose up from the women, as they began the *zuggarit* in celebration of the good news. The two fathers shook hands and kissed, beginning a round of congratulatory greetings among the family members. Though both Muhammad and Noura were congratulated by each person, they refrained from coming in contact with each other. Muhammad had to be satisfied with a mere smile from his fiancée-to-be until the official engagement took place. It was then and only then that he would be allowed to touch his future bride.

Before they left for the night, arrangements were made for the engagement and timeframe prior to marriage. Since Muhammad did not yet have an apartment, it was agreed that the engagement would be at least a year in order for preparations to be made. Ahmed refrained from trying to think now how he would manage such a feat for his son within a year's time, knowing that the engagement could be extended if need be. The important thing for the moment was that his son was engaged and would have something to keep him occupied and looking toward the future with hope.

Chapter Twenty-Eight

Though it was against her better judgment to leave her children as they prepared for exams, Phardos could not refuse her husband's insistence to go down to Ein al-Soukna for the day with a group of their friends. It had been a long time since they had been out of town, and with the warming temperatures of May, she was actually looking forward to the break from the pollution and heat of Cairo. Marcos and Gigi had a beautiful villa at the Stella del Mar resort where they would all gather for a day of relaxation and food. Though the seashore in Ein al-Soukna was not exceptional in comparison to that of Sharm al-Sheik in the southern Sinai, the fact that it was within about an hour's drive from the city made it accessible for more frequent trips. Plus, everyone knew that Stella del Mar was the most exclusive resort in the area and had beautiful gardens and multiple swimming pools.

The dream of owning such a villa was not within the realm of possibility for Girgis and Phardos, but having friends like Marcos and Gigi at least gave them opportunities to enjoy the good life more than most. They joined their hosts and three other couples around 10 that morning, to find a table set in the garden with breakfast delights. Gigi had come down the day before with her maid to have everything ready for their visitors. She greeted them as they came out on the patio:

"Welcome, welcome," she said, kissing Phardos on both cheeks, "it's been so long since I've seen you."

"Thank you, Gigi," replied Phardos, "it really has been too long. Thank you so much for inviting us."

"We're so glad you could come. I know you didn't want to leave the children, but am so glad you did."

"I feel bad that I am enjoying this beautiful day and they have to sit in their rooms and study," replied Phardos with a nod. "I hope they will forgive me."

"Now, don't you feel guilty, Phardos," came another voice from behind her, "you've had your share of studying."

"Charlotte! I'm so glad to see you," Phardos rang out, as she kissed her friend on the cheeks. "I have had my share of studies, but still... I'm their mother and should suffer with them."

"Oh, please!" replied Charlotte with a laugh, "Why is it that Egyptian mothers feel they have to carry everything for their children?"

"Most likely because our mothers did it for us," said Gigi.

"Well, it's time to break tradition!" Charlotte chimed.

Laughing, Phardos turned to greet the other guests of the day. Charlotte was there with her husband, Magdy. He was in plastics and had a big factory and made good money. Renee was an old friend from Phardos' early school days. She and her husband, Tawfiq, owned several private schools in the city. Ruth was a schoolteacher at the British school, which was a very good job. She had excellent English and taught math. Her husband, Wagdy, was a medical doctor. Phardos had not seen him much, so was looking forward to really seeing what kind of man he was. Ruth was so simple and kind, she could not imagine Wagdy being anything but the same.

This was an elite group—not the super rich, but of the higher class in Egyptian society and living the good life. Once greetings were complete, Gigi encouraged everyone to help themselves to the breakfast buffet, which they all did willingly. Though she was petite and slim, she had prepared food for an army, not allowing anyone to think her inhospitable or lacking in graciousness. The table was adorned with croissants and pastries of several kinds as well as *fatir*, a buttery, layered Egyptian bread to be eaten with molasses or aged cheese, both of which were served. She had also prepared *foul* and *tamaiya*, traditional Egyptian dishes, mostly associated with the lower classes, but enjoyed by all. Boiled eggs, cucumbers, tomatoes and a variety of cheeses were also available, allowing each person's tastes to be fulfilled.

The couples stayed together during breakfast, catching up on one another's news. As Phardos listened to them talk, she could not help but feel at ease with this wonderful gathering of her peers. With nothing to distract them or hinder the subjects of conversation, they were free to discuss all issues, including the political and religious ones of the day. Of course, the men expressed unified worry over the growing pressures from the Muslim Brotherhood along with the rising food prices, knowing that this meant potential unrest for the country.

"Wagdy, my friend," she heard Marcos say, "you must put some of your money outside the country. You don't know when things may suddenly go under."

"I agree with Marcos," Magdy joined in. "In fact, we have already applied for immigration to Canada, just in case."

"You wouldn't really think about leaving, would you?" asked Ruth, looking concerned.

"It's not that I want to, Ruth," replied Magdy, "but with rising inflation and a change in government coming soon, we want to be ready."

"Surely not everyone can just leave?" responded Ruth, now clearly upset.

"It doesn't have to be forever, Ruth," said Charlotte. "but you have to be realistic that the future looks grim."

Ruth's husband, Wagdy, now spoke his peace. "I agree that the future looks grim, but we cannot just leave. We as Christians have a responsibility to our country. How can we just leave it to the Muslims to ruin? I will not leave my country, my homeland, no matter what happens."

"That is very admirable, Wagdy," Marcos said soothingly, "but you need to realize that when trouble comes, who are the targets of violence?"

"The Christians," Girgis replied. "I know that, but the Christians can also bring balance. The Muslims need us, and they know it, no matter what they may say from the mosques about us."

"They may know they need us, Girgis, but when the mobs start moving, there is no reasoning with them," said Tawfiq. "The best thing to do is get out of their way until they calm down."

"That's all fine and good," said Wagdy, "but what about our interests in the country, our investments and homes?"

"We just have to pray that God will protect them," Magdy responded. Everyone nodded.

"This conversation is depressing," sighed Gigi, "can we change the topic?"

The direction of conversation was changed quickly enough, but everyone knew that this issue was not going away. It was a perpetual fear and tension in the lives of the Christian community that the day would soon be coming when the country would once again go through an upheaval. In many ways they were at the mercies of the Muslim majority and government, and they could only hope and pray that the Lord would protect their people when the inevitable took place. Though they did not have the means to do so, Phardos knew that many Christians were in fact putting a good chunk of their money in foreign banks and applying for immigration. Had she not seen her own church's congregation shrink in the past 15 years at least by half due to immigration? There was no family who did not have someone in the States, Canada or Australia. She wondered if there would soon be no Christians left in the country.

Later in the day, the group naturally divided, allowing the women to talk about more enjoyable subjects than politics. This was definitely an area they preferred to leave to the men. While the men stayed outside in the shade, the women moved into the salon and drank tea as they sat on the sofas and soft chairs. Conversation remained light as they talked about their children and latest events within their social worlds.

Charlotte changed the subject to tell the women about a wonderful ministry of the church in which she had recently participated. She joined a group of young people in visiting the homes of the sick and elderly in order to sing Christian hymns, read from the Bible and allow the priest to give them Holy Communion. Her friends were uniformly impressed with this special service and complimented Charlotte on her participation in it.

"You know, I thank God for the wonderful good works the Orthodox Church does for so many people," Renee spoke up.

"Yes, there are so many needs. We just need more people to participate," said Charlotte.

"I really should get involved," admitted Ruth, "but my time is so limited."

"That is my problem too," Phardos added.

"Well, anything you can do would be welcomed," Charlotte assured them. "If you can't help yourself, perhaps you can give money for a certain ministry."

"Charlotte, you must keep us informed of the needs," Gigi urged. "I know we would all be glad to help out."

"I will be sure too," Charlotte replied.

Seeing that the subject had changed to religion, Phardos felt she could easily talk to her friends about the issues on her mind. She decided to begin with the more acceptable topic.

"Which priest would you recommend to invite to the house to talk to my Philippe? He has been having some questions lately, and I would like to have someone come and talk to him." She looked up at her friends in quiet expectation.

"I would not have any priest in my home!" Gigi quickly and resolutely responded.

"I know what you mean," agreed Renee.

"I don't know what you mean." Phardos replied, puzzled.

"Oh, Phardos, where have you been?" Gigi looked at her in shock and continued, "Didn't you hear about the affair that the priest, who will not be named, had with the wife of the one of his own members?"

"No, I never heard of such a thing? A priest?"

"Yes, a priest," assured Gigi, "and the horrible thing is the woman went as far as to leave her husband and children completely for him."

"No, it cannot be true." Phardos said incredulously.

"I'm afraid it is, my dear," affirmed Charlotte, with sadness in her voice. "The woman's husband was caught with a gun in his car, ready to murder the priest in revenge, but came to his senses before he was able to do the deadly act."

"Phardos, all women know that you never leave a priest alone with a girl," Renee added. "Certainly I would never trust my daughter with one."

"How can you say such things?" Phardos implored. "They are priests, men of God!"

Charlotte, put her hand on Phardos' shoulder. "Yes, they are men of God, Phardos, but they are also human beings, though some would not think of them as such. Power corrupts, and I'm afraid that it is true that when some priests gain that power, they use it wrongly and give into earthly desires."

Ruth had remained quiet throughout this interchange, but she now spoke up.

"I cannot let you all defame the good name of the priests in our church like this! OK, maybe there are some bad priests, but there are some very good ones too. My favorite is Father Marcos. I've never known a kinder and more godly man."

"Yes, yes, there are good priests, Ruth," assured Gigi, "we know that. But it's important for Phardos to know that there are many bad ones too. She has to really ask around and get the right one to help her with Philippe." Turning to Phardos, she then asked: "What's his problem, anyway?"

"Oh, he had some questions about the Holy Communion, and was not comfortable about the sermon."

"Was it not a good sermon?" Ruth asked.

"No, I thought it was fine, but Philippe felt that the priest's heart was not in it or something. I'm not really sure what his objection was. I told him it was not for us to question the priests, but this new generation seems to be all about questioning things."

Charlotte spoke up, "Yeah, you know my son the other day asked me what priests are eating. He said he knew they went into the priesthood skinny, but come out fat!" She looked at her friends and smiled. Everyone laughed, grateful for the comic relief provided by this old joke.

The day continued with food and conversation both in generous supply. The liberal sprinkling of alcoholic beverages also helped in the loosening of tongues. Phardos could hear Girgis laughing in the garden, as the men enjoyed their drinks and ate an amazing selection of nuts and seeds. She was afraid he would have a hard time driving home if he continued to drink long.

The women were no less inebriated, but kept their voices at a more respectable level. Though they had avoided the topic of religion as the day wore on, Phardos looked for an opportunity to ask her best friends an important question. When Renee began talking about one of their Christian girl students running away with a Muslim boy, Phardos seized the moment to ask:

"Do you think a Muslim can become a Christian?"

The women became silent and stared at her like she had committed a crime. After a moment, Charlotte spoke up. "Are you out of your mind, Phardos? What would make you ask such a question?"

"I don't think she's crazy," began Ruth.

"I asked you a question," Charlotte continued, without taking notice of Ruth's comment.

"Well, it's an honest question," Phardos tried. "I mean, I have heard things, and it is not like the issue is not in the papers. I just wondered what you all thought about it."

"You cannot believe everything you read in the papers, Phardos," added Renee. "Our priest has openly condemned the man."

"Yes, but I understand that is only for diplomatic reasons," said Phardos.

"A priest would not lie just for political reasons," replied Renee. "He is bound by the truth."

"Now that sounds a little funny after our earlier conversation," Ruth interjected.

"This has nothing to do with that," Renee retorted heatedly. "Besides, we said there were good priests and bad ones. They would never allow a bad one speak for the Church."

"I agree," added Charlotte, "but I think this issue may have more to do with the television than the papers. Am I right, Phardos?"

"What do you mean?" Phardos questioned, now regretting the whole thing.

"I mean, I think you have been watching Father Zacharia on that Christian satellite station. Am I right?"

"Charlotte, why are you grilling her like this?" Ruth asked. "She has not committed a crime. So what if she has watched his show?"

"So what?" exclaimed Charlotte, "He is a heretic and has given the Church more troubles than I can name!"

Phardos got her courage in hearing Ruth take her side. "Whatever you may think of Father Zacharia is not the point. My question is the same — can a Muslim become a Christian?"

"This is absurd!" Charlotte expressed with exasperation.

"Why?" Phardos asked with all sincerity.

"Because Christians are born Christian, Muslims are born Muslims. There is no point to discuss it further."

"Oh, Charlotte," Ruth began in a soothing tone, "you cannot believe that is it. Did not Christ come to earth to die for all mankind? Isn't that what the Bible says? It is my understanding that anyone who confesses Christ as Savior becomes Christian."

"I have heard that Jesus has even come to many of them in dreams," Gigi finally spoke up and said. "They come to the priest because they have seen a man in white, surrounded by light, calling to them."

"That is ridiculous!" retorted Charlotte, "Jesus comes to only the Christians in dreams, not Muslims."

"Oh, please, Charlotte," begged Ruth, "you cannot be that closed-minded. Why would the Lord Jesus refrain from revealing himself to Muslims?"

"Because they are a filthy, demon-possessed people!" Charlotte's face was full of rage.

"And they probably think the same about us, my dear," Ruth added, trying to calm her friend down. "I find it hard to think that one so eager to do good works for the Church can be so hard on those outside of her walls."

"Phardos," Gigi turned to her friend, "have you met a convert from Islam? Is that why you are asking this?"

"No, Charlotte is actually right. I happened upon Father Zacharia's show a few months ago, and it made me wonder."

"Well, though I have never met any either, I have friends who know of some. They are very complimentary of their faith and say they are actually very close to God and behave better than Christians do," Ruth shared. "I think it is good to be open-minded and willing to accept them when they come into the Church."

"You have got to be kidding," Charlotte exclaimed. "Next thing you know you'll be wanting our daughters to marry them!" She got up and walked out of the room.

Phardos felt so bad about allowing her silly question to cause such a problem with her best friends. She went to apologize to Charlotte and then as well to Gigi for causing the stir. Forgiveness was all too quickly granted and Phardos knew that this had put a strain on the friendships. Somehow, however, she now felt a certain bond with Ruth. She would look for later opportunities to visit with her.

Chapter Twenty-Nine

Um Muhammad was pleased to have something good to think about these days. As she made preparations for her son's engagement, she began to have hope for the future. She tried hard not to let her concerns for Rachid put a dark cloud over Muhammad's good fortune. No, she saw this as a good sign of things to come for her family. She hoped it would be the first of many marriages in the near future. Though Abdel-Karem might need to wait a while, there was no reason that either Nawal or Eptisam would have to wait long to marry—the younger the better in the eyes of the Muslim community. The challenge would be in finding suitable husbands for them. She could only hope that they would have one as good as Ahmed had been for her. While she knew he could be harsh with words, she was one of the lucky wives who had never actually been beaten by her husband. She could only thank God for this.

The eldest of her girls, Nawal, was spending more and more time at her friend, Nancy's house, as they prepared for final exams. Um Muhammad did not worry about this, as she knew the study group helped Nawal, and she was not the only Muslim in the group. Nawal knew that if her mother really knew what was happening at Nancy's house, she would never let her go. Though she had in fact been studying for exams, two other, very critical things were taking place each time Nawal visited Nancy. The first began early in May when, alone in the house, Nawal pressed Nancy about Christianity.

"I want to convert to Christianity, Nancy."

"Nawal, do you know what you are saying?"

"I do, and I am serious. Can you help me?"

"Why do you want to convert?" her friend questioned.

"Because the life you lead is the life I want," Nawal replied honestly.

"That's all good and fine, but don't you know what your family will do to you?"

"I do, but they will not have to know."

"How can they not?"

"I will work that out. Please be my friend and help me."

"You will need to see the priest," Nancy suggested.

"Fine, can you take me to him?"

"I'll arrange a meeting."

"Thank you, Nancy," Nawal said, hugging her, "this means everything to me."

While Nancy was actually pleased that Nawal wanted to convert, she did not realize the real reason for this life-changing decision. She was oblivious to the reality that her own brother, Emir, had continued in seeking to win Nawal's heart.

Two weeks later, Nancy managed to arrange a meeting with a sympathetic priest, Father Antonius. She had Nawal meet her a block from the church and they walked together to the side entrance to find the priest waiting for them in his office. Though the priest was required to have any Muslim requesting conversion to first see his own imam, this was rarely done, as it was known that the potential candidate would be quickly and quietly taken into hiding until the thought of conversion was forgotten. Father Antonius asked Nawal several questions about her own religion and the Prophet Muhammad, in order to know the depth of her loyalty to them. Realizing that she was in fact turning her back on Islam and wanted to convert to Christianity, he agreed to baptize her into the Church. He took her and Nancy into a room on the second floor of the church, where a woman came in with a robe for her to put on. Once she had changed, she came into a larger room to find the priest and Nancy waiting beside a large baptismal pool, which looked like a well. She climbed into the pool. The cold water came up to her neck. She started shivering. The priest quickly prayed as he dunked her under the water three times. Nawal was terrified, thinking she would drown, but the ritual was completed before she could protest. Coming out of the water, the priest anointed her on different parts of her body with holy oil, again praying something that Nawal did not understand as he did so. The woman came around her with a towel and led her back into the room to get dry and change into her own clothes.

A mass was in process while the priest had been baptizing Nawal, so he led her and Nancy downstairs to the main church and indicated for them to sit on the women's side. At the appropriate time, Nawal joined Nancy in taking her first Holy Communion as a Christian. She understood little of what was said or done during the mass that day, but was pleased she had taken the first step toward being accepted by Emir.

For the next two weeks, Nawal continued to sneak away from her home to attend mass at every opportunity. She wore her veil to within a block of the church and then would take it off before arrival, so as not to attract extra attention. This however, did not prohibit Father Marcos from taking her aside one day before she entered the building.

"My daughter, you must be careful."

"Why, Father?" Nawal asked fearfully.

"Surely you know National Security will eventually see you come here and ask to see your ID."

"What can I do, Father?"

"I can arrange for you to obtain new papers."

"Papers?"

"Yes, if you are to remain committed to the Church so openly, you will need a new identity card, but it will cost money."

"I don't have any money, Father," Nawal replied.

"Ask the friend who helped you in the beginning."

Not feeling comfortable attending mass that day, Nawal went over to Nancy's house where she told her about the encounter with the priest. She was surprised to hear Nancy actually agree with the priest's assessment for her need to obtain a new identity. Nancy told her that she would talk with her parents, who had been aware of the situation from the beginning and were willing to help in any way possible. Again Nawal was amazed at the love shown her by these Christians, and hugged Nancy for all she was doing.

"I want to get a cross tattoo like you too," Nawal said as they were walking to the door.

"You know that would be dangerous as long as you are with your family."

"I hope I won't be with them for long," Nawal replied with bitterness in her voice.

"I will call you in a few days, once I've talked with my parents and Father Marcos again."

While still studying for exams, Nawal found it very hard to keep her mind on school. It was another week before she received the call she had been waiting for from her friend.

"We are to meet a man in front of the Almaza telephone office at 3:00 this afternoon. Can you come?"

"Yes," replied Nawal. "What do I need to bring?"

"Nothing, I have everything."

"Thank you, Nancy."

Telling her mother she was going to Nancy's to study was becoming a routine excuse to get out of the house for

Nawal. This meeting was the first of three required to finish the process of gaining a new identity in Egypt. By the third visit, Nawal learned from the one preparing the fake ID card that her new name would be Miriam Fahim Girgis Milad.

As they met for the final time the man told her, "You need to remember this name and forget your old one. Do you have your identity card with you?"

"No, I did not think I would need it."

"That's too bad," he replied frowning. "Well, you make sure when you go home to get your things that you get it and tear it up. You are dead to your old life and have risen anew in Christ to the new one."

Nawal did not respond, but looked at Nancy again for understanding. She did not know how she could just tear up her identity card. It did not seem right, somehow, but then again, she did not know what was right in this situation. Things were definitely moving too fast. Nancy looked at her, smiled and said, as if oblivious to Nawal's confusion:

"I like the name, Miriam. It is the same as the Virgin Mother's. What a blessing."

"And you come from Mallawi, in the Al-Minya province. Your parents died when you were young, and you were raised among your relatives. You are 20 years old and have education up to first preparatory."

This was too much for Nawal to take. "First preparatory! I am graduating in a few weeks from Saint Claires! And I am only 18, not 20. No one would ever believe that."

"Calm down, girl," the man said. "You did not think that your life could be the same once you took this step, did you? No, you must forget everything from your past and prepare for following a different path now."

Nawal did not know what to do. She had not fully realized what this decision meant for her life. She did want to get away from her home, she wanted to be like the Christians she knew, but she had really not thought through what all this meant in reality for her. When the man handed her the final papers, Nancy walked her to a nearby coffee shop and bought her a drink. Still thinking about the facts of her new identity, Nawal vaguely heard Nancy say something about finding a place to stay.

"Nawal, oh, yes, Miriam," she began, "I'm afraid I will not be able to help you there. Your family will naturally come to my house looking for you, so it is better if you find someone outside of our school that you can stay with until your family gives up. It is better that I don't know, so I would not be lying when they ask me about you. I'm sorry to tell you that, but is it all right?"

Nawal looked at her friend in shock, but found herself saying: "That's fine, I understand." However, she did not understand. As a matter of fact, she did not understand anything of what had happened in the past few weeks, for no one had bothered to really explain any of this to her. She had no idea that becoming a Christian would mean becoming another person. What had she done? Was it really worth it? Then she remembered the real reason behind her action—Emir. Did he know what was happening? Had his sister told him? When would she be able to see him again?

All these questions and more were screaming in her brain as Nancy continued talking. "Nawal, I'm so happy for you," she began. "This is such a wonderful day."

"Thank you, Nancy," Nawal replied with a weak smile, "I could never have done it without you."

"You know it would be better for you not to try to contact me again for a while. Call me in a few weeks once we know things have calmed down."

"I cannot think that far, now, Nancy."

"I know, I know," she replied, patting her friend on the hand. "I will be praying for you."

"Thank you, and please give your family my thanks as well."

"I will."

Leaving the coffee shop alone, Nawal, now Miriam, walked out into the bright sunshine, not knowing what to do. She wondered aimlessly for several blocks when she spotted a garden by a mosque. She walked into the grassy area, lined with trees, found a bench, sat down and cried.

Chapter Thirty

The weeks had passed and with her children in the midst of exams, Phardos felt compelled to go to the church and light a candle for each of them. The students in her own school were almost finished with their tests, and Phardos took a lunch break one hot Monday morning to walk over to the church to pray. As she walked she felt the stress of all the exams of Egypt upon her shoulders. It was always the hardest time of the year for families, as they kept vigils over their children as they studied and worried over their results. This was also the worst time to be the director of a school, as it never failed for countless parents to come crying to her at all times of the day and night for her to show mercy on their extremely smart child who somehow had failed a test.

How she longed for a break, but the end was not yet in sight, for she had to oversee the testing and then the grading of the tests. She was thankful that for the most part, her teachers were honest and fair in their marking of the papers, but it did not mean that one of them would not try to help a favorite student in some way. She realized the pressure was intense on them as well, for parents would offer many incentives to encourage them to grade with leniency. A month, a month of this painful process and then she could rest.

Coming into the cool of the church, Phardos immediately felt peace. She smiled up at the picture of the Lord

Jesus and Virgin Mother, gladly crossing herself at the sight of their familiar faces. The church was empty, and Phardos walked over to the candles and quickly pulled some bills from her wallet and deposited them in the small slot next to the stand. She decided to light three candles instead of two, remembering to pray as well for her students who were working hard to do well. Their success, after all, was hers and the school's. After placing the lit candles in the stand, she moved over to a bench to pray.

She began with praying a familiar prayer from the liturgy that she had known since she was a child, then moved to ask God to be with Philippe and Marianne as they took their tests that day, especially Marianne, who had not been studying as well as she should. She prayed as well for her students, that they would make the school proud and that parents would be happy and not bother her too much this year. When she felt that sounded selfish, she asked God to forgive her. Her mind came back to Marianne. Something had been different about her daughter in the last several weeks. Several times Phardos had tried talking to her, but felt a distance growing between them. When she asked Girgis about it, he told her it was probably just the stress of the exams. While that could easily be true, something inside her told her there was more. Not knowing how to tell God about this, she did not. She was not used to praying personal prayers to God.

Then she remembered Naema. How had she prayed? She tried to remember the words she used, but could only remember the last statement:

Ease her mind, give us your answers, that we may know your truth in all these matters and be drawn closer to you. In the precious Name of Jesus our Lord, I pray. Amen.

Drawn closer to you...how she longed for that; to draw closer to Jesus. Yet, even now the pressure of exams was calling her back to school. Before she stood to leave, she quickly prayed: "Dear God, please draw Marianne closer to you. In the precious Name of Jesus our Lord, I pray. Amen."

Feeling pleased with that effort, she rose and turned to leave the church. Just as she crossed the threshold of the main door, she saw Ruth coming up the stairs. A smile came on her face as she greeted her friend:

"Good morning, Ruth, how are you?"

"Morning of roses, Phardos, what a nice surprise. I'm fine, how are you?"

"Praise God, all is well."

"I'm impressed you say that in the middle of exams."

"Well, I am trying to be positive," Phardos responded, laughing. In reality I was here lighting candles for my children and students."

"Good for you. I'm doing the same."

"May the Lord hear our prayers."

"Amen."

Ruth took Phardos by the arm and led her under the patio of the church and out of the bright sun. "I have been meaning to call you," she began.

"You have? Why?" asked Phardos.

"I just wanted to tell you how sorry I was about the way the other women responded to your questions that day in Ain al-Soukna."

"Oh, that's all right. I was not hurt by it. I know that not everyone thinks the same."

"I am sorry to say that some of us in the church are more closed-minded than is good for us."

"Yes."

"As a matter of fact, I know of a monk who could be very helpful in answering your questions."

"You do?"

"Yes, and if you would like, I could take you to his monastery one day to meet him."

"That is very sweet of you, Ruth, but it will have to be after exams are finished."

"I understand. Just call me when you are free."

"I will, I promise."

"Good."

"I am sorry, but I have to get back to the school now. I am so glad I ran into you."

"Me too. Have a good day."

"You too. Bye."

"Bye."

Phardos made it back to school only to find one of her teachers reprimanding a student in the hallway over his efforts to cheat on the exam. As she intervened in the situation, she wondered to herself if God had heard her prayers at all.

Marianne was hoping someone was praying for her as she struggled with the test page before her. Not only was the subject hard for her, but the air was so stifling, she could hardly breathe. The room was packed with 40 girls all hovering over their papers, and even though the ceiling fan was going at full speed, it was barely moving the hot air. How she wished she were going to one of those modern, private foreign schools instead of this very old-fashioned Franciscan school. At least she could have an air-conditioned class room.

She tried to concentrate on the test but found her mind wondering. Soon, she thought, I'll be out of school and free. I never want to sit in another class again! I'm so sick of this—nothing but studies day and night. Nothing was worth all this pain. Her teacher called out the 10 minute warning, and Marianne immediately snapped back to reality. Write anything, she told herself...just finish! Would this day never end?

Being a more diligent student, Philippe had actually breezed through his marketing exam. He was a natural for business, and actually enjoyed most of his classes, which made it easier to study for them. Now he was heading home by bus to rest and then start studying for tomorrow's exam. His friend, Stephen, was sitting beside him, having caught up to him just before he boarded the bus. Philippe had not talked to him after the visit to Stephen's church. He did not really know what to say and felt embarrassed for running out. Stephen, sensing what his friend was feeling, tried to allay his fears:

"Hey, man, it's been a long time. I hope you're not mad at me."

"Hey, Stephen, it's good to see you," Philippe replied with sincerity. "Of course I'm not mad at you. I'm sorry I never called to say thank you."

"Thank you for what?"

"For letting me come to church with you."

"Anytime, man, no problem. I hope you were not offended by it."

"No, no," Philippe stuttered, "I think my brain just could not take it all. I had to get some fresh air."

"Yeah, I know it can be pretty overwhelming to new folks, but I do hope you liked it."

"I did, really, I did. It just gave me a lot to think about."

"Yeah, I'm sure. That preacher is not what you hear every day in our church."

"Hmm."

"But I really liked him and actually I've started going to a class he's teaching during the week."

"Really?" Philippe was curious. "What kind of class?"

"A class about how to grow as a Christian. He calls it discipleship."

"Never heard of it. Do you like it?"

"Yeah, I really do. He's amazing at how he gets us to think and discuss issues. The best thing I like is how he makes us look to the Bible for answers to our questions. He doesn't just give us an automatic answer because he's the pastor, he takes us to the Bible and has us read what it says about stuff."

"Wow, you don't hear of that every day," Philippe said, really interested now.

"No, you don't," agreed Stephen. "Hey, you know, I'm sure you would be welcomed to join us if you like."

"Well, I don't know," Philippe said with hesitation.

"Think about it and call me if you want to come. It's on Wednesday nights at 7:30. We meet in one of the class rooms in the church."

"How many are in the group?"

"Just ten of us, mostly our age, but there are a few who are older adults. What's neat is that they get just as excited about the discussions as we do. It's like they never had a study like this before."

"Cool," Philippe replied. He sat in silence for a while, thinking about this. Didn't he still have questions after his visit to the church, and then even more after going to mass with his mother? What would it hurt to listen to what this man had to say?

Stephen sensed that Philippe was not completely comfortable with the conversation, so made a change in the topic.

"I forgot to ask you how your exams are going?"

"I wish they could all be as easy as the last one I just took," Philippe replied, relieved to be talking of something else.

"May the Lord give me an easy one!!" exclaimed Stephen. "You're lucky."

"Well, they won't all be like that."

"How many do you have left?"

"I still have three more, what about you?"

"Four painful ones!" Stephen moaned.

"Sorry."

"Me too."

The bus neared the stop where Philippe was due to get off. With the crowd, Philippe knew he had better start moving toward the door or he would not be able to make it. He rose and said to his friend,

"I have to get off here. It was good to see you."

"You too. Study hard."

Philippe crossed in front of Stephen and held on to the seat for balance, "You too. Hey," he added as an afterthought, "I might just join you some time for that class."

Pleased that Philippe was still interested, Stephen responded. "That's great. Come anytime you can. Wednesday's at 7:30."

"OK, thanks. Bye."

"Bye."

Chapter Thirty-One

Nawal had not been ready for all the events of that day by any means, and she now tried to get her thoughts clear before taking another step. After the tears subsided, she went over the options.

She could go home, quietly pack her bags and leave. But where would she go? And how could she just leave her family without saying goodbye. For this she was just not ready.

She could go home and continue life as normal, finish her exams, and then figure out how to move out. Yes, that seemed the better option. Otherwise, she would be on the streets alone, and she did not want that. Nancy would not be happy to see her back at school, but right now she felt that this was the better course to take. How could she not finish her exams, even if they meant nothing later on? At least she would have the satisfaction of knowing she had graduated. Surely Emir would understand that.

Wiping her eyes with a tissue, Nawal then straightened her veil and began the walk home, not sure what would be happening when she arrived. The meeting had taken longer than expected.

"Where in the world have you been?" exclaimed her mother as she finally walked in the door of their apartment. "I have been worried sick about you!"

"I'm sorry, Mother," replied Nawal, "I was studying with Nancy and completely forgot the time. I should have called."

"Yes, you should have. You will be in big trouble with your father for certain."

"Is he already home?"

"Yes, he came in to eat something before going back to the shop. When he did not find you here, he was very upset."

"Please, Mother, please don't let him be angry with me," Nawal begged.

"I can promise you nothing, Nawal, you know how he is. Now, go get cleaned up and come into the kitchen. I will fix you something to eat."

"Yes, Mother," Nawal was glad to escape this first attack, but worried what would happen when her father saw her. It did not take long to find out, for as she came out of the bathroom, her father caught her in the hallway and grabbed her by the wrist.

"Girl, don't you know you had us worried to death about you? How dare you stay out so long."

"I'm sorry, Father, I forgot the time. I was just studying at my friend's house."

"Is this what happens when you spend too much time with those Christians? They teach you to show disrespect to your parents?" He twisted her arm till Nawal winced.

"No, no, Father. They would never do that. It is my fault. We were studying for tomorrow's exam, and I just did not look at the clock. It is only my fault."

"Since that is how you see it, you only will take the blame. You are forbidden to go back to their house during exams. Forbidden, do you hear? I will not have them ruining my daughter."

"Yes, Father, yes. Please, you're hurting me." Tears started coming to Nawal's eyes as his grip tightened.

"Go to your room. I'm ashamed of you!" And he loosened his grip and pushed her toward her bedroom door.

Nawal fell toward her room and opened the door to get away from him as quickly as possible. She almost fell over her sister as she did, for Eptisam had been listening to the confrontation from behind the closed door. Trying not to alert their father to the problem, they refrained from crying out as they both fell to the floor of the room. Eptisam quickly closed the door.

"Are you all right, Nawal?"

"What were you doing behind the door? Do you want Father to be on you too?"

"No, I'm sorry. I was just listening. I didn't know you'd come flying in here."

"Yeah." Nawal pulled herself up and sat on her bed, drawing her arm to her chest in an effort to work out the pain.

"Did he hurt you?"

"I'm all right," though she was not sure of herself as she said it. Tears started flowing.

"What is it, Nawal? Is it broken?" Eptisam went and sat by her sister's side, putting her arm around her shoulders.

"No, it's not the arm."

"What then?"

"You would not understand," Nawal said with exasperation.

"Maybe I would," Eptisam answered with the confidence of a 15-year-old.

"No, you wouldn't. Never mind." Nawal wished her sister was not around, and she knew she would never let her be.

"Tell me, tell me please, Nawal!" Eptisam was now begging for information.

"No, I have an exam tomorrow, as I'm sure you do too. Leave me alone. I've got to study!" She pulled herself angrily from her sister, hoping she would get the message and leave her alone.

"Be that way then!" shouted Eptisam. "Forget I even bothered to make you feel better." She went over to her bed and sat down in a huff.

Nawal went through the motions of getting her books out to study, but her heart was not in it. She also had a growing hunger in her stomach, realizing she had not eaten since the morning. She looked over to her sister, who was reading through her notes for the next day's exam.

"Eptisam, could you please go to the kitchen and see if Mother will give you something for me to eat. I'm starved, and I don't want to face Father again."

Eptisam pretended not to hear. "Please, Eptisam, I'm sorry that I yelled at you. It is just not a good time to tell you everything, but I promise, after exams are over, I will. I will."

Eptisam stirred in her place, not willing to give in too quickly to her older sister. Nawal looked at her with pleading eyes and again said, "Please." Thankfully, this worked and Eptisam went toward the door, but not without a comment: "You owe me, sister, and I will expect to hear every detail of this after exams."

"Yes, yes," agreed Nawal. "Please just get me some food."

The weeks of exams passed all too slowly for the students in Abu Muhammad's household. Nawal knew that she barely passed if at all the last two of her exams. Since her conversion to Christianity, her mind was overwhelmed by the thoughts not only of what she had done, but of what was to come. She was surprised that she was able to sit through the tests at all. When she, Abdel-Karem and Eptisam were all finished with exams, Um Muhammad made a big dinner for them. At last they could relax some until the results were published.

The first way they relaxed was by sleeping. Nawal felt as though she had not slept in years. She slept till 2 p.m. the day following her final exam and remained in her pajamas until she went to bed again that night. Her brother and sister were no better, and it was not long until Um Muhammad had had enough of her lazy children and tried to think of ways to get them to move.

Nawal had avoided Nancy during the last days of exams, though she saw that her friend was shocked when she walked into the classroom for the first exam after her conversion. Knowing that Nancy would be nervous around her, Nawal simply left her alone and tried her best to focus on the exam at hand. Now that school was over, she longed to see her best friend and her brother as well, but knew it was risky. There was also the problem of her father. He had become hardened to the idea of her spending so much time in a Christian home, but Nawal was hoping that her mother would help her out.

"Please, Mother," she begged Um Muhammad a week into summer vacation, "all my friends will be at Nancy's, and you know they are not all Christian. I don't understand what is so terrible; they are my classmates."

"You know your father would not be pleased," her mother responded. "You proved yourself untrustworthy as a result of your association with them. They are a bad influence on you."

"No, Mother, that is not true. They had nothing to do with my being late that day. What am I to do all summer if I cannot see my friends? Please, Mother, I will go crazy in this house!"

"Perhaps you need to start thinking about getting a job."

"A job!" Nawal exclaimed, "I just finished school. I need a break first. Besides, we don't know if I passed yet or not."

"The Lord willing, you have passed, my daughter," her mother replied. "Will you not give me a moment's peace?"

"Mother, I can go and come back before Father gets home," Nawal continued unrelenting. "Please let me go."

"All right, but if you are not back by 4 p.m., I will never let you go again. Do you understand?"

"Yes, Mother, I understand. I'll be back before four." Nawal kissed her mother on the cheek. "Thank you, Mother."

Nawal was filled with anticipation as she virtually ran down the stairs to the main door of the building. She was so happy that Yvonne had called her the day before, inviting her to join them at Nancy's house the next day. Nawal was sure that Yvonne had no idea about all that had happened between her and Nancy, and was glad for this innocence, as it allowed her an opportunity to see both Nancy and Emir again. She hoped that they would be equally as happy to see her. By the time she arrived at Nancy's flat, she was out of breath. She took a deep breath before ringing the bell. Nancy's mother opened the door.

"Oh, Nawal," she said, as if taken by surprise. "Welcome. It's good to see you."

"Thank you, Madame Ghada," Nawal replied as she stepped into the house, "I hope you are well."

"Yes, thank the Lord. Please," she said, pointing toward a door down the hallway, "Nancy and the girls are in her room."

Nawal walked down the hall, and knocked on Nancy's bedroom door. She could hear laughing on the other side.

"Come in," she heard a chipper voice reply.

"Hello," Nawal rang out as she walked through the door.

"Nawal!" came the response from three of the four girls in the room. There was one who was very quiet—Nancy. No one noticed as Yvonne, Fatma and Mary all jumped up to kiss Nawal upon her arrival. Nancy recovered from her shock as they all finished exchanging greetings.

"Hi, Nawal," began Nancy, as she also rose to kiss her friend on the cheeks. "How are you?" Her look was slightly too serious.

"I'm fine, Nancy;" replied Nawal, "how are you?"

"OK, I guess." All too suddenly, she took Nawal by the arm; then, turning to their friends, said with a smile on her face, "excuse us just a minute, girls, I need to ask Nawal something in private. We'll be right back." Before they could respond, Nancy had taken Nawal out of the room and closed the door. Still holding her tightly by the arm, she led her friend into the kitchen.

"What are you doing here?" she asked, clear distress in her voice.

"I had to see you," replied Nawal. "Please don't be mad at me."

"I don't understand what you are doing. First you come back to school and finish your exams, and now you are here. Don't you know that we could both get in big trouble?"

"Don't worry, Nancy," Nawal tried to reassure her, "my family doesn't know anything yet. I just had to finish my exams. Besides, I didn't know what to do or where to go. I needed time to think before I ended up out on the streets. Surely, you understand that?"

"All I understand is that my family went through a lot for you and could get into big trouble for it. I would think you would be more considerate of our situation."

"I am considerate and appreciative of all they have done, believe me. I wanted to say that to your mother just now, but was not sure who was in the house. But you have to realize that no one is suspicious yet, so you won't be in any danger. I just had to see you. I missed you—you're my best friend."

"You're my best friend too, Nawal," replied Nancy, softening. "I'm sorry if I overreacted. I just want you to be safe. Let's go back to the girls. They will wonder what we are doing. We can talk more later."

"I hope so, but I have to leave by 3:30 at the latest today. I'm only here because my mother agreed to let me come.

My father got mad at me during finals, and didn't want me coming here any more."

"That's not a good sign. Well, you just make sure you're home on time today. We don't want any problems."

They went back to Nancy's room and joined their friends who were in a lively discussion about the exams and what they wanted to do now that school was out. There was no question that Yvonne and Mary, as well as Nancy, would go on to college. It was expected in most Christian families with any income that their children, girls and boys, would achieve a higher education. Because their families were traditionally smaller in size, they did not have to immediately rush to find employment after graduation from high school, but could continue their studies, which would allow them to find higher-paying jobs later in life. As for Fatma and Nawal, college was not a given, for two reasons—because the large sizes of Muslim families usually required every available adult to work in order to bring income into the household, and also because it was not universally accepted that girls needed higher education. They were expected to marry young and begin their own homes. The families of these two girls had already made great sacrifices to get their daughters into private school, and for Nawal, that was as far as her father was willing to go. Fatma's father, however, had better means, and therefore was encouraging his only daughter to continue her studies if she made it into the college of her choice.

Nancy's mother prepared a lovely breakfast for the friends and soon called them to the dining room to eat. As they began to sit down around the table, Emir walked into the room.

"Hi, ladies," he greeted them with ease in his voice.

"Hi, Emir," they all replied in unison.

"Emir, leave us alone," scolded his sister.

"No, I am starving. I want to eat too," he said rebuking. "I don't think your friends will mind, will you ladies?"

"No."

"Please sit down, Emir."

"This is your table." Melodic voices rang out all at once. Emir chose, however, to sit down next to the only one who had not spoken since he entered the room—Nawal.

"Hi, Nawal," he said, as he smiled at her.

"Hi, Emir," came a soft reply. Nawal was afraid to look at him for fear of giving away her feelings. As they all began eating, she relaxed somewhat, but was still afraid to talk to him or look directly at him. Emir did not seem upset, however, and kept a lively conversation going with the rest of the girls. They laughed at his jokes as they enjoyed the breakfast of eggs, pastrami, *fatir*, molasses, honey, cheeses, *foul*, and *tamaiya*.

Eventually the girls finished and began moving back to Nancy's room. Nawal excused herself to wash her hands in the bathroom. When she came out, the hallway was empty. Before she had a chance to go to Nancy's room, Emir came toward her from the other end of the hall. He took her by the hand and led her to his room. He closed the door behind them.

"Emir, what are you doing?" Nawal asked him, trying not to let her voice rise.

"Is it true, Nawal?" he asked, a serious look on his face.

"Is what true?" She was afraid to respond too quickly.

"I heard my parents talking to Nancy about it. Did you convert?"

Nawal looked at him without responding. He shook her by the shoulders and asked again with impatience. "Did you convert to Christianity?"

"Yes."

"Really?" He asked, dumbfounded.

"I said, yes," she replied. "and I did it for you."

"For me?" He took a step away from her.

"Yes, for you. Now there will be nothing to separate us from one another."

Emir started pacing around his room, running his fingers through his hair in nervous agitation. Nawal was immediately sorry for the words spoken, as the response given was not what she had anticipated. She sat down on the bed, tears beginning to form in her eyes. Seeing her eyes become moist, Emir rushed to her side, putting his arm around her.

"No, Nawal, don't cry," he began soothingly, "I did not mean to upset you. I am just so overwhelmed that you would do such a thing for me. You have taken such a risk."

"Yes, but you are worth it, Emir."

"But what about your family, your religion?"

"They hold nothing for me anymore," she replied. "I've been disillusioned for a long time now by my father's faith, and there is no reason for me to stay with my family. They would only want me married off soon, anyway, so I would no longer be a liability to them. The question is," she continued, "what do I do now? I know I will soon be found out, but I don't know where to go, who to turn to. I cannot come to your family, as they will be the first my family will accuse."

"Yes, that's true," Emir agreed. "You need to give me time to think. I will help you, but need to figure out how. We can't talk about this now. Nancy and the girls will be wondering where you are. Don't worry, my love," and he kissed her forehead, "I will find us a way."

"But how will we meet? I cannot call you. In reality this should be the last time I come to your house."

"You can call my cell phone," Emir replied. He went over to a desk and wrote the number on a small piece of paper. Handing it to her, he said, "Give me a few days before you call, so I can see what to do."

Nawal took the paper and moved toward the door. Before her hand touched the handle, Emir touched her arm, making her turn once again to face him. He drew her near and kissed her on the lips. This was the first time Nawal had ever been kissed. She felt every part of her body tingle with excitement and yet, also with fear. On impulse, she said quickly, "I must go, Emir. Thank you."

She moved quickly through the hallway and into Nancy's room again. Slightly out of breath, the girls all stared at her as she entered.

"Where were you?" Nancy asked.

"I'm sorry, I was not feeling too well. I think something upset my stomach."

"Something or someone?" Yvonne snickered.

The girls laughed. Nawal turned red.

Chapter Thirty-Two

Marianne slept for almost three days solid following the completion of her exams. She thought the day would never come that she was finally finished with school. Now, rested and relieved, she was ready to explore the possibilities of a relationship with Emad. She wondered if he had found a job since she last saw him. Was he really serious about her? Lying on her bed, she looked at his number in her cell phone. "Do I call him?" she asked herself out loud. "Not here, for sure." Putting the phone down, she got up and began to get dressed, ready to go out to meet her destiny.

With both her parents at work, Marianne was able to go out as she wished, so she headed to a popular coffee shop for Heliopolis youth—Cilantros. As she walked, she dialed Emad's number. A sweet voice answered:

"I thought you would never call," he began. "How are you?"

"I'm fine," she replied, "and you?"

"I'm fine now," he said.

She smiled.

"Where are you?" he asked.

"I'm walking to Cilantros in Corba. Can you join me?"

"I will be waiting for you there," he replied.

"Oh, wow, that's fast. Are you not working?"

"I'll tell you all about it when I see your beautiful face."

"All right. Bye."

"Bye for now."

Marianne picked up her pace in anticipation of seeing Emad again. She wondered why he was not working now, but trusted that it simply meant he was off now for lunch or did not go in till later. Surely he had found work. She moved briskly along the streets, taking care to cross the larger ones, as traffic was heavy. Finally, she arrived at the coffee shop and entered. She found Emad sitting at a table waiting.

"You really did make it here before me," she said, sitting down in the chair he offered her.

"I was close by," he replied, smiling. "I'm so glad you called. I missed you."

Marianne took a quick look around to make sure she did not recognize anyone. "Well, I'm finally done with school," she sighed. "I never thought I would finish."

"Congratulations."

"Well, I don't have my results yet," she admitted, "but I think graduation is almost guaranteed at this point."

"I'm sure you did fine," Emad assured her, then continued, "but let's don't talk about the past, let's talk about the future."

"What would you like to say about the future?" she asked, with feigned innocence.

"I would like to say that the future includes us together."

"And how do you propose that to happen?"

"I have a plan."

"You do?"

"Yes, I do. Would you like to hear it?"

Her curiosity raised, Marianne wanted nothing more than to hear Emad's proposal. She was still nagged, however, by what she saw as the slight possibility that he was not sincere. This led her to be cautious.

"Emad, before you tell me your plan, I have a question."

"Yes, my love?"

"Tell me about your new job."

"Oh, yes," he replied, sitting up straight in his chair, "I am moving too fast as usual. I told you I would find a job, and I have. I'm sorry that I did not tell you about it first."

"That's all right," she comforted, "but just tell me now."

"All right," and he straightened himself again in the chair. "Oh, first, why don't you order something. You haven't even done that. What would you like?"

"I will have a Pepsi," she replied.

"Something to eat?" he asked.

"No, just the Pepsi."

"OK" Emad rose to go to the counter to order the drink. He returned shortly to her and gave her the drink. "Here you are."

"Thanks."

"Now, about my job. My uncle has a business which deals in stocks and commodities. It's a relatively new business, and when I asked him about it, he was very excited to have me come aboard. There are three shifts of workers, as the work is 24/7. I oversee the third shift, which is at night. It's not too hard. I just have to get used to staying up all night and sleeping more in the daytime."

"That sounds great," Marianne encouraged him. "Does it pay well?"

"I can't complain," he said.

"Wow, I'm amazed you found something so quickly."

"Praise God," Emad replied, then changed the subject. "Now, can we talk about us?"

"Yes, of course."

"I want us to be together, Marianne," he began.

"I want that too," she agreed.

"We can't talk about us in a place like this."

She looked around her, realizing there were people at nearby tables. "No, I supposed we can't."

"I have a place for us to go."

"You do?" She looked concerned.

"Don't worry, Marianne," he assured her, "I would never do anything to hurt you. I just want us to have a quiet place to make our plans together, plans for the future, for marriage. Don't you want that too?"

"Of course, Emad," she admitted. "What kind of place is it?"

"Well, if you must know," he smiled as he replied, "it is to be our future home."

"What?"

"Yes, it is the apartment my family is preparing for me when I marry. It's empty, and not completely finished, but will give us a great place to make our plans."

"Really, Emad?" she was now excited. "I would love to see it."

"I was hoping you'd say that. Let's go!"

"Now?"

"Of course now, why not now?"

Marianne hesitated and again looked around her. "What if someone sees us?"

"No one will see us. It is not the building where my family lives, and we can go in separately if you like. It's a big building, with lots of apartments. No one will know we are together."

"Well, if you think it's safe."

They quickly finished their drinks and left the coffee shop. Emad explained to Marianne where the building was, as they would need to take the metro there and arrive separately. It was on the far side of Heliopolis, so it would take some time to get there. They got on the same metro, but different cars. Marianne was nervous and constantly looking around to see if anyone knew her. Emad was smiling to himself and pleased that he had so easily deceived the girl into believing him. He could not deny that his sexual desires were high for her, so he contemplated carrying out the charade for as long as possible in order to enjoy the game even more. However, he could not wait until the moment came when he was done with her and able to throw her triumphantly out on the street. He would show those Christians not to try to keep their girls away!

At the appointed stop, both Emad and Marianne got off the tram and walked the short distance to the building. Emad arrived first and went quickly up to the flat he had prepared for their encounter. It belonged to a friend whose family had recently immigrated to Australia. This particular apartment had been intended for his friend upon marriage, but with the departure of his parents, the work on it had stopped. Abdel-Aziz had readily agreed to give Emad the key, as it was not uncommon for friends to share available flats for rendez-vous' with girls.

When Marianne reached the flat, she nervously rang the bell, looking up and down the hall to make sure no one saw her entering. She did not have to wait long, as Emad quickly opened the door and pulled her inside the apartment. Before she could take a breath, he was kissing her. She allowed his passion to overtake her. Holding her by the waist, he pulled her toward a bedroom. She realized as they walked that the flat was actually partially furnished and the room where he took her actually held a full-sized bed, properly made up with sheets and pillows.

"Emad," she protested, "I was not expecting the flat to be furnished."

"That was my little surprise," he said, smiling, as he tried to unbutton her blouse.

"Wait, Emad, aren't you moving a little too fast?"

"Am I?" he asked, "Don't you know I have thought of nothing but you since the night of the wedding. You know we are going to be together forever; what should stop us from starting forever now?" He started kissing her on the neck.

"I don't know," her protest grew weaker with the touch of his kisses.

"Please, Marianne," he pleaded softly, "I love you."

"I don't know..." the reply dwindled, as he took her fully in his arms and overpowered her with his body. They fell onto the bed lost in love.

Lying under the sheets, Marianne did not know what had happened. She must have fallen asleep. Now, as she felt Emad's body wrapped around her, she felt both intense fear and pleasure. She had given herself to him without reservation; it was an ecstasy she had never known. Yet, she rebuked herself for allowing it to happen. Wasn't she a good girl? Should she not have waiting until they were properly married? What would her mother say? No, no, she would not think about that now. The important thing was that this man loved her and wanted to marry her. She would deal with the complications of the situation later. Wasn't this a lovely flat? The bedroom was large, and she was sure the rest of the house was very nice as well. They could be very happy here. What time was it? As she stirred to look for a clock, Emad squeezed her tightly in his sleep. She smiled and slowly worked her way out of his grip to go to the bathroom.

Marianne had washed and gotten fully dressed before Emad actually began to wake up.

"You're dressed," he said, sitting up in bed and taking notice of her standing before him.

"I really should go," she said.

"Why? It's early yet."

"Don't you have to go to work?"

"Not until later. Please don't go."

"I should. My mother will be coming home from work soon."

"We haven't had time to talk about our plans."

"No," she agreed, "you seemed to have forgot about talking."

"No, no," he argued, "I just figured we would have more time."

"Well, I really can't talk now. I've got to go." She moved toward the door.

"When will I see you again?" he asked, then added, "so we *can* talk?"

"Only talk?" she looked at him with a slight smile.

"Talk first, play second. How's that?"

"Well, if you promise we talk first, then maybe I could come again tomorrow."

"That would be nice..." He got up out of the bed, wrapping the sheet around his waist. "What about the same time, but just come straight here?"

"Well, since it is our house." She was feeling the kisses again on her neck.

"Yes, our house," he agreed. "Til tomorrow?"

"Tomorrow." They kissed once more; a long, drawn out kiss. Then Marianne pulled herself away from Emad, straightened her clothes and went toward the front door. He stayed at the bedroom door and waved. She liked the way he looked with that sheet around him. He really was good-looking. Boy, was she lucky.

Chapter Thirty-Three

There were now two goals in Muhammad's life—to marry Noura and to find out more about what he was reading in the *Injil*. As marrying Noura was now conditional on his parent's helping him set up an apartment, he wanted to help as much as he could to find a place that his father would be able to purchase.

"Father." Muhammad did not waste time approaching the topic as they worked in the shop.

"Yes, my son?" Ahmed replied.

"I know the responsibility of finding me a flat weighs heavily on you."

"God will provide," came the uniform answer.

"Yes, I believe God will provide," agreed Muhammad, "but do you mind if I start looking for something reasonable? We do not have to have a castle. I just want a simple flat that we can begin life in."

"I was intending to call Mahmoud to seek his help."

"You do not need to bother Mahmoud with this, Father," Muhammad argued. "I am very capable of searching for a flat. Will you not let me use the evenings to do so?"

"I need you in the store."

"Yes, but I am sure you can do without me for a few hours. Besides, you could have Abdel-Karim come in now.

He's not doing anything since school finished. I'm sure he could help you here."

"Well, now, that would probably be good for him. All right, son, you may take off after our lunch break and do your searching. Let me know if you find anything."

"Thank you, Father," Muhammad said smiling, "I will."

This was an amazing development in the eyes of Muhammad—his father actually agreed to something he suggested! Would wonders never cease? He was so pleased with himself for thinking of having Abdel-Karim come and work. He knew, of course, that his brother would not be happy for it, but what did he care? Had anyone asked his opinion when he was told to come and work for his father all those years ago? And, maybe his younger brother would actually learn to like the work and agree to stay with Father in the store. He could only hope so.

Now, armed with evenings free, Muhammad was also able to pursue his second goal of finding out more about the *Injil*. How he would go about it, he did not know, but he knew that he needed someone to talk to. For several months now, he had been secretly reading the book, engrossed with the stories of the Christ and his disciples. Yet, as he read, questions arose, and he longed to have someone to ask them and discuss the passages he had read. He remembered passing a small bookshop in the area that was obviously Christian, for the name had *love* in the title. Maybe someone there could answer his questions or point him to someone else who could. Finding the shop, he quickly stepped inside.

"Peace be upon you," Muhammad said as he crossed the threshold.

"And upon you be peace," came the response from a middle-aged woman. "Can I help you?"

"Uh, do you have..." Muhammad did not want to ask directly anything related to his quest, "paperclips?"

"Yes," the woman replied. "Would you like large or small?"

"Uh, large." A small girl came into the store. Muhammad started looking around at the merchandise on the shelves. The girl asked for an eraser and quickly made her purchase and left. Muhammad looked toward the door, making sure no one else was coming in. He moved back toward the counter and noticed a book lying there.

"What is this book?" he asked.

"This is the Holy Bible," the woman responded.

"The *Injil*?"

"Well, it includes the *Injil*, but also holds what we call the Old Testament, which is the Torah, Psalms and books of the Prophets."

"Oh," Muhammad said, looking up at the woman's face. "I haven't heard of that;" and then added without thinking, "all I have is the *Injil*."

A smile came upon the woman's face. "So you have read the *Injil*? Muhammad shifted uneasily on his feet. "Well... yes. I have been reading it, but..." he looked again toward the door, "I do not understand everything."

"That is understandable," the woman answered kindly.

"It is?"

"Yes, many times people have questions when reading the *Injil*."

"Yes, questions," Muhammad almost shouted, "yes, that is what I have. In fact, I am looking for someone who can answer my questions. Can you answer them, Madame?"

"No, I am sure it would not be good for me to try to answer your questions, young man, but if you come back tomorrow at the same time, I will find you someone who will."

"You will?"

"Yes, if you really want to understand." She stared at him intently in the eyes, as if to discern his sincerity.

"I do."

"Then come back tomorrow."

"Thank you, Madame." Muhammad turned to leave.

"What about your paperclips?" she called after him, holding up the box.

"My what?" he questioned her, then remembered, "oh, yes. How much are they?"

"They are my gift," she smiled.

"No, I could not take them," Muhammad insisted.

"Oh, but you must. Then I will know you are sincere."

"I will show my sincerity by returning tomorrow," he replied. "Thank you for your generosity." He quickly moved back to the doorway. "Peace to you."

"And peace to you," she smiled as she watched him step out onto the busy sidewalk and disappear.

Muhammad spent the rest of the evening searching for apartments. It was not an easy task, and he did not know how to even go about it. He started by asking several men at area coffee shops if they knew of available apartments; however, the prices of those available he knew were far out of his father's range. He did not desire to put any extra financial burdens on his father than he already carried. Since the time was getting late, he decided that the next time he would move further from his own neighborhood into areas which were more crowded and most likely cheaper. He wondered if Noura or her family would be ashamed of her living in a lower class area. He determined to cross that bridge when he got to it. The first order of business was to even find a flat.

The following day was busy with repairs and customers, for which his father was grateful. Though he had not seen his little brother, he knew from his mother that Abdel-Karem had not been too happy about having a summer job. His father, however, seemed relatively pleased with his work, making a comment as they worked that perhaps his brother was a more natural repairman, like himself. Muhammad smiled as he saw in his mind the noose tightening around his brother's neck, while envisioning new freedom in his own life. There was hope!

As the time approached, Muhammad made his way to the small bookstore he had visited the day before. He was nervous and wondered who the person would be that would meet him. He walked past the bookstore twice before entering. The kind lady was smiling as she heard his greeting. After they exchanged pleasantries, she handed him a small piece of paper.

"What's this?" he asked.

"He is waiting for you there," she indicated, pointing to the paper.

Realizing that she was trying to be careful, he thanked her and, without opening the note, left her shop. He rounded the corner and walked for another block before he took a chance to read the words written. He recognized the name of a nearby restaurant and memorized the description of the man he was to meet. There was no name given. It took Muhammad another twenty minutes to reach the destination. He entered the restaurant and began looking around for the man. When he spotted him sitting in a corner, Muhammad nodded. The gentleman nodded in return and pointed to a chair in welcome.

"Peace be upon you," Muhammad said, as he came up to the table.

"And peace to you," came the reply. "Please sit down. We have a mutual friend?"

"Yes." Muhammad sat down cautiously in the chair. He began looking around the restaurant to see who was around them.

"I am having tea, can I order one for you?"

"Yes, thank you," replied Muhammad.

The man motioned to a waiter and ordered the tea plus a plate of local sweets. He introduced himself as he waited for the order to be delivered.

"My name is Dr. Samuel."

"I am Muhammad."

"It's nice to meet you," the elder man replied.

"Thank you for meeting me," Muhammad said.

They continued some small talk as the waiter finally made his way back to their table. Having deposited the tea and sweets, he left them once again. Dr. Samuel looked up at Muhammad.

"I understand you have some questions," he began.

"Yes. Do you know about the *Injil*?" Muhammad asked.

"I have studied it for most of my life," the man responded. "We will trust the Lord to show us the truth."

"Many of my questions come from reading the Gospel according to John," Muhammad began. "I find that the Christ speaks of himself many times as a son, and refers to God as father. How can he call God, "father"? He is associating himself with the One God—how can that be?"

Dr. Samuel kept his voice low as he began his reply, "My dear brother, Muhammad, when you read the words of Christ in the *Injil*, what word was used to refer to himself as a *son*? Do you remember?"

"Yes, I believe it is *ibn*," Muhammad replied.

"And yet there is another word that also carries the same meaning, is there not?"

"Yes, *walid*."

"Very good, my friend," the man smiled. "When you ask me how the Christ can say he is the son of God, you may use one word, but your mind is thinking another."

Muhammad did not want to show the man that he was right so quickly, so remained quiet and let him continue.

"The Qur'an states that God has no son, nor has he ever begotten a son; yet, the word it uses is *walid*, which refers to a physical son, born as a result of sexual intercourse between a man and woman. In this, I agree with the Qur'an, for we do not, as Christians, believe that God had sexual relations with the Virgin Mary, causing her to become pregnant and give birth to Jesus. This would be blasphemy to think so."

Muhammad could not help himself now. "Yes, yes, it is blasphemy."

"This is why the word used in the Bible to refer to the sonship of Christ is so important," continued Dr. Samuel. "Christ is the *ibn Allah*. This means that he is the son in the sense that he comes from God. He comes from the same essence of God. It was God's Spirit that breathed life into Mary. Her pregnancy did not come as a result of a sexual relationship. We would never think of God having such a relationship with a human. Does that make sense?"

"I understand what you are saying about the meaning of the words, but I do not understand how God, who is One, can be three, as you Christians say."

Dr. Samuel looked around the restaurant to make sure no one was noticing them talking or seemed too interested in their discussion. He took a sip of his tea before continuing. "All your life I know you have heard and repeated that God is One." Muhammad nodded in agreement. "This is another point on which we agree. As Christians, we also hold to the belief that God is one, but unlike you, we do not see God as a number, indivisible. In the Holy Bible, God has revealed himself to us as a being or person with three different essences."

Muhammad interrupted, "What does that mean?"

"I know it is difficult to understand," Dr. Samuel admitted, "but even in the Qur'an, God shows himself to have a Spirit, isn't that true?"

"Yes," Muhammad replied hesitantly.

"Well, we see that God has revealed himself in three ways: God, the Father, who is the Almighty One, who sits on the Throne, the Creator of all things. We also have God, the Son, who is Jesus, the essence of God which came down to earth in the form of a man, that we might understand more about God the Father and learn how to have a relationship with him. Then, we have God the Holy Spirit, who has helped man throughout time to hear God's voice and to know his will. Since Jesus' return to heaven, the Holy Spirit has been made available to all who follow Christ, helping them to live according to God's will, in a way that pleases God. These are not three separate people or beings, but one. Perhaps some have misunderstood our understanding of God because of the false conception that we believe in God, Jesus and Mary as the Trinity, but this is not the case."

Muhammad could not say anything for quite a while, but simply tried to take in all he had heard. In many ways it made perfect sense, and he now saw how Muslims had misunderstood the beliefs of Christians. He also felt that all that this man was saying was in perfect agreement with what he had heard from Fouad on the bus and Thawrat on PalTalk. Most importantly, it affirmed all he had been reading in the *Injil* itself. This sense that truth was being spoken could not be denied. The question now was what to do with it? He took a deep breath and looked up at Dr. Samuel.

"You said something about the reason for Jesus coming in the form of a man was for us to understand how to have a relationship with God."

"Yes," Dr. Samuel replied.

"I have heard about this before, but do not understand what it means."

"Do you remember the first two people God created?" asked Dr. Samuel.

"Yes," answered Muhammad, "Adam and Eve."

"Well, when God created Adam and Eve, he created them perfect, free from sin, and they lived in a garden, where all their needs were provided. Because they were without sin, God came to the garden and met with them, talked with them—they had a close relationship with the Creator."

"OK," nodded Muhammad with some hesitation about where this was going.

"The problem was, that when Adam and Eve sinned by eating the fruit from the tree they were told not to, they lost that perfect status; they were no longer holy and so God was not able to be in their presence, because he is a Holy God and can have nothing to do with sin. The sin that began with Adam and Eve continues in every human born on earth and even affects the earth and environment.

"The good news is, God knew this was going to happen so had a plan. That plan was to send his son to pay the price for our sins, so that we could return to that great relationship that he knew with Adam and Eve."

"That is the same as when they talk about Christ being the ransom for us."

"Exactly," Dr. Samuel said, smiling and pointing his finger in agreement. "So you have heard about our need for a ransom."

"Yes, I read it somewhere."

"Then I think the Lord is trying to get the message to you, my brother," said Dr. Samuel. "The question now is: will you accept this good news?"

"What does it mean if I do?" Muhammad asked in all sincerity.

"The first thing it means is that you will have a relationship with God. He will now not only hear, but answer your prayers. You will be guaranteed eternal life, and will have the peace in your heart to prove it. It also means that the Holy Spirit will dwell in your heart, allowing you to understand the Holy Bible in a special way. It means so many things, but maybe I can sum it up by saying it means you will have an abundant life!"

These words stopped Muhammad. How could this man know it was these very words that drew him toward Christ? Was this a sign from God? He did not know, but what he did know for sure was that ever since he started reading the Bible and talking with Christians, he felt nothing but peace about the way of Jesus, and that is what he wanted in his life—peace. He could not help what came out of his mouth next:

"That is what I want!" Muhammad said, allowing his voice to rise to a level which caused others to turn around and look toward him.

Noticing the curiosity, Dr. Samuel leaned toward him across the table and said in a lower voice: "I want you to have it too. Would you mind coming with me to my office. This may not be the most appropriate place to continue our discussion."

The two men rose from the table after the bill had been paid. Each one should have been nervous at taking such a step of confidence with a person who had previously been a stranger, but neither expressed doubt or fear at their action. Dr. Samuel led Muhammad several blocks to a building which held several medical offices. They entered and took the elevator to the 11th floor. Dr. Samuel opened the door with a key, as it appeared no one else was in the office. Muhammad entered to find a modestly furnished flat with two couches in the reception area, and a large conference table to the side. He was led down a small hallway to what appeared to be Dr. Samuel's personal office, complete with a messy desk and chair. It also contained two armchairs and coffee table. Dr. Samuel invited Muhammad to sit down and left the room.

Muhammad took a moment to look around the room and was struck by the simplicity of the place. A single picture hung on the wall. It was of a kind-looking shepherd, knocking on a door. He was not sure, but thought that it must be Jesus, since this was a Christian's office. He wondered where the door led.

Dr. Samuel returned to the room with two glasses of water, as well as two soft drinks in glass bottles. Offering them to his guest, he then sat down in the neighboring chair. He took a moment to drink from his soda, and then said to Muhammad's surprise:

"Now, my friend, the Lord Jesus is knocking on your heart's door, are you ready to open it up to him?"

Muhammad turned his head quickly toward the picture.

"Yes, yes, Muhammad," Dr. Samuel continued, realizing what had happened, "that door is the door to the human soul, your soul. He never forces his way in, nor tricks us into following him. He simply presents himself to us, and asks us to make the decision whether or not we will follow him and make him Lord of our life."

"Amazing," Muhammad said simply.

"Yes, it really is," agreed the older man. "Would you like to pray to accept Jesus as your Lord and Savior?"

"Yes."

"I can tell you what to pray and you can do it yourself, or you can repeat after me. Whatever you prefer."

"I will repeat after you," Muhammad replied.

"That is fine, my brother. Let us pray."

Dr. Samuel closed his eyes, which indicated to Muhammad to do the same. He then listened and repeated these words:

> "Heavenly Father, I admit that I am a sinner and deserve nothing but the fires of Hell. Yet, I believe, as your Holy Bible says, that you sent your son Jesus to show us the way of eternal life, and that he paid the price for my sin by dying on the cross. Because he rose again from the dead, I can have a new life with you. Forgive me, Father, for all my sins. I ask Jesus to come into my life to cleanse me and to make me whole. I commit myself to him as my Lord and Savior, that I might live in a way that pleases you.

> Thank you, heavenly Father, for the eternal life that you guarantee me as a result of my decision to follow Christ. Fill me with your Spirit, that I will know your will for my life from this point forward. In the name of Jesus, I pray, Amen."

After he said, "amen," Muhammad thought the prayer was through, but he realized that Dr. Samuel was continuing on in prayer for him, asking God to strengthen him and teach him more about how to live a life of faith as he revealed himself in his Word. He prayed that the Devil would not be able to cause him troubles, but that he would truly live that victorious life in Christ without fear. As the man prayed, Muhammad felt a strength flow through him that he had never known before. Maybe this had to do with the Holy Spirit, he thought to himself. When Dr. Samuel finished praying, he raised his head and looked at Muhammad.

"Now, when I call you *brother*, I can say it as a true statement of our brotherhood in Christ." He rose and moved toward Muhammad, giving him a hug and kiss on both cheeks.

Tears began to flow down Muhammad's face. He had never experienced anything like this before, and though he could not explain it, he knew that it had to do with God. He felt like a new person and was full of a joy he had never known before. He smiled through the tears.

"Those are the tears of joy," Dr. Samuel said, himself smiling and stepping back from Muhammad, though still holding him by the shoulders. "May the Lord just flood you with his presence and peace, my brother."

Muhammad did not want this moment to stop, and when Dr. Samuel sat back down, he was hoping that more great things were to come. He was surprised, however, at what came out of the man's mouth.

"You know Satan will not like what you have done," he began. "He is never happy when a person gives his life to Christ, and you must be prepared for his attacks."

"How do I prepare for them?" Muhammad asked.

"You need to be daily in God's Word and prayer," came the response. "The faster you grow and the deeper you go with the Lord, the stronger you'll be when Satan works to bring you down. There is nothing better for Satan than to cause a Christian to feel defeated. He can do this in many ways: by troubles from your family, leading you to fall back into bad habits, keeping you away from other believers, or making you lazy to read the Bible and pray."

The sky grew dark outside as Dr. Samuel and Muhammad continued to talk in the small office. When Muhammad realized the late hour, he rose quickly to excuse himself.

"Thank you, Dr. Samuel, for all you have done for me today."

"It is the Lord Jesus who has done it, my son," replied the old man.

"Well, he used you," smiled Muhammad, shaking his hand.

"It was a pleasure to be used by him. God bless you, Muhammad, and be with you as you walk anew in Christ."

"Good-bye, Doctor."

Leaving the building, Muhammad walked out into the darkness of the night. For some reason, however, to him it still seemed like the light of day.

Chapter Thirty-Four

While his sister's life was in turmoil over a boy, Philippe was suffering from a different kind of turmoil—that of his spiritual condition. He could not reconcile the struggle that was happening in his heart since attending the Evangelical church. He was aching to know more, to understand about the prayer the pastor asked people to pray. Wasn't he born Christian? Had he not been baptized in the church as a baby? Why were the words of that man bothering him so much?

He was encouraged that Stephen was not angry with him and even encouraged him to join him for the class on Wednesday nights. Now that he was finished with exams, he did not think it should be hard for him to slip over to the Evangelical church at least once to see what the pastor had to say. He decided not to call Stephen, just in case he backed out at the last minute. He did, however, hope his friend would be in attendance, so he would not have to sit among strangers.

When Wednesday night came around, Philippe was still at home, having taken a nap after an especially delicious meal his mother cooked. It was already 7 p.m. when he woke up. Looking at the time, he quickly washed his face and put on his clothes before heading for the door.

"Where are you going in such a hurry?" his mother asked, having seen him rush from his room.

"Just going to meet a friend," Philippe replied.

"What friend?" Phardos asked, in her best motherly tone.

"You don't know him, but his name is Stephen."

"Where are you meeting him?" the questions continued.

"Mother," Philippe said with exasperation, "do I have to have all these questions? I am in college now!"

"I am perfectly aware that you are in college, my son," his mother replied, "but that does not mean that I stop being your mother or stop showing concern for you."

Philippe realized he was not going to be able to stop her until he allayed her worries. "Mother, I am meeting Stephen at church, after, which we will most likely play some basketball. I should be back by 11. I will not talk to strangers. Does that answer all your questions?"

His mother smiled, pleased even with her son's mocking compliance. She walked to him at the door and gave him a kiss. "Have fun, Philippe. Be careful."

"Yes, Mother," he replied with a smile. "Bye."

Due to the slight delay, Philippe now moved briskly down the stairs and out into the street. The night was relatively cool for June, and he enjoyed the opportunity to walk. When he passed his own church, he kept his eyes straight ahead so as to not make eye contact with any acquaintances there. He crossed to the opposite side of the street as he neared the Evangelical church, so that he would not appear to be heading there directly. Once in front of the building, he looked in both directions before crossing the street and entering the gate, making sure that he saw no one he knew. As he did not know where he was going, he asked a man standing in the courtyard where there was a meeting that evening.

"There are many meetings here tonight," the man answered. "Do you know who is teaching it or the name of the group?"

"I think it is called discipleship," Philippe responded hesitantly.

"Oh, yes, that must be Dr. Raouf," replied the man, smiling. "I will take you up to the room."

Philippe followed the man to a building behind the main church facility and up a flight of steps. The man indicated a door, through which Philippe walked. He found a wood-paneled room, with a large conference table in the middle. Around it sat about 15 people, including the pastor Philippe recognized from the Sunday service he attended.

"Philippe!" his friend Stephen shouted as he saw him enter. He stood up and came toward Philippe, kissing him on both cheeks and leading him to a vacant chair by his own. "I'm so glad you came. Please sit down." Then, turning toward the pastor, he said, "Dr. Raouf, this is my friend, Philippe."

"Welcome, Philippe," the pastor said with a smile. "We were just getting ready to begin. Let's open with a word of prayer."

Philippe watched as everyone in the room instinctively closed their eyes. The pastor began praying, asking the Lord to bless their time of study and discussion, enlightening their minds through the Holy Spirit in order that they would grow to be more like Jesus and serve him more effectively. Philippe had no idea what all this meant; he had never heard a prayer like it before. It definitely didn't sound like any priest he knew.

After the prayer, the pastor asked, what seemed to Philippe, a very odd question:

"Do any of you have anything you want to share with the group as to how the Lord worked in your life this past week?" He looked around the room in anticipation of their answers.

There was silence for a while, but then a middle-aged lady spoke up:

"I have been so amazed at what God is doing in my life as I have learned more about how to pray according to his will," she began. "First of all, my prayer time in the mornings is so much more meaningful, and I am really enjoying it. I don't feel like it is a duty at all, but just a really intimate time with God."

"What has changed?" the pastor asked.

"The way I pray, for one thing," she responded. "I like the way you taught us how to divide our prayer time into different parts—praise, confession, thanksgiving and supplication. Now I really feel like I am worshiping God in prayer."

"I know what you mean," agreed a man who looked not much older than Philippe, "but my worship is happening most of all during church services."

"Was it not happening before?" questioned the pastor.

"No, because I never expected it to," the young man replied. "But now I come to church prepared in my heart to hear something from God. It has taken some time to get into the habit, but now I take the time to pray before attending any kind of religious service and ask the Holy Spirit to speak to me through the music and message. Now I know that when I make myself ready to hear him, he speaks, even if the speaker is not the greatest!!"

The room erupted in laughter. As it died down, the pastor began to speak again. "Now I know that we could keep talking all night about what we are learning, but let's get down to some new concepts tonight and hopefully we'll have time to talk more later."

Everyone in the group had a small folder and began to open it up. Stephen pushed his own toward Philippe, so they could share. Philippe thought that it was strange that no one questioned his being there, since it was now obvious that this group had been together for several weeks and were following a program of study. However, he decided to simply listen to what they had to say and then make a decision about whether or not to continue.

The pastor began talking about something he described as the disciple's cross. Philippe watched as he stood and went to a white board and began drawing the shape of a simple cross. As he asked questions to the group and they responded, he continued by writing words on and around the cross. The first thing he wrote on the cross was right in the center, and that was the word *Christ*. Philippe came to understand that the vertical beam represented man's relationship with God through Christ, while the horizontal one referred to man's relationship to others. The important thing was, as the pastor stressed, that Christ was the center of all our relationships. He went on to remind the group that without Christ being the Lord of one's life, we cannot have a relationship with God, nor can we have proper relationships with those around us.

Philippe's mind became cloudy with this thought as the discussion continued for the next hour. Though the group went on to review a passage in the Bible they had all studied and even talk about opportunities for witness, Philippe could not take it all in. Finally, one of the group was asked to lead in a closing prayer, and the people began to scatter. Stephen nudged Philippe on the shoulder and told him he wanted to introduce him to the pastor. He rose to follow his friend to where the man was saying goodbye to those leaving.

"Dr. Raouf," Stephen began, "this is my friend, Philippe."

"Welcome, Philippe, we're so glad you could join us tonight."

"Thank you, sir," Philippe replied.

"What did you think of the time?" Dr. Raouf asked.

"It was very interesting," came the answer.

"I felt as if you may have had some questions about what we discussed."

Philippe shifted uneasily on his feet. He did not know if he was ready to show his ignorance to Dr. Raouf or to his friend. "Well," he hesitated, "I guess there were some things which were not clear to me."

"I would be glad to talk through them with you," the gentleman replied. He then looked at Stephen, who seemed to get the hint.

"You know, let me go and get some drinks. You two start without me. I'll be right back." Stephen was quickly out the door.

"Come, sit down, my son," Dr. Raouf said to Philippe, pointing to some chairs. "Tell me what is confusing to you."

Philippe sat down next to the older man and tried to put his thoughts together. Before asking a question, he decided to make his situation clear. "I heard you preach a few weeks ago," came the matter-of-fact statement from his mouth.

"Oh, you did? Did you like the sermon?"

"It was, was…very different," Philippe replied, "not something I'm used to."

"You come from the Orthodox church?" Dr. Raouf asked.

"Yes."

"Well, I'm sure it was a different experience for you, then," he replied. "But don't worry, Philippe, there are many in the Evangelical church who found it different too; so you are not the only one!" He smiled at him reassuringly.

Philippe was put completely at ease by the man's demeanor. He did not hesitate now to ask him a question. "I do not understand why I have to ask Jesus into my heart, as you said that night. I was born Christian."

"Let me ask you a question," the man replied. "When you look at Christians in Egypt, can you really say that all of them act like God would want them to?"

"No, I don't suppose so," Philippe replied honestly.

"If then, a Christian does not act Christ-like, what guarantees him eternal life or what separates him from someone not born into a Christian home?"

"I don't know."

"Nothing does, my son," Dr. Raouf replied with force. "That is why being born into a Christian home does not cut it with God. Even if I was good, went to church, and obeyed the priest, I would not be guaranteed a place in heaven, because the Bible is clear to say that it is not by works we are saved, but by faith. If it were by works, then we might have a reason to show off, to boast in our own abilities. The problem is that sin is spiritual in nature and cannot be wiped out by a physical act. It took a perfect being to pay the price for our sin, and that's what Jesus did on the cross. It is only through our faith in him that we can come into a true relationship with God. That's what we were talking about tonight."

"Why doesn't the Orthodox church talk about this?" Philippe's question came from the bottom of his heart.

"That is a big question, Philippe," Dr. Raouf replied, "and not easy to answer. All I can say is that somewhere along the way, the church lost sight of grace."

"What does that mean?"

"Grace is what God shows us through Christ. We do not deserve his salvation or redemption, and yet, the Bible says, *while we were yet sinners, Christ died for us*. He did it because of his great love for mankind. The problem with man was that he rejected God's love and tried to do things on his own."

"If I believe what you are saying, does that mean I have to leave the Orthodox Church?"

"Your questions are very deep, my son," Dr. Raouf responded. "I am not going to tell you what church to belong to, but I will share with you two things that are important to remember. Your relationship with God through Christ is more important than any Christian label a person may put on you. Does that make sense?"

"Yes," Philippe replied.

"Secondly, when we become a child of God through our faith in Christ, we instantly become part of a larger family of faith, the Church universal. The Church finds many expressions and carries many names or what we might refer to as denominations, but the central teaching in all of them is that Christ is the Son of God and it is by faith in him that we become part of his family and gain eternal life. I will not tell you that you have to leave the Orthodox Church, and you may find there a group of believers who are in relationship with God through Christ and are growing in their faith and witness. If, however, you do not find a group of believers with whom you can go deep into the Word and grow in your faith, then you do need to find such a group. It is essential for a person's growth as a Christian to be part of an active and growing body of believers. The neat thing is that the Holy Spirit will show you what to do at the right time."

"The Holy Spirit?" Philippe asked.

"Yes, when a person asks Jesus to be Lord and Savior of his life, the Holy Spirit comes to live in his heart, serving as his guide and counsel for living the abundant life in Christ."

A light knock came from the door. Stephen entered with hesitation, carrying three soda cans. "I hope I am not disturbing," he said as he handed them their drinks.

"No, not at all," Dr. Raouf responded. "I was just getting ready to ask Philippe one final question." Stephen sat down as both he and Philippe looked to the pastor to hear what he had to ask.

"What is hindering you, Philippe, from asking Jesus to come into your heart tonight and beginning a new life with him?"

Philippe's mind was racing. He had heard so much and found it fascinating. All that came to his mind was the question of what his mother would say. Would she be furious with him for even being at an Evangelical church? Maybe they would call the priest in. Was he shaming his family that had been Orthodox for centuries? Did this mean that the Orthodox Church was wrong? He could not find his way through these nagging questions.

"I need to think about it," he replied to the pastor.

"Well, I hope you will think about it, Philippe," he said with kindness, "but I also want you to make sure that before you sleep tonight you ask God what he thinks. He will give you the answer if you truly seek his will. Then I hope you will call me or Stephen and let us know what you finally decide."

"I will, sir, thank you."

"Philippe," Dr. Raouf continued, "I must warn you of one thing."

"Yes?"

"When God gives us an opportunity to accept Christ, we never know if that will be the only opportunity, because no one knows what tomorrow will bring. My son, I encourage you not to delay in making your choice. It is a choice for eternity."

Stephen rose, as he realized that the meeting was finished. Philippe joined his friend in shaking the pastor's hand and thanking him for his time. It was now late as they left the church property and began walking down the street. Stephen tried to keep the conversation light, as he knew it had been a hard night on his friend. Philippe wasn't listening, but walked in silence and with the feeling that a weight had placed on his back that he could not shake off.

Chapter Thirty-Five

His father was pacing the floor when Muhammad entered the shop that morning. Afraid that it had something to do with his visit with Dr. Samuel, he asked nervously:

"Are you all right, Father?"

"I have just received some distressing news."

"About?" Muhammad asked, the fear rising in his voice.

"About?" Ahmed looked up at his son and stopped pacing, "About what do you think? Of course, your brother, Rachid!"

The relief Muhammad felt appeared instantly across his face. He caught himself, and tried to show concern, "What is the news, Father? Tell me."

"You are not to talk about this to anyone, do you understand?"

"Yes, yes, Father, I will never mention it."

"I have heard that your brother has left the country."

"Would that not be a good thing?" Muhammad asked, confused.

"Not when he has traveled to Pakistan."

It took time for this news to settle in Muhammad's mind. He moved toward the back of the store and sat down on a stool behind the workbench. If his brother had gone to Pakistan, that meant only one thing. He looked up at his father.

"Are you sure about this, Father?"

"Yes, Mahmoud has a friend in airport security. He has been keeping his eyes open for us."

"Why did they not arrest him at the airport then?"

"Rachid is nothing. They want to catch the ringleader of the group, so they are watching and waiting to see when he comes back. I was told they are already in contact with the authorities in Pakistan."

"Father, what does this mean..." Muhammad asked slowly, "for us?"

"I don't know, my son," he replied, "I don't know." The old man sat down in a nearby chair and put his head in his hands. Muhammad was moved by his father's distress. He stood and moved closer to him, touching him gently on the shoulder.

"God will protect us, Father, I am sure of it. We must put this in his hands."

"I wish I could be so confident, my son," his father replied, taking his hand and placing it on Muhammad's. "I see nothing good coming from this."

"I will pray for Rachid, Father."

His father did not respond. Muhammad took this as a good sign that at least he could say such a thing and not get into trouble. If only his father knew to whom he was now praying! It had been several days since his visit with Dr. Samuel, but he knew what he had experienced was real. Never before in his life did he know such peace. Even with all the troubles with Rachid, marriage, work and his family, he was confident that God would help them through them all. He was taking time every day to read in the *Injil.* He wondered if there were other people out there in Cairo like him.

The store was extra busy that day, and Ahmed was thrilled to have the business. It not only helped put thoughts of Rachid out of his mind, but it was a great boost to their income. Things were getting so tight in Egypt these days, everything was going up, and he had seen a drop in business as a result. God was good to give them a good day.

Muhammad was tired by the time he was able to leave the shop. He walked with his father to the metro stop to catch the trolley home. Thankfully, his mother had a great meal waiting for them when they arrived.

"Praise be to God for your safe return," she greeted them.

"God's peace be upon you," the two men said in unison.

"Something smells wonderful, Mama," Muhammad continued, drawing in a deep breath with his nose.

"Lord willing the food will be even more pleasant than the smell," his mother responded, smiling. "Wash up, and I will put everything on the table."

The men obeyed and then came to the table to find a meal of chicken, rice, okra, and various salads. The other children came out to join them.

"So, how's the easy life?" Muhammad asked them as they all began eating.

"It never lasts long enough," Abdel-Karem responded.

"You should not be complaining, my son," his father said, "be glad I don't make you work all day in the shop!"

The boy dropped his head in defeat at the thought, "yes, thank you, Father, for that blessing."

"And what are my daughters doing all day long now?" Ahmed looked at Eptisam and Nawal.

Before they could answer, Abdel-Karem responded for them, "Sleeping. At least that's all I see them doing."

"That's not true," Eptisam piped up. "We are helping Mother around the house."

"I don't see much evidence of it," Abdel-Karem said in rebuttal.

"That's enough, children!" Ahmed cried out. Everyone got quiet.

Noticing that Nawal had remained quiet through this interchange, her father looked at her and said, "I trust you are keeping close to home, Nawal. You will keep your distance from those Christians this summer, do you hear?"

"Yes, Father," Nawal answered softly.

"I did not hear you, daughter," he said with emotion rising in his voice.

"Yes, Father," she repeated, more to his satisfaction.

Muhammad wanted to know what this was all about, but kept quiet. He was too tired from work to think about it now, so he decided to take a shower and nap. He slept longer than he anticipated, and when he woke, his father and brother were already out of the house to reopen the shop for the evening shift. Muhammad slipped into the kitchen to fix a cup of tea to wake up. He found his mother there, cleaning and snapping beans.

"Peace be upon you, Mama," he said as he entered the room.

"And upon you be peace, my son," she responded with a smile. "Did you sleep well?"

"Yes, but too long. I really need to go out and look for an apartment."

"Well, it is not too late, my dear, I am sure you will still have time for your search. Would you like some tea?" she asked, rising from her seat at a small table.

"I would, but you stay there, Mama," he replied, "I will fix it myself."

"The Lord bless you, Muhammad," she said, returning to her chair.

"He already has, Mama," Muhammad answered, "he already has."

Thinking that he was referring to his future bride, Um Muhammad said, "Yes, I think the Lord has blessed you with Noura. She will make you a good wife."

"Noura is one of the blessings of God, I agree," Muhammad smiled at his mother, then added, "but he has been especially good to me lately. I wish I could explain to you how."

"I would love to hear about it, my son." She looked up at him expectantly.

Muhammad found himself unsure of how to proceed with his mother. He had started it, but did not know how to finish it without getting himself into trouble. Of course, he wanted to tell his mother; to tell her what a difference his decision to follow *'Isa* the Messiah had been in his life; to tell her that he now had hope for the first time, but he could not figure out how to say it in the right way. He took a deep breath and asked the Lord for wisdom. Then he found himself changing the subject completely:

"Mother, I wanted to ask you about what Father said to Nawal at the table today. What was he talking about?"

His mother looked at him in surprise at the sudden change in conversation. "You do not need to concern yourself with that my son," she answered bluntly. She focused once again on her beans.

"But it is my concern, Mama," he replied with a rise in his voice, "just like Rachid's actions are my concern. Everything any of us does affects the other. Is Nawal in some kind of trouble?"

"Well, not exactly," Um Muhammad replied. "She stayed too late one day with that Christian girl she studies with and your father got angry. He has forbidden her to see them again."

"Don't you think that is a little extreme?"

"It does not matter what I think. Your father's word is final in his house."

"Yes," Muhammad agreed, "but you can influence his decisions."

"Do you think it is all right for Nawal to have such a close relationship with Christians?"

Muhammad was surprised that his mother would ask him such a question. "I have never had such a friend, but if you don't see that they have a negative influence on Nawal, I do not see what the problem is. In fact, I have heard many people say that if there are any people we can trust our daughters to, it's Christians."

"I would like to agree with you, my son, but I am also fearful that she could stray from the Faith if she stays too much among Christians."

"Mama, be reasonable," Muhammad responded, as he sat down at the table with her. "We are not overly religious as a family. What can it hurt if she spends time with her girl-friends? It's not like she is with Christian boys."

"God forbid!" her mother let out in reply.

"Do you have any doubts about Nawal's behavior as a result of her relationship with this girl or her family?"

"No, in fact, her grades have been some better since she started studying with them two years ago."

"Then what is there to lose?"

"Yes, but now she is finished with school. She really has no reason to continue seeing them."

"Mother," Muhammad sighed, "they are her friends. You can't stop her from seeing them just because they are not studying. Be reasonable."

"Well, it is your father that has to be convinced and reasoned with."

"I won't be the one to bring it up, but I will say that if he keeps putting restrictions on her, Nawal will just be tempted to go behind his back. It's a natural reaction."

"I'm afraid she has already gone behind his back," his mother admitted sheepishly, then added, "I even helped her."

"Mother!" Muhammad exclaimed.

"Well, she wanted to see her friends after the exams. Besides, some of the group are Muslims, so I felt like it was not so bad. She was back before her father returned from work."

"Oh, I'm not angry with you, Mother," Muhammad said, soothingly. "I just don't want you to get in trouble with Father, but don't worry, I won't say a word."

"I know you won't, my son, thank you."

"In fact," Muhammad continued, "if it were up to me, I would encourage her to have relationships with Christians. I believe we have much to learn from them."

"You are sounding like your aunt Amal now," she said.

"Why what did she say?" Muhammad asked, sincerely interested.

"She said that it was not only important for us to study Islam, but to study Christianity too. She even suggested that I get a Bible. Can you imagine?"

"I don't see anything wrong with it, Mother," Muhammad replied, now very pleased with the way this conversation had turned. "Would you be interested in studying it together?"

"What? You want to study Christianity too?" she asked, surprised at her son's warm attitude.

"To tell you the truth, I have been very interested to read the teachings of *'Isa* for a long time. Besides the Qur'an tells us to ask the People of the Book if we have questions, so why not go to the book itself?"

"Your aunt Amal said we could even buy one here."

"Yes, I have seen a small shop in Midan al-Gamaa that sells them," Muhammad affirmed. "I can buy one for us if you like, then we can read it together. What do you think, Mother?"

"Your father would be furious, Muhammad."

"Father does not have to know everything," her son replied. "Besides, we are just doing a study of the religion, not becoming Christians. We can compare it to the words of the Qur'an. That would show that we are just being students of religion. What do you think?"

"Can you buy the Bible without getting into trouble?" She asked, looking worried.

"Don't worry about that. No one will know."

When his mother did not say anything else, Muhammad took this to mean that she was in agreement. He quickly finished the last of his tea, rose, and kissed his mother on the top of her head before leaving the room. He dressed and left the house, excited about this amazing development in his life.

"Thank you, Lord," he said out loud as he started down the stairs.

Chapter Thirty-Six

No one relaxed in the country of Egypt until exam results came out. Phardos and Girgis were among the few parents who had something to smile about, for their children had passed. Though Girgis was not pleased with Marianne's marks, at least she would graduate and be able to go on to college, though not that of her father's choice. Phardos invited the entire extended family for a special meal following the school's graduation ceremony. As congratulations and gifts were offered, the obvious questions were "which college?" or "what major?", but no one took notice of Marianne's non-committal replies. If only they knew that college was the farthest thing from her mind right now.

Summer vacation could now officially start with old and young alike ready to get out of the city. For the Orthodox community this meant only one word—conference. From the time test results were out, the line of buses never stopped in front of the churches. There were conferences for families, women, youth, children, sports, and a host of other special interest groups. Philippe was the first to leave, joining his friends for a trip to the largest Orthodox conference center up on the north coast. For college students, it was an opportunity to be away from parents and be able to mix with the opposite sex—though still under the watchful eyes of required chaperones and priests.

Marianne, though reluctant to leave Emad for an extended time, knew she would be expected to join her friends for the special conference for all high school graduates. Her mother did not understand her lack of enthusiasm, as she knew this would be a highlight of her life, for the group would stay in a 5-star hotel in Sharm el-Sheik on the Red Sea. Marianne found her solace in knowing that Emad would just be a phone call or SMS away.

Thus with her children safely shipped off to various destinations, Phardos was encouraged by her husband to join a group of women from the church in a trip to a well-known convent. As with the monasteries in the country, most religious orders had accommodations for groups. Phardos was particularly excited to go on this trip because her friend Ruth was going. She was looking forward to getting to talk to her more, for she sensed in Ruth a peace which reminded her of Naomi.

"Are you sure you will be all right without me here?" Phardos asked Girgis as she closed her suitcase on the bed. "I have never left you completely alone before."

Girgis was sitting on the overstuffed chair in their bedroom watching his wife pack. He smiled as he replied, "Maybe it is about time you did."

"What is that supposed to mean?" she asked, putting her hands on her hips in exasperation.

"It just means, my dear," Girgis began, as he stood and walked to her, then pulled her toward him, "that you have spoiled me long enough. It is time for me to suffer some so I will appreciate you more."

"Oh, Girgis," she smiled, kissing him lightly, "you are the one who spoils me. Thank you for letting me go. I need this. I want to hear God speak, and I am trusting him to do so at the convent."

"As long as you don't come back a nun, he can speak to you all he wants!" Girgis held tight to his wife and smiled. "But I will miss you."

"I will miss you too, my dear."

Phardos thought about this last encounter with her husband as she sat on the bus to the convent. It was good to be loved, she thought. God had given her a good man, and she needed to thank him more for that, as she knew many were not as fortunate. She was awakened from her thoughts by her seatmate:

"You must be thinking of something very special," Ruth said, nudging her friend.

"Well, as a matter of fact, I was," Phardos replied, with a smile, but without looking at Ruth.

"Well?"

"Oh," Phardos said, now turning to address Ruth, "yes, actually, I was thinking of what a good husband I have."

"Wow," Ruth replied in astonishment, "I don't think you'll find many women on this bus smiling when they think of their husbands."

"How can you say that?"

"Oh, I'm kidding to some degree, but then again, surely you know, Phardos, that many women have very tough marriages."

"Yes, actually I do know that's true, but it is still a shame to think that it would include most of the women on *this* bus."

"Why do you think they want to go to the convent to pray?" Ruth smiled.

"Oh, Ruth," Phardos nudged her with her shoulder, "You are bad."

"If we don't joke about it, we'd have to cry about it."

They laughed as they realized both the humor and sadness of this truth. However, it was no time for serious conversation, the bus was full of noisy women, passing food to each other and catching up on the latest news and gossip. Phardos did not dare open any important subject with Ruth now. She knew there would be quieter times when they could talk about the issues that troubled her. For now it was time to relax and just enjoy the company of women, which was a nice change from that of students and teachers at her school.

Convents and monasteries in Egypt are always places of wonder. Most are located in the desert and yet seem to teem with life, as their early founders dug wells and planted trees and gardens. During troubled times, they were not only safe havens but spiritual refuges, and many continue to be so today. Phardos was touched upon entering the large gates of the convent at the contrast from the stark desert landscape they had driven through for hours. The main church building was surrounded by palm trees, full of ripening dates, as the season for harvest was near. The grounds were covered with rows of plants and flowers that flourish in the desert environment, many sold to provide a steady income for the order.

There were several buildings on the walled-in property. Besides the church, the other main building was that which housed the nuns. There was also a substantial facility for female guests, complete with a common dining area. Any priests or monks who came were housed to themselves in a small lodge connected to the quarters of the residing priest. The last of the ancient buildings was that of a workhouse, which housed animals and several large rooms for projects to which the nuns attended. Phardos could not help but feel at peace as she walked the grounds, taking special notice of Bible verses carved on buildings or religious symbols interspersed among the flowers. Surely God must be pleased with such a place, she thought.

Ruth and Phardos were roommates for the trip, and as they unpacked their bags, Phardos was glad to finally have some quiet time to talk with her friend.

"Isn't this a lovely place?" she asked.

"I look forward to coming here every year," replied Ruth.

"Every year?" Phardos was astonished.

"Yes, Wagdy knows that I need the time at the convent, away from the rush of life in Cairo. He sees how I come home refreshed and happy, so he is always glad to let me come."

"But doesn't it get boring to come to the same place every year?"

"It's not the place, Phardos," Ruth responded smiling, "it's the time I have with God."

"What do you mean?"

"For me this trip is not to be with other women, though that is enjoyable; it is for me to spend some truly concentrated time in Bible study and prayer. With all the distractions of work, family and crowded city life, I find myself longing to get away just to hear God better."

"Can't you do that at church?"

"Yes, God does speak to me during mass, and even when I read my Bible at home, but they are short times. It's like when you read the headlines of the newspaper, but not the whole story, because you don't have time or can't focus. That's the way it is for me most of the year. He speaks, and I hear him, but I want time to pour myself into his Word for hours, not minutes. That's why I come here."

Phardos looked at her friend in amazement. She had never heard an Orthodox woman speak like this. Most were satisfied to get their spiritual food from the priest. She knew few who actually read the Bible for themselves, much less wanted to spend hours doing so; especially not a woman under the age of 60.

"Ruth, I don't think there are many in this group who have the same goal as you."

"No," Ruth responded laughing, "I'm sure there are not, but that does not bother me. I know what I need, and don't worry about their motives in coming."

Phardos did not know how to ask her next question, but decided to take the chance. "Ruth, please forgive me if I offend, but there is something different about you. Ever since our day in Ein al-Soukna, I have wanted to talk with you. You were the only one who was even open to the idea of a Muslim becoming Christian. I was touched by how you did not make me feel bad for even asking the question that day."

Ruth put her suitcase in the closet, as she was finished unpacking. She sat on her bed and pointed to the other, "Why don't we sit for a minute," she began. Once Phardos had settled on the bed opposite her, she took a deep breath and smiled, as if trying to decide where to begin. "Phardos, not too many of our friends know this about me, as I don't talk openly about my relationship with God. There are too many closed minds within our church, and the Lord has given me peace to simply live out the change that has taken place in my heart and allow him to be the one to draw those to me who really want the same." Seeing the confused expression on her friend's face, she paused and said, "Well, maybe I had better back up. I am glad you see me as different from others, for that is what I want to be. It is hard to describe what God has done in my life, but I will try."

"Yes, please tell me," Phardos encouraged her. "I really want to know."

"That is what I like to hear," responded Ruth, "OK, here it is. About five years ago, Wagdy and I were in Sharm el-Sheik for a vacation. Our marriage was on the rocks, neither of us had time for the other, and the children were suffering because of our constant arguing. A friend recommended we get away together, and I think out of desperation, we agreed to do so. We were not bad people, Phardos. We both were in church on a regular basis, and I had helped with Sunday School for years, but I can safely say that religion was designated to our time at church only. Neither of us really new God."

"Did something happen in Sharm?" Phardos asked, really interested now.

"Something amazing happened," replied Ruth. "Something life-changing."

"What was it?"

"We met Jesus."

"In Sharm?" Phardos asked. "Did you see a miracle?"

Ruth smiled at her friend, "The miracle is what happened to our lives, my dear. I know we as Orthodox love miracles, but it was not like that at all. Let me tell you what happened." She took a deep breath and sat up straight. "Wagdy and I were sitting by the pool one day having a drink when a young couple with three children came near. The kids jumped in the pool, and the parents sat on chairs next to ours. Well, of course, we greeted them. They were so sweet and warm. Their names were Mamdouh and May. When Wagdy asked Mamdouh his occupation, he said he was a pastor. We knew right away that they were not Orthodox, but Evangelical. Though this would normally have been cause for alarm and suspicion, we were both put at ease by their warm personalities and loving spirits. We talked for hours as we watched their kids swim and play. The amazing thing was that for some unknown reason, we simply began to tell them our problems."

"Your marriage problems?" Phardos said in shock, "To strangers?"

"Yes," Ruth replied. "it just poured out of both us. But the couple did not condemn or criticize, they just listened and let us get it all out. Then, as we finished our story, Mamdouh began to speak. He said he wanted to ask only one question. When we gave our assent, he asked, 'How is your relationship with God?'"

"Really?" asked Phardos.

"Yes. Well, of course, Wagdy and I just looked at each other. Here we had been telling about our marriage troubles and they wanted to know about our religious life. It seemed like a non-issue, a useless question. When Wagdy asked Mamdouh what that had to do with anything, Mamdouh responded that it had everything to do with it. He then went on to tell us the story of Adam and Eve, like we had never heard it. But of course the way he told it, it seemed we never had. He talked about how God not only created us to have a relationship with him, but that marriage is his special creation which allows a man and woman to experience that unique union we have with God through Christ. When our relationship with God is not right, then our other relationships are not right, and this especially affects the relationship of marriage, as it is the most intimate."

"But what did he mean by relationship with God?" Phardos asked. "Didn't he know you were Christians?"

"Oh, yes, he knew," her friend replied, "but he said being born Christian is not what saves us. He made it very clear through Scripture that we must accept Christ as our personal Lord and Savior. We don't inherit our salvation."

"What did you do then?"

"We asked a lot of questions, but in the end, we knew he was right. Neither of us really knew God. We rarely even opened our Bibles to see what his Word said, and we had never prayed together as a couple or family. In reality, the only thing that showed that we were Christian was that we had crosses tattooed on our wrists and went to church every now and then. Then Mamdouh asked us another question. He asked what was hindering us from giving our lives to Jesus right then and there and beginning again with him and as a couple dedicated to the Lord. Wagdy and I looked at each other and nodded in agreement. This is what we wanted, it was what was lacking in our personal and married life. We knew it would be the thing to make the difference. So, right there by the side of the pool, we prayed for Jesus to forgive our sins and asked him to come into our hearts to be the true Lord of our lives."

"And that was it?" Phardos asked, sitting on the edge of the bed.

"That was it."

"How did you know?"

"Because we had a peace that could not be explained. From that day on, Wagdy and I began to read our Bibles together. We started praying together as a couple and then included our children. Our love for each other was restored, and we began to serve each other as never before. Jesus transformed our home."

"So are you Evangelical now?" This was a typical question from the Orthodox point of view.

"Well, I will be honest with you," began Ruth, "we did think about leaving the church. We would have done whatever Pastor Mamdouh told us at that point, but he did not tell us what to do. Instead, he said we should pray about it, and seek God's will on the matter. He did add that maybe God wanted to use us from within the Orthodox church to help others come to a true relationship with God through Christ. We tried going to Evangelical churches, but never felt peace that that was where God wanted us. We then realized that it was from within that we were to make a difference."

"But you said you don't talk about your decision."

"Yes, but that does not mean that I don't speak at all. I talk about what God's Word says, especially when we have ladies' meetings. I live out my faith so that others see the difference. See how it worked with you?" Ruth smiled.

Phardos nodded and laughed, "OK, you're right. I was drawn to you in an amazing way. I could not put my finger on it, but I knew you were different."

"The question is now," Ruth began, "what will you do with what I've told you?"

"Yes, that is the question," Phardos could not deny it.

Chapter Thirty-Seven

Nawal felt like his number was burning a hole in her pocket as the days and weeks passed. She was slowly dying all cooped up at home, not able to get out or make a call to Emir. What made it worse was her sister Eptisam's persistent pestering as to what had happened during those last weeks of school. Though Nawal would have loved to just unload all her emotions and thoughts on someone, she knew that telling Eptisam could be dangerous. Her sister might get upset and tell her parents, leading to even more problems.

"Let's go out, Eptisam," Nawal said in a burst of insight.

"Where?" her sister asked with excitement. "Will Mother let us go out alone?"

"She will if we are just going to the sewing store. I want to get some yarn for a new project."

"Oh, it's so hot outside, Nawal," Eptisam exclaimed in disappointment. "Can't we at least go to the mall?"

"You know Mother will never let us go to the mall alone! Come on, let's go ask her if we can go to the store. At least we will be getting out of the house."

Having gained permission from their mother, after many tears and pleading, Nawal and Eptisam took the metro to the Midan el-Gamaa area, near their father's shop. They wanted, however, to avoid any contact with him or their brother, so they made sure to keep watch as they walked in the area. Nawal led her sister to the shop and made her purchase. Eptisam suddenly got interested in a project and decided to purchase a needlepoint pattern and yarn as well. While her sister argued with the clerk over colors, Nawal, having already bought her yarn, moved outside of the shop to wait. As she did, she spotted a shop that offered cell phones for calls. She quickly went back into the shop to tell her sister she would be just across the way and to look for her when she came out. She then nearly ran to the shop, asked to use a phone and fumbled for Emir's number in her pocket. She nervously dialed the number.

"Hallo." She thought his voice sounded melodious.

"Emir, this is Nawal." The sound was quiet on the other end, and Nawal looked around nervously as she waited for a response.

"Nawal," he said finally in an excited tone. "Where have you been? I have been so worried."

"I'm fine, I'm fine," she replied. "I just have not been able to get out of the house until now."

"We must meet. Can you come by the church now? I will meet you there."

"I'm with my little sister, but I will think of something. Yes, I'll meet you. Just wait on me."

"I will, my love."

"Good-bye." She found herself unable to say anything else in response.

Nawal had to see Emir, but she was at a loss as to how to get rid of Eptisam. She had just finished her call when she saw her sister cross the road to meet her. Nawal grabbed her by the arm and began walking toward the church a few blocks away.

"What is it Nawal?" her sister asked, while trying to pull her arm from her grip. "Where are we going? Is something the matter?"

"Yes, everything is the matter," Nawal replied sharply, "and I can't take it anymore."

"What is it? What's wrong with you, Nawal?" Fear rose in Eptisam's eyes. "Stop holding on to me, people are watching."

"I will, but you keep walking, or I'll grab you even harder." Nawal did not even look at Eptisam as she talked, but just kept going with a furious speed. They crossed the metro track and headed down another street. About a block before the church, Nawal suddenly turned into a small side street and stopped by a wall to catch her breath. Eptisam, leaned against the wall, panting from the experience.

"Tell me what this is all about, Nawal," she insisted. "I know something is terribly wrong."

Nawal looked at her sister straight in the eyes. "All right," she said in exasperation, "but remember I did not want to tell you, and if you breathe a word about it, I will make your life miserable."

"All right, I won't tell anyone," Eptisam promised.

"I am going away."

"Where? When?" her sister questioned. "Why would you leave us?"

"Because I have an opportunity to have a new life."

"What are you talking about, Nawal? This doesn't make any sense."

"I cannot tell you any more than that, Eptisam. Don't you see, I'm trying to protect you. If you don't know anything, then Father cannot be angry with you. Now, I've said enough already. This is what I want you to do. I want you to wait right here for 15 minutes. Don't watch where I am going or follow me. I will be back. That's all I can tell you right now. Wait right here." She began to walk away.

"Nawal, what if you don't come back," her sister yelled after her.

"I will, don't worry."

This was the beginning of the break that Nawal knew would have to come with her family. If she could not tell her closest sister her secret, she could tell no one. She met Emir that day, who told her he had a family who was willing to take her in for a short time as he prepared everything for them to marry. She would have to meet him that night again with as much as she was able to bring from home without her family becoming suspicious. They made plans to meet, and she then rushed back to her sister, whom she found pacing up and down the street where she left her.

"I was worried sick, Nawal," she exclaimed. "Are you all right?"

"I'm fine," Nawal responded matter-of-factly. "Let's get home."

Though Eptisam tried to get more information from her sister, she realized it was now useless to try. She had no idea what was happening, all she could deduce was that perhaps Nawal had gotten a job somewhere that offered her some freedom. She would never have imagined the chain of events through which her sister had passed nor the future that was before her.

When they got home, Nawal acted as normal and showed her mother the yarn she bought for her newest project. Eptisam tried to put up a good front, but her mother caught a disturbing look in her eyes.

"Are you all right, Eptisam?" she asked, walking toward her youngest child and putting her hand on her shoulder.

Nawal quickly responded before her sister had a chance. "Oh, it must have been that candy bar that I bought her. Maybe with the heat, it upset her stomach."

"Haven't I told you about buying food on the street during the summer?" Um Muhammad exclaimed.

"I know, I'm sorry, Mama," Nawal offered. "Come, Eptisam, let's take this stuff in our room and you can rest there while we look at it."

"That's a good idea," she agreed, "you two go and try to cool off for a while. I'm working on lunch."

"Thank you, Mama," Nawal called, as she escorted her sister to their room.

Once in the safety of their room, Nawal let down her guard and began going through her closet as Eptisam sat submissively on the bed. Choosing several skirts and two pairs of pants, Nawal tried to figure out how she could wear as much as possible under her galabiya, leaving only her school backpack to carry out with her.

"Why are you leaving like this," Eptisam asked almost in a whisper.

"It's the way it has to be, Eptisam." Nawal looked at her with compassion and then moved over to her bed and sat beside her. "Listen. I am going to a better life. If I don't take this chance, I may never get out from under Father's thumb. I want to live differently, think differently, and be able to make decisions for myself."

"But aren't you taking a big risk leaving this way, without Father knowing?"

"It could never happen otherwise." Nawal stood up and began going through her things once again. "But you know. I will miss you. Will you try to remember me as a good sister?"

Eptisam jumped up and ran to her sister and hugged her tight. "You know I will miss you too. What will I do without you? It will just be me and the boys!"

"Oh, you'll survive," Nawal assured her. "Plus, I'm sure they will find a good husband for you before too long."

Nawal continued her organizing as Eptisam rested on her bed. They did not talk further except for Eptisam to ask when she was leaving. Nawal told her she would not tell her, so she would not have to say she knew anything to her parents. They ate the late lunch with the family, acting as if nothing where happening. Once her father and brothers again left the house, Nawal, Eptisam and her mother cleaned up the kitchen and sat down to watch television in a room just off of the salon. As the night wore on, Nawal excused herself to say she wanted to take a shower and change for the night. While she did take a shower, it was not her pajamas she put on, but several layers of clothes followed by a large galabiya. She covered her head with a black scarf and put on her now heavy backpack and grabbed her stuffed purse, which carried two separate identities. Quietly passing the room where her mother and sister relaxed, Nawal slipped out the front door, closing it quietly behind her.

It wasn't until her husband came in late from the shop that Um Muhammad realized Nawal must have gone to bed much earlier.

"Eptisam, my dear," she said, as she rose to go to her own room, "can you tell Nawal that I need her to help me clean the carpets tomorrow?"

Eptisam was not sure whether her sister had left or not, but she definitely did not want to the be the one to find out. "Mama, I want to watch this next show, can you just tell her when you go to your room, I'm sure she's still up reading."

Without responding, Um Muhammad walked down the hall and gently knocked on her daughter's room door. When there was no response, she opened the door and looked inside. The room was empty. She turned and looked across the hall to the bathroom, but found that her husband had just walked in there, closing the door. She then went to the kitchen, but found only Muhammad eating a late-night snack. Returning to the living room, she looked at Eptisam, "Where is Nawal?"

Eptisam looked up at her mother as innocently as possible, "I don't know, Mama, I've been sitting here with you. I thought she went to bed."

Um Muhammad began running through the house, throwing open every bedroom door and calling for her daughter. Hearing the commotion, Ahmed came out of the bathroom exclaiming, “What is going on here? What are you yelling about, woman?”

“Nawal, it’s Nawal,” his wife screamed, “she’s gone!”

Chapter Thirty-Eight

While her mother soaked up the fresh air and spiritual refreshment of the convent, Marianne struggled to even survive the days in Sharm. Though they should have been the highlight of her life, the days seemed to drag by. Her friends worked hard to understand what was bothering her, but eventually gave up trying as Marianne increasingly isolated herself from all those who thought they knew her best. She was no longer the gentle, loving girl who had grown up with them both at church and in school. All she cared about was being with Emad, and she told him that over and over again during the long phone calls between Sharm and Cairo.

Emad was thrilled with the way things were developing, and when he learned during one of their conversations that his friend, Reda, was at the same conference as a group leader, he knew the time was right to bring his plan to completion.

"I have a surprise for you," he told Marianne on the phone one day.

"What is it?" she asked with anticipation.

"You'll find out tomorrow. I have to go now. You sleep well, my darling."

"May your dreams be sweet too," she replied dreamily.

"They can only be sweet, because I dream only of you."

"I love you, Emad." Her voice was full of desire.

"I am counting on it," came his reply.

Marianne slept well and even listened more carefully than usual during the morning session. The topic was marriage, and the priest spoke to them from the second book of Paul's letters to the church in Corinth: "Do not be yoked together with unbelievers. For what do righteousness and wickedness have in common? Or what fellowship can light have with darkness?"

Marianne perked up as he commented on the passage. "My children, take heed of these instructions from God's Word. How can uneven members carry the same load? If one is tall and the other is short, the load will fall or spill. It is the same in marriage. We must be united in our belief of God and dedication to the Church in order to have a blessed marriage. We are the majority among Christians, why would any of us be encouraged to marry outside the Orthodox Church? Evangelicals are to marry only Evangelicals, and Orthodox only Orthodox. If we mix them, then the church is corrupted with their false teachings. If you want to stay blessed by God and within the good favor of the Church, keep your eyes from wondering outside her walls."

As the priest continued his discourse on marriage, Marianne began thinking about what he was saying. Of course he was only talking about Orthodox and Evangelicals, what if he knew that she was going to marry a Muslim? But as soon as this thought came to mind, she dismissed it, because Emad had told her he would convert. However, she realized that in the days of their bliss together, they really had not talked any more about this. She determined in her mind to make sure the next time she saw him they would talk about making an appointment to meet the priest. He should be thrilled that she was bringing someone into the Faith.

Sitting on the beach that afternoon with her friends, Marianne was watching those playing in the sea when she noticed a familiar face swimming close by. She sat straight up in her chair and then looked around to see if anyone noticed her. When she sat up, the person in the water caught her attention and motioned for her to go to a nearby refreshment stand. He then went back to swimming and left the water a short distance away. Marianne told her friends nonchalantly that she was going to buy a drink and would be right back. Leaving them talking, she practically ran to the stand to find Emad waiting for her with a big smile on his face.

"What are you doing here?!" she exclaimed, but then quickly looked around again.

"I told you I had a surprise for you," he relied. "Can I buy you a drink?"

"Emad, you shouldn't be here!" Marianne grabbed him by the arm and pulled him around the side of the drink stand. "You could get me in big trouble."

"No one has to know," he said coolly, "and besides, I couldn't live without you in Cairo."

"How did you get off work?" she asked, suspicious.

"I told my uncle that I had to visit a sick friend for a couple of days. He let me off." He moved closer to her but without touching and lowered his voice. "I have a room all to myself in the same hotel as you. What do you think?"

"Emad, I think it sounds dangerous." She began to back away.

He touched her gently on the arm and ran his fingers up and down her skin. "I've missed your touch," he said with a sadness in his eyes. "You could easily get away while everyone is in on the beach. Please, Marianne, I need you."

"Well, we do need to talk," she said, half-heartedly. "I was reminded this morning that we need to think about when you can meet the priest."

"Yes, yes, you see," he agreed, "we need to be alone. There is much to discuss. My room is 209. I'll be waiting for you there."

"I don't know when I can safely get there."

"It doesn't matter, I can wait all day...and night. You are worth it." He backed up quickly from her and said with authority. "Now, get back to your friends. You wouldn't want them to think anything is up."

She looked at him and hesitated.

"Go, go," he said, motioning for her to start moving.

Lost in the confusion of her emotions and thoughts, Marianne returned obediently to her place on the beach with her friends. They were caught up in conversation about summer vacation and boys and did not even notice her return. After she sat there a while and finished her drink, she told Nadia, her roommate, that she was going to go inside. She was not feeling too well and wanted to get out of the sun. Marianne covered her swimsuit with a flowery cover-up she had with her and headed back to the hotel. Instead of going to her own room, however, she went directly to 209, continually looking over her shoulder to make sure no one saw her on that floor.

As promised, Emad was waiting for her and quickly opened the door upon her knock. He was very pleased that she was still in her swimsuit and pulled her toward him, closed the door, and kissed her all in one swift movement. Marianne was at a loss to get any conversation started as Emad was obviously hungry for her affections and moved her immediately toward the bed. The sheets became stained with her suntan oil as they became lost in love.

As they finally came up for breath, Marianne whispered into Emad's ear, "I'm so glad you came. I love you so much and was miserable without you."

"I'm glad I came too. You are fantastic."

They remained in bed and continued to enjoy each other's kisses and touch, though Marianne did manage to get some conversation going as well. She told Emad that it was important to see the priest, because she would not be able to keep up the hiding for long. As he enjoyed the shape of her body, Emad promised he would go with her to the priest as soon as they returned to Cairo.

Then a new thought came to Marianne: "Wait, you know what? It is better if you go alone or with another guy, or the priest will definitely suspect something."

"Yeah, that's true," Emad agreed. "I would not want to get you into trouble."

"But you will go?" She asked, looking him straight into the eyes to test his sincerity.

"Of, course," he replied without blinking. "Hey, you know what? Didn't you say Reda is here? He can take me. I know him well from college. I'm sure he'll help me out."

"Yes, he's a nice guy and very faithful to the Church. Oh, but of course, you can't let him see you here!"

"No, no," Emad replied, "but even if he did, that doesn't have anything to do with you. He doesn't know we know each other."

"Well...but still I think it's better if you wait."

"Whatever you say, my love. You know I would turn the world upside down for you."

"Oh, Emad, I love you." She kissed him long and hard, and then laid back on the pillow and continued, "Besides, you will be so happy in the Church. The people are good and will take you in and love you."

"Yes, I'm sure they will."

Emad had Marianne promise to join him again later in the night. After all, since he had the room, they might as well enjoy it. She hesitated, but told him if possible, she would try. He knew she would not let him down. Later leaving him to return to her room and then attend the afternoon session, Marianne cautiously decided to take the stairs back to her floor. Emad remained in the bed, contemplating his next step. His flight was at 12 noon the next morning, so he would have to get it together soon.

It was during the late evening meal that Emad began to execute his plan. The group from the church was sitting at two large tables in the main restaurant of the hotel. Marianne had just helped herself from the buffet when she saw Emad enter. Though he caught sight of her, he did not indicate in any way that he knew or recognized her; instead, as the waiter was escorting him to a small table, he glanced in the direction of the large group and noticed his friend, Reda. Allowing the waiter to seat him, he then placed an order for a drink and rose as if to go to the buffet, but then moved toward the large table. Marianne froze at the buffet as she watched Emad call out Reda's name and greet him.

"Emad!" Reda exclaimed as he rose from his chair, "what a surprise to see you here! How are you?"

"I'm great. It's good to see you. How are you, man?" Emad replied, kissing his friend on the cheeks.

"I'm fine. What are you doing here?"

"Oh, I'm just getting away for a couple of days of fresh air. It is so hot in Cairo."

"Yeah, tell me about it," Reda agreed. "Are you here with someone?"

"No, not really. I'm open to any possibilities, though." Emad smiled. "This is a big group you're with."

"Yeah, it's from the church. I'm chaperoning." Reda was now uncomfortable with his Muslim friend so close to a table full of beautiful Christian girls. He shifted on his feet.

"Well, I don't want to keep you from your dinner," Emad offered, knowing what his friend was feeling. "Anyway, it was good to see you."

"Ah, yeah, you too." Reda watched Emad move toward the buffet. All of a sudden he saw Marianne standing with her full plate in her hands, watching Emad as he came toward her. Fear rose in his eyes as he saw her suddenly come to her senses and quickly move to the other side of the counter. However, he continued to watch as Emad now took a plate for himself and went to the opposite side of the same buffet. As the two looked at each other through the salad dishes on display, Reda felt a rage rise in him. He quickly walked over to the buffet and came up beside Marianne, startling her so, that she nearly dropped her plate.

"Marianne, did you find enough to eat?" He began, trying not to act like he knew something was happening. "The girls were looking for you."

"Oh, yes," she replied weakly, "I think I've gotten more than I can even think of eating." She looked briefly up at Emad and then down again as she moved toward her table.

"She's a cute girl," Emad offered across the buffet, as Reda watched her to return to her seat.

Looking up at him with a look of wrath in his eyes, Reda replied, "Emad, I don't know what you are up to, but please, stay away from the girls. I'm responsible for them here, and I would hate for something to happen to them."

"I have no idea what you are talking about, my friend," Emad said in innocence. "I was merely making a comment. I think I have freedom enough to do that."

"Yeah," was all Reda could say without blowing up completely. He returned to his table without another word.

Marianne was nervously eating her dinner and trying not to watch what was happening between the two guys. Her friend, Lucy, looked in the direction she noticed Marianne watching.

"Wow, that's a cute guy," she said, smiling. "Do you know him?"

"No, not really," Marianne replied, "but I think Reda does."

"Yeah, maybe I'll have to ask him about him. What do you think?"

"What would I know?" she said sharply. "Do what you want."

"All right," Lucy retorted, looking at her friend in disgust. "You don't have to get so uptight about it."

"I'm not uptight." Marianne felt like she was losing it. "I'm sorry, Lucy."

She continued through the meal, merely picking at her food. Emad made no effort to look at her or get her attention. She had no idea what was happening, but knew she had to talk to him. He was going to get her into trouble like this. Afterwards, the group went to the conference room for a fun time of music and games. It was after midnight before they began moving toward their rooms. Marianne went with Nadia back to their room. Thankfully, Nadia was tired and wanted to sleep. Marianne told her she was going to read for a while on the balcony.

While her roommate settled in for the night, Marianne listened to the sounds of the sea and looked out at the star-laden sky, reflecting on her life. What had once seemed to be the answer to her dreams was now a way that appeared only dark and murky. Was Emad not the man she longed for? But he was so willing to go to great lengths for her, to change his religion, to get a good job…what was wrong? There was no peace in her heart. Yes, she was experiencing sexual gratification for the first time in her life. She knew what it was like to be loved by a man, and the feeling was intoxicating, but somehow it did not seem to be enough. Why did the world have to be so complicated by divisions? Who cared if someone was Muslim or Christian?

Then Marianne realized something in her own heart—she was not really Christian anyway. Sure, she had grown up in church and had all the marks of what makes a good Copt—the tattooed cross, the certificate of baptism, the Christian name and heritage, but in reality she knew that they were merely outward symbols; inside was empty. There was no mark on her heart.

Not knowing what to do with these feelings, all Marianne could think about was talking to Emad. She must go to him and let him know something was not right. She wanted to slow things down so she could really be sure about marriage. Yes, she knew that it would be better if they married, since they had already consummated their relationship sexually, but she didn't care. She could not continue without some kind of certainty that this was what God wanted for her life. Anyway, she reasoned, if Emad was serious about her, he would wait on her and convert to show his sincerity. Once she was convinced of his decision to become Christian, she would consider him again—nothing more, nothing less.

She slid the glass door open and peeked into her room to see if Nadia was asleep. Being assured that she was, Marianne quickly put on her clothes and slipped out the door and down the stairwell. Arriving at Emad's room, she tapped lightly on the door, hoping he would hear but the neighbors would not. She had to knock twice more before he answered the door, dressed only in his boxer shorts.

"My love," he smiled, pulling her into the room, "I'm so glad you came. I was afraid you wouldn't."

"Well, I had to wait until my roommate slept," Marianne replied. "Emad, we need to talk."

"Yes, of course, my love," he agreed eagerly, still leading her by the hand. He kissed her on the forehead and then the lips. As he tried to move his lips down her neck, Marianne pulled away."

"Emad, I want to talk first, please." She moved toward a chair. Emad sat disgruntled on the bed and crossed his legs.

"What do you want to talk about?"

"What happened tonight at dinner?"

"Oh, nothing," he replied, "I just think Reda was surprised to see me and worried that I would take advantage of one of his girls."

"It was not smart for you to have met him like that," Marianne offered matter-of-factly.

"Not smart?" Emad's voice rose in anger. "Are you telling me I don't know what I'm doing, that I'm not smart?"

A look of fear came to Marianne's eyes as she had never seen Emad get angry. "No, no," she offered weakly, "maybe that was a poor choice of words. I just mean that I was afraid Reda would suspect something if he saw you here before you talk to him about converting when you see him later in Cairo."

"Well, now, that's my business," retorted Emad. "Besides, Reda needs to know that he is not in charge of 'his girls' and I can talk to any one of them I want to."

"What does that mean?"

"It means exactly what it sounds like. He thinks he's so special and you girls are so off limits because you're Christian. Well, he should know better than to try to withhold anything from us."

"From us?" Marianne looked at him like he was a total stranger.

"Yes, us—Muslims. How dare he think he can deny me something I have every right to take under the *Sharia*."

"Well, you must understand his position, Emad," Marianne tried, "I mean after all, no Christian would allow his daughter to marry a Muslim just like that."

"And what are you doing?"

"Well, you are different," she said slowly, "I mean, you said you would convert to Christianity for me. Isn't that right, Emad?" Her eyes were pleading for some kind of confirmation.

"Well, for your information, I have a right under the laws of the Holy Qur'an to lie to a Christian in order to gain his or *her* confidence. And in this case, that lie was to you, my dear."

Fear rose into Marianne's eyes and extended throughout her entire body as she listened to these words from Emad and watched a sinister smile come across his face. She had been sitting in the chair with her legs under her, and as she instinctively began to pull them out in order to get up and run, Emad came leaping toward her, grabbing her by the arm.

"Don't you scream, or you will have everyone in this hotel know what a bitch you are!"

"Emad, please don't!" she urged, "I loved you. Why have you done this?"

"To prove a point, my dear, to prove a point." He pulled her off the chair and onto the bed with him. "And now I will have one more point to prove before I'm finished with you once and for all."

"Emad, don't! Please don't!" But it was too late, Marianne had no way to escape the one last encounter with the man she thought to be her future husband. She now knew him to be a beastly deceiver who had ruined her life forever.

Chapter Thirty-Nine

Um Muhammad was beside herself in anguish. She had to be forced to take a sedative in order to calm down, and Eptisam was put in charge of watching her mother as she now lay in her bed. Abu Muhammad was close to a nervous breakdown of his own, as the weight of not just his son but now Nawal's disappearance weighed on him. The first thing he did was call his friend, Mahmoud, hoping that at least one rational head would help them to make better decisions. While they waited for Mahmoud's arrival, Muhammad and Abdel-Karem were sent out to walk around the neighborhood in search of their sister, though without raising the suspicions of neighbors. The thought of the neighborhood knowing that their daughter had run away was beyond shame!

As Muhammad roamed the streets, he felt miserable about the turn of events in his family's life. First, Rachid, and now Nawal—what was happening? He looked up at the dark sky and wondered if this had any relation to his new faith in Christ. Didn't Dr. Samuel warn him about attacks? Maybe this is what he was talking about. Was this Satan trying to discourage him from following Jesus? Not knowing what to do, he continued wandering the streets looking for any sign of Nawal. A thought then came to his mind that he could pray. He did not know much about it, but had enough faith to trust Jesus to help him. As the streets were relatively quiet due to the late hour, it was not hard to find a secluded spot on a small side street to stop and mediate. An old bucket was sitting upside down next to a garage gate. Seeing that no one was around, Muhammad sat down on the bucket and closed his eyes.

> Merciful and gracious Lord God, in the name of Jesus I lift a prayer to you. Please forgive me if I do not know how to pray, but know that my heart desires for you to hear as you promised in your Holy Word. Lord, you know the problems my family is facing now. Please show us where Nawal is and how to bring her back. Keep her safe, dear Lord, and watch over her. Help my parents to have peace. Keep them calm through all these troubles. Especially watch over my mother, as I want her to know you, Lord, as I now know you in Jesus. Lord, also I want to pray for Rachid. It is not easy to do so, but I know I should. Bring him away from these evil men he is associating with, dear Lord. Do not allow him to do harm to others. Help me, Lord, to find an apartment, to marry Noura, to follow you in a way that pleases you. Forgive me of my weaknesses and show me how to live for you. I know that in the Name of Jesus you will hear my prayer. Amen.

Muhammad continued sitting on the bucket with his head in his hands, just taking in the silence of the moment. So much of life was noise and confusion, it was good to sit and be quiet and rest in God's care, for that's what he felt as he closed his prayer to the Lord—a warm arm around his shoulders, giving him the comfort and peace that had been so rare before in his life. He savored the feeling and then looked up with a smile on his face and took a deep breath. "Better get home," he said out loud. He rose and headed back to the apartment.

While the initial search had begun, Nawal and Emir were already in the final stages of their escape. After meeting him in the designated location, Emir's friends had helped Nawal pack the layers of clothes she wore out of the house, along with her other items, in a small suitcase. Emir had his own ready as well. As they quickly completed this needed step, they were then hurried to a waiting car and driven to the airport. Since the moment they met, Emir explained to Nawal that they were leaving the country and flying to Cyprus. The friends had made arrangements through a church there and there would be people waiting to meet them as they landed, at which time, Nawal would request asylum as a Muslim convert.

"What about your family?" Nawal asked Emir as they were almost to the airport.

"They will come to understand," he replied, squeezing her hand.

"But how will we travel," she asked, we aren't even married?"

"We have taken care of that," he said, slipping a gold band on her left finger and smiling.

"Emir, what is this?" Nawal looked shocked.

"It is a wedding band."

"Yes, I see that, Emir, but we aren't married."

"Well, this paper says we are in case anyone asks, but don't worry," he rubbed her hand, "we will do it officially once we are in Cyprus. There is a priest there waiting for us."

"This is all happening too fast," she exclaimed.

"You don't want to marry me?" He had a sad look in his eyes.

"No, no, it's not that," she said, consolingly. "It's just that I did not expect it to be like this."

"Then you are happy to marry me."

"Of course, Emir," she managed a smile, "why do you think I am doing all this?"

Final instructions were given by the man driving the car. He made sure before letting them out that Nawal had given him all her Muslim identity papers and was carrying only the Christian ones. She left the car with Emir and entered the airport, leaving behind Nawal Ahmed Muhammad Rachid and becoming forever Miriam Fahim Girgis Milad, newly married wife of Emir Magdy Estafanos Boulos.

Mahmoud's knock on the door startled everyone in the house. Muhammad quickly went to open the door for his father's closest friend, who rushed through it with a hurried "peace be unto you." Abu Muhammad rose to greet his friend.

"Ah, Mahmoud, my friend," he began as he kissed him on both cheeks, "I'm so glad you've come. We are in terrible straights."

"Tell me, Ahmed, what has happened? I was so worried. Is it Rachid?"

"No, no," Ahmed shook his head, motioning for his friend to sit near him on the couch. "I am afraid that it is our daughter, Nawal."

"What? Ahmed? What?"

"She has disappeared."

"Yes, well, what do you suspect, Ahmed? Why has she disappeared?" Mahmoud was looking for details from his distraught friend.

"I really have no idea. Everything was fine. No suspicions, nothing."

"Come now, think, Ahmed, there must have been something that has happened. Have you had any cause to be angry with her lately? Has she been out of the house a lot in recent weeks?"

His sons watched as their father stood and began to pace the floor.

"Well, she finished her exams. She did well. Nothing unusual there. I have no knowledge that she has been out of late. The only thing that I had cause to reprimand her for in recent months was the excess of studying at the home of a Christian classmate. She came in late one time, and I forbid her to return."

"That could be the key," Mahmoud said, as Ahmed finished his processing. "Do you know how to reach this Christian family?"

"Actually, I have no idea," Ahmed replied, "but perhaps her mother does." He went toward the back bedroom to talk to his wife.

No one dared speak, but all listened intently to see if there were any clues to come from the conversation in the distant part of the house. Muhammad looked at his brother as he heard his mother's voice rise sharply. Though they could not make out the details of the words, they knew that their father had acquired something useful, for as he opened the door to return to the salon, they could hear their mother crying.

"I have a phone number, Mahmoud," Ahmed said, as he returned to the room. "It is for a Professor Magdy, from Ain Shams University. Apparently he is the father of the girl who was a classmate of my daughter."

"The hour is late, Ahmed," Mahmoud cautioned. "Perhaps we should wait until morning to call."

"How can I wait, Mahmoud? I must find out what is happening with the girl."

"All right, but can you do it without causing a wrong response?"

"Boys, leave us." Ahmed shot a look at his two sons which meant instant obedience.

As the boys left the room, Ahmed again sat down on the couch near his friend. "You must calm yourself, Ahmed. Take a deep breath and think before you call."

"Let me get you a drink, Mahmoud. I did not even extend you that courtesy. Then I'll call."

"No, I'm fine, Ahmed. I do not need anything at this hour."

"Please forgive me for calling you at such a time as this. I know you must be tired."

"We are closer than brothers, my friend. Do not worry. I know you would do the same for me."

"Yes, yes, I would. Thank you."

Ahmed then proceeded to pick up the telephone and call Nancy's father, not knowing that their own home was in turmoil as well. When Magdy picked up the phone on the second ring, Ahmed was shocked, but tried to speak calmly.

"Professor Magdy?" he began.

"Yes, who is this?" came the agitated reply.

"I'm sorry for calling at such a late hour. My name is Ahmed Muhammad Rachid Abdullah, and our daughters have been in school together. My daughter's name is Nawal."

"Ah, yes, yes," replied a shaken Magdy.

"Again, I'm sorry to disturb you, but I was wondering if you or your daughter perhaps had seen my Nawal tonight."

"Your daughter," he paused in reply, "why, no, no. We have not seen her. She used to come here to study, but I haven't seen her in weeks."

"Well, thank you. Again, I am sorry to have disturbed you. Good-bye."

"That's all right. Good-bye."

Ahmed put down the phone and shook his head at his friend with a disappointed look on his face. Professor Magdy put down the phone and yelled for his wife and daughter. "It's that Muslim girl, Nawal! She's the one! Come, come quickly!"

Chapter Forty

Marianne's terror continued throughout the night. By morning light, she laid huddled in a fetal position on the bed. Emad was taking a shower. Though it would have been the best opportunity to escape, Marianne had no strength in her to even move. She was sore and bruised and completely exhausted from the constant struggle. She prayed as she laid on the bed that he would simply get dressed and leave her alone.

Though her wish came true for him to dress and leave, unfortunately, it was not Emad's intention of completely leaving Marianne alone. Carrying his bag with him, he paid his bill at the front desk, but before leaving the hotel, he passed through the main restaurant. Spying his friend, Reda, standing by the breakfast bar, he placed his bag on a nearby chair and went over to speak to him.

"Good morning, Reda," he said, cheerfully, patting his friend on the back. "How are you today?"

"Emad," Reda replied, startled, "Good morning. Are you having your breakfast?"

"No, I've got a plane to catch. I just wanted to let you know something."

"What's that?"

"That precious Christian girl that I met at the wedding back in the Spring, remember her?"

"Uh, yeah, I guess so." Reda admitted hesitantly. "Why?"

"Well, remember you said that I could not have her? You even said you would do all you could to prevent me from seeing her?"

Reda stepped back from Emad and looked at him with new suspicion in his eyes. "What's this about Emad?"

"Just wanted to let you know that nobody could stop me from seeing her or from taking her—not even you."

"What are you saying, Emad?"

"What I'm saying, my friend, is that you will find that your filthy Christian flower has been plucked and tasted and found lacking. I wouldn't marry her in a million years—even if she became the best Muslim in the world!" A sinister smile came across his face.

Reda slung his plate of food on the bar and moved toward Emad to grab him by the shirt. "Emad, you bastard! What have you done? Where is she?"

"I did only what she wanted me to, brother. You'll find her in room 209. I'm sure she hasn't moved."

Though he should have punched Emad out and called the police, Reda's first reaction was in relation to Marianne. He pushed pass Emad and ran toward the door, calling over his shoulder for two of the other chaperones to come with him. In all the excitement, no one noticed that Emad calmly took a piece of bread from the buffet, walked to the door and picked up his bag, disappearing out the door of the hotel. He would be on the plane and back to Cairo before they had a chance to think of looking for him.

Finding the door unlocked, Reda and the others burst into room 209. Marianne could only raise her head slightly at the noise of their voices before she passed completely out. Reda hurried to cover her with the bed sheet as the other chaperone, Marcos, called the front desk and asked for a doctor. Reda sat next to Marianne, tears running down his cheeks.

"What have I done? What have I done?" he wailed.

Along with the doctor, Madame Cecile was called from her room, as she was the lone woman chaperone on the trip. She brought with her, Nadia, Marianne's roommate. Both gasped when they saw Marianne's condition, as the doctor was now examining her.

Walking back into the other room where the men were waiting, Madame Cecile asked Reda: "Who has done this?"

"It was a boy she met at a wedding back in the Spring. His name is Emad." He paused, before he could speak the next words. "He's Muslim."

"No!" both women exclaimed. "Why? How would our sweet Marianne ever get mixed up with a Muslim?"

As Reda now reflected on Emad's actions and words to him, he realized what had happened. "I remember the night he met her. We actually were friends from college. Emad rode in the same taxi with me that night. He was really impressed with Marianne and wanted me to help set him up again with her. When I refused, he got angry. Actually, I never saw him again after that night—until yesterday."

"What are you saying, Reda?" Marcos asked.

"What I think I'm saying is that Emad obviously wanted to prove to me that he could have a Christian girl if he wanted to, and that it's legal for him as a Muslim to take her. If I had known she had seen him again, I would of course have stopped it, but I had no clue. She must have been hiding the relationship, since her brother, Philippe never said anything about it."

They were talking as the doctor was finishing his examination. He came into the room and closed the bedroom door behind him. "Does this girl have any family here?"

"No, Doctor," replied Madame Cecile, "she was here with a church group. We are the chaperones, except for Nadia here, who was her roommate."

"Miss Nadia, please, if you don't mind, I would rather talk about this with the chaperones only." He looked at the girl, who looked on the verge of tears.

"It's all right, Nadia, please just go back to your room right now," Madame Cecile offered, patting her on the shoulders, "and please don't talk to anyone about this until we have had a chance to work things out."

"Yes, ma'am." The girl turned and left the room.

The doctor motioned for the group to sit in the available chairs. "Please sit down, we need to talk about this." Everyone obediently complied. "What church are you from?"

They looked at each other, before Reda answered, "St. Marcos Church, Heliopolis."

"Oh, a very good church," he replied, "I'm from St. Fatima's, nearby. My name is Doctor Hany Estaphanos."

A huge sigh of relief came upon each of the three chaperones. Their thoughts were almost visible as they realized they were dealing with a Christian doctor.

"Please, Doctor Hany," began Madame Cecile with more confidence now, "how is she?"

"Well, I'm afraid to say she has experienced extreme trauma of a sexual nature."

"She's been raped?" Reda verbalized what they were all thinking.

"Yes, that is the case," the doctor affirmed. "She also has some bruises on various parts of her body and is now suffering from exhaustion and shock due to the experience."

"Is there anything we can do?" asked Madame Cecile.

"In reality, there is nothing to give her. She needs some rest, and I would suggest moving her back to her original room. I assume this was the room of the perpetrator."

"Yes, that's correct," Reda offered.

"Of course, her parents would need to be notified. I'm sure they would want her returned home or will come and get her."

"Yes, yes," agreed Michael, the other male chaperone, "we will have to call them." The three looked at each other, trying to decide who might be the unfortunate one to take this grave duty.

"It's my responsibility," Reda spoke up, "I will call them."

"I will be glad to talk to them once you do, son," offered the doctor. "You can call them from my office in the lobby."

"Thank you, doctor."

"There are two other matters, however," the doctor continued, changing the subject.

"Yes?" Madame Cecile asked.

"She will need to have a pregnancy test within the week to see if she is pregnant as a result of the attack." There was silence in the room. "And, you need to decide if you are going to make a police report." The silence continued, but the eyes were busy studying the reactions of each other.

Marcos was the first to speak on the later issue, "Do you think it would do any good?"

"Do you not want to catch the perpetrator?" the doctor asked.

"He was Muslim, Doctor," Reda answered without any further comment.

"I see," Doctor Hany mused.

"Perhaps we can ask that question when we talk with the parents," suggested Michael.

"Good idea," Marcos agreed.

"Doctor, is it all right to move her to her room now?" Madame Cecile asked.

"Yes, I will call the porters to bring a small mattress to move her on."

As they stood to make these arrangements, Michael asked, "Reda, where is this guy? Can we get him?"

"No, I am sure he has already made his escape back to Cairo," Reda declared angrily. "Should we try to get him at the airport?"

"What, and make a scene—Christians going after a Muslim guy?" Marcos interjected. "We would be attacked in minutes."

"No, let's not get involved in that," Madame Cecile added, "We can leave that to the parents. We are going to have enough trouble ourselves—remember we're the ones who are supposed to be protecting the young people." This worrisome reality settled into everyone's minds for a moment as they remained silent.

The doctor spoke up: "Please, don't worry, I do not believe it is your fault."

"How can you say that, doctor?" asked Michael.

"Because, I can tell this was not the first penetration for the girl," he said matter-of-factly.

"What? She had known the guy before?" Madame Cecile responded in shock.

"Whether this guy or another," the doctor began, "she was not new to sexual intimacy."

Chapter Forty-One

Both houses were in an uproar, the Muslim one, still not knowing why or to where their daughter had gone; the Christian one, because they did now know the why, but were still unclear about the where. While Emir's family called his friends and acquaintances to see who might have information, Nawal's called the police. There was no other choice.

Calling the police had risks of its own. The family was already marked because of Rachid and his actions, and Abu Muhammad knew that they could turn this into a full security investigation. However, if he did not make a report, any actions of his daughter would reflect badly on the family and cause disgrace. It was better to report her missing and to show the community that they were innocent in relation to whatever their daughter might be doing.

Though she knew she should mention it to her parents, Eptisam was terrified of their reaction, and in reality, she knew nothing. All that she had been able to understand from Nawal was that she was leaving and making a new life for herself. What that meant, Eptisam had no idea, but she knew that her sister had changed in recent months. As she lay in the darkness of her room, listening to her parents arguing in the salon, she made a decision to keep quiet. There was no reason to bring problems on herself.

While Eptisam contemplated her role in the matter, Muhammad and Abdel-Karem were in their room trying to listen to their parents' conversation in order to know what was going to happen.

"He's calling the police," Abdel-Karem said, leaning with his ear against the door.

"He must be going to make a report," Muhammad whispered. "That makes sense, he did the same with Rachid."

"I can't believe this is happening," his brother groaned. "What could Nawal be doing?"

"The less we know, the better," Muhammad offered. "It's times like this when it's better to ignorant."

"You think Eptisam knows?"

"I hope for her sake, she doesn't say anything."

"How can you say that?" Abdel-Karem came over to his brother's bed.

"Because your father would beat her for not confessing earlier and then make her life miserable for even knowing." The harshness of this reality fell on them both, yet they knew it was true. "All we can do now is pray."

"Pray," Abdel-Karem questioned. "The call to prayer hasn't come yet. It's only 2 a.m."

"Oh, Abdel-Karem, can you be so dumb?" asked Muhammad with an indignant look on his face. "Do you think God cannot hear prayers at any other hour besides those of the regular prayer times?"

"Well, no, but why pray? God knows everything already."

"Yes, that's true, brother," Muhammad said, nodding his head, "but sometimes I think he would like to hear us ask him for something, like a father likes to hear his small son ask for help. It pleases him as much as the five regular, repetitive prayers. When we ask him for something, he knows we need him."

Abdel-Karem looked at his older brother, and at that moment Muhammad realized that he probably thought he was speaking nonsense. After all, what good Muslim would talk to God like a father—that was a blasphemous thought right there, if ever there was one. No, Muhammad knew that he probably should have kept quiet, but it had just slipped out.

"Let's try to get some sleep," Muhammad offered, trying to save face and get Abdel-Karem to forget the conversation.

"Yeah, you're right. I am sure we won't have any peace once the sun comes up." He moved to his bed and climbed in. "Good-night."

"Good-night, brother." Muhammad sighed inwardly as they now lay there in the darkness. He began to reflect on all that had been happening in his life. Since his decision to follow Christ only a few days back, everything had turned upside down. The only positive thing was that his mother wanted to read the Bible with him; otherwise, disaster was all around them. He then thought of Noura. What would she think of what was happening in his family? Would her father still allow her to marry him with such family problems? What if she did not like the idea of his following Christ? Would that end their relationship and future? He wanted to believe that Noura would have an open mind. Surely she would come to accept his decision.

"Gracious and Merciful God," Muhammad began praying in his heart, "please be with my family. You see all these problems with Rachid and now Nawal. Help my parents to make wise decisions and to not be worried. Keep Nawal safe, wherever she is, Lord, and help her to get in touch soon. Lord, you know that I want to marry Noura. Please don't let anything hinder her accepting me and becoming my wife. Show me how to talk to her about all these things. In the name of Jesus, I pray, Amen."

Um Muhammad was beside herself with worry about Nawal. She was glad that her husband had figured out the

Christian connection on his own. This kept her clear and from having to say anything about it. What she didn't understand was why Nancy's father had said they had not seen her. Was he covering up? She knew she would never know for sure, as she would have no access to the family, nor could she really call them up and accuse them of lying and hiding their daughter. No, she would have to leave it to God to bring her Nawal back. When the police knocked on the door, Abu Muhammad quickly urged his wife to go to her room; he and Mahmoud would handle the report by themselves. Um Muhammad was happy to be able to run down the hall to her room, collapse on her bed and have a good cry.

What no one in the family could have possibly known was that Nawal had left the country under a new identity. Tracing her would be impossible. If her identity papers were eventually found, it would be assumed that she had died and the body was missing. While they would write her off as dead, imagine their shock in years far away when their daughter would contact them to share the news of the birth of a grandchild.

Yet, this was the future, and the present was still in play. Muhammad and Abdel-Karem were again sent out once daylight came, to search the streets of the area for their sister. While he wandered the streets, Muhammad decided to go into the Midan al-Gamaa area and pick up a Bible. He knew the time perhaps was not right, but somehow he felt that if he could just read to his mother many of the comforting words of the Bible, she would find peace about Nawal.

"Peace be unto you," he said as he stepped over the threshold of the shop.

"And to you be peace," came the reply from a familiar voice.

"How are you today, Madame?" Muhammad asked, smiling.

"Oh, it's you!" she exclaimed, apparently pleased to see him. "How are you?"

"Praise God, I am fine," he answered. "I wanted to take the opportunity to thank you."

"Thank me?" she asked, "for what?"

"For showing me the way to eternal life."

"Praise be to Jesus!" came the happy response.

"Yes, praise his name." Muhammad began looking around to see if anyone was near the door or preparing to come in. "Madame, I would like to buy a Bible, please."

"A Bible?"

"Yes, it is for my mother," he replied, matter-of-factly.

"May I then offer you one as a gift for her?" She pulled a large book off of the shelf and placed it before him.

"That is very kind of you, Madame," Muhammad answered, "but I insist on paying. It will mean more to me if I did."

"Well, if you insist."

"I do."

Making the business transaction, Muhammad then left the shop with a now gift-wrapped Bible in his bag. He momentarily forgot that he was supposed to be looking for Nawal, and when he realized his mistake, he began again in earnest to look for her face up and down every street he passed. The more he walked, the closer he came to Dr. Samuel's office. He wished he had a cell phone to call the man before just barging in, but he felt certain that the doctor would understand. He walked around the block again, just to make sure that no one was following him, before entering the building and going up to the floor of the office. The reaction of the doctor was the confirmation that there had been no need to fear.

"Muhammad, my son, welcome!" came the warm greeting. "How did you know I had been thinking of you?"

"Our spirits must have been together?" Muhammad replied, stepping through the doorway, "How are you, doctor?"

"I am fine, fine. I'm so glad to see you. Come," he moved and motioned toward the office, "come into my office."

Sitting in the chair offered to him, Muhammad began, "Dr. Samuel, I'm so sorry I did not call before coming, but I really needed to talk to you."

"Don't worry about that, my son," the man replied kindly, "you are always welcome. What is it you want to talk about?"

"First of all, doctor, I must tell you that I am so grateful to you."

"For what, Muhammad?"

"For showing me the way to Jesus."

"I am grateful that he chose to use me in your life."

"I have such peace now, and I am certain of my decision to follow him."

"Praise God."

"Do you remember what you warned me about, Doctor, that day we met?" Muhammad asked.

"Would it be about Satanic attacks?"

"Exactly."

"They have come?"

"Like a pouring rain," Muhammad replied simply. "First of all, we learned one of my oldest brother's is in trouble with security. Then yesterday, my sister disappeared."

"Disappeared?" Dr. Samuel's face looked worried. "Why?"

"We don't know. It may have something to do with a Christian family she knows, but we have no proof."

"Well, it certainly does seem like there is definitely an attack on your family."

"But guess what, Doctor?"

"What is it, my son?"

"My mother wants to read the Bible with me!"

"Why, that's wonderful, Muhammad. Praise Jesus."

"Yes, and even with all the problems today, I just went and bought her one. I felt peace that maybe the Bible was exactly what my mother needs right now to calm down."

"Well, I'm sure that it can give comfort, that is without doubt, but you will still need to be cautious."

"Yes, I will. That is why I came to you. Please pray for my family, Dr. Samuel. Ask the Lord to give me wisdom in how to act. Also, please pray for my fiancée."

"Your fiancée?"

"Yes, I have been engaged for a few months only. Of course, Noura—that's her name, doesn't know anything about all that's been happening, good or bad, so pray that when she does find out she will still want to marry me."

Dr. Samuel, who was sitting in a chair opposite Muhammad, now leaned forward and put his hand on the young man's knee.

"Muhammad, my son," he began, "I want to tell you something. The Bible is very clear that we are not to be unequally yoked. Do you know what that means?"

"No."

"When a person marries, he joins with another not only physically and emotionally, but also spiritually. God instituted the act of marriage when he first joined Adam and Eve in the garden. Marriage is from him, but not all marriages are blessed by him. Those that are truly blessed and have an effect for the Kingdom are those that are between two believers in Christ. If I have a relationship with Christ but my wife does not, I cannot serve him as effectively as I could if we were both united in faith. Marriages between couples of different faiths are always stormy and difficult."

"Are you saying I should break my engagement with Noura?" Muhammad looked very worried.

"What I am saying is that you need to pray about this issue and ask the Lord what he wants you to do. It may mean breaking the engagement, or it may mean telling her about your change in life and seeing how she reacts. Whatever you decide, I am here for you."

Muhammad wanted to stay longer and talk about this new revelation. It seemed that following Jesus was going to be a lot harder than he realized at first. Now, however, was not the time for such a long discussion; he had a duty to perform for his father, so he must be on his way.

"I wish I could stay, Dr. Samuel," he said, rising from his seat, "but I really must go. I am supposed to be looking for my sister."

"I will be praying for you, my son," the doctor said, taking his hand as he rose to see him to the door. "May the Lord give you wisdom."

"Thank you, Doctor."

Muhammad walked out to the street, dazed not only by the brightness of the sun but by the words of Dr. Samuel: "You may need to break the engagement..." Still holding the Bible in his hand, he walked back toward his neighborhood, no longer certain that following Jesus was worth such a cost.

Chapter Forty-Two

Phardos had two beautiful days of prayer and reflection as the women went through a very simple routine of morning mass, followed by breakfast, exercise in the garden, prayers again and Bible study with the priest, lunch, and then leisurely afternoons of quiet activity and visiting, and a simple evening meal. During her personal time, she read passages that Ruth suggested to her, saying they would help her in understanding what she had been hearing. She began with the first few chapters of Genesis, reading for what seemed the first time the story of creation and the Fall of man. However, it was the passages from the New Testament that spoke to her the most, and she would many times find herself lost in reading long past the call to dinner.

Later that second evening, Phardos sat in her room, talking with Ruth about what she was discovering.

"Ruth, I cannot tell you how much God is showing me!" she exclaimed like a school girl.

"I am so pleased that you are discovering the richness of God's Word." Ruth smiled back at her friend.

"One of my favorites is this passage from Matthew," she began, pointing out to Ruth the verses found in the eleventh chapter. "Come to me, all you who are weary and burdened, and I will give you rest. Take my yoke upon you and learn from me, for I am gentle and humble in heart, and you will find rest for your souls. For my yoke is easy and my burden is light."

"That is a beautiful passage," agreed Ruth, "and one of my favorites too."

"In many ways, I feel like I have no reason to think of my life as heavy. I have a wonderful husband, two great kids, and a good job. Many people could not dream of such a good life. But somehow, I know that my heart is not right with God. I want the peace his Word speaks of. This picture of Jesus lifting the yoke makes me feel so much at ease, like I have to do nothing but allow him to lift the weight."

"That's exactly right," Ruth nodded. "He's just waiting for you to ask him to do it." She paused and allowed the silence to hang in the room. "Would you like to give him that load tonight?"

Phardos looked up at her friend, tears now running down her cheeks. "Yes, Ruth, yes," she nodded, "that's exactly what I want to do."

The next day passed as a dream for Phardos, as she savored the peace that came with her decision the night before to give her life completely to Jesus. She spent most of the afternoon with Ruth, talking about how to read the Bible for herself and have a quiet time with the Lord each day in order to grow stronger in her faith. As they packed their bags and headed to the bus for the ride home, they looked forward to talking even more before being forced to separate in Cairo.

Girgis picked her up late that night, as the bus stopped at the corner of the church property. He was greeted by a tired, but happy wife, and was inwardly pleased that he had insisted she go and that she had enjoyed herself as a result.

"There is so much to tell you, Girgis," Phardos said to her husband, as they sat in his car for the short ride home.

"I want to hear all about it, of course, my dear," he replied. "I'm glad you had a good time."

"Oh, Girgis, I cannot tell you what a wonderful time I had. I feel as if I have touched the face of God!"

"Is that so?" he mused, "Well, I hope it will not keep you from touching the face of your husband tonight?"

Phardos awoke from her reverie and smiled at her husband, "Oh, Girgis, you are terrible!" and she let out a laugh, one that he had not heard from her in years. "You know nothing could keep me from touching your sweet face." She let her fingers caress his cheek. "I've missed you."

"I've missed you too," he answered, smiling.

Alone in their home, Girgis and Phardos were able to relax and enjoy each other's company that night and sleep in the following morning. Girgis was in the kitchen, fixing himself a cup of Nescafe, when Phardos came into the room.

"I could have fixed that, my dear," she said, sleepily.

"I know, but you looked so beautiful and peaceful, that I did not want to disturb you," he replied. "Besides, I've gotten used to fending for myself this week."

"Well, I won't say that's not good for you," she smiled, sitting down at the kitchen table. "So, will you pour me one too?"

"Of course."

They sat at the table together, allowing their bodies and minds to awaken with the caffeine. Phardos was just beginning to tell Girgis about her trip when the phone rang.

"I'll get it," he said.

"Who could that be?" she wondered. "Oh, maybe it's one of the kids." She stood up to follow him to the phone in the other room.

"Yes, this is Mr. Girgis Philemon," she heard him saying into the receiver. "Yes, my daughter, Marianne...what? What's that you say?"

"What is it?" Phardos looked at him in alarm.

"No, no!" he screamed, "It's not possible! Oh, my God!!" He stopped to listen to the person talking to him. Phardos was beside herself with worry, pulling at his sleeve. He shrugged her off and made a sign for her to be quiet. "No, I cannot believe it. What? All right, I will talk with the doctor."

"Doctor?" Phardos, urged, "what is it Girgis?"

Agitated, he turned to his wife: "It's something with Marianne. Be quiet now, and let me hear what they are saying." He turned back to the phone.

"Yes, hello, Doctor. Yes, thank you. Oh my God! What's her condition? All right, good, thank you. Yes, we will come right away. Can I talk to Reda again please? Thank you, Doctor Hany." Phardos grew pale and sat on the couch as she watched her husband continue the conversation.

"Reda, how could this have happened? OK, OK, I'm sure you are not to blame. We want to come right away. Remind me of the hotel. Yes, I've got it. We will be there as soon as we can. Give me your number, Reda, please. Yes, OK, I've got it. Please, Reda, take care of my little girl." He hung up the phone and stood with his face to the wall. Phardos could not see it.

"Girgis, what is it? What's happened to Marianne?"

Turning to sit down slowly on the couch next to his wife, Phardos now saw that huge tears were running down her husband's face. "Oh, Phardos!" he exclaimed, sobbing, "our little girl has been raped!"

"No! No! God!" screamed Phardos, pulling at her hair. "How, how could this happen? Where were the chaperones? Is she all right?"

"She's all right, but of course in shock. I don't have all the details of course. I'm sure they are waiting to tell us face-to-face. What we need to do right now is get a flight down there. Please, Phardos, I know it's hard," he put his arm around her, "but you must go and pack a small bag for us. I will call the airline and get us a flight." When his wife did not move, he shook her slightly, "Please, Phardos. Go, pack a bag. Our daughter needs us."

All the joy, the peace, the euphoria of the last several days had been vaporized. Phardos rose in a blur, her eyes stinging with tears, and moved toward their bedroom. She took a small bag from the wardrobe and began filling it with assorted clothes and underwear, not really aware of what she was doing. After seeing it sufficiently full, she went to the bathroom to wash her face, though it was a useless effort as her tears kept falling. Girgis came back to the room, shortly thereafter and began dressing.

"I booked us a flight," he said in monotone. "They will deliver the tickets in 30 minutes. It leaves in two hours."

While they waited for the tickets, Girgis called his workers to tell them that the store would need to be closed for a few days, as he had an emergency. Phardos could tell that it took every ounce of energy in him to control his voice. He assured them he would call them in another day or so.

She did not remember the flight or the ride to the hotel. Phardos felt that all the life had been sucked out of her. It was only when Madame Cecile led her to Marianne's room that she suddenly snapped out of her shock to face the only daughter she had. Tears poured down everyone's face in the room. Madame Cecile quietly slipped outside the door.

"Oh, Marianne," Phardos exclaimed, "What has happened to you, my sweet girl?"

Marianne, who had now been resting for almost 8 hours, was overcome with remorse upon the sight of her parents. "Oh, Mama, Baba!" she exclaimed, "I am so sorry!" Tears rained down her face.

"No, my darling," her father said softly, coming to the other side of the bed to take her hand in his, "you have nothing to be sorry for."

"Yes, we're just happy to see that you are all right," her mother added.

Marianne was so emotional that she was not able to say any more to her parents. They hugged her and tried to comfort her as much as possible, but her tears just kept pouring out. Leaving Phardos at their daughter's side, Girgis left the room and went into the hallway. He found Reda, Marcos and Michael talking with Madame Cecile.

"How is she doing?" they all asked at once.

"She's very emotional, as can be expected," Girgis replied. "She hasn't been able to tell us anything yet. Can you tell me what you know?"

The chaperones looked at each other questioning who would be the brave one to speak up. Though the youngest, Reda felt the responsibility lay on him.

"Sir, I regret to inform you that the perpetrator was a young man your daughter met at a wedding some months ago."

"Wedding?" Girgis questioned. "So she knew the man?"

"Yes, Sir," Reda affirmed. "Unfortunately, I also know him. Actually, the night of the wedding, he, his name is Emad, asked me if I could get him to meet her again. He liked her very much, but I told him it was impossible and that I would actually do all I could to prevent him from seeing her."

"Why would you have said that, son?"

"Because he is Muslim." Reda said no more, knowing the news had to sink into the father's mind.

"Muslim!" exclaimed Girgis. "Tell me, no!"

"Yes, I'm sorry, Sir, but from what I am figuring out now is that Emad wanted to prove that he could have a Christian girl if he wanted, because he basically told me that this morning when I saw him at breakfast."

"You saw him? Did you not stop him?"

"We did not have the chance. My first instinct was to see if Marianne was all right, because he told me I would find her in his room. I was so afraid something even worse had happened to her, that I rushed up to the room, leaving Emad the chance to get out of town and fly back to Cairo. I'm sorry, Sir." Tears began to well up in his eyes as he looked at the distraught father.

Girgis leaned against the wall of the hallway, overcome with grief and emotion. As they were standing there in silence, Doctor Hany emerged from the elevator and came toward them. He was introduced to Girgis by Madame Cecile.

As Girgis learned from the doctor the extent of his daughter's injuries, he could no longer hold back the tears and lost all control. Doctor Hany tried to comfort him, and yet kept the conversation going as he reminded the man that there was more to be worried about.

"I hate to tell you this, Mr. Philemon, but you do realize there is a possibility that your daughter has become pregnant as a result of this attack?"

The tears stopped in an instant as Girgis looked up at the doctor in complete shock. Yes, his daughter had been raped, and yes, he knew what that meant, but that it might result in pregnancy never crossed his mind. All he knew was that his daughter had been soiled, spoiled for the future of a happy married life. Anger now took over where grief had dwelled.

"I will kill the bastard!" He declared, causing Madame Cecile to gasp and cover her mouth with her hand. "I must have justice!"

"Calm yourself, Mr. Philemon," the doctor said as he patted him gently on the shoulder. "If you want justice, you must let the authorities get it, not you. You know what could happen if you as a Christian try to take revenge on a Muslim boy. No, if you want to press charges, submit a report to the police. You have all the right to do that."

Girgis appeared to come to his senses as the doctor talked and he reflected on his advice. "Yeah, but what will the police actually do? Nothing. You know that; all of you know that. In reality, we have no recourse as Christians. They will think it's funny and just let the guy go free."

"If I may speak," Michael said with a cough. "While that may be true, things are not the same now in the country, Mr. Philemon. We have more avenues to prosecute Muslims now. Human rights groups can be called in and Coptic groups from the West. They will get the message out internationally, and then the government will be forced to act." The others nodded their heads in agreement.

"Yes, Mr. Philemon, if that is the way you wish to proceed, I will be glad to testify. It is your decision."

Girgis knew that he was in no condition to make any rational decision right now. He would think it over and talk with Phardos first. Now, he realized, the important thing was to make sure his daughter was all right and to get her home as soon as possible.

"I just want to take my daughter home." He said, weakly.

"Yes, of course," replied Doctor Hany. "She should be fine to travel at anytime, as she's been resting well."

"Our group was set to leave tomorrow," Madame Cecile offered.

"Yes, well, I may not want her to travel with all her friends watching her. Let me see if she might be willing to leave tonight."

"I will have the front desk call the airline and see if there are empty seats on the 10 p.m. flight," offered Doctor Hany. "You and your wife are free to stay with her in her room. We have moved her roommate into another one for her privacy."

"Thank you, Doctor."

Though, in many ways, he did not want to return to the room, Girgis forced himself to open the door and go back to his wife and child. Child, that's what she was. How could this have happened to his baby? "God," he cried out in his heart, "why have you let this happen?" He found Phardos and Marianne sitting together on the bed. Marianne was now sitting up and leaning on her mother's shoulder. He sat in a nearby chair and looked at them in silence.

It took a long time, as her tears and emotions kept hindering her ability to talk, but Marianne was eventually able to tell her parents the whole story of her affair with Emad. They listened with their mouths wide open, unable to even comprehend that their sweet Marianne could be capable of such deception. However, as she shared the details openly, Marianne, herself began to realize that she should have been more aware of Emad's own deceptions and not so gullible to his advances. As she finished, she cried out to both her parents, "I'm so, so sorry, Mama, Baba! I was so stupid, so wrong. I know God will curse me for this wrong! I deserve whatever punishment you give me."

Girgis looked at Phardos, tears streaming from his eyes, as his pain for his daughter was raw and real. "Oh, my dear, sweet daughter, how could we ever punish you? You have already received the punishment for your deeds. Would we presume to add to them?" He looked at his wife, who was nodding in agreement. "We will leave everything in God's hands. Now, we only want to get you home."

"Home," Phardos let the word come softly from her lips, "Yes, let's go home." She put her arms around Marianne and hugged her deeply.

Chapter Forty-Three

Ahmed knew that he needed to have someone at the house to watch over his wife. He was worried she might get herself worked up into a real state and have to go to the hospital. He preferred to keep things calm and not add to their already multiple troubles. Women were weak creatures, but it was his responsibility to make sure she did not suffer a breakdown. He decided to call her sister, Amal. After all, she was the one Fatma loved the most, and he knew he could trust her to keep her mouth shut. God forbid that her sister Myriam find out—then everyone in Cairo would know their problems.

By the time Muhammad walked in the house, his aunt had arrived. Though surprised to see her, he was in a sense relieved that there would be someone who could watch over his mother and keep the house running too. He greeted his father, who offered no new information on his sister, and then excused himself to check on his mother.

"How are you, Mother?" he said softly as he pushed open the door to her room.

"Praise God, my son," came the weak reply. "Muhammad, your aunt is here."

"Yes, I saw her. I'm glad she can be with you."

"It was kind of her to come."

Muhammad moved to his mother's bed and sat down beside her. "Can I get you anything, Mother?"

"No, my son, thank you."

"Mother, I have a surprise for you," he offered, looking behind him to make sure no one was at the door.

"Perhaps it is not the right time for surprises, Muhammad."

"No, Mother, this is something that will encourage and comfort you."

"What is it?"

"It is the Holy Bible," he replied. "Remember we talked about reading it together."

"Oh, Muhammad," she cried, her weak eyes pleading, "please don't let your father see it. With all that has happened, I cannot imagine what he might do."

"Don't worry, Mother," he patted her hand. "I won't let him see it. When we have a quiet moment together we can read it…not even today, but sometime. I know you will like it."

"Like what?" came the question from the doorway. Muhammad turned his head quickly. It was his Aunt Amal.

"Oh, nothing," came the non-thinking response from her nephew. He kissed his mother on the forehead and rose to leave the room.

"Amal," Um Muhammad spoke up, "would you mind getting me a cup of tea?"

"Of course not, my sister," came the reply. "I'll bring one right away." She turned and left the room.

"Thank you, Mother," Muhammad said as he kissed her once again.

"Be careful, my son."

"I will. Get some rest, now."

Muhammad returned to the salon to find his father talking with Mahmoud, who must have come to the house after his own return.

"Nothing," he was saying. "I can find no record of her traveling at the train station or airport. Perhaps she's just vanished in the city."

"Are there other avenues we can pursue?" His father asked, acknowledging Muhammad's presence and motioning for him to sit down.

"No, I'm afraid not." Mahmoud shook his head. "We've informed the police, so they will be on the watch for her. Otherwise, it will just depend on someone who knows her spotting her."

"That does not give us much hope."

"It is in the hands of God," his friend offered.

"Then we will leave it with him." Muhammad watched as his father's shoulders sank and he allowed the rest of his body to do the same into a nearby chair.

"Is there anything I can do, Father?" Muhammad asked with compassion.

"No, my son," his father replied. "The best thing you can do now is just go and open the shop so we don't lose any more business as a result of all this."

Though it was not what he would have preferred to hear, Muhammad rose obediently and went into the kitchen to fix himself a sandwich before leaving for the store. His aunt was standing by the sink, washing up the many dishes that had been piled up since the day before.

"Thank you for coming, Aunt," Muhammad said, as he stood by the refrigerator.

"I am glad I can help my sister," she responded. "I know she is beside herself with worry for Nawal."

"Yes, but we pray for God's peace," he said quickly as he stuck his head intently into the now open door of the appliance, pretending he was determined in his search for food.

"God's peace..." came the words from her mouth. "Yes, we all need that."

Muhammad stopped his search and turned toward his aunt, "Are you all right, Aunt?"

Amal caught herself and moved toward him, "Oh, yes, I'm fine, Praise God. Can I fix you something to eat, Muhammad?"

"Oh, that's all right. I can do it myself, thank you." He pulled some luncheon meat and cheese from the refrigerator and closed the door.

"I wish my boys would say such a thing," she smiled, relaxing.

"I am sure they are spoiled by your good cooking, Aunt." He took some bread and began composing his snack.

"Well, perhaps," she admitted, "but I have to say they are not willing to do anything on their own in the house. Oh, that I had more daughters!" she moaned.

"May the Lord grant you good daughters-in-law!" he smiled.

"May the Lord hear you and make it so!" she chimed.

Having fixed his small meal, Muhammad rolled up the sandwich and began walking to the door. "Take care of my mother, Aunt Amal," he called over his shoulder.

"You can be sure of that, Muhammad. Go in peace."

"And to you be peace."

Muhammad walked through the salon to leave the house and passed his father, who was sitting on the couch, lost in his thoughts.

"Good-bye, Father," he said, as he continued walking.

"Good-bye, my son," came the rote reply. "Oh, Muhammad," his father said, suddenly aware of his son's presence, "I will send Abdel-Karem to you once he gets home. It is better if the two of you are at the shop."

"Yes, Father. That's fine," Muhammad returned. "Don't worry about anything there. We will take care of it."

"You are a good son."

On these small words of encouragement, Muhammad left his home and began the walk to the shop. The weather was hot and unusually humid, but Muhammad did not notice. His thoughts were occupied in all that was happening in his family. Opening the store, Muhammad saw that repairs had piled up, so he got busy right away, forgetting his sandwich for several hours. When his brother finally walked in, Muhammad looked up from his work, sweat pouring from his brow.

"Where have you been?" he asked Abdel-Karem with irritation in his voice.

"I was out looking for Nawal."

"All this time?" Muhammad questioned sarcastically. "Give me a break, Abdel-Karem."

"Well, I was, most of it," he retorted.

"Don't you think it's time you stopped being a baby and take some responsibility for your life?"

"I am not a baby! I did what Father asked. Besides, I didn't think he would even open the store today, so get off my back!"

"All right," Muhammad responded, calming down, "come on, there are some deliveries to make. I've finished this pile over here. Can you take that tape player to Hagg Hassan? And go ahead and take this one too. It goes to the guy at the children's clothing store on the next corner."

"Yeah, all right. I'll take care of them." Abdel-Karem knew not to continue arguing but obey his older brother. He dutifully began checking the addresses and preparing to carry the items to their owners. "I'll be back," he said as he moved toward the door.

"Hey, will you pick me up a soda? I'm dying of thirst."

"Sure," Abdel-Karem replied. "Anything else?"

"No, thank you, little brother…Hey, look at me." Abdel-Karem took his hand from the door and turned to look at his brother. "Thanks for your help. Father says you are doing a great job here."

"Really?"

"Yeah."

"Well…thanks." As he turned again, Muhammad could just catch a sliver of a smile come across his brother's face. Pleased, he returned to his work. His stomach rumbled as the door closed. Realizing he had forgotten all about his sandwich, Muhammad stood up, stretched and pulled it from his bag. Leaning against the table to eat, his mind wondered to a subject that had troubled him earlier…Noura.

Why was it that Dr. Samuel had to ruin his day by talking about being unequally yoked? Good wives were so hard to find, would God really make him wait to find one that followed Jesus? In Islam, a man could marry anyone he wanted, though most women converted to their husband's religion. He began to think that the abundant life that Christ promised did not necessarily mean the easy life! He knew he was going to have to talk with Noura about this. In reality, he just needed to talk with her. It seemed like days since he had called her. She must be wondering if her fiancé had forgotten her or not. Maybe this was as good a time as any, since he was alone in the shop. He went to the shop phone and dialed her home number. A kind voice answered:

"Hallo."

"Peace be unto you."

"And to you be peace."

"Um Sayed, this is Muhammad, the son of Ahmed. How are you?"

"I am fine, my son, praise God. Your mother is well?"

"Yes, she is, praise God." Muhammad did not think it was the time to reveal the truth of the matter.

"Please give her my greetings."

"I will." Muhammad cleared his throat and asked, "Is Noura home?"

"Yes, she is."

"May I speak with her?"

"Of course. One moment please."

Muhammad waited patiently as he heard the woman put down the receiver and call for her daughter. He could faintly hear her sweet voice responding, and then the reality of it when she answered the phone. "Peace be unto you."

"And unto you be peace and all God's mercies and blessings," Muhammad rang out, suddenly thrilled to be talking to her again.

"How are you, Muhammad?" she asked, "I have not heard from you in days."

"Yes, please forgive me," he replied, honestly. "We had a family emergency, and I have not been free to call until today."

"Oh, I hope everything is all right," she replied, alarmed at the news.

"We pray to God it will all be fine soon, thank you."

"Is there anything I can do?" She was trying to get more information.

"I wish I could tell you everything, but you have to be patient and know I will when the time is right. No, there is nothing you can do, but lift our family to God. It is up to him to act now."

"Yes, yes, I will. Lord willing, all will soon be well."

"Noura," Muhammad wanted to change the subject. "I really want to see you. If I can get away in the next couple of days, can I come to your house and visit?"

"Of course, Muhammad," she replied, uncertain of why he was taking such a formal approach, "you are my fiancé now; you can come anytime you want. Do not feel you have to call for an appointment."

"Yes, I realize that, but am still not used to the idea, so please forgive me. I would not want to do anything that displeases you or your family."

"What could you ever do to displease us? My parents like you very much."

"And you?"

"And me."

"You are a blessing, Noura—truly the light of my day, as your name says."

"Thank you, Muhammad. That is very sweet."

"So, I will call you soon to tell you when I am coming, all right?"

"Yes, I will be waiting for your call."

"Good-bye."

"Good-bye," came the drawn out sweet reply.

Hanging up the receiver, Muhammad leaned on his hands at the desk. How could God deny me such an angel? Surely he wants her to follow Christ just like I have. He went back to work with confidence that God would open the way for the yoke of marriage to be perfectly even.

Chapter Forty-Four

Though there had been sunshine and warmth, Phardos felt as if that day had been only darkness and cold, from the moment they learned the tragic news till arriving at home with their broken and bruised daughter. She was selfishly relieved that they had arrived back during the wee hours of the morning, which prevented any of the neighbors from seeing Girgis carrying Marianne from the taxi to the building and up the elevator to their flat. They could now allow her to rest and recuperate in the privacy of her own room, far from the eyes of friends and family with wagging tongues. Of course, she was worried about the kids from the retreat group, but Reda and the other counselors assured her that only Nadia, her roommate knew, while the others thought she had just been taken ill and had to return early. She prayed it would remain with only the few.

Now lying by Girgis' side in bed, Phardos was exhausted, but unable to sleep. She could hear the soft snores of her husband, and was thankful he could rest. She knew he would want to open the store that day, and trusted he would be able to get several hours sleep. If only she could sleep herself. When it refused to come, she rose quietly from the bed and went into the living room. Suddenly aware of her emotional overload, tears began to pour from her eyes as she knelt down beside the couch, head in her hands.

"Lord, Lord," she cried out in a loud whisper, "Why have you let this happen? Why has Marianne, our sweet Marianne, been forced to go through such a trial? Are you so angry with her? Have we done something to displease you? Oh, Lord, take this stain from our hearts, from our family. If I can carry any of it for her, please Lord, give it to me, that her pain might become less."

At the moment she spoke those words, Phardos felt a presence in the room and words, she knew were from scripture, came to her in an almost audible sense.

"Who are you, my child, to carry the weight of her sin?" the kind, but stern voice spoke. "Are you capable of carrying such a burden?"

Phardos replied to what she appeared to be hearing, "I do not know, but maybe you can give me the strength to do it."

"No, my precious one, you cannot, and that is why my Son had to come. Did you not believe what you confessed, my child?"

Reminded of her decision to follow Christ the day before, Phardos was filled with remorse. "No, of course, Lord, I do believe!" she cried.

"Then you must give Marianne the chance to do the same, for it is only in Him that she will have peace and healing."

"Yes, yes, I will, but Lord," she paused, as if afraid to ask the question. "What if…what if she does not accept?"

"Then she cannot know forgiveness, mercy…eternal life."

"Lord," Phardos dared to ask another question…but she felt the presence leave. She knew it…he was gone. She remained on her knees, exhausted and spent. As the moments passed a verse came to her mind: "Come to me all you who are weary and heavy burdened, and I will give you rest." They were the words of Jesus that she and Ruth had discussed at the convent. She stood up and began to return to her room. Yes, God had meant for her to recall this, because it was in

Jesus carrying her load that she would be allowed to sleep, to really rest. She was not just resting...she was resting in him, in Christ's care for her, her daughter, husband and son. He was there to take all her worries, because he loved her and cared for her. With the comfort of these thoughts in her mind, she put her head on the pillow and slept till morning.

When she woke up, Phardos felt as is she had been asleep for ages. Then, realizing that she had a daughter who might need her, she quickly jumped out of the bed and went down the hall to Marianne's room. As she opened the door, Marianne rolled over in her bed and looked at her mother. Her eyes were wet from tears, but she managed a smile.

"Good morning, my princess," Phardos sang out, as she walked to her bedside.

"Hi, Mom," came the weak reply. "When did we get home? Did I really sleep through it?"

"You were so exhausted, my dear. Your father just laid you in your bed. I hope you slept well."

"I must have, because I don't remember it. I woke up about an hour ago, I think."

"Are you all right to stand up and walk around? You might like to take a shower."

"I'm sore, but I think I can manage," Marianne answered. "A shower is a good idea." She began slowly swinging her legs over the edge of the bed to sit up. Realizing that she was sorer than she anticipated, she sat for a moment, her mother just watching her. Tears again started to flow. "Mama, I'm so sorry!" she cried. "What have I done?"

Phardos rushed to Marianne's side and sat on the bed with her arms around her. "Oh, Marianne, it's all right. Yes, I know you feel terrible and regret all this, but that is actually a good thing."

Marianne looked at her mother through her wet eyes. "It is?"

"Yes, because you regret it that means you knew it was wrong. Isn't that true?"

"Yes, of course I know it was wrong. I just could not help myself and let it get way too much out of hand."

"Well, the beginning of forgiveness and healing come with the feeling of regret and remorse. If you weren't sorry for what happened, then God could never forgive you, but now you have a chance."

"God?" Marianne, spoke the word with sadness in her voice. "Do you think God would ever want to forgive me?"

"Oh, Marianne, my sweet girl," Phardos replied, hugging her tighter, "that is what God is all about, giving us what we do not deserve. That's grace. Forgiveness is part of that."

Though she wanted to go on, Phardos was afraid that it was too much for her daughter to take in in her weak state. "Why don't you take your shower, and we can talk about it more when you are feeling up to it?" She helped her daughter stand up and get to the bathroom, where she saw to it that she was steady enough on her feet to take care of her self. As she left Marianne, she rushed back to her bedroom and changed into a pair of slacks and a short-sleeved top. Girgis was still sleeping, so she tried hard not to wake him.

She went into the kitchen to fix some coffee and grabbed the phone. "I have to call Ruth," she kept telling herself, "she will know what to do." She dialed the number. When Ruth answered, Phardos tried to explain without going into details that her daughter had had a crisis but was now very close to being ready to accept Christ into her life. She begged Ruth to come over to help her talk with her and lead her in the prayer of salvation.

"You don't need me to come," Ruth said, matter-of-factly.

"No, no, I do. I don't know how to talk to her," Phardos' voice was full of panic.

"Phardos, there is no magic formula," her friend replied. "All you need to do is to see if she realizes she's a sinner, needs Christ for salvation, and is ready to turn her back on sin to begin a new life under his lordship. I think you can handle that."

"You are not going to help me?"

"No, I will help you." Ruth answered.

"Oh, wonderful, you'll come?"

"No, I'll pray."

"Thanks." Phardos was not encouraged.

"Phardos," Ruth's voice softened. "Just remember what you prayed and believed. The same will work for her. Besides, what a joy you will always have to know that you led your daughter to the Lord."

Phardos let this thought sink in. "All right, Ruth, I'll do it, but please don't stop praying for me until I call you back!"

"That I can do!" her friend laughed. "Call me as soon as you have news. I don't want to be burning up the prayer waves for nothing!"

"You know I will. Thanks. Bye."

"Bye, my dear."

Phardos sat in the kitchen and bowed her head in prayer.

"In the name of the Father, the Son, and the Holy Spirit, Amen. Lord, I lay my fears before you right now, even as the verse you gave me and are giving to Marianne. I am giving you my load right now, my fear in taking this step with Marianne. But you know, Lord that she needs you and she must know your forgiveness. Only then can she find peace after this horrible ordeal she's been through. So, help me, Lord Jesus, to share this good news with her that she will come to know you as Lord and Savior. For it's in your name I pray, Amen."

Phardos lifted her head, sighed with new contentment that the Lord would walk with her through this, and began drinking her coffee. She enjoyed the peaceful quiet of the house for about half an hour before she heard Marianne walking toward the room. When her daughter entered the kitchen, Phardos greeted her with a wide smile.

"How do you feel, my dear?" she asked the girl.

"It was very refreshing," replied Marianne, "thank you."

"Would you like a cup of coffee?" Phardos rose from her place at the table and went toward the stove.

"Yes, please." Marianne sat down. "Do we have any croissants, Mama? I realized I am starving."

"Oh, let me fix you an omelet instead, it will just take a minute."

"No, please don't. I really just want something simple."

"Well, let me see if I still have some in the freezer." Phardos said, walking to the refrigerator and opening the freezer door. She found two croissants and put them in the microwave to thaw. "I think I will join you. I'm quite hungry too."

As they ate their breakfast, an uneasy quiet hung between them. Marianne was working hard to control her emotions and was managing to keep the tears at bay, but her mind kept reviewing the events of the past several months with horrifying vividness. Phardos did not want to push her daughter, but she could see on her face some of the mental struggle she was experiencing.

"Marianne, my dear one," Phardos began hesitantly, "I want you to know that God loves you, just like your Father and I love you. It doesn't matter what you've done; that love will never change. The even harder thing it might take for you to accept is to love yourself."

The tears that were so close to the surface began to flow. "If I cannot forgive myself, Mama, how can God possibly forgive me?"

"Because he is the one who created us and his love is unconditional. And that's the whole reason he had to send his Son, Jesus, to die on the cross. Man was weak and could not overcome the urge to sin, but Jesus paid that price on the cross, allowing us a way to be free from sin's control. If you admit that you are a sinner, Marianne…"

"Oh, that is without a doubt," the girl interjected with ease.

"Then because you know that, all you have to do is believe that Jesus came to pay the price of your sin on the cross and accept that reality, that gift. Then you ask him to take control of your life—you agree that you will no longer seek to run things your way, but will obey his leadership. With that comes the guarantee of our faith, the Holy Spirit, who will help us to live lives pleasing to God." Phardos paused a minute and then continued, as she watched her daughter try to process all she was saying. "Do you know why I am telling you this, my dear?"

"Because you love me?" Marianne guessed.

"Well, that is one reason, but also because I want you to know that I made this same decision only two days ago, and I have never felt more at peace—even with, even with all that has happened, I know God has a reason for it and will help us through it."

Phardos stopped talking and looked at her beautiful daughter. No longer was she the vibrant, innocent high-schooler she had known just a few weeks ago. No, she was now a broken and prematurely experienced young woman, marked for life. Marianne stared open-mouthed at her mother, who had been saying things she would never have imagined her to say. Though she had always believed her mother to be faithful to the church, she never saw her as overly religious; she certainly didn't expect her to talk about being saved. These were not words that Orthodox Christians used. Maybe her mother had been brainwashed by Evangelicals. However, even though the source may have been questionable, in reality, Marianne knew the words were truth. They burned to the depths of her troubled soul.

"Mom, I don't know how or from where you learned all this," she began with the strength returning to her voice, "but I can tell it's real…that it's truth."

"Yes, my dear, it is," Phardos nodded back to her.

"If I wanted to do what you said you have done, how do I go about it?"

"That's the easy part," Phardos replied, perking up. "All you have to do is repeat a short prayer with me, confessing to God that you are sinner, that you believe his Son, Jesus, came to die for your sins, and that you want to follow him for the rest of your life. Would you like to do that?"

"That's it?" Marianne had expected much more than that. It wasn't very mysterious-sounding, like most Orthodox practices.

"Yes, I know it sounds too simple, but there is one thing."

Marianne thought: I knew it. "What is it?" she asked.

"You have to believe it in your heart."

"All right."

"All right?" Phardos could hardly believe her ears. "Well, then, OK, let's pray."

The mother-daughter team bowed their heads and held hands across the small kitchen table. As Phardos led her in prayer, Marianne repeated the simple words spoken. Tears were pouring down their faces, making it hard sometimes for Marianne to understand her mother or Phardos to hear her daughter, but in the end, the accomplished the task and sat in silence gripping tightly each other's hands. Phardos finally looked up, smiling at her daughter, who was managing to get a smile on her face as well, despite the tears. Letting go of her hands, Phardos rose up and went to hug Marianne, kissing her and laughing.

"Oh, Marianne," she cried, "I am so happy for you. Now you are not just my daughter, but my sister."

"Thank you, Mama," her daughter answered. "I love you."

"And I love you." She handed her a tissue to wipe her face. Marianne pulled another from the box to offer her mother. They laughed as they realized what kind of sight they must look.

Once they were able to get their emotions under control, Phardos said with confidence, "Marianne, now I can say that no matter what the days ahead may bring, the Lord will help both of us get through them. He will give us strength to keep going, to have hope for the future. Oh, my sweet daughter, I know this is not the end for you, though it may have seemed so; no, it is only the beginning. The chance to start again with a clean slate, for that is what Jesus has given you."

Marianne hugged her mother tightly. "You don't know how much that means to hear those words, Mama."

They stood there in silence, savoring the wonders of the moment, when suddenly Marianne cried out, "but what about Father and Philippe?!"

Chapter Forty-Five

Um Muhammad did not stay down long. Though she grieved over Nawal's disappearance, she was quickly made aware by her husband that there was really no more they could do, and she might as well consider her dead. This declaration was unfortunately made in front of her sister, Amal, who could not control herself and yelled at her brother-in-law in anger.

"How can you tell her that?! Can't you see it would break her heart? It's her daughter, her own flesh and blood!"

Ahmed withheld the urge to slap his wife's sister, but did not subdue his own angry response. "I am fully aware, Amal, that the girl is her daughter. Remember, she is mine as well, but what good will it do for us to keep grieving over her. It is God's will. She is gone. If he had wanted us to find her, we would. She is in God's hands now."

"I am not as confident as you are, Ahmed, that this is God's will. I think he gives us some choices in this life," she retorted, "but it is important that you allow her mother to grieve. It's natural and cleansing for the soul."

Ahmed had no intention of being lectured to by a woman. "Most women will spend their whole lives grieving and moaning if you let them. This is my house, and I have no intention of allowing my woman to mope around and become useless. She has work to do, as do I. Your time is finished here, Amal. Thank you for coming."

Amal knew there was no use in saying more. She looked at her sister, who had been sitting on the couch, silent as the argument took place before her. She felt bad now that she would be forced to leave quickly and not have a chance to be of real encouragement to her sister. Nodding to Abu Muhammad, she went to the bedroom that she had been sharing with Eptisam, to pack her things. She could hear Ahmed yelling commands at Fatma before declaring that he was going to the shop. She heard the door slam.

After quietly packing her belongings, Amal returned to the salon where Fatma had remained unmoved. She sat beside her sister.

"I'm sorry I got angry at your husband," she said softly, her head hanging.

"Oh, that's all right. I would not have dared to say it, but am glad you did."

"Well, I guess I should go. Can I do anything for you before I leave?"

"Do you think my Nawal has become Christian like that girl you told me about?"

The question stunned Amal, though she was in some ways glad Fatma had asked, for she knew it must be weighing heavy on her heart. "We may never know, Fatma," she replied. "But can I be bold enough to say, there could be worse things she could do."

"What does that mean?"

"Well, in my experience I have seen nothing that makes me think bad of Christians. Remember I said I knew a Muslim woman who had converted before?"

"Yes."

"Well, I can testify to the fact that before she changed religions, she was miserable, lazy, a liar and even sometimes known to steal. But after she converted, all that changed.

She worked harder than anyone else in the factory. She was happy, and the boss came to trust her even more than the rest of us. So, there must be something to it, that makes people act so good."

"Hum," Fatma mused. "It would be interesting to learn more about it. Remember what you said about studying Christianity just like I would study Islam?"

"Yes, I think it's important to know both religions."

"Well, can you believe that my son, Muhammad bought me a Bible to study with him?"

"Really?" Amal raised herself up on the couch in added interest.

"Now, you promise you won't tell anyone, Amal?" Fatma was suddenly worried that it might cause trouble for her son.

"No, no," she comforted. "Your secret's safe with me. Will you tell me what you find out? I have only read one of the books of the *Injil*; I have never been able to get a whole Bible. I'd like to know what it says."

"Do you want me to get Muhammad to get you one too?"

"No, no," Amal hastily assured her. "I would be too afraid Mustafa would find it. Just have me over every once in a while to visit, and we can talk about what you are learning. What do you think?"

"I will. Oh, Amal, I am going to miss you. Thank you for all you've done for me. I would not have made it without you." She hugged her sister warmly.

"It was my duty and pleasure. I am just happy you are getting better. Please let me know if you hear anything from Nawal."

"I will."

The two sisters parted company, and as Um Muhammad turned toward the salon again, she sighed. Though she would have preferred to return to the couch or go straight to bed, she knew she must press on and get back to work. Nawal never left her thoughts as she took up her wifely duties.

Muhammad was greatly relieved when his father entered the store by surprise that night. Thought Abdel-Karem had been there as long as he had, he quickly showed his father the work they had accomplished, sales made, and jobs pending before excusing himself for the evening. It all happened so fast that his little brother did not even have a chance to voice his objections. Muhammad saw his chance and took it.

The first place he went was the office of Dr. Samuel. It had been several days since he had seen the man, and he longed for a moment with him to pray and counsel. As he was entering the elevator of the building, he was surprised to see Dr. Samuel coming out.

"Oh, Muhammad, my son, how are you?" he exclaimed with a warm smile.

Muhammad stepped back from the door and allowed the man to exit the elevator. They stood in the lobby, talking. "I was just coming to see you."

"This is unexpected, but a very good opportunity. Are you free?"

"Well, as a matter of fact I am."

"Good," Dr. Samuel replied, looking around, self-consciously. "I want you to go with me somewhere special."

"Where?" Muhammad was curious.

"I'll tell you in the car."

"All right." He obediently followed the man to his car, parked nearby.

As they drove, Dr. Samuel explained to Muhammad that he was not the only Muslim that had made a decision to follow Jesus. There were actually thousands like him, and some of these meet together in small groups to pray, worship, and study God's Word. He shared that though he has contact with many of these groups, he only actually attended one of them regularly, and considers it his church. Muhammad knew what a church was—Cairo had hundreds of them, huge ornate buildings with large crosses on top.

"No, my son, I'm afraid that is not the kind of church I'm talking about," he said laughing. "We can say that's a church building perhaps, but the real church consists only of people who follow Christ as Lord and Savior. When they meet together on a regular basis and share certain actions, then we can consider them a church. It doesn't matter where they meet. In the Bible, we read that some met by the side of a river, others in homes, and some in open, public places. It was only after these early years that they began to build big buildings, but I'm afraid that with that, the true nature of the church life was affected."

"So who will be at this 'church'?" Muhammad asked.

"You'll see." He slowed the car and paralleled parked. "We need to walk a ways, but it's not far. I just prefer to be safe."

"I see." Muhammad said, as he followed the man, consciously looking around him as he did so.

They eventually reached a tall apartment building, which was obviously full of both private flats as well as a large number of offices. They took the elevator to the seventh floor. The floor held at least six flats, as Muhammad quickly glanced around. Dr. Samuel walked to the end of the hall and rang the bell for apartment six. A young man, with a moustache answered.

"Ah, Dr. Samuel, welcome," he said warmly. Muhammad followed the older man across the threshold as he was shaking hands with the host.

"Welcome to you as well," Dr. Samuel replied, "Salama, I would like you to meet my friend, Muhammad."

"Welcome, Muhammad," Salama said, as he shook his hands.

"I did not have a chance to tell you in advance that he was coming, but I am thrilled that he's with us," Dr. Samuel shared, making sure that others that Muhammad now noticed were sitting around the living room could hear. "He has recently given his life to Christ and is need of fellowship."

"Congratulations, Muhammad," Salama exclaimed, echoed by several other words of congratulations by various guests. "Please, come, let me introduce you." He took Muhammad by the arm, and began walking him around the room, giving the name of each person. Once introductions were made, Muhammad was encouraged to sit next to Dr. Samuel. The doorbell rang once more just afterwards, and Salama welcomed yet another person into the house. His name was Aatif. Muhammad had the sense that once Aatif arrived, the group was expecting something to happen. It was confirmed when Dr. Samuel quietly shared with Muhammad that Aatif was the leader of the group.

"Of course, we don't call him that, but in general he is the one who keeps things moving smoothly, though he is not always the one who shares from the Word." Muhammad had no idea what this meant, but worked hard to take it in. Everyone was talking among themselves until Aatif finally took his seat and began to speak.

"Brother Salama, will you please begin our time with a word of prayer?" Muhammad watched as everyone bowed their heads, though some held their hands up as he knew Muslims to do during their prayer time, palms toward heaven.

"Oh, Gracious and Merciful God, our Heavenly Father, we come to you today in wonder of who you are. You are strong and mighty, the Great I am, the Alpha and Omega, Faithful One, Loving and Compassionate, our Lord and our Redeemer. Thank you for your presence in our lives, for making yourself known to us. Thank you, most of all, for your Son, Jesus, who came and lived among us and gave himself for us, that we might have life eternal with you." As he prayed, several in the group were voicing *amens* or *in the name of Jesus,* in seeming agreement with the words Salama spoke.

" Oh, Lord, we are not worthy of your love for us, but we are so grateful for it, and want to ask you to strengthen us to live more and more like Jesus on this earth. Cleanse us of our sins, fill us with your Spirit, that we may be victorious day in and day out in a dark and dying world. Be pleased now, dear Lord, with the praises we offer you, for it's in the Name of Jesus, I pray, Amen."

Muhammad hesitantly lifted his eyes, as he realized others were doing so as well. He had been extremely moved by the prayer, having never heard something so personal and spontaneous offered to God, and by a Muslim no less. But he knew that this was no longer a Muslim, but a follower of Jesus, just like himself. Actually, he was shocked at the number of people, all former Muslims, who by sitting in this room, were showing their alliance with Christ. It was not a big group, 15 at the most, but it was certainly more than Muhammad had imagined where like him. And had Dr. Samuel not told him that there were many more? Amazing.

The group had begun singing, not loudly, but with joy on their faces. No instruments were used, obviously because of the fear of being heard by the neighbors, but their voices were pleasant, though not trained. One of the women, Salama had introduced her as Habiba, was taking the lead in beginning the songs and carrying the tune for the rest of the group. They were working hard to follow her lead, though it seemed to Muhammad that not all of them knew the song. He listened to the tune and tried to follow the words. It was catchy, and easy to sing along as they repeated the chorus.

My heart is happy, because I'm walking with Jesus.
Walking with Jesus, walking with Jesus.
My heart is happy, because I'm walking with Jesus.
Every day, I am walking with Jesus.

Hallelujah, I am walking with Jesus, walking with
Jesus, walking with Jesus.
Hallelujah, I am walking with Jesus,
Every day, I am walking with Jesus.

It seemed like a simple children's song, but it did not seem to bother the members of this group. Their joy was evident as they sang, and Muhammad could tell they would have loved to raise their voices to the roof if it did not mean possible retribution.

The next song was slower, but the words were powerful to Muhammad, and he listened hard in order to remember them for later.

I love you, Lord Jesus
I love you, Lord Jesus
There's no one for me but you.

I will follow you always
I will follow you without return
I praise your holy name
There's no one for me but you.

It was a love song, but not like any love songs Muhammad had ever heard. This was a love song to Jesus. What an amazing idea—singing love songs to God! Even singing to God was unheard of in Islam. What were these people doing? Yet, Muhammad felt the song inside himself longing to come out. He had never been much of a singer, he hummed along with popular Egyptian music like everyone else, but here, in this place, with this group of people, it was obvious that following Jesus meant singing praises to God. It wasn't worship of a slave before his master, but of a grateful heart before a loving father. This new joy meant a desire to sing!

Several other songs were sung before Aatif spoke up.

"Let's take some time in prayer, thanking God for his goodness toward us, and remembering those in need. If you have a request, instead of sharing it, just lift it in your prayers that we may all join you in asking the Heavenly Father to intervene and meet needs."

The group again took different postures for prayer, and Muhammad found himself bowing his head as he had known Dr. Samuel to do. What he heard next was something amazing. One at a time, various members of the group began praying. Though they praised God as Salama had done at the beginning, they now asked him for very personal needs. One woman asked for her mother to be healed from illness, and not just healed for healing's sake, but in order that she would recognize the power of Jesus and accept him. A young man asked for the Lord to provide him with a job, while another asked God to give him boldness as a witness with his family. Almost all of them prayed for lost family members.

Muhammad did not dare pray. He had no experience in making himself vulnerable before a group of strangers, though it did not seem to bother these people. As a Muslim, he would never let non-family members know that he needed a job, or there was sickness in his family, or any other kind of need. Needs made people look weak, and the society he knew was all about looking strong, keeping the upper hand, even if it meant that a person forfeited the chance for someone else to help. Yet, as he heard these other requests, in his heart he wished he had the courage to pray for Nawal, his mother, and his marriage to Noura. He was interrupted from these thoughts by the voice of Dr. Samuel, next to him.

"Heavenly Father, you are so amazing in your timing, and I want to thank you for your perfect timing in allowing our brother Muhammad to join us today. Bless him, Father, as he experiences church, the Body of Christ, for the first time. Teach him new things about yourself and strengthen him in his faith."

Amens were ringing in agreement, as the man prayed. This time continued for a short while longer before Aatif brought it to a close with one final prayer and an amen. Muhammad could not explain the emotions that were rising up in his heart after this very moving experience of prayer. Dr. Samuel must have sensed his feelings, for her reached over and grabbed the young man's hand and squeezed it. Muhammad managed a weak smile as he then let go. All eyes had now turned to Aatif as he began to speak.

"I want us to look today at a passage of Scripture and talk about something you may find strange—a movie. However, let's look at the Word first. Abdel-Rahman, will you please read from the book of John, chapter 12, verses 23-46? I want us to read this whole passage to see the situation, but we'll only talk about a few points. This is Jesus speaking shortly after his entrance into Jerusalem, when all the people were praising him, especially those who had seen him raise Lazarus from the dead." He nodded to Abdel-Rahman to read.

> Jesus replied, "The hour has come for the Son of Man to be glorified. I tell you the truth, unless a kernel of wheat falls to the ground and dies, it remains only a single seed. But if it dies, it produces many seeds. The man who loves his life will lose it, while the man who hates his life in this world will keep it for eternal life. Whoever serves me must follow me; and where I am, my servant also will be. My Father will honor the one who serves me.
>
> "Now my heart is troubled, and what shall I say? 'Father, save me from this hour'? No, it was for this very reason I came to this hour. Father, glorify your name!" Then a voice came from heaven, "I have glorified it, and will glorify it again." The crowd that was there and heard it said it had thundered; others said an angel had spoken to him.

Jesus said, "This voice was for your benefit, not mine. Now is the time for judgment on this world; now the prince of this world will be driven out. But I, when I am lifted up from the earth, will draw all men to myself." He said this to show the kind of death he was going to die.

The crowd spoke up, "We have heard from the Law that the Christ will remain forever, so how can you say, 'The Son of Man must be lifted up'? Who is this 'Son of Man'?"

Then Jesus told them, "You are going to have the light just a little while longer. Walk while you have the light, before darkness overtakes you. The man who walks in the dark does not know where he is going. Put your trust in the light while you have it, so that you may become sons of light." When he had finished speaking, Jesus left and hid himself from them.

Even after Jesus had done all these miraculous signs in their presence, they still would not believe in him. This was to fulfill the word of Isaiah the prophet:

"Lord, who has believed our message and to whom has the arm of the Lord been revealed?" For this reason they could not believe, because, as Isaiah says elsewhere: "He has blinded their eyes and deadened their hearts, so they can neither see with their eyes, nor understand with their hearts, nor turn-and I would heal them." Isaiah said this because he saw Jesus' glory and spoke about him.

Yet at the same time many even among the leaders believed in him. But because of the Pharisees they would not confess their faith for fear they would be put out of the synagogue; for they loved praise from men more than praise from God.

> Then Jesus cried out, "When a man believes in me, he does not believe in me only, but in the one who sent me. When he looks at me, he sees the one who sent me. I have come into the world as a light, so that no one who believes in me should stay in darkness.

"Yes, I know it is a long passage, but I want us to think about a few things," Aatif began. "Who has seen the movie, *Hassan and Morcos*?" he asked. Two or three in the group raised their hands. Muhammad had heard about this film, but had not seen it. He had little time for the cinema these days. "Though I'm sure most of you know, but just in case, it is a film about two men and their families. One man is a sheik, but moderate in his views. He is not liked by the fundamentalists, and after an assassination attempt is forced to go into hiding with the help of the security forces. The other man is an Orthodox priest, who, like the sheik, is more tolerant and moderate. Again, fundamentalists in his religion try to kill him, so he is also taken into hiding. Of course the funny thing in this film is that they are given fake identities behind which to hide as a family—the Muslim becomes a Christian while the Christian becomes a Muslim." There were several chuckles in the group.

Aatif continued, "In the process of this change, they both learn things about the other's religion, so we are able to see how each religious group views the other in an inoffensive way. By chance, these two families are put in apartments opposite one another, and of course, there is a love affair—the Christian (now Muslim) boy falls in love with the Muslim (now Christian) girl."

Muhammad's eyes widened as he processed this development. Though he had heard of the movie, he did not know the details. Of course, he knew that it would be impossible for the Christian boy to marry the Muslim girl. He eagerly awaited Aatif to tell them what happened.

"I wish I could tell you that this very good film gave us some solutions to the problems between Christians and Muslims today, but I cannot. As with most of our films, it ends abruptly without any solutions or even political statements. In reality, I was more depressed from watching it, though it was meant to be a comedy, for it shows the truth of our sad situation in Egypt. However," and he paused to take a breath and look at the group, "that is not why I brought up the film." Of course, now, he had everyone's attention.

"You know as well as I do that many of us struggle with being Christians in Muslim clothes." Several heads nodded at this statement. "We love the Lord, but struggle to freely exercise our faith in Christ. I mean, we can't even sing too loud or use instruments because we are afraid of being caught.

"As a result, some believers, and we've all known a few, choose to change their identities, becoming like Omar Sherif in this movie, "Christian" in the eyes of the community and before the government. I'm not going to talk about the legality of this issue today, because I want us to learn a spiritual truth. I want us to think about what it means to follow Jesus, really follow him.

"Jesus said, in the passage Abdel-Rahman read that the person who loves his life will lose it, while the man who hates his life in this world will keep it for eternal life. What does that mean? Does it mean I give up being "Muslim" in order to live for Christ? Is that the life he's talking about? Identity? I don't think so. If you remember in some of the letters of the Apostle Paul, he talks about being satisfied in the situation you find yourself when you come to faith in Christ. Remember some of the early Christians were slaves. He did not tell them to escape, to run from their masters. No, he said be a better slave, work harder, respect your master, and God will be glorified as a result.

"Some of us may feel that our Muslim identity is a kind of slavery, but I will tell you that any earthly identity is such. Look at the passage again that we read, see what it says about the Pharisees? Some of them actually believed in Jesus, but they were afraid to declare their belief, why? Because they loved praise from men more than praise from God. If we go back and think about the movie too, you will see that the Christian priest had just as much of a hard time as the Muslim did to try to live in a new identity. We have to remember that this movie is not showing us Christians who are true followers of Christ, who have an intimate relationship with him, but nominal Christianity. It can be as much of a slavery as our Muslim religion. I know of Orthodox Christians who have just as much persecution and struggles in living as believers in Christ as we do."

Of course, this remark brought a lot of shaking heads, but Aatif was not put off and continued, "Yes, my friends, whether we are Muslim, Orthodox, Buddhist, or Atheist, we are enslaved—enslaved to a life of man-made rules, traditions or values that keep us from God. Once we come to a saving faith in Jesus Christ, we begin to chaff against the former life, whatever it was. We are no longer at ease on this earth, but I want to tell you that we need to learn to be content where we are. No, I no longer am a practicing Muslim in the sense that I believe what I am doing, but I can still remain among my people in order to be a light for them. We are now sons and daughters of light, and Christ commands us to let that light shine. It's not a new "earthly identity" but a heavenly one that matters. It is my prayer that each of us will ask the Lord to give us wisdom and boldness to live for Him within our specific situations. Even our Lord came and lived among a stubborn and hard-hearted people, would we dare want to do less?"

Muhammad was so moved by the words Aatif spoke, and was even more encouraged because Aatif then asked for comments and questions. That opened a long discussion as most members of the group offered opinions and even other Scripture passages to back up what Aatif had shared. It was an amazing time of learning from one another. Muhammad could not imagine any lecturer in an Egyptian classroom allowing his students to comment on the talk! This was radical, but he liked it.

As the discussion drew to a close, Habiba was asked to lead in one more song before they prayed and dismissed. Of course, the end of the time together was not *the* end of the time together, for as they then stood and enjoyed some drinks and cookies, conversations continued around the room. When Dr. Samuel finally walked out with Muhammad, he asked him what he thought of the time.

"Amazing," was all Muhammad could reply.

Chapter Forty-Six

When Girgis woke up that day, he was immediately hit with the memory of the recent events, and rushed to Marianne's room to check on her condition. When he did not find her there, he looked further until he found her and her mother in the kitchen, sitting calmly at the table, their breakfast plates empty and looking up at him with smiles on their faces.

"Oh, Marianne, Phardos, I'm...I'm glad you're all right," he stuttered. "Ah, good morning."

"Good morning, Baba," Marianne said softly.

"Good morning, Girgis," Phardos echoed, rising from her place and kissing him gently on the cheek. "Can I get you some coffee?"

"Ah, yes, yes, of course," he replied, confused, looking at his daughter. "How are you feeling, Marianne?" he asked, touching his daughter on the shoulder.

"I will be all right, Baba," she replied. "Really, I will." Her eyes looked at him and began to well up with tears, but she kept putting on a brave smile.

"Girgis, come," Phardos called, motioning to the table, "join us while you drink your coffee. I can fix you some eggs. We've already eaten."

Girgis did not know what to make from the calm demeanor of his wife and daughter. Where they in denial of what had happened? Maybe they were just trying to block it all out. It made him nervous and unsure of how to react. "No, I need to take a shower and dress," he said, taking the cup from his wife and backing toward the door. "Excuse me, there is much to do today."

He left his wife and daughter wondering what was going on, but they rationalized that he was still distraught over the affair and not able to handle being with them as yet. Phardos encouraged Marianne to return to her room to rest, as she knew she was still in a very fragile state along with dealing with physical pain. Her daughter complied willingly after kissing her and thanking her again for making a new way known to her.

Phardos was very happy that it was still summer vacation and she did not have to go back to the school yet. This would allow her time to care for Marianne, though in reality, she only had two more weeks before she had to begin to ready the school for the new year. She was also glad that Philippe would be arriving home today. He had been away for over a week now at his conference on the north coast. The only problem was that he knew nothing of this crisis, and she prayed he would be able to take the news without exploding.

There would be an explosion of another kind, however, before Philippe managed to get home. It began when Girgis arrived at the house around 2 p.m. with a priest.

"Phardos!" he called out, as he led the priest to the salon to wait.

"Yes, Girgis," Phardos was saying loudly as she came into the front hall. She stopped short as she saw the priest. "Oh, forgive me," she stammered, "I didn't realize you had a guest with you."

"That's all right," Girgis offered. "My Dear, this is Father Philemon. Perhaps you remember him?"

"Ah, yes, of course, Good afternoon, My Father," she said, bending to kiss the priest's hand as he held it out to her.

"Blessings to you, my daughter," the priest declared, as his free hand raised slightly above her head in blessing.

"Can I get you some water, Father?" Phardos asked, knowing her duties.

"Yes, please," he replied. "Thank you."

Phardos retreated to the kitchen, her heart and mind racing as to the cause of the priest's visit. Of course it had to do with Marianne, but what must Girgis be thinking to have a priest come without telling her? She did not have time to think it over, but moved quickly back into the salon where the men waited. As she offered the priest the glass, her husband began speaking.

"Phardos, I asked Father Philemon here on behalf of Marianne. He knows the whole story now, and of course wants to pray with her once he hears her confession."

"Confession?"

"Yes, my daughter," the priest replied, "she cannot possibly expect forgiveness and reconciliation to the church without confessing her sins."

"Yes, Father," came the submissive response.

"Of course, we will need to discuss her rehabilitation as well," he began, "but once I have seen the girl."

"Yes, Father," Girgis replied. Phardos merely sat in shock, not sure what rehabilitation he could possibly mean. She knew the Church took severe action when girls were threatened by Muslim men, or had thoughts of converting. She had known of a family in Upper Egypt whose daughter was essentially kidnapped by the Church and put in hiding in a convent until all thoughts of conversion to Islam passed. But for Marianne, this was not the case. She had, in a sense, been saved by the horrible deeds of the boy, for now she had no desire whatsoever of leaving her Christian faith, and as of this morning, she actually had one to hold on to.

Girgis interrupted her thoughts, "Phardos, please," he was saying. "Go get Marianne."

"Oh, yes," she replied, standing quickly, "I'll be right back."

She hurried to Marianne's room and softly knocked on the door. At her daughter's response, she opened the door and entered the pastel-colored, neatly-kept room.

"I'm sorry to disturb you, sweetheart," she began, as she walked to the side of her bed and sat down.

Marianne pulled herself up to a sitting position and leaned back on her pillow. "That's all right, Mama," she replied. "Is someone here? I heard the door earlier."

"Yes, it was your father. He's brought a priest to see you, my dear."

"A priest? Why?" Marianne's eyes widened.

"You must have expected something like this to happen, Marianne," her mother said, trying to sound like she was not surprised herself. "It is expected in such cases for the priest to come and pray with the victim."

"Well, yeah, maybe," the girl replied weakly. "I just have not been completely alone with a priest before."

"You won't be alone, I'm sure," Phardos said, patting her hand. "Your father and I are here."

"Mother, I don't think he will hear a confession with you around." Marianne concluded logically.

As it had been several months since Phardos herself had actually gone to confession, she had to realize her daughter was probably right. "Yes, I suppose, but you don't have anything to be afraid of. Your father and I will be close by."

She helped her daughter get up and dressed in blue jeans and a t-shirt before going out to the salon. She grudgingly introduced Marianne to the priest.

"Father Philemon, this is our daughter, Marianne."

As Marianne, knelt to kiss his ring, he smiled and gave her a blessing. "Sit child," he commanded kindly, as she rose from her humbled position. "I am very grieved over what I hear, child," he said, casting a look of disappointment to the girl.

"Yes, Father," Marianne said softly, her head hanging.

"Look at me, child," he spoke up firmly, "so I can see your sincerity." Phardos bristled at the attitude she felt the priest was taking toward her daughter, but knew better than to speak. Marianne raised her head and kept her gaze on the priest.

"Now, you know there are consequences to your actions, child," he continued, "but we will discuss them with your parents after I have heard your confession." He looked at Girgis and Phardos, and without speaking they rose up and left the room, retreating to the kitchen.

Once on the other side of the door, Phardos could not help herself and quietly let her feelings be known to Girgis. "How could you, Girgis? Look at the way he is talking to her! I do not trust him." She moved toward the door to see if she could hear what he was saying to Marianne.

"Phardos, get away from the door!" Girgis commanded. "What did you expect me to do? Go to the police! You know I can't do that, so the church is the only solution. Besides, unless you want Marianne to be excommunicated, she has to make a confession and go through penitence."

"What more penitence do you want her to go through, Girgis?" Phardos replied, trying to keep her voice low. "She was raped, for God's sake! Does she really need to endure more suffering?"

"She has to know she did wrong, Phardos." Girgis felt like the argument was weak.

"Girgis." Phardos moved closer to her husband and took him by the hand, and led him to sit down at the kitchen table. "I had a long talk with Marianne this morning."

"You did?"

"Yes, and she confessed her sins before the only person she needs to—Jesus."

"What are you talking about?" Girgis looked confused.

"I'm talking about the real cleansing of her soul, my dear," she replied.

"Well, that is all good and well," he retorted, "but unless she confesses to a priest, she can forget being a part of the Church. Not only that, but we can be reprimanded as well."

"Girgis," Phardos tried to reason with him, "what is more important, our standing with the Church or her standing with God?" She looked him straight in the eyes for a response.

"The Church and God are one and the same, Phardos," came the reply. "If she is not right with the Church, then she cannot possibly be right with God."

Phardos was looking at her husband in disbelief. She knew she should have expected such a response, for this was what she believed as well until a few months ago, when she became increasingly disillusioned with the domineering role of the Church in the lives of her members. But now when it had a direct affect on their own daughter, she wanted to believe that Girgis would feel differently. He did not, and she needed to respond carefully. She remembered Ruth's words about bringing change from within the Church...maybe this was her opportunity, beginning with her own family.

"I do have to disagree with you, my dear, on this, but only on a point," she began slowly, trying to read the response in his eyes. "I will always believe that God is the highest authority in a person's life, for he is our Creator. We cannot say that about the Church. However, I do believe God uses the Church to confirm his will and vision for a person's life. So, if Marianne has to confess to the priest, that is fine, but she should not do it before having confessed to God first."

Girgis looked at his wife with a furrowed brow. "I don't know what happened to you at that convent, but you are definitely coming up with new opinions, my dear." He then smiled at her. "You know I have never been very religious,

Phardos, so I will leave this matter in your hands. I just want to see that Marianne is all right. She needs our protection."

She stretched her hand across the table and took her husband's, thankful that God had given her such a loving man. "You are a good man, Girgis, and I know you mean the best for Marianne. She is going to need both of us in the weeks and months to come," she paused, "but most of all, she will need the Lord. We just need to trust her into his hands."

They sat quietly for a moment, when they heard a commotion in the other room. Rushing to the door, Girgis opened it quickly as he and Phardos moved toward the salon.

"You have a very insolent daughter!" the priest exclaimed, as he saw them come into the room.

"What are you talking about?" Girgis asked in anger. "Our daughter has never been anything but respectful to authority!" He looked at Marianne, who had run toward her mother's side.

"He put his hand on my leg!" Tears began flowing, but she tried to keep her control.

The priest rose from his seat, and took a dominant stance, "She was distraught, and it was hard to hear her. I merely leaned over to be able to hear her confession and give her comfort."

"That was not a touch of comfort!" the girl shouted at him.

"Marianne, now," her father tried to calm her, "maybe you misunderstood Father Philemon."

"I am not a child, Baba," she retorted, "I know what he was doing. Please, Baba, let me go to my room."

"Take her to her room, Phardos," Girgis looked contritely at his wife, so sad that he had let his daughter go through more pain, and this time on his account.

As the women left the room, the priest continued his defense. "Whatever the girl implies, she is wrong, Girgis. She has yet to make a full confession or to pay penitence.

You can find others, if you like, but this matter needs to be settled. Until then, she is not to enter the Church." He picked up his small handbag, and moved toward the door.

"I will be talking to Father Andraos about this matter," Girgis assured him as he walked just behind the priest, to show him out. "I am very disappointed about this, Father. My daughter does not need more pain, and I was depending on you to bring her relief, not add to her troubles."

The priest turned to him sharply, and stared into his eyes. "Rest assured, my son, it is she who brings the troubles, not I. If you had not so quickly taken her side, but trusted your priest, she would have finished her confession and be on the way to forgiveness. As it is, she will have to suffer in her sin a while longer." He turned toward the door without waiting for Girgis to reply and left.

"Of all the nerve!" Girgis exclaimed...but to an empty room.

Chapter Forty-Seven

Muhammad was floating on air for several days following the service he attended. Though the circumstances had changed little in his house, he felt confident that the Lord would see his family through these trying times. He continued to go to work in the mornings and apartment hunt in the afternoons, sneaking time in between to read his Bible. He longed however, for two things—to see Noura and to read the Bible with his mother. The second wish came first.

Almost a week following Nawal's disappearance, he found himself alone in the house in the late afternoon. His father and Abdel-Karem had returned to the shop, and Eptisam was visiting her cousin for a week. Unknown to him, Um Muhammad had arranged this visit in order to allow Eptisam to feel better about her sister's disappearance, for she knew she missed her terribly. Her sister, Amal, had graciously offered for her to stay with them for a week, saying that her daughter, Ranya, would love the company. So when Muhammad woke from his afternoon nap, he realized it was just he and his mother in the flat. He pulled the still-wrapped Bible from his drawer and went to see his mother, who was sitting in the salon, crocheting.

"Hi, Mama," he began as he entered the room, "that's a lovely piece you are working on." She looked up at him as he touched the fine lace doily and stretched it out to see the design.

"Thank you, son," she replied, smiling. "I am making it for your grandmother."

"She will like it, I'm sure."

"I hope so. Are you going out to look for apartments?"

"No, I wanted to sit with you for a while first, if that's all right."

"Of course, come, sit down." She patted the couch beside her.

"Here is what I promised you, Mama," he handed her the package.

"Oh, Muhammad," she replied, rubbing her hands over the wrapping. "You did not have to do this."

"I wanted to, Mama." he smiled. "Open it."

She carefully pulled off the paper and took in her hands the strong, handsomely bound book. She lifted it to her mouth, kissed it and touched her forehead. "God be praised," she said. "Thank you, son."

Muhammad was so anxious to show her what the book contained, that he began immediately explaining to her the divisions in the book, the difference between the Old and New Testaments, and how the book was set up. He showed her the table of contents, which would enable her to find a certain book more easily. But then he told her with enthusiasm about a beautiful passage he had recently read.

"Mama, I know your heart is troubled for Nawal as well as Rachid." Tears started to well in her eyes. "It's all right, Mama," he assured her, "God knows a mother's heart and gave us words of comfort. Listen to this from the book of the Prophet Isaiah.

> Comfort, comfort my people, says your God. Speak tenderly to Jerusalem, and proclaim to her that her hard service has been completed, that her sin has

been paid for, that she has received from the LORD's hand double for all her sins.

A voice of one calling: "In the desert prepare the way for the LORD; make straight in the wilderness a highway for our God. Every valley shall be raised up, every mountain and hill made low; the rough ground shall become level, the rugged places a plain. And the glory of the LORD will be revealed, and all mankind together will see it. For the mouth of the LORD has spoken." A voice says, "Cry out." And I said, "What shall I cry?" "All men are like grass, and all their glory is like the flowers of the field. The grass withers and the flowers fall, because the breath of the LORD blows on them. Surely the people are grass. The grass withers and the flowers fall, but the word of our God stands forever."

You who bring good tidings to Zion, go up on a high mountain. You who bring good tidings to Jerusalem, lift up your voice with a shout, lift it up, do not be afraid; say to the towns of Judah, "Here is your God!" See, the Sovereign LORD comes with power, and his arm rules for him. See, his reward is with him, and his recompense accompanies him. He tends his flock like a shepherd: He gathers the lambs in his arms and carries them close to his heart; he gently leads those that have young.

Who has measured the waters in the hollow of his hand, or with the breadth of his hand marked off the heavens? Who has held the dust of the earth in a basket, or weighed the mountains on the scales and the hills in a balance? Who has understood the mind of the LORD, or instructed him as his counselor? Whom did the LORD consult to enlighten him, and who taught him the right way? Who was it that taught him knowledge or showed him the path of understanding?

Surely the nations are like a drop in a bucket; they are regarded as dust on the scales; he weighs the islands as though they were fine dust. Lebanon is not sufficient for altar fires, nor its animals enough for burnt offerings. Before him all the nations are as nothing; they are regarded by him as worthless and less than nothing.

To whom, then, will you compare God? What image will you compare him to? As for an idol, a craftsman casts it, and a goldsmith overlays it with gold and fashions silver chains for it. A man too poor to present such an offering selects wood that will not rot. He looks for a skilled craftsman to set up an idol that will not topple.

Do you not know? Have you not heard? Has it not been told you from the beginning? Have you not understood since the earth was founded? He sits enthroned above the circle of the earth, and its people are like grasshoppers. He stretches out the heavens like a canopy, and spreads them out like a tent to live in. He brings princes to naught and reduces the rulers of this world to nothing. No sooner are they planted, no sooner are they sown, no sooner do they take root in the ground, than he blows on them and they wither, and a whirlwind sweeps them away like chaff.

"To whom will you compare me? Or who is my equal?" says the Holy One. Lift your eyes and look to the heavens: Who created all these? He who brings out the starry host one by one, and calls them each by name. Because of his great power and mighty strength, not one of them is missing. Why do you say, O Jacob, and complain, O Israel, "My way is hidden from the LORD; my cause is disregarded by

> my God"? Do you not know? Have you not heard? The LORD is the everlasting God, the Creator of the ends of the earth. He will not grow tired or weary, and his understanding no one can fathom. He gives strength to the weary and increases the power of the weak. Even youths grow tired and weary, and young men stumble and fall; but those who hope in the LORD will renew their strength. They will soar on wings like eagles; they will run and not grow weary, they will walk and not be faint.

Um Muhammad had closed her eyes while listening to her son read, longing to visualize the words, which were already so descriptive—smooth valleys, withering grass, the hand of God, a handmade idol, and a youthful runner. All these were amazing illustrations of God's power and care. Care, yes, that's what she felt, from the first word of comfort to the final promise of renewed strength. She looked up at Muhammad and smiled.

"Beautiful, my son, beautiful."

"This book is full of such words, Mother," he declared. "I wish I could sit and read to you all afternoon."

As she agreed with him, he told her of another passage, and put the bookmark there for her to read later—Psalm 23. Muhammad told her of how the Lord touched his own heart with this passage of the Good Shepherd. But he wanted to read just a couple of verses before he had to leave, then they could talk about them another day. "Oh, Mother, listen to these words of the Lord Jesus Christ," he urged as he read to her from the book of Matthew.

> Come to me, all you who are weary and burdened, and I will give you rest. Take my yoke upon you and learn from me, for I am gentle and humble in heart,

> and you will find rest for your souls. For my yoke is easy and my burden is light.

Tears started to well up in her eyes, as she felt the desire for rest rise inside her. Muhammad sensing her emotions were raw, touched her hand as he finished.

"Mother, I know these days have been very hard for you, but I believe that you can find rest in Jesus the Christ. Take this book, read it, and then we can talk. Don't worry about anyone knowing. It will be between you and me, for you see, Mother, I have found that rest in him."

She looked up at her son, in awe of the overwhelming peace that was evident in his face. "Thank you, my son," was all she could say. She leaned forward and took his head in her hands and kissed his forehead. "You are a good son."

Muhammad had never experienced such a close moment with his mother. Yes, she had cared for him, fed him, met his every need, but all that was seen as her duty, by him and her. Now, however, he felt love, love for which he had longed to know from his parents his entire life. He was deeply touched. He leaned down and kissed her hand, tears now dripping from his face. With both of them in such a state, his mother wiped his tears with her hand and said, "Go, Muhammad, you will be late in looking for a flat. Go."

He took this as the right opportunity to leave. He rose and went first to the bathroom to wash his face, and then, after freshening up, left the house to face new challenges ahead.

Though rejoicing over the amazing time with his mother, Muhammad knew that he really needed to see Noura. He missed her, for one thing, as he had had precious few chances to visit with her since their engagement, and he knew she must know the truth about him before continuing this commitment toward marriage. Though he talked to her on the phone, he had never gone into details about recent events. She knew that a family crisis had occurred, and Muhammad wanted to talk to her to tell her that he had nothing to hide. It would be a new approach for the typical Muslim fiancé, for family secrets where never revealed prior to marriage and sometimes, not even afterwards. Muhammad did not want to be secretive, however, but brutally honest, no matter the cost.

He arranged to visit Noura the following evening, and began the long journey across town just after finishing his shift at the store. Her mother welcomed him at the door, "Peace be unto you, Muhammad, welcome, come in." She showed him through the door. "It has been a long time since we've seen you, my son. I trust all is well with you and your family."

"Yes, it has been a long time, Um Sayed. We have been busy at the shop, and I have used my extra time in looking for an apartment."

His future mother-in-law was very pleased with this response. "That is quite all right, my son, please sit down." She pointed toward the salon area, "Noura will be right with you. What can I get you to drink?"

"Please do not trouble yourself," he replied courteously.

"No, you must drink something."

"Well, if you insist, I would like some water."

"Just water?"

"Yes, that will be more than enough." He sat in a large arm chair as Um Sayed left to get him not only water, but a soft drink and a plate of sweets.

Muhammad sat quietly, trying to catch his breath from the hot, bothersome ride across town. Noura really did live too far away for his taste, and in the heat of summer, it made coming just that much more taxing. When she walked into the room shortly thereafter, however, all that effort seemed to go out the window. She came in with a shy smile on her face, her head covered in a stylish veil of two layers, the first of which was a dark green and the second of a sheer slightly ornate green, which matched well with the first as well as her long-sleeved linen shirt. Instead of a skirt, she wore loose fitting wide-legged pants. She was modern, modest and attractive all in one shot. Muhammad could not help but smile back.

Before either had a chance to speak, Um Sayed entered the room with a tray of drinks and refreshments to feed and army. "Here is a little something for you both," she declared, as she sat the tray down on the coffee table. "Help yourselves."

"Thank you, Mother," Noura said, as she watched her mother just as rapidly return to the kitchen without another word.

"Yes, thank...you..." Muhammad tried, but realized that she was already gone. "Your mother is very kind...and sensitive," he said to Noura, as she sat down on the nearby couch.

"She likes you." Noura offered him a glass of water, which he took, just slightly touching her hand as he did so.

"That is good to hear," he replied. "I hope she will always do so."

"What is that supposed to mean?" his fiancée questioned.

"Noura, there has been so much going on lately, and I wanted to come earlier and talk to you."

"Yes?" her brow furrowed.

"Do you remember that you told me that the most important thing you wanted in a husband was kindness?" he asked.

"Yes, that's right."

"Well, I believe that with kindness comes honesty, for in honesty, I am showing that I care for you and am being kind by not leaving you in the dark on any aspect of our life together."

"What are you trying to say, Muhammad?"

"Something has changed in my life, Noura, something that I think will make me an even better husband to you. But

I need to know from you that you will hear me out, and let me share everything. Can you do that?"

"I think so," she replied, slightly unsure of herself.

"Several months ago, before I met you, I met a man on a bus. He started me on a path toward a greater knowledge and understanding of the teachings of *'Isa* the Messiah. I learned more about him as I read from the *Injil*."

"The *Injil*?" she questioned.

"Yes, the book of his teachings that is found in the Holy Bible of the Christians." He could see her eyes getting round with fear, but he pressed on. "Anyway, in that book, I was so touched by how Jesus taught his followers to live and to have a relationship with God. I have always been a moderately good Muslim, but I have never been a satisfied Muslim. Something always seemed to be lacking in the practice or essentials of our faith. I found the answer in the *Injil*—abundant life."

Muhammad went on to tell a stunned Noura about his journey from seeker to believer, including how the Lord helped him in finding her as a wife. He even went as far as to tell her about the house group that he had recently met with, and how he learned that he was not the only follower of Jesus from a Muslim background in the city, but just one of many. He then told her of what he had been learning and understanding about unity in marriage, that it was essential for two people to be united, not only intellectually and emotionally, but spiritually as well.

"Noura," he began as he tried to finish his detailed report, "I am not asking you to make any kind of judgment right now. I know I have just thrown you into a lot of confusion about me, and maybe you are even angry with me. That's all right. What I want you to promise me is this: think about what I've said and even take time to ask God about it in the quietness of your room. I am confident that he will show you whether what I am saying is right or wrong. Know this. I want you to know Jesus; I want you to marry me, but I only want you to make the decision if you think it's right. And if you don't, I will understand that too, and allow you to break the engagement. However, I have to say this. Please do not tell your parents or mine about this. There are other things happening in our family right now, and I do not want to upset them. You need to know that my brother, Rachid, has left the country, following a radical sheik, and my sister, Nawal, disappeared last week. We still don't know why. As you can imagine, both have upset my parents very much, so I do not want to make things worse right now, but I will tell them...in the right time." He stopped talking and sat back in the chair, looking at her, trying to read her thoughts.

After a few minutes of silence, she spoke, "Well, when you want to be honest, you are honest." He shrugged at her remarks and made a weak smile. "I don't know whether to beat you and throw you out of the house forever, or just say, all right, if that's how you feel, then fine. I'm not sure how kind are you being to me by telling me the truth, though, Muhammad. Do you not realize what this means, could mean for us?"

"I do."

"Well, I don't know if I can pay that price. You will have to give me some time."

"I was expecting to do that," he said quietly.

Noura suddenly stood up. "Thank you for coming. I know it was a long way," she said matter-of-factly, making clear her indication that the visit was over.

"Thank you for listening, Noura," Muhammad said as he stood. "Can I call you soon?"

"Give me some time."

"I will, but how will I know when to call?" his heart began to ache.

"Your God will show you, right?" She tested him with her sarcasm.

"Yes, I'm sure he will," Muhammad did not want her to see him lack in confidence at such a challenge, but rose to the occasion and boldly put his trust in God. "I will be praying for you, Noura," he said, moving toward the door.

"I will need it. Good-bye, Muhammad."

As he passed her to go through the door, he put his hand out and touched hers. "I know God will show you what's right. He knows how much it means to me for you to trust what I've said." He smiled, and she dropped her eyes, as the electricity between them rose. The door closed between them.

Chapter Forty-Eight

When Philippe arrived home that evening, oblivious to the recent events. His father was the first to greet him as he came in the door.

"Ah, Philippe, my son," he said, greeting him with a kiss on the cheeks, "praise the Lord for your safe return. You should have called me, I could have picked you up from the church."

"Thank you, Baba," Philippe answered, "but it wasn't necessary; a friend dropped me off."

Phardos heard the voices, and came into the foyer, "Welcome home, my dear," she called, as she came forward to hug and kiss her son. "I'm so glad you are safely home."

"How are you, Mama?" Philippe asked. "You look tired."

"I'm fine, I'm fine," she brushed him off, "but how was your week? Did you have a good time?"

Philippe put his bags down and walked with his parents into the salon. "It was fine. There was a very good speaker, and the weather was great. I had fun."

"That's wonderful," his father responded, though looking at his wife with a questioning glance.

"What is it?" Philippe caught the look between them.

"It's nothing, my dear," his mother replied, "why don't you go and take a shower. We can talk once you've changed. I know you're tired."

"No, I'm not that tired, it's still early. What is going on? I want to know."

Phardos looked at her husband. He was tired. It had been a trying day, and he feared the worse in telling his son. Yet, it had to be done. He began speaking as Phardos nodded her head at him to share the story. Philippe sat in shock as he listened to his father, with the help of his mother, gradually reveal the events in regard to Marianne. He remembered back to the night of the wedding, recalling how Marianne wanted to leave so suddenly. It never registered to him at the time that something had happened. He blamed himself for not being more aware and protective of his sister.

"You cannot possibly blame yourself, my dear," his mother comforted.

"Yes, how could you have known, if she did not tell you?" his father agreed.

"Well, I should have seen it happening at least!"

"It does no good for you to do this, Philippe," Girgis ordered. "If anyone is to blame, it's me."

His son and wife looked at him blankly. "You? But why?" they asked together.

"Because I am her father, I should have never let her go to the wedding in the first place. I knew she was much too young for such an environment."

"Who is closer to her than her mother?" Phardos insisted. "She tells me everything. I knew something was not right during the last weeks of the school term, but I did not push to know. I was busy. I should have spent more time with her."

"It is no one's fault but my own," came a quiet, but firm voice. They all turned to see Marianne standing in the doorway dressed in her bathrobe. Phardos rushed over to hug her and lead her to the couch.

"No, no, my dear," she comforted, "how could you have known that boy was so evil?" Philippe looked at his sister, obvious pain coming over his face at the sight of her as he thought about what happened.

"Mother, whether the boy was evil or not is not my concern. I was responsible for my actions. He never pushed me until the final day. Before then, I willingly met him and continued the relationship. I allowed my hatred of studies and desire for escape to lead me to follow my emotions—even if they were wrong ones." She looked at each one of them in the eyes in turn. "Now, I don't want to ever hear of you blaming yourselves again. I did wrong and I will pay the price. The only thing I ask of each of you is to forgive me. I have asked God to, and I'm trusting that you will find it in your hearts to as well." Tears started flowing profusely.

"Oh, Marianne," her mother began, "you know we forgive you." She hugged her daughter.

"I need to hear it from Father and Philippe too." She turned her pleading eyes to the men in her life.

Girgis' face was awash with tears. "Oh, my darling daughter," he cried, "you know I forgive you. I just wish you would forgive me. I'm so sorry I had that priest come today. He just made things worse."

"It's all right, Baba," Marianne replied, "I know you meant well, really."

Marianne now looked at her brother. He was so distraught and full of conflicting emotions as he processed not only this scene but all that had happened to his sister. He pulled several tissues from the box on the table and blew his nose. He felt as if Marianne's gaze would bore a hole through him.

"What can I say?" he said, looking up into her eyes. "The guy hurt my little sister. You know I don't blame you, Marianne. I could never hold you responsible."

"But Philippe, don't you see?" she asked. "Whether you hold me responsible or not is not the issue. I have done something to disgrace our family, and I need to know you will forgive me for that." Phardos could be heard weeping deeply at this thought.

"No one is perfect, Marianne." Philippe replied. "In fact, this will make us a stronger family, not weaker, because people will see that we love each other despite problems and we have come together to work through it."

Girgis looked at his son in wonder. "Son, that is a beautiful thought. May the good Lord give us the ability to see it through."

"Jesus will help us," Phardos chimed in, wiping her face. She blew her nose loudly. Everyone laughed in relief. "Sorry," she said, sheepishly, "I have a request."

"Yes, my dear," Girgis replied.

"If we are going to overcome all the obstacles before us, like gossip of those around us, Marianne's physical and emotional healing, and how to handle this with the priests, then I would like us to come to Jesus in prayer as a family. Only with him and the Holy Spirit's help can we make it."

"Ah, yes, dear," Girgis replied hesitantly, "that's a wonderful idea." Girgis had never prayed a spontaneous prayer in his life, and he was unsure of how to do so now. His family knew this made him uncomfortable, and they wanted to help. Philippe spoke up.

"May I pray, Baba? That is, unless you want to?"

Relieved, Girgis answered, "No, that would be great, son, please go ahead."

They bowed their heads, and Philippe led them in a prayer, remembering the things he'd learned from Steven and Dr. Raouf.

"In the name of the Father, and of the Son, and of the Holy Spirit. Amen. I want to thank you, Heavenly Father, that my sister is all right. Thank you for protecting her and keeping her from more harm. Heal her, dear Lord, in Jesus' name, that she will once again be strong and healthy and ready to face a great life ahead." He cleared his throat and continued, "We come to you, dear Lord...we come to you as a family, because we need you to give us wisdom and grace during these difficult days. Maybe people will talk or the church will take a stand. We don't know what lies ahead, but we are trusting that you know all things and will help us to face whatever comes. We want to please you, dear Lord, as a family. Help us. I pray, in Jesus' Name. Amen."

No words could express the love and joy that filled the hearts of each family member at that moment. Girgis was so proud of his son. He could not quite figure out what had happened in his family, but he was not opposed to it. They seemed to him to be drawing nearer to God, and that was good. He wished silently in his own heart that he were a better Christian. He knew his relationship with God wasn't what it should be. He trusted God would be pleased with him because of what was happening with his children and wife. Surely, he could get some credits for that!

Philippe hugged his sister tightly. He then excused himself to take a shower and change. He grabbed his bag from the front hall and headed to his room. His mind was racing with all that had happened, and as he showered, he tried to figure out what it all meant. Exhausted from the experience, as well as the trip, he laid on his bed to relax. He was almost instantly asleep.

While her children rested, Phardos cooked a wonderful meal of their favorite dishes. It was good to be back in the kitchen and cooking for her family after having been away at the retreat. She was so happy to have everyone back in the house. Though the weather was still hot, she did not mind the heat, knowing that her loved ones would be pleased with her offering. She made goulash, with its fine layers of filo filled with minced meat and spices. Marianne's favorite was macaroni with béchamel sauce. For Girgis, she made veal panné and fatouche, a Lebanese salad. The sweat was rolling down her face by the time she finally turned off the oven.

She quickly went to the bathroom to shower and change and then called the family to the table.

The love offering was an overwhelming hit with her target audience, as they exclaimed their delight and appreciation while sitting at the table. No one had eaten well in the past several days, so they were thrilled to have their favorite dishes from their preferred cook.

"Oh, Mama," Philippe exclaimed, "You have outdone yourself. This looks wonderful. You wouldn't believe how tasteless the food was at the camp."

"I have my suspicions," she replied, smiling. "Please, eat up, everyone." She looked over at Marianne, who was sitting to her left. She caught sight of the tears brimming in her eyes. She quickly reached her hand over and touched her daughter's face. "My dear," she said softly, "enjoy your meal. It's all right."

"I know, Mama, I know." Marianne tried to stop the tears. "I just do not deserve such a wonderful family." She looked from her mother to her brother to her father.

Not wanting this to turn into a sad moment, Philippe spoke up quickly before the tears developed more in his parent's eyes. "Marianne, we're not that wonderful," he said with a smile on his face, "you get to wash all the dishes!" He laughed and added, "Now eat up before I finish everything on this table!"

"Oh, no you don't, my hungry son," his father replied, taking a fork to stab a piece of panné, "You're going to have to compete with me tonight!" The laughter spread, and Marianne relaxed, as she joined them in attacking the various dishes with gusto.

Later in the kitchen, it was both Philippe and Marianne who cleaned the dishes, as they jointly forbid their mother from returning to the hottest room in the house. Though still tired and sore, Marianne had enough strength to sit on a high stool and dry dishes as Philippe washed. She complained several times that he was getting more water on the floor than on the dishes, but did not take his offer to switch places.

"I think you are feeling better," he said lightly. "You're already bugging me, so it can't be too bad."

"I think I would have to be dead not to bug you, brother," she laughed.

"That's probably true," he shrugged. Silence hung between them for a while, before he spoke again. "Marianne, I really am sorry for what happened."

"I know, Philippe. Thank you." She worked hard to keep from crying again.

"What was his name?"

Marianne was taken back by the question. "Philippe, don't worry about it. You don't even know him."

"I know, but I still want to know. I need to be aware of it if he ever shows up again."

"I don't think he will."

"Well, even so." He tried not to give away his feelings.

"His name was Emad. Apparently he was a friend of Reda's, though I didn't know it until I was in Sharm. Mom and Dad told me that Reda had been with him that night at the wedding, but when Emad tried to get him to fix us up again, Reda refused because he was Muslim. Apparently that is when he decided he would get me no matter what, and I fell for it!"

Philippe looked at his sister's face and saw the hurt and regret that were so deep in her now. He would give anything to get this guy, Emad—to revenge his sister's shame. But what can a Christian guy do against a Muslim? He shrugged to himself and took a deep breath and went back to washing the dishes with a vengeance. His mind was spinning with ideas.

Chapter Forty-Nine

Though he knew he should have been worried about Noura's reaction to the bombshell of news that he dropped on her, he really was not. He had done what he felt like the Lord wanted of him, and he would have to be satisfied to leave the results to him as well. After all, had the Lord not blessed him with Noura? Would he not help her to accept the change in Muhammad's life? He just knew something good was going to happen.

The atmosphere of his home had changed since Nawal's disappearance. It was always evident at the dinner table when the family gathered and there was only he, Abdel-Karem and Eptisam at the table with their parents. On more than one occasion, he saw his mother lift her eyes, brimming with tears, as she served them food, and his heart broke for her. Knowing that his father allowed no mention of the two missing children, it seemed impossible for anyone to make conversation during meals, which made the setting even more depressing.

Wanting to flee from this oppressive environment, Muhammad was thrilled to be able to go with Dr. Samuel once again to the weekly gathering of believers, though this time it was in a different home. As they walked together through some narrow streets in a distant area of town,

Muhammad was able to share with the older man about the visit with Noura.

"I am very proud of you, Muhammad," said Dr. Samuel, as Muhammad finished the story. "No matter what happens, no matter her response, you have been obedient to the Lord, and he will reward you for it."

"Thank you, Doctor," Muhammad answered.

As they made their way up several flights of stairs, they could hear faint music coming from inside the flat. As the door opened in response to their knocking, the music stopped. Abdel-Rahman greeted the two men, who stepped quickly through the doorway. They refrained from greeting everyone else and merely took the seats offered them, as they realized the meeting had already begun. Muhammad recognized some of the faces from the last meeting, but saw a few new ones as well. It was a group of about ten with them included. The songs were being sung in a much lower voice than the week before, obviously because of thinner walls in this building, but it did not hinder their enthusiasm for the message contained in each one. The words of the final song were easy to remember:

Bless the Lord, oh, my soul and do not forget all his benefits
Bless the Lord, oh, my soul.

It was Aatif who spoke up as the song ended.

"I wanted us to sing that song tonight for a special reason," he began. "How often do we remember all the good the Lord blesses us with? I am afraid that we are quick to complain, to see the bad, to succumb to evil, and forget that there are good things in our lives as well. Is this not true?" He looked around for a response. Muhammad saw many heads shaking.

"You are being nice and agreeing with me, but some of you might be thinking that you do not see too many of the Lord's benefits in your personal life. Why do we as believers in Christ from Muslim backgrounds have to suffer so for our faith? Why can't we just live for him openly and freely like Christians in other parts of the world? Oh, if only I could get out of here, then I'd be able to be a better Christian." He paused for a moment to let the ideas sink in. "Tonight we are going to do something different," Aatif said, looking at each face in the group. "We are going to talk about all the bad things that are happening. Now, believe me, it may take a while, because I already know personally of many bad things that have happened in the lives of believers I know, so that is not counting what may be happening in your life or the lives of your friends. Let's talk about it...bring it all up and out in the open. Why, you may ask? Because I want us to see two things—first, that your situation is no worse than anyone else's, and two, that God can bring good out of even a horrible situation. OK? Are we ready to talk?"

The room grew deathly quiet as heads began to turn in every direction, some down, in order to avoid comment, others to their neighbor to see if they would share, and others at the ceiling, wondering why they had even come tonight. As the minutes passed, it was a man named, Sayed, who spoke first.

"OK, I will start. This is hard for me, Aatif." Tears welled up in the man's eyes.

"It's all right, Sayed," Aatif consoled, "we are with you. I'm glad you are going to share."

Sayed took a deep breath to gain control of his emotions. "Some of you know that my younger brother came to know Jesus last year." Heads nodded in response. "I was so thrilled for him. Now he was not just my brother, but my spiritual brother as well. Things were great. We read the Bible together, and I saw him have such an excitement for Jesus. The problem was that he got a little too excited and wasn't wise. We have another brother who is a very strong Muslim. Ahmed wanted to share Jesus with him. Before I could warn him and help him to be careful in how he approached our brother, Ahmed blurted out the truth. The house turned upside down. Our brother got a gang of people from the mosque he attended and they took Ahmed out and killed him. That was it. No discussion, no recanting, no chance for forgiveness. One day he was alive and happy. The next day he was dead."

Aatif moved over to Sayed and put his arm around him as the tears began to flow freely from his face. Aatif looked up at the group as he continued holding Sayed in his grip, "What do we do with this? What happened to Sayed as a result?" He looked at his friend and asked him, "Can you tell us or would you rather I share the rest?"

Unable to speak, he indicated to Aatif to continue the saga. "Yes, this is bad, horrible and an unspeakable injustice. Having walked with Sayed through this time, I can tell you that Sayed was beside himself in grief. He felt the guilt of the world upon him, as he believed himself to be the cause of his brother's death. It took a long time for him to even want to talk to God again, much less acknowledge Jesus. But do you know what? God helped Sayed through it. He walked through the valley of the shadow of death, like it says in Psalm 23, but the good news is he came out on the other side! The first thing he had to realize was that now Ahmed was with the Lord, and that was a good thing. What good is it to live 100 years and die and go to hell? No, the Lord began to give Sayed peace in the assurance that Ahmed was with Jesus. Now, what has happened in Sayed's life? I think when he's able to talk more, he will tell you he still struggles. He has to be careful with his family, but he is seeing God open their hearts to the Truth, and he is planting seeds until the moment comes for harvest." He hugged Sayed. "Thank you, brother, for sharing this hard thing." Turning back to the group he said, "OK, who wants to go next?"

Emira was a young woman of about 23 years of age. She dressed conservatively in a long skirt and long-sleeved shirt. Her veil hung loosely now around her shoulders, revealing jet black hair which gave stark contrast to her hazel eyes.

"I want to share something that has been hard for me. It's not like what Sayed went through, but it still has hurt."

"We are not comparing experiences, but just sharing," Aatif assured her. "Please, go ahead, Emira."

"I have been a follower of Jesus for about five years, and when I first came to faith, I wanted so much for my sister to know him too. I wanted her to have the same peace I had. I tried to find ways to share with her, but it was difficult. When I came to faith, she was already engaged to a man from our village. He had a lot of control over her. I talked to her about him and said he was not a good man and that God had a better way for her. She didn't want to listen. She said he would get better after marriage. She knew she could change him. I really worried about her. When he started beating her, I went crazy. I tried talking to my parents about it, but they said it was none of my business. In their eyes they were already married and he had the right to treat her as he wanted.

"I prayed for her. I had to trust that Jesus wanted something for her life too, but he did not seem to answer because she married him. I was devastated. Of course, once she married him, I didn't see her as much, but when I did, I knew things were bad. She couldn't change him and he kept beating her. But now things were worse...she was pregnant. The marriage didn't last long; he was such a vicious man. So, now my sister is back at home, divorced and about to give birth to her first child. Where was God in all of this? Why didn't he answer my prayers?"

It was Habiba who spoke up as the silence in the room lasted several minutes.

"Emira, I know what you are feeling. I felt the same thing when a friend of mine got married. She had come to faith the same time as I had, and we were very close friends because of it. However, her family, when they learned of her change decided to take action. They could have had her killed, but did something more wicked instead—they had her married to a fundamentalist Muslim in order to bring her back to the Faith. I could not take it. I cried out to God for his mercy on her life. Death would have been preferable to being married to such a man! But he did not allow her the easy way, the way that leads to ultimate freedom. She has been with him now for three years and I've watched her suffer under his oppressive hand, but do you know what? Though I don't get to see her much, because she is closely watched, I do know that she is still a believer in Christ. She holds tightly to him, and I think God is using her even more to touch other women because of what she's going through. No, God doesn't always answer in the way we want, but always it is the way which brings the most fruit for his glory."

"I have a friend who has troubles because of other issues," Sara spoke up. "She's like us and became a Christian, but in the beginning it was only in order to marry a Coptic man she was in love with. In order to do that, she had her id changed and tries to live a new life. In the process of living in the Christian community, she made a real decision to follow Jesus. While this has been great as far as her faith and future, her present is still a mess. For one thing, she can't work. She was already graduated from college when she converted. Her new id says she has education only up through high school. Her mother, who has accepted her daughter's change, is still Muslim and cannot control what she says when she visits her. Her Christian friends wonder why her mother has such a Muslim sounding vocabulary. Of course, this leads to lie upon lie in order to keep their past covered up, but it also leads to a lot of stress in their lives. Really, she is just overwhelmed by problems, and of course, now they have a baby."

"I think this is just the tip of the iceberg," Aatif spoke up. "We can also talk about Mustafa's difficulties at work, Salama's marriage issues, and even maybe Muhammad has some things troubling him." He looked at Muhammad and made eye contact. All Muhammad could do was nod silently in affirmation. Aatif smiled slightly, looked back over the group and continued. "So what do we do with problems? How do we handle them? Do we turn our backs on God when he asks us to face trials or when he doesn't answer things the way we expect? I want us to look briefly at a story found in the book of Daniel."

Muhammad had never heard of this Old Testament book or the prophet. Dr. Samuel helped him to find the designated chapter. They read along as Aatif had Abdel-Rahman read aloud the story of Daniel's friends, Shadrach, Meshach, and Abednego when they faced the fiery furnace. It was an exciting read.

"Now, here we have three young men living in a foreign land where they were not free to live according to their faith as they had been in their own land. You may say, 'we're not living in a foreign land,' but if you think about it, our experience is basically the same. We've become foreigners because of knowing Jesus. We're not free to worship as we desire. OK, what did these guys do when they were called in for not worshiping the idol of gold?"

"They took a stand," Emira answered.

"That's right," Aatif confirmed. "But what was the consequence they knew they would face?"

"The furnace," Muhammad offered mildly.

"That's right, Muhammad," Aatif assured him enthusiastically. "But why were they willing to take such a chance?"

Muhammad looked down at the Bible in his lap. He read over the verses again. "Because they trusted God to save them?"

"Yes, Muhammad, these young men trusted God. Now, my question to you all is this: why didn't God save them from the furnace? They had been bold in their faith. Shouldn't he have allowed them to avoid the trial?"

The room was quiet for a moment. Muhammad really didn't know what this meant. He agreed in his mind that it would appear that God should have saved them, but he didn't. He was glad when Abdel-Rahman spoke up.

"Because if God had not allowed them to go through the fire, he could not have received the recognition from the king he deserved."

"Yes, my brother, I think that is a great part of it." Aatif affirmed. "God really showed his power and might by allowing the men to go through the fire untouched, and not even smelling like smoke! As a result, his name was honored in all of Babylon. Yes, I do believe that is the ultimate reason—for God to receive all the glory. But I also want to propose another reason, one more personal, that affected the three young men themselves."

"Three things could have happened in this story," he began. "God could have delivered them from the fire completely. In doing so, I believe their faith would have been greatly encouraged. They would have celebrated their release or escape from danger and given glory to God. God does this sometimes, doesn't he?" Heads nodded. "When he does allow us escape, we're encouraged and even emboldened in our faith, but then sometimes that fades with time. We forget." He took a breath and paused.

"OK, we have another option here. God delivered the men through the fire. They had to experience the trial, go through the valley like Sayed did, but in the end, there is deliverance. Maybe some trials leave us a little more smoky smelling than these young men, but deliverance is evident just the same. When God allows us to go through a trial, what happens to our faith? Think about gold." He paused for an answer.

"Ah, we are refined," Salama spoke up.

"Yes, Salama, that's right. Our faith is refined, made more pure, sharpened. These kinds of experiences last longer with us. They not only encourage and embolden our faith but enable us to trust God even more the next time. We've experienced his deliverance and are not afraid to face new challenges."

Aatif looked toward Sayed as he began to share the last scenario. "There is another kind of deliverance, and many times we do not consider it as such. Sometimes God chooses to deliver us by the fire into his arms. He could have just as easily chosen this option for these young men. And if you notice in verse 18, they were prepared for this as well. They trusted God, whether he allowed them to escape the flames, go through them untouched, or be consumed by them. Of course, by being consumed by the trial, our faith is perfected, for we are with Jesus face-to-face. God chooses that for some of us, as he did for Sayed's brother. The question we want to ask today is and to close in prayer with is this: Will I trust in God no matter the trial before me? Let's pray."

As Muhammad closed his eyes during the time of prayer, his spirit was overwhelmed with all he had heard. He questioned himself as to if he could have such a faith in God as those three men who were willing to be thrown into the flames of death for his sake. What did all this mean for his life? He did not know, but asked the Lord to show him and give him peace.

Just as the prayers ended, there was a knock on the door. Abdel-Rahman went to answer it, opening only the top glass part that allowed him to talk through an iron grill to any visitor without opening the door completely. Everyone grew quiet as he began talking with a woman in a full niqab.

"Yes, yes, I understand," he was saying. "Thank you, thank you, my sister. Oh, what a blessing. May the Lord give you strength and bless you richly. My wife, Habiba would love to visit with you sometime. Do not fear, we will take precautions. Please, know you have family here if ever you need us. God bless you. Good-bye."

It was like listening to one side of a phone conversation. Everyone was eager to know what the woman wanted. Abdel-Rahman closed the door and returned to the salon.

"You will not believe it," he said, sitting down. "That was our neighbor, Um Osama. She came to warn us that her husband is planning an attack on our meeting. He is a strong Sunni and knows something is going on here."

Everyone shifted nervously in their chairs. Even after the earlier lesson, it brought tension into the room. "Why did she tell us?" Aatif asked.

"Well, that is what is amazing," Abdel-Rahman replied, "she told us because she is a secret believer!"

"Praise be to God!" several called out in astonishment.

"Yes, isn't that amazing. Of course I told her that you would love to visit with her, Habiba, and that she had a family here."

With that news, the group began thanking the Lord for his protection and goodness. Prayers were offered up on behalf of the woman and her family and the growing risk. However, even though the group did discuss avoiding meeting for a while in this particular home, they were not in favor of avoiding it completely. God had protected them once. He was sure to come to their aid again, and they would not fall prey to fear.

Chapter Fifty

Phardos had prepared to spend the day washing Philippe's dirty clothes from camp and tending to the needs of her daughter, but all that was interrupted by a frantic phone call from her older sister, Manal.

"Phardos, Phardos!" she cried into the phone. "Can you please come over, I cannot wake Makram. Please, please come!"

Phardos assured her elderly sister she would be there immediately. She reasoned in her mind as she quickly dressed that Manal had called her because she was the closest to her house. Makram had been ill for several years, but nothing indicated that he was this close to death. She tried to push the thought out of her mind as she rushed to her car, calling Girgis on her way to tell him of the incident.

"Yes, yes," she was telling him as she maneuvered through the streets, "I will call you as soon as I know something. Girgis, can you check on the kids later? I left them both asleep. Thanks."

When she arrived at her sister's flat, she was greeted by a frantic Manal. She went with her to the bedroom and when she saw Makram, she knew. He was gone. Phardos stopped in the doorway, unable to move into the room. Manal pushed past her and went to her husband's side, gently shaking him and kissing him on the forehead. Phardos forced herself to go to her side and took her gently by the shoulders.

"Manal, my dear," she said quietly, "he's gone."

"No, no!" her sister wailed, "it's not possible. We were just talking last night, and I was preparing his breakfast just now. How could he be dead?"

Phardos put her ear toward her brother-in-law's open mouth. No sound, no breath. She tried his pulse. Nothing. She moved her sister to a chair and told her she would call the doctor.

"Yes, yes," Manal urged, "let Dr. Philemon come. He will see what's wrong with him. He's had spells like this before. Maybe he can help."

Phardos left her sister, who had once again risen to tend to her husband, and went to the other room to call the doctor. She explained the situation and he assured her he would come over immediately. After ending that call, she then dialed Girgis and a couple of other family members. Each one would be there within minutes.

Death comes without warning and never at an opportune moment in life. In Egypt, it meant that whatever may have been planned for that day was cancelled, for the dead are buried immediately. After the doctor came to confirm the death, a certificate had to be issued by the health department with his signature to authorize the burial. Girgis and other men were asked to prepare the body, first wrapping the head with a bandage to keep the jaw shut. Then washing and dressing him in his best suit. All this was done as Phardos sat with Manal and a growing number of family members in the salon. Girgis was able to call the church and obtain the services of two priests for the burial. Makram was not a wealthy man or high in society, so two was an adequate number for his status in life. They were all just grateful that the church was available and there were priests around. The shop which provides caskets for most of the Christian community in Heliopolis was called and a casket ordered. All this was done within two hours of the death.

By the time the hearse arrived with the casket, Manal had accepted the fact that her dear husband of 42 years was indeed with the Lord. She was now dressed in black. Phardos had gone quickly home and changed as well, waking her children and urging them to get dressed for the funeral of their uncle. They returned with her to the house as the men carrying the casket were going up the four flights of stairs to retrieve the body. The entourage followed the hearse and arrived at the church where others who had been contacted shared their condolences and filed into the sanctuary.

Phardos sat by her sister on the front bench and grieved with her, knowing that she would be lost without her husband, for they had no children. She listened to the priest present the mass and prayers for the departed and family. It went by in a blur.

Philippe was sitting on the other side of the aisle with the rest of the men, and as he listened to the service, he wondered why the priest said nothing of significance about his uncle. Here was a man who had lived a good life, worked hard to provide for his wife and served the community and church, yet his name was barely mentioned. Was this how a life should end? Was this how he should be remembered by the church? Philippe asked himself as the scent of incense increased with each passing moment, would this be the way he wanted to be remembered? No, then and there, Philippe knew that all he was hearing and reading on his own in the Bible was what he wanted. He wanted a real relationship with God, one where he talked with him and knew his presence in his life. He wanted a relationship with other Christians too that was real and intimate, so intimate that when he did die, they would talk of him and remember him and share about what he did in his life for God. Yes, that's what he wanted—not this.

He bowed his head as the chanting of the priest faded into the background. Right there, in the midst of the Orthodox church, in the middle of a funeral service, Philippe asked Jesus to forgive him of his sins and become Lord and Savior of his life. He thanked the Lord for freeing him from the bondage of tradition and allowing him to experience new life in Christ. He raised his head and opened his eyes, still sitting in the dark church, but now full of a new inner light he could not deny.

He looked over at his sister, sitting just behind her mother on the women's side, and wished in his heart that she might know what he had. He hurt for her and knew she needed Jesus more than ever in her own life. He vowed to share with her the truth. He could not wait to talk to Steven and Dr. Raouf. As the service continued, he sent a short text message to his friend, telling him of his uncle's death and asking for prayer.

When the service ended, the family again followed the hearse to the Orthodox cemetery. There, the deceased was laid to rest in a family mausoleum. Phardos struggled to keep her sister standing strong as the priest offered a short prayer while the casket was pushed through a small door in the structure. Then it was done. Death came, life went on.

The next three days were taken with the compulsory visits. They first had an opportunity for friends and family to share their condolences at the church hall, which was rented for the evening. Phardos was so thankful for Girgis, as he handled all the arrangements for this and made sure everyone who served was paid and taken care of. She saw more of her family in those three days than she had seen in a year. It reminded her how distant they had all become and made her wish for a happy occasion in which to gather.

The third day following the death, a priest came to the house and prayed over the home to release the spirit of sadness there. He used water, parsley and bread as symbols of life and hope. As they faced toward the east and listened to him pray, Phardos wished for the same hope to be found in her home which had been so saddened by Marianne's troubles. As her daughter came to mind, she realized she had not yet had her checked by a doctor. She made a mental note that this had to be done the following day.

While his mother spent as much time as possible with her sister, Philippe found some time to call Steven and set up a visit with Dr. Raouf. It worked out that there was a gathering at his home that evening, and he welcomed Philippe to come early with Steven to visit before the meeting began.

"I'm so glad to see you," Dr. Raouf said as he greeted Philippe at the door that afternoon. "Come in, you are welcome."

"Thank you, Dr. Raouf, for seeing me and for having me in your home," Philippe replied.

As they sat in the salon, Steven was the first to get straight to the subject. "Philippe has some good news to share with you, doctor."

"Yes, well tell me, then Philippe," the older man urged.

"I have asked Jesus to come into my life."

"Praise God. Tell me, how did you come to that decision?"

"I was at a funeral."

"Oh, I see..." the doctor said, knowingly.

Philippe went on to share with Dr. Raouf how the Lord had been working in his life, including the events in the life of his sister. This brought a concerned look to the man's face, but saw that there was possibility for redemption in the eyes of the Lord. When Philippe told him how he was praying for the opportunity to share with his sister, Dr. Raouf affirmed that line of thought and encouraged him to do so as soon as possible. They talked for several minutes about various issues dealing with Philippe's new faith in Jesus and how his life would change. Dr. Raouf stressed the importance of

Bible study and prayer in his daily life. Steven then joined into the discussion.

"Of course you have to get baptized."

"Baptized?" Philippe questioned.

"Yes," Steven answered, "baptism is an outward symbol of the inner change in your life. It shows the church or body of believers that we have made a decision to follow Christ."

"But I was baptized as an infant."

"Yes," Dr. Raouf affirmed, "most of us were. Steven may be going a little fast, but it is not wrong to talk about it. Philippe, I was like you are, older when I asked Christ to be my Lord and Savior. I had grown up in the church and been baptized as an infant as well. However, when my life changed radically because of this very personal decision, I realized that the Bible was clear that I needed to show that in a tangible way to other Christians by being baptized. When we go under the water—yes, we go fully into the water, we are representing the our dying to sin and rising to new life in Christ, just as he literally died on the cross for our sin and rose to life to give us the opportunity to live in eternity with him. Does that make sense?"

"Yes, it makes sense," Philippe agreed, "but where do I do it?"

"That's a good question." Dr. Raouf looked at Steven and smiled. "I don't know what Steven has told you about the meeting tonight, but what we have here is basically a church."

"In your home?" Philippe looked confused.

"Yes, in my home," the man affirmed. "But it is not always in this house. Those in our fellowship use their own homes as well, so we rotate where we gather."

"But why do they meet in homes and not in the churches?"

"I can answer that, doctor," Steven offered.

"Please son, go ahead."

"We are a group of about 20 people now," Steven began. "Each one of us has a different story and we all came from various church backgrounds. What we hold in common is a personal relationship with Jesus Christ, a desire to go deeper into the Word in Bible study and to be actively making a difference for Christ in our communities. For various reasons, we are not satisfied with what we have been receiving in our own churches. Some of us still work in the church and try to make a difference, but for all of us, this is our real church family. The place we grow and get encouragement in our walk with Christ."

"It is important that you know, Philippe," Dr. Raouf interjected, "that we are not against the established church. As Steven said, several here, including myself continue to work with the churches and serve in them. However, we believe that a person needs to be free to worship in whatever way he is led by God, as long as it is according to Scripture. And, as you know, the earliest gatherings of believers in Christ took place in homes. So, we are not doing anything that has not been done before, and for many of us, this is the best environment for growth and service. We don't advertise what we do, because we do not want to draw extra attention to us from either the government or the Church. We do welcome all who want to see if this is where the Lord would have them. We only have two requirements."

"What are those?" Philippe asked.

"That you share your testimony, allowing everyone to know that you have made a personal decision to follow Christ as Lord, and that you be baptized. Now, if a person has been baptized by emersion in another church, that is fine and we accept that, but if not, we ask that they be baptized."

"Where do you have the baptisms?"

"It could be in a bathtub, as long as the person can get under the water. Unfortunately, my bathtub is too small, so we use a baptistery that a friend has built on the roof of his apartment building."

"On the roof!" exclaimed Philippe.

"Yes, but it is protected, so no one can see it. We've actually celebrated eight baptisms there."

Philippe was amazed at all this information and surprised that things like this were happening in Egypt. His friend, Steven, was definitely very happy with the group and he could tell that he had a strong faith in Christ. As he reflected on what this would mean for him personally, he realized that the person most affected would be his mother. What would she say? Would she disown him? He knew the Orthodox Church worked hard to keep their youth from going Protestant. Would this destroy his family?

"You will have to give me some time to pray about it," Philippe finally said. "But I will consider it."

"Good," Dr. Raouf replied. He began writing down something on a small slip of paper and then handed it to Philippe. "Take this home and read through these passages. They will help you get a clearer picture of the church and baptism."

"Thank you, doctor."

The doorbell rang. Philippe heard a woman's voice welcoming several people into the house. As she showed them into the salon, he realized it was Dr. Raouf's wife. He had not met her before, and the host took several minutes in introducing both his wife and the other guests to Philippe. She then left the group and came back with glasses and a pitcher of water for everyone. After the doorbell rang a couple times more, the room was full to capacity. It was a very mixed group of people gathered, Philippe realized. There were two or three couples and several singles, varying in age from 25 to 45.

After Dr. Raouf took a minute to welcome everyone and especially introduce Philippe, he surprisingly turned over the service to younger man he called Magdy. Magdy began by leading in prayer, thanking the Lord for being in their midst and asking him to bless their worship and study. Another young man, named Joseph, led the group in several songs. Philippe recognized one of them from the Evangelical church meeting he had attended, but did not know the rest. Of course, they were easy to follow and the tunes pleasant to his ears. Magdy then did something that Philippe thought was really amazing. He asked for prayer requests.

Several people then began sharing needs. One woman asked for prayer for her mother, who was sick. Another asked for the salvation of his father, who was a violent man and beat his mother. Steven asked that the Lord would help him witness to his Muslim friend, Abdel-Aziz. When all had been shared, Magdy told the group that they would lift these before the Lord and opened the time up for prayer. Philippe listened as person after person began voicing very personal prayers to the Lord, asking for his help in the matters of the group. He was amazed that a relative stranger would be praying for the need of another person's mother, father, or friend, but he was very moved by it and thanked the Lord in his heart that he had led him to such a group of believers.

The prayers ended and as they did someone began singing a song.

Come among us, remain among us
And take from our hearts a place for you to live.
We are hungry, you are our bread
We are thirsty, you are our water
From you is the best food
Our desire is that you answer our supplications.

As they sang it for a second time, Philippe lingered over the words in his heart, making them his own personal prayer to the Lord.

Magdy now began talking again and asked the group to look at the book of Acts. They read in turn several long passages from three chapters of Acts which talked about difficulties the Jewish believers were having in accepting Gentiles coming to faith.

"You know," Magdy shared, "something was happening in this tenth chapter of Acts that was new for the believers of the church in Jerusalem. Does anyone know what it was?" He looked around the room to see if anyone would answer.

A woman spoke up, "Was it that Gentiles were coming to know Jesus?"

"That's right, Nadia," Magdy affirmed. "For the first time Gentiles were coming to faith in Christ without first becoming Jews. See before that, most of the conversions were among Jews or Gentiles who had already been in the synagogue as converts to Judaism. Now, however, they were coming straight to faith in Christ without knowing anything about the Jewish faith first. This was radical, and that is why God had to prepare Peter by giving him a vision of the unclean foods. He wanted him to know that God accepts men and women from every nation who put their faith in Christ.

"The problem was that the Jerusalem church was not ready for this. They still expected that anyone who came to Christ needed to be Jewish first. Do you know what the major requirement for that would be?"

"Circumcision," rang out a voice from the corner of the room.

"Right," said Magdy. "They did not yet see that salvation was really by grace alone—nothing else. However, when Peter told them that the Holy Spirit had been given even to these uncircumcised Gentiles, they were convinced that God must be accepting them too. The problem was that though they made this initial acceptance to the Gentiles, there were still some among them who did not. Even nine years after this first meeting with Peter, there were still some Christians who were teaching that a person had to be circumcised first before coming to Christ. So, the whole matter had to be brought up again in Jerusalem and finally a compromise was made—not to put conditions for coming to faith but to help Gentile believers not be offensive to those from Jewish background by not eating food sacrificed to idols, meat with blood or that had been strangled, and by not practicing sexual immorality.

"Now," Magdy paused to ask, "why do you think I'm talking about this issue with you today?"

There was silence in the room, and even Philippe was trying to understand what this meant. Eventually, a young man sitting next to him spoke up.

"Magdy, is it because we have the same problem today?"

"What is that problem, John?" Magdy asked.

"That some in the church do not accept others coming to Christ?"

"Who would be the others, in your opinion?"

"Would it be Muslims?"

Magdy smiled and looked around the group,

"I think John is on to something here. If his idea is correct, how can we make a comparison between this past event and our situation today?"

"Well, if we think about the Jewish background church in Jerusalem," a young woman shared, "then we can relate that to the Orthodox Church today."

"How?" Magdy asked.

"Because just like the Jewish background church, it has a lot of traditions and customs, and this makes it harder for someone from the outside to have not just faith in Christ but join the church as well."

"Yes, but I think we could say the same about the Evangelical Church too," John again spoke up.

"Do you think so?" Magdy urged.

"Well, sometimes even in those churches, they are not accepting of someone from the outside, meaning from a non-Christian background, coming into the church."

"In a way, I think you are both correct." Magdy affirmed. "Anytime we are dealing with a structure that has been established for a very long time, like both the Orthodox and Evangelical churches, we run into a tendency for members to believe that what they are practicing as church is the way things ought to be. So, if someone comes to faith from a totally different background, then they either have to *do church* their way or not be accepted. OK, we may find agreement on this comparison. What about this? God did something that made them uncomfortable—he allowed Gentiles into the Kingdom. Is he doing the same today with Muslims?"

Philippe was amazed at such a question. He had never really thought about a Muslim coming to faith in Christ. Could it really happen? Then he remembered the story in the paper about the Muslim man who had become Christian and wanted to change his identity card. Maybe it was real. He waited for someone to answer the question.

"I think I can speak to that question." It was Dr. Raouf's voice. He had not spoken the entire meeting, which Philippe thought was very unusual, since as the oldest person in the room and the host of the meeting, he should have been the main speaker. However, he was quickly learning that things were done differently here. "Muslims are coming to faith in Christ all over the world and even here in Egypt. I know many. They are amazing believers, as they have to go through so much and take such risks for even accepting Jesus. We need to be aware that their numbers are growing, and they are meeting just like we are today, in houses all over the city."

Philippe saw some heads nodding in agreement with Dr. Raouf as he spoke. Others seemed to be just contemplating the possibility of his words.

"Thank you, Dr. Raouf," Magdy said. "Now, if God is allowing Muslims into the Kingdom, who are we to think that we could oppose God? This was the question of the early church and it is our question today. What are we going to do with the growing numbers of Muslims coming to faith in Christ. Do we separate ourselves from them or even oppose them? Or, do we accept them and even make changes on their behalf in order for them to feel comfortable among us? What do you think?"

With the last question, it seemed that the earlier moments of silence were shattered with everyone talking at once. Some were answering Magdy directly, others talking to their neighbor, but it appeared that everyone in the room had an opinion. Magdy finally had to shout to get the room quiet again and bring order.

"OK, OK," he proclaimed, "I see that this is opening you up now. Let me try to get a consensus. Who thinks that we should either keep separate from Muslim believers or oppose them completely?" Several hands were hesitantly raised. One man spoke up.

"I am not opposed to Muslims coming to faith, but I do think we need to keep separate," he said. "First of all, we have to consider that they are different from us. They will do things differently and use different language to do it. Neither of us can be comfortable with the other. Also, for security's sake. If we are seen mixing with Muslims, the government will come down on us big time. It's better to just leave them alone and safer for them too."

"If our faith does not cost us something, what good is it?" Nadia asked. "Look at what we just read, Medhat. The Jerusalem church took a risk in accepting the Gentiles. It cost them increased chance at persecution, but they were willing to do so, because they knew they could not oppose God. How can we just ignore the Muslims coming to faith if God is not? Besides, aren't you taking a security risk just being in this group, Medhat?"

Everyone's eyes turned to the man. His head went down for a moment, as he contemplated this challenge to his argument. He took a deep breath, raised his head and said,

"You're right. If I can take the risk to come here, which was a really big step for me, what is one more step in worshiping with a Muslim background believer?"

Magdy smiled as Philippe heard an audible sigh of relief from the group.

"This is God at work. I think we need to just stop here and pray. Obviously, this issue will touch each of us in a different way, but I want to challenge us in two ways today. First, as an individual, ask God how he would have you to respond. We already see what he's asking of Medhat. But you will have to hear that from God to you. However, I also want us, as we give time for God to work in our hearts, to speak to us as a church and show us what this means for us in the days and months to come. Let's pray."

Philippe left that meeting with his head and heart full of amazingly wonderful and complex feelings and thoughts. Between the idea of baptism and now Muslim believers, he did not know how much more he could handle!

Chapter Fifty-One

In the days that passed since his visit, Noura had thought of nothing but Muhammad and the words he spoke to her. Her mother had grown concerned as she noticed her daughter had stopped eating and lacked concentration. Noura knew that if she accepted what her fiancé had shared, they could have a very difficult life. They could be ostracized or even killed by their families. He could lose his job. How would they raise children? Why had God given her such a nice man to marry and then ruined it all by allowing him to become a blasphemer?

Lying on her bed, eyes wide open, Noura could not sleep. Was Muhammad a blasphemer? He still seemed so nice, and he was so blatantly honest with her. Most men would never confess all that to a woman, especially one they had not yet married.

"Oh, God!" she cried out in an audible voice. "What do I do?"

Closing her eyes, she tried to sleep. Though her mind continued to race, she eventually found rest. As the sleep deepened, Noura had a dream. She saw herself dressed in white, standing at the back of a room full of people who were watching her and smiling. She did not recognize the place. It was not a mosque or a church, but it was someplace pleasant and comfortable. There was a man, dressed in white, standing at the front of the room. He was so bright that Noura had to shade her eyes to look at him. She was hesitating, not ready to walk to the front of the room, but then the man in white spoke to her.

"Noura," he called her by name, "Noura, my daughter, it is all right to come and take Muhammad's hand."

That's when she saw him. It was Muhammad, dressed in a nice suit and looking so handsome. He was standing next to the man in white. He was smiling at her too.

"But I'm afraid," Noura heard her own voice call out.

"You have nothing to fear if you trust in me," the man assured her. "What Muhammad has told you is true and good. Choose the same path, and you will find peace for your soul."

"Who are you?" she heard herself question.

"I am the one who gave his life for you," he replied. "I am Jesus."

She woke up suddenly. Noura now knew what she had to do.

Muhammad had been very busy in the past couple of weeks. Between work at the shop, searching for an apartment and attending the weekly meeting, his plate was full. He had also purchased a cell phone for himself. Now that he had contact with a wide variety of people, from those in his weekly fellowship to realtors showing him flats, he felt he needed his own number. Everyone had a mobile phone now, even the guards, maids, and trash collectors, so it was time for him to spend some of his earnings and get better connected to the world.

Though he had yet to hear from Noura, he had peace that God would work things out. He continued to look for a flat, trusting that whether married or single, he would need a place of his own. Though the family still had no word of either Rachid or Nawal, a hesitant peace had come over the house, as everyone felt it better to just leave them to God.

Muhammad saw his father gradually relax as time passed since Nawal's disappearance, though he knew that in reality his heart was broken over his wayward children.

The only visible negative result was in his relationship and treatment of Eptisam. She had become a virtual prisoner now in their house and Abu Muhammad critiqued her every move and action. Only last week he had discovered a poem Eptisam wrote for a school project. While poetry is highly appreciated in the Arab world, Abu Muhammad was not pleased with his daughter's achievement in the least as he found the subject of her work to be love. Muhammad cringed when he remembered the grilling his father had given the teenager, asking her who she was referring to in the poem. Though she assured him with tears that it was simply a poem and had no relationship to her life, he angrily tore up the paper and forbid her from writing further poems. As Muhammad and his mother discussed this later, they were very sorry for his reaction, because it had been obvious that Eptisam had a gift. Now they would never know how great it could have become.

Almost three weeks after his visit to Noura, Muhammad got two phone calls in the same day. The first was from Abdel-Rahman, telling him in encrypted language that a time and place had been set for the baptism. He had been talking with Muhammad about the importance of baptism in the life of all believers, and Muhammad had prayed and decided that even if this would lead to a trial like that of the men in the book of Daniel, then he was ready to face it. He looked forward to meeting Salama, as Abdel-Rahman had told him, and going together to the designated place the following evening.

The second call that day was from Noura. His heart skipped as he heard her voice on the other end of the line.

"Peace be unto you, Muhammad," she said.

"And to you be peace," Muhammad replied.

"How are you?"

"I'm fine, praise God, how are you?"

"I'm better now," she said softly.

"Have you been sick?" he asked, "I didn't know."

"No, no, not sick. I just mean that I've had time to think things over."

"Oh,"

"And I want to tell you about my decision."

"Yes?" He was dying with anticipation.

"Can we meet?"

"Uh," he hesitated, "of course. Do you want me to come to your house?"

"No," she said quickly. "I would prefer, if it's all right with you, to meet outside somewhere."

"Well," he responded, trying to think quickly, "we could meet downtown. That would be halfway for both of us. Though I don't mind, of course, coming to Giza."

"No, downtown is fine. That was what I was thinking. On the Cornish, perhaps, by the Blue Nile boat. We could walk there."

"That sounds great. When?" he asked.

"Tomorrow afternoon?"

Muhammad worried that he would not be able to get back to Heliopolis to meet Salama in time. "Could we make it the day after? I am sorry, but I already have something tomorrow. I feel bad."

Noura was surprised that he had not jumped at the opportunity to see her, but she tried not to show her feelings. "Well, OK, the day after is fine."

He agreed on a time and hung up. His mind was racing with possible scenarios. Why did she not want me to come to her house? Is she afraid I'll make a scene? Maybe it would be easier for her to break off the engagement in a public place, so she can quickly get a taxi and get away. Maybe she just wants to be freer to talk. Maybe she is willing to accept me as I am. Muhammad did not get anything else done that day, his mind was so preoccupied with Noura.

The next evening, as he was finishing getting ready for his baptism, Muhammad went into the kitchen where he found his mother reading the Bible. They had read together a few times over the past weeks, but he did not realize how much she had continued to devour the book he had come to cherish.

"Oh, my son, you startled me," she said, as she saw him come through the door. He saw her put the book quickly on her lap, where it did not show.

"I'm sorry, Mother," he replied, joining her at the table, "I did not mean to interrupt."

"It's all right, my dear," she said warmly, "I think you saw that I was just reading."

"Yes, and I'm so glad," he answered smiling. "Are you enjoying the book?"

"I cannot tell you how it soothes my soul. There are many things I do not understand, but I trust God will show me one day."

"Mother, I wish I had more time to talk to you now, but I have an appointment. But I want you to know that you can easily understand more."

"How, my son?" she asked.

"By trusting your life to Jesus Christ. When you do that, he gives you the Holy Spirit, who helps us to understand his Word."

"Muhammad, how do you know all this?"

"Because, Mother, I am following his teachings now." He sat back for her to react.

"Muhammad, what have you done? You have converted to Christianity?" Fear rose in her eyes.

"Mother, I have a relationship with God now. I have peace. It has changed everything for me, Mother. I finally have hope for once in my life. Please do not be angry or afraid. Keep reading that book in your lap. God will show you that it is truth." He stood up and went to her side, bent and kissed her cheek. "I want to stay, to talk this through with you, but really, I am late. I need to leave. We will talk about it later, I promise. I love you, Mother."

He left her sitting stunned in her chair. She was not sure if it was because she had come to know her eldest son was a Christian or because he told her he loved her.

Chapter Fifty-Two

Phardos was not sure where the time had gone. Between keeping vigil with her grieving sister and carrying for Marianne, the days had passed quickly. She was thankful, however, that her daughter was better, though the doctor had confirmed their worse fears—she was pregnant. The news had come like an explosion on the entire household, with Girgis being the most aggrieved. He, of course, suggested that she have an abortion, but Marianne was adamantly against the thought and stood her ground with her father, declaring that she had to take the responsibility for her actions but an innocent child did not need to die as a result.

It was incredibly hard for Phardos to allow her daughter to basically throw away any chance at a good marriage by carrying this child, but in so many ways she was extremely proud of her. They took time every day to pray together, asking the Lord to give them strength to get through these months and to give them a love for the baby no matter what. They knew as a family that as word got out tongues would wag, even among their closest friends and family, yet they determined to stand united and support Marianne. She had not yet gone to confession, so no one had actually been to church in quite a while, but Ruth had come over a few times to pray with her and Marianne and read the Bible together. The love she showed her as a friend was overwhelming.

Though Philippe had struggled with his sister's condition, he sought council with Dr. Raouf and was encouraged to join his mother in supporting her and loving her through this. When he recognized that something had changed in his sister's life, he became even more courageous in sharing with her and his mother about his own new life in Christ.

"Philippe, my dear," his mother exclaimed, "I am so happy. Now I have both my children secure in Christ."

"I am so glad you feel that way, Mother," he replied, hugging her. "It really is a wonderful feeling to be at peace."

"Thank you, Philippe, for being so supportive. I could not do this without you and Mother by my side." Marianne shared in the hug with her mother and brother.

"None of us could do it without Christ," Phardos exclaimed.

Philippe excused himself from this special moment, saying that he had to meet a friend.

"Pray for me tonight," he called to them, as he moved toward the door. "I'm getting baptized."

"Baptized!" they ladies exclaimed together, but Philippe did not hear them. He was out the door.

Walking through the streets of Heliopolis, Philippe thought back over the past few weeks that led him to this moment in his life. The meeting at Dr. Raouf's house had been a turning point for sure. He had taken time to read the scriptures that the man had given him concerning baptism. He prayed and talked to Steven about it as well. He asked God to give him confirmation. He found it one day while he was reading his Bible.

He was reading in the book of Acts and was fascinated by the story of his namesake, Philip, when he was walking on the road to Gaza. He met an Ethiopian eunuch, of all people, which was unusual in itself, but even more weird that he was reading from the Old Testament book of Isaiah. Being a great evangelist, Philip simply asked the man if he understood what he was reading. The man did not, so Philip took time to explain the scripture and share the Gospel. The amazingly simple and obvious response of the man was to not only to accept this good news, but when he saw some water on the side of the road, he asked Philip, "Look, here is water. Why shouldn't I be baptized?"

To Philippe this was the faith he wanted. When faced with a command of Jesus, he wanted to answer, "Why not?" or "Why shouldn't I?" Now he knew that he had no reason to oppose baptism, but needed to act on the Word of God. He was now on his way to meet Magdy, who had a car and could take him to the place for the service. As he waited on the designated corner, Philippe was afraid he had gotten the time wrong. After about 20 minutes, an SMS came over his cell. It was Magdy telling him that he had gotten stuck in traffic but would be shortly there.

When Magdy did arrive, they were more than an hour behind schedule. Though this is not unusual for Egyptians, Magdy felt bad and phoned their host tell the group they would be there shortly. They eventually arrived in another part of town, found a parking place and began the short walk back to the building they needed to be in. They were welcomed into a nicely furnished apartment by a middle-aged man with graying hair.

"Welcome, Brother Magdy," he said, shaking his hand at the door.

"Thank you, Pastor Sami," Magdy replied. "This is my friend, Philippe."

"Welcome, Philippe, welcome."

"It's nice to meet you, sir," Philippe said, shaking the man's firm grip.

"Come on in, I think everyone is here."

"Please forgive us for being late. The traffic was much heavier than I anticipated."

"Well, that's all right," Pastor Sami consoled him. "However, I must tell you all that because of your late start, we may have something of a problem."

"A problem?" Joseph asked, stepping forward to greet Magdy and Philippe.

"Please, let's all sit down," Pastor Sami motioned to the salon area. "Mira, can you please get some drinks, my dear?" His wife came through the doorway with a tray as the words were coming out of his mouth. "Oh, thank you. Please, everyone, help yourself."

Philippe drank a big glass of water, hot from the wait and ride over. As the group finally settled down again with their drinks, Pastor Sami started speaking again.

"This doesn't happen often, but it seems today I have two groups scheduled for a baptism."

"Well, that is fine," Dr. Raouf assured him. "We can do it together. What time are they coming?"

"Oh, they should be here within half and hour," he confirmed. "What you might want to know is the ones being baptized are from the majority background."

A silence came over the room. Eyes got big as they looked at one another in shock. Then Magdy began to laugh, and then Steven, and then Nadia, and soon the entire group was in tears.

"Praise God!" Magdy exclaimed.

"Hallelujah!" Nadia shouted.

"What an amazing God." Steven declared.

Pastor Sami and his wife watched in disbelief.

"Are you all all right?" he asked.

"Yes, oh yes, I'm sorry," Magdy offered. "You need to know, Pastor Sami, that just a few weeks ago, the Lord gave us a great lesson on the church, and it seems that he wants us to live up to what we learned today, that's all."

"Ah, I see..." the man had a confused look on his face. He looked at his wife and shrugged.

Dr. Raouf then took the time to share with the couple the events of that very crucial study and how God had changed so many hearts that day to accept and welcome Muslim believers. The only thing was no one had really, besides Dr. Raouf, actually met a Muslim believer in Christ, so it was difficult for them to know how they could carry out the practice of inclusiveness. Obviously, God had something up his sleeve.

Pastor Sami was so pleased that he was able to witness this great event in his own home.

"How about we take some time to thank the Lord, then, and pray for those coming, that the Lord will be glorified in this act of obedience and very special time of fellowship?"

Philippe was moved by the man's prayer and that of several others who joined in. His eyes grew misty as he realized that his own baptism would take place at such an important moment for the church. He wished his mother and sister could be here with him.

Chapter Fifty-Three

The doorbell rang several times over the next few minutes as the group Muhammad was in gradually made their way to Pastor Sami's apartment. They had come separately or in pairs, spacing their arrival at the building to avoid attention. Thankfully, it was a tall apartment building which included private homes and several businesses, so heavy traffic was not unusual. Muhammad was immediately taken by the host's kind smile and warm welcome. As he followed Salama into the flat, he stopped short when he saw a large group of strangers in the salon. Pastor Sami assured them they were friends.

"Please, come in, my brothers," he encouraged them with a wave of his hand. "You are among the family of God. Come, sit down, I have wonderful news to share with you all."

Once the entire group had arrived and everyone had been served refreshments, Pastor Sami shared with the new arrivals what he had just learned from the earlier group. Cautious smiles came from the Muhammad and his friends, as they nodded in understanding.

Dr. Samuel, who had arrived just before Muhammad rose and warmly greeted Dr. Raouf. He then turned to his group and shared.

"My friends, this is a work of God today. You do not know it, but my brother, Raouf, here is an old friend and together we have been praying regularly for the growth of the church in Egypt. Though he is not with us each week, his heart is and much of what I have learned in this ministry is from him. We have been asking for God to work a miracle in the lives of believers from all backgrounds, praying that he would bring them together in his way, in his timing. My brothers and sisters, I believe today is not an accident but the beginning of a new era for the church in Egypt."

Muhammad's heart was racing as he took in the impact of these words. What a privilege to be part of such an historic event, he thought to himself. What an honor to be among those who would be baptized. He then looked up as the man about whom Dr. Samuel had spoken began to speak.

"I love this man right here," he began, putting a strong arm around the shoulder of his friend. "And I thank the Lord for what he has done through him. As I look into your faces and see the peace of Christ, my heart rejoices. But I want to tell you, my brothers and sisters, the faces you see across the room are going through many of the same things you are today, as they have made a decision to follow Christ fully and completely no matter the cost. We are one in Christ Jesus." *Amens* and *hallelujahs* echoed around the room.

"We are old," he continued, looking at Dr. Samuel and smiling, "but you are young. You are the ones who will make the biggest difference for the Kingdom in the coming years and generations. I want you to remember this day and note it as a spiritual marker in your journey with Christ, because believe me, there will be days when you want to quit, when you think there is nothing good to come of this land, and your heart will be tempted to grow cold. Beloved, don't grow cold, though wickedness will surely increase in the days to come, keep your hearts warm for God, keep the fire burning and keep sharing your faith till the end. Now, I could go on..."

"Yes, he could," affirmed Dr. Samuel with a laugh.

"But we have some more important business to do today. Is the water ready, Pastor Sami?"

"Yes, ready and waiting."

"Good," Dr. Raouf replied. "Now, before we go upstairs, I want us to take some time in prayer and then we want to hear the testimonies of each one who will be baptized today.

Muhammad felt like the building was shaken by an overwhelming power as prayers were offered up to the Lord. He had never heard a Christian believer pray, and though they used some different vocabulary in their prayers, he felt the Spirit's presence and power in their words. It was a moving and memorable experience of unity in the Body.

Following the prayer time, those who were to be baptized began sharing their testimonies. Magdy had helped Muhammad know how to share what had happened in his life in a few short minutes. Though he could have gone on for a long time, he learned it was important as well to be able to share about his journey to Christ in about five minutes, just like he remembered from Fouad on the minibus. He grew nervous as his time neared, but realized that many of the testimonies had similar issues. He laughed with the group as he heard a young man named, Philippe, share that he actually prayed to receive Christ while attending a funeral. When he told about his sister's rape and pregnancy, he thanked God that he could help a guy who should have every reason to hate Muslims and be angry with the Lord find peace and hope.

After Philippe finished, Muhammad was asked to share. He took a deep breath.

"Like my brother, Philippe, here," he began, "I had every reason, or so I thought, to be justifiably angry at the world and God. As the eldest, I was basically forced to work with my father to carry on the family business, though I never liked it. My brother has run off with a fundamentalist group. My sister has disappeared, and I can't find a single apartment I can afford so I can get married. Life should be the pits for me, but I can stand here today and tell you it is not, because God saw fit for a young man named Fouad to tell me about an opportunity of a lifetime—a chance to have an abundant life. From the moment I heard those words, I was on a search, and God guided my every step from an internet café, to a bookstore, and finally to Dr. Samuel with whom I made my decision to follow Christ. Now, I cannot tell you that a lot of my life has changed for the better. I'm still working for my father, my brother is still radical, my sister still gone, I still have no flat, but my life is abundant. That is all because of Christ."

His hands were shaking and sweaty by the time he sat down, but Muhammad immediately felt warm affirmation and encouragement from the group as they offered up words of praise and thanksgiving. When all the candidates for baptism had finished sharing, they were led to a room to change into robes. Muhammad had been told to bring his swimsuit to wear underneath, and Abdel-Rahman had offered him a white robe to wear. He finished and walked with the others, following Pastor Sami up some inside stairs to a door which led to the roof. Though normally the roof of every building was open to neighbors, obviously Pastor Sami had prepared this private area to be hidden, as he had built a covered walkway which led to a large makeshift room, completely walled in and covered. Inside was a large box-like concrete pool, completely tiled on the inside and full of water. It had steps going up the side and then into the water.

The man named Magdy was the first to go into the water, as he would be the one to baptize those in his group. As he stepped down into the pool, the wall came up to his chest, meaning the water was about a meter in depth. He called the first candidate to enter the water. It was the one named Philippe. Muhammad watched as the young man went into the pool. Magdy looked at him and asked:

"Brother Philippe, have you accepted Jesus as your Lord and Savior?"

"I have," Philippe declared.

Magdy put his right hand raised above the man's head and said: "Philippe, in obedience to the commands of our Lord Jesus Christ, and upon your confession of faith in him as Savior and Lord, I baptize you in the name of the Father and of the Son and of the Holy Spirit. Amen." He then slowly lowered Philippe down into the water and raised him back up.

Muhammad's heart stirred and he got shivers across his skin as he watched and heard the joyful *amens* in response. Magdy continued after Philippe left the pool, baptizing three others in their group. He then left the pool and Abdel-Rahman entered. Muhammad's knees grew weak as he watched two from his own group participate in baptism. He moved as he heard his own name called and walked up the steps. Abdel-Rahman took his hand and led him into the water.

"My brother, Muhammad," he asked, "have you accepted Jesus as your Lord and Savior?"

"I have," Muhammad replied.

"Muhammad, in obedience to the commands of our Lord Jesus Christ, and upon your confession of faith in him as Savior and Lord, I baptize you in the name of the Father and of the Son and of the Holy Spirit. Amen."

Muhammad gripped tightly Abdel-Rahman's arm as he felt his strong hand on his back controlling the dip into the water. He held his breath as the water rushed over his head and face. As he came up out of the water, tears were running down his face.

"Thank you, Jesus," was all he could say.

"Praise God," he heard Abdel-Rahman whisper. "God bless you, brother. Walk now in newness of life."

As he came out of the pool, the last of those being baptized that day, a song rose quietly among the group.

I have decided to follow Jesus.
I have decided to follow Jesus.
I have decided to follow Jesus.
No turning back, no turning back.

As they stood in a circle around the pool, holding hands, Dr. Raouf spoke up in a loud voice.

"As the Scripture says, 'Anyone who trusts in him will never be put to shame.' For there is no difference between Jew and Gentile, Muslim and Christian—the same Lord is Lord of all and richly blesses all who call on him, for, 'Everyone who calls on the name of the Lord will be saved.' Amen and Amen. Go in God's peace. This is the hope for the world, the hope for Egypt."

Chapter Fifty-Four

She entered Chez Louis salon with fear and trembling. It had been months since she had seen her hairdresser, and she knew he would be horrified to see her present condition.

"Madame Phardos!" Carmon called out. "How are you? It has been too long."

"Bonjour, Carmon," Phardos replied. "Yes, much too long, I'm afraid."

"You just sit right here," Carmon said, pointing to a nearby chair. "Here is a magazine to look at. Alex will be with you shortly. Can I get you some tea?"

"Yes, please. That would be lovely." Phardos sat down and took up the magazine of hairstyles. As she waited, another patron walked in. She was modestly covered in a light blue veil. Carmon saw her as she was bringing Phardos her cup of tea.

"Madame Fatma, welcome," she called.

"Good morning, Carmon," came a soft reply. "How are you?"

"I'm fine, Madame. You look lovely today," Phardos could tell Carmon was being honest in her praise. The woman did seem to glow.

"Thank you, my dear." She sat next to Phardos on a small couch.

"What can we do for you today?"

"I would like a special coiffeur, if possible."

"Of course, what's the occasion?"

"My son is getting married," the proud mother smiled.

Carmon moved to the back of the shop to prepare a tea for Madame Fatma. Phardos looked over at the woman and smiled.

"Congratulations on the wedding of your son," she said.

"May the Lord grant the same for your children," Fatma replied.

"Weddings are always blessed times, aren't they?" Phardos asked.

"Yes, I am blessed to have a wonderful son and be gaining an even more wonderful daughter-in-law."

"My, that is a blessing," Phardos agreed. "I don't hear many mother-in-laws saying such things."

"Well, God has been especially good to me, and I'm grateful."

"He is a good God."

"Yes," Fatma affirmed. "I cannot do enough to praise him. Do you have children?"

"Yes, a son and daughter."

"The Lord bless them," Fatma replied.

Phardos felt something was different about this woman. It was just not normal to be having such a conversation with a Muslim. She vaguely remembered seeing her in the past, but had never talked with her. As she sipped her tea, she could not help but feel there was a special bond between them. She took a chance.

"What is your son's name?" she asked innocently.

"Muhammad."

Phardos could not help but think she was taking a risk. After all how many Muhammads were there in the city? "Is his fiancée's name Noura, by any chance?"

Fatma looked at Phardos with shock. Who was this Christian woman, she wondered. How would she know Noura and Muhammad? Then she figured it out. "Is your son's name Philippe?"

Phardos put down her tea cup, and cupped her hand over her mouth in wonder. "Yes, it is. I can't believe it! You're Um Muhammad!"

"And you're Madame Phardos! I'm so glad to meet you!"

"Me too."

Carmon came into the room. "Madame Fatma, Simone will see you now. If you will follow me to the back."

"Of course, my dear, of course." Fatma rose, reaching out her hand toward Phardos as she did. As Phardos touched her finger tips, they both nodded, a smile on their faces.

"We will talk soon." Phardos said.

"Yes, we must." Fatma replied, leaving her to get her hair washed.

Carmon looked at them in surprise. "Would wonders never cease?" she thought to herself. "And in my shop of all places!"

Glossary

aied	holiday or feast time
Al-Ahram	The Pyramids (the title of a local newspaper)
corban	the communion bread
fatir	a light, buttery, layered bread eaten with molasses, honey or cheeses
foul	fava beans
galabiya	long, wide robe worn by both men and women in the Middle East
habibi	my dear one (male)
habibti	my dear one (female)
hajj	pilgrimage (here referring to Mecca). The term can also be used as a title for a person who has completed the pilgrimage.
hayati	my life (term of affection)

ibn	son
ibn Allah	son of God
Injil	The Gospels (or could refer to the New Testament)
in sha Allah	if God wills
'Isa	the word used for Jesus in the Qur'an
jizya	ransom paid by non-Muslims to remain in their religion
moloukhiya	a green leafy vegetable cooked like a thick soup and eaten with rabbit or chicken and rice or bread
niqab	a black veil which covers a woman's head and face, leaving only her eyes showing (though sometimes even these are covered with a sheer piece of black material)
Sharia	Islamic law
tamaiya	a fried patty composed of leeks, chick peas and spices rolled in sesame seeds
Um	mother (Um Muhammad = Mother of Muhammad)
walid	son (physical)
zuggarit	shrill sound made with the tongue to celebrate a special event such as a wedding or birth

CPSIA information can be obtained
at www.ICGtesting.com
Printed in the USA
LVOW11s1112141117
556165LV00001B/3/P